Disraeli Rising

Disraeli Rising

A Novel by

Maurice Edelman

STEIN AND DAY/*Publishers*/New York

First published in the United States of America in 1975
Copyright © 1975 by Maurice Edelman
All rights reserved
Printed in the United States of America
Stein and Day/*Publishers*/Scarborough House,
Briarcliff Manor, N.Y. 10510

Library of Congress Cataloging in Publication Data

Edelman, Maurice, 1911-
Disraeli rising.

1. Beaconsfield, Benjamin Disraeli, 1st Earl of,
1804-1881. I. Title.
DA564.B3E33   942.081′092′4[B]   74-26940
ISBN 0-8128-1675-7

To my brother Jack

Chapter One

'Marriage is all the rage,' said D'Orsay. 'You must get married, Ben.'

'The Queen – ' Disraeli began.

'She's bespoken, I fear,' D'Orsay went on. 'Tomorrow's the Coronation. Then there'll be a betrothal. In a year or two an heir. Marriage is going to be very fashionable. You'll really have to hurry.'

The tall Frenchman, sauntering with Disraeli down St James's Street in the late summer evening of 1838, paused to look at the reviewing stand where workmen were hammering into position the base of a gas illumination in the shape of a crown and the letters VR. He tapped his tight doeskin trousers with his pink cane, and said in a cadenced voice, 'I prefer your simple Saxon style to our own *tourbillons* of colour.'

Disraeli took his hand away from the filigree chains looped over his embroidered waistcoat.

'Yours symbolizes order,' D'Orsay went on. 'Rococo and revolution go hand in hand.'

'I agree,' said Disraeli. 'The Queen represents the domestic principle, and whatever anyone may say, this is a domestic country. The only explosions you'll hear tomorrow will be the fireworks in Hyde Park.'

All along the street as far as the triumphal arch, the lamps in arabesques of Brunswick stars and laurel wreaths began to glow yellow against the blue sky.

'Happy Albion!' said the Count. 'In France when we overthrow the monarchy, all we do is replace one ugly man by another. We choose someone to hate whereas you choose someone to adore.'

'We have the advantage that the hereditary system predetermines our choice.'

'Everyone believes in the principle. It's just that in France

7

we don't respect it. Our system is based on heredity tempered by usurpation.'

'Marriage has much to commend it,' Disraeli said as they walked on towards Crockford's Club. 'But there must be exceptions for men of independent spirit. Myself, for example. Surely it must destroy anyone's nerve to be amiable *every* day to the same human being? I've observed among most of my friends that marriage is the guarantee of lifelong infelicity. Can you persuade me to the contrary?'

D'Orsay frowned at the thought of his own abortive marriage to the fifteen-year-old daughter of his friend and protector, Lord Blessington.

'Every marriage is different,' he said. 'Ideally it should be the sum of two people.'

'In your case?'

'Division. I'm afraid my wife was too young. There's no quick cure for inexperience.'

'And if I were to marry?'

'You'd add greatly to your resources. After all, you're a bachelor of – what is it? Thirty-five?'

'Thirty-four.'

'You've been a Member of Parliament for Maidstone a whole year. You're a handsome man, and you make up a table – and all that's excellent. But every year there's a new crop of good-looking bachelors to put next to the dowager ladies.'

'The difficulty is,' said Disraeli, 'the rich and pretty women are either married or their mamas are prudent. No one's in a hurry to surrender a precious young daughter to a debt-ridden novelist.'

They handed their cloaks to an usher, and stood for a moment at the foot of the staircase leading from the vestibule to a landing supported by four Doric columns, above which the huge dome with the massive chandelier gave Crockford's the air of a classical temple. The opulent drawing-room and dining-rooms with pastoral scenes after Watteau seemed more secular. It was as if a ducal palace had been built on to a place of worship where Crockford – Crocky to his familiars, the

8

Fishmonger after his father's trade to the disgruntled – was both Duke and High Priest.

The crystal chandeliers made the reception rooms as bright as day, but in the Gaming Room it was always night. The shuttered windows excluded sound, and the muttering gas-lamps that shone over the green baize tables left the rest of the room in a penumbra except for the changing-counter lit by a small light in the far corner. The Room was like a warm tomb, except that at ten and at dawn footmen removed the shutters, trying to banish from the curtains and the carpets the persistent smell of cigar smoke.

Thronged after the House rose with politicians, diplomats and officers, some in uniform but most of them in fashionable blue coats with brass buttons, stiff white neckcloths, short, richly-studded waistcoats and ornamental shirts, Crockford's was as fashionable and exclusive as the Carlton or White's.

With grave nods to run-of-the-mill peers, throwing a word like largesse to more favoured ones, and inspecting the liveried servants without addressing them, Crockford, impeccably dressed in a black coat and trousers strapped under his shoes, greeted Disraeli on the landing with an elaborate bow that stopped short of the reverence he reserved for the Duke of Wellington.

'Hello, Crocky,' said Disraeli negligently. 'What are the chances tonight?'

'As always,' said Crockford, 'in favour of the bank. Can I offer you gentlemen a little champagne?'

They moved to the drawing-room, and Crockford handed them the glasses from a footman's tray.

'The art of gambling,' he said, 'is like the art of painting. You've got to know when to stop.'

'I've always regarded you as more of a collector than an artist,' said Disraeli.

'Perforce,' said Crockford blandly. 'Perforce! My collection is, for the most part, a museum of ruined men. I could restock the National Gallery with masterpieces left in pledge.'

His pallid, heavy face broke into a smile.

'But then, you have to consider that the object of my otherwise agreeable guests – ' he bowed – 'is to ruin me. It's a duel the whole time.'

Disraeli was anxious to move into the Gaming Room, where the clamour of voices calling the bets alternated with silences broken only by the clack of dice and their dribble against the cushioned side of the table.

Crockford followed his glance, and said, 'Yes – later on it'll be hard to get near the game.'

'*Écarté?*' asked D'Orsay.

'Tonight,' said Disraeli, 'we'll play hazard. Just for a change.'

His friend, Edward Bulwer, joined them at the entrance to the Gaming Room.

'Well, Disraeli. Are you going to the Abbey after all?'

'Yes,' said Disraeli. 'Lumb's promised to deliver my court dress by six o'clock this morning. Will you be there?'

'I think not.'

'A radical principle, no doubt,' said Disraeli.

'No, a matrimonial one. Mrs Bulwer's arriving from Taunton. It means I have duties in Cheltenham.'

Bulwer made a bow to Count Pozzo di Borgo, the be-whiskered Russian Ambassador, who paused in his progress to say, 'Mr Bulwer, I must tell you how greatly I enjoyed your *England and the English.*'

Bulwer acknowledged the compliment.

'A superb book,' said D'Orsay. 'I've lived in England for many years and can confirm Mr Bulwer's insight into England's virtues.'

'And you've no desire, Count, to become naturalized?' the Ambassador said ponderously.

'No,' said D'Orsay, 'I was born French and will die French.'

'You see, Excellency,' murmured Disraeli. 'No ambition!'

'Ah,' said the Ambassador, his hand on the Order of St Michael, 'I esteem your patriotic *amour propre*. I have read your new novel too, sir. *Augusta*, I think.'

'No, *Venetia*.'

'Ah, yes – it has a most felicitous portrait of Byron . . . But you are too young to have known him.'

Disraeli brightened.

'He was a friend of my father, Your Excellency.'

The Ambassador in his grandeur didn't feel it necessary to follow the sequence of other men's conversation.

'*La Reine!*' he exclaimed irrelevantly. 'What brilliance! What majesty!'

Without waiting for comment, he moved on like an Admiral's flagship with his deferential entourage towards the crowded table where the Honourable Henry Stanley, the younger brother of Lord Stanley, the Chief Secretary for Ireland, was playing for heavy stakes against the bank.

Almost seven years had passed since they had become acquainted on board ship when Disraeli was returning from his tour of the Near East. They had learnt to play cards in the officers' mess when they stopped at Malta, and on reaching Falmouth, Henry Stanley decided that before he joined his family he would try out his new skills in London at Effie Bond's rooms, a gambling 'hell' in St James's Street, where at his request Disraeli had introduced him.

To begin with, Henry had been lucky and won eighteen hundred pounds. Collecting his winnings, he was about to leave when Effie Bond himself invited them both to visit his shooting gallery in an underground cellar.

'My friends need to keep their hand in,' he said, scratching his broken nose. 'Just in case . . . You will be staying, gentlemen, a little longer?'

He poured a glass of brandy each for Henry Stanley and Disraeli, who glanced quickly at each other and then at Bond's bullies hemming them in.

'My dear fellow, we're most anxious to,' said Disraeli.

'If you need refreshment, my lord,' said Bond, 'one of my young ladies will supply it. And then you'll be very welcome at the tables.'

They returned to the dice. After another twenty-four hours, Henry had lost over seven thousand guineas. Disraeli himself had lost a hundred pounds, the balance of the sum he had received from his father's bankers at Valetta.

'Well, that's that, Mr Bond,' said Henry. 'You can draw on me for what I owe.'

Bond passed his fingers through his thin red hair.

'Oh no, if you can't pay on the nail I'll take you in pledge, young man,' he said. 'Your family is one of the richest in the land. They'll have to bail you out. Tell you what. I'll give you credit for another two "thou".'

And so, while Henry Stanley settled down at Bond's, distracted by dice, brandy and Mr Bond's hostesses, Disraeli spent the days distractedly hurrying from money-lender to money-lender, seeking a loan to get his companion out of pawn. At last, in despair, though against Henry's wishes, he sent a message with Bond's doorman to Lord Stanley, asking him to deliver his younger brother from a detention which he described as 'the unfortunate consequence of a debt of honour'.

The reply, together with the money, came at once in the hand of Lord Stanley's servant.

'Sir, your involvement in these affairs has been a matter of concern to the Stanley family. I ask you to spare us your future interest.'

The insult had smarted; the wound had been deepened several years later in the House of Commons when Lord Stanley spoke immediately after Disraeli's disastrous Maiden Speech without condescending to notice it. On his release, Henry had let it be known to his family that he had gone to Effie Bond's at Disraeli's insistence, and that for all he knew, Disraeli might well have received some commission for his introduction. At any rate, Disraeli had got him into trouble, and was no gentleman, and on that assumption Henry was restored to the family's regard.

Now, at Crockford's, Henry greeted D'Orsay in the press of the crowd, calling their bets for the croupiers to lay them on the main line, but he ignored Disraeli's nod. He had put a thousand guineas at odds on number three, and several others joined him with smaller sums. Unabashed by the snub, Disraeli, making his first bet, laid a hundred guineas at evens on seven.

The caster rattled the dice in the box. One player crossed himself surreptitiously. Others, leaning over the backs of the chairs, tightened their grip till the chairs themselves seemed to sweat.

'Seven,' called the croupier indifferently.

The losers withdrew a little like a disappointed tide. The croupier scooped up the rattling counters and pushed Disraeli's winnings towards him.

By two o'clock in the morning, D'Orsay had lost two thousand six hundred guineas, Henry Stanley had lost three thousand guineas, and Disraeli had won over two hundred pounds. The dice leapt, the casters muttered, the croupiers called the points, cravats were loosened, faces like wet chalk under the chandeliers dripped in the hot room, and the men-servants moved quietly to and from the buffet table with peaches, champagne and cold meats.

At a quarter to three the chief croupier sent a note to Mr Page, the accountant, who sent it on to Mr Crockford. It read, 'Hon. Henry Stanley – down £4000.' Mr Crockford, with a benevolent expression, touched Henry Stanley's elbow and whispered, 'I'd like your advice, sir, about a filly.'

'I think,' said Disraeli over his shoulder to D'Orsay, 'our young friend needs your help.'

At Crockford's touch Henry looked up angrily, then slowly rose, and his place was immediately taken by another player. D'Orsay drew him aside as he followed Crockford.

'Can I be of service, sir?'

The young man, half-drunk, yet controlled in his movements by an old discipline, said, 'The only service you can offer me, my dear D'Orsay, is – is – an introduction to a Jew. Any Jew – ' he stumbled – 'except that one,' pointing to Disraeli, who was out of earshot. 'When Crocky wants to tell me no more credit, he always asks me about a horse . . . I need five hundred guineas to recoup.'

Accustomed to these occasions, Crockford looked on with a neutral expression.

'How much on one of these studs, Mr Crockford?' said D'Orsay negligently, pointing to the diamond studs of his waistcoat.

13

Crockford raised his eyeglass.

'Four hundred.'

'Make it five.'

Crockford hesitated, then agreed.

'For you, Count.'

D'Orsay detached his bottom stud as Henry Stanley observed him with wonder.

'But your waistcoat?'

'Don't worry,' said D'Orsay. 'Tomorrow all the gentlemen of fashion will be wearing their waistcoats unbuttoned at the bottom.'

Disraeli and D'Orsay left Crockford's at dawn, when the spectators were already beginning to line the route and assemble in the reviewing stands, although the departure of the Coronation procession from Buckingham Palace wasn't due till ten o'clock.

The fresh morning air revived them after the night's gambling, and Disraeli felt cheerful since in his final throw he had won a few hundred guineas. He had lent D'Orsay two hundred pounds in cash, and backed a bill, drawn on D'Orsay by Crockford for three thousand pounds at a rate of interest which they'd both forgotten. He stood on the steps of the club with a feeling of virtue added to success, while the carriage horses stamped restlessly on the macadam.

'Hazard,' said D'Orsay, ruminating, 'is a very complicated game.'

'Not really,' said Disraeli. 'But some people like Henry Stanley, poor fellow, will never learn that with six spots each on two dice, there are three ways of adding up to seven – five plus two, six plus one, and three plus four. But only one of adding up to eleven – five plus six. Chance, my dear D'Orsay, is a matter of arithmetic.'

D'Orsay smiled at Disraeli's self-satisfied instruction. He knew that only the previous week Disraeli had lost most of the quarterly allowance his father gave him.

Wherever Disraeli now looked, he could see the crowds

steadily getting thicker and hear the accumulating sound of shuffling feet as new contingents arrived from East London. In Piccadilly, beneath a huge silk banner inscribed 'Long Live the Queen', a ragged company of out-of-work Spitalfields weavers were already in position behind the barriers, cheering the Rifle Brigade detachment as they marched past in good order to line the route, while street-sellers with trays of flags and favours, pies and gingerbread, called out their wares and crossing sweepers scraped up the horse-droppings. Then the sun rose, diamonding the windows and transforming the grey morning light into the blue sky of a summer's day, and the mood of the public rose with it in anticipation of the festival.

'I'll make my toilette at Duke Street and go straight to the House of Commons,' said Disraeli. 'You know, D'Orsay, I have a very fine leg.'

'Indeed?'

'Yes, my tailor says so. So does Mrs Wyndham Lewis.'

'You mean the widow of your lamented colleague has already seen your leg?'

'At Lumb's. She accompanied me to my last fitting.'

'What has she got?'

'Gaiety – warmth – sympathy.'

'You can't live on that. How much a year?'

'About five thousand a year, I think, and a lifetime reversion in Grosvenor Gate.'

D'Orsay raised his hat to Disraeli in a parting salute, and the sun illuminated his handsome features.

'You must marry her. I told you. Marriage is going to be the rage. You must marry her.'

'Impossible. She's twelve years older than I am.'

'Couldn't be better. It'll encourage her to appreciate you.'

The Chamber of the House of Commons was filling rapidly as Disraeli arrived, and he picked his way carefully over the feet of Members of Parliament in the second row to the place he'd chosen for himself on the Opposition benches behind Sir Robert Peel, the Tory leader. Except for those who wore naval or military full-dress uniform with orders, decorations and plumed helmets, the Members were either in court dress or Windsor uniform. The crowded benches, the half-light from the leaded windows, the dark oak panelling, the intimate conversations swelling and falling as the places were taken, and above all the familiar Parliamentarians, O'Connell, Follett, Hobhouse, Sugden, Sir James Graham, Lord Landon and Lord Euston, metamorphosed by their garb into courtiers, made Disraeli feel he was being admitted into the mysterious ritual of some privileged secret society.

An usher at the door shouted 'Mr Speaker!' in a bugle voice, and the roar of talk stopped at once, with Members struggling to their feet like a bivouacked army at reveillé.

'Mr Speaker at Prayers!' another usher called towards the lobby, and the Speaker's chaplain read the Litany, praying for the welfare of the most gracious Sovereign and that Members might be delivered from partial affections and guided in their deliberations by divine grace. Then, facing the wall on both sides with their backs to the Mace, the Members recited the Lord's Prayer aloud, adding at the end an emphatic 'Amen!'

'Speaker in the Chair!' came the usher's wail.

Disraeli's neighbour said, 'Barbarous to make us rise so early.'

'Frankly,' said Disraeli, 'I find it rather late, not having been to bed since yesterday. It's as well for our complexions that the Chamber's so dark.'

But as the bewigged clerks drew the names from the black ballot box at the table in the draw for seats in Westminster Abbey, Disraeli's anxieties rose. One by one the Members were called and left the Chamber, and Disraeli felt his calves in their silk stockings beginning to get chilled. Was he, with his colleague Mr Fector, successor at Maidstone to the late Mr Wyndham Lewis, to be among the left-overs on the benches? Was it for nothing that he had acquired a costly court dress and doubled his debt to his tailor? In the gossip at dinner-parties about the Coronation would he alone have to invent the scene that others had witnessed?

In despair he watched the dwindling queue of his colleagues disappearing through the door beyond the Bar and behind the

Speaker's Chair as the clerks intoned. 'The Honourable Members for Devon,' 'the Honourable Members for Glamorgan,' 'the Honourable Members for Northumberlandshire . . .'

Then at last, like a benediction, he heard them announce his own county and his own name. Cheerfully he made his way towards St Stephen's Entrance to the accompaniment of a thunderous salute of cannon that sent the pigeons fluttering from the roofs in alarm and brought a great cheer from the crowds, held back by rows of footguards. The salute was a coincidence. But the omen, he felt, was there.

At the sight of Mr Fector in his magnificent braided uniform, a wag in the crowd called out, 'Make way for the Sheriff of Maidstone!' Fector was unmoved by public ribaldry. He regarded the pageant with awe. After all, Mr Wyndham Lewis was only three months dead, and his own election was recent.

In Westminster Abbey two galleries reserved for Members of Parliament had been built above the altar, and Disraeli and his colleagues sat together on the blue and gold seats.

'Great loss!' said Mr Fector. 'Great loss! Poor Wyndham Lewis! Cut off like that. He wanted to see the Coronation.'

Disraeli looked at his neighbour's contented face and recalled that Mr Fector had tried for two frustrated years to take over the ailing Member's seat.

'Mind you,' said Fector, 'he was never a man for much display – not in his private life. Thought it a waste of money. But there you are. Iron and steel. That's a grim trade. Smoke and darkness. That's your iron works in Monmouthshire. It was his whole life.'

Once he'd begun to talk, Mr Fector felt a compulsion to continue.

'Pity about poor Mrs Wyndham! She'd have enjoyed all this pageantry. Widow's weepers. All very sad. Still, it's the natural order of things. He was a good twenty years older than she was. She'll be able to enjoy herself at last.'

'Indeed,' said Disraeli, studying the pews and galleries that were already full with murmuring onlookers. The processions of Ambassadors in their scarlet cloaks and lace were advancing down the aisle, and he didn't want to be distracted by Mr Fector's chatter.

'Speaking as a corn merchant with the Tory interest at heart,' Mr Fector had begun to say, when suddenly, in a single impulse, the congregation rose and craned forward to see Napoleon's Marshal Soult, the hero of Austerlitz, England's old and defeated enemy, entering with his retinue.

'Never too late for a *Te Deum*,' said Disraeli, 'provided you survive.'

From outside came another salvo of artillery, followed by distant cheers getting louder, shouted orders, the clank of presented arms and the quaver of military music. Then within the Abbey there was a silence with every face turned to the entrance. Opposite the Members of the Commons, the choir-boys with surplices and red hoods, flanked by the orchestra in scarlet, waited. A cough emphasized the hush. In the south transept, the peers rose unfurling like a crimson wave, and the whole attendance followed their example as the pre-bendaries and the Dean of Westminster in full canonicals appeared at the door. A fanfare blared. The Queen was arriving in procession. Everyone craned forward, and the choir and the organ and the musicians joined in the anthem, 'O pray for the peace of Jerusalem: for there is the seat of judgment, even the seat of the House of David. Glory unto the Father and to the Son and to the Holy Ghost . . .'

Disraeli watched the procession intently as it advanced into the Abbey.

Chamberlains and chancellors, pages carrying coronets, archbishops in rochets, attendants, the Princesses of the Blood Royal, the Duchess of Kent, the Queen's mother in purple velvet with a circlet of gold on her head, her train borne by Lady Flora Hastings; the regalia, the golden spurs and the sceptre carried by peers of the realm; the Princes of the Blood and Lord Melbourne, the Prime Minister, carrying the Sword of State; the golden orb borne by the Duke of Somerset; and St Edward's Crown carried by the Duke of Hamilton, attended by two pages; and the Bible in the hands of the Bishop of Winchester. The cortège with the pale young Queen in the centre moved slowly into the choir, its members dispersing to their places as Victoria, alone, passed through the body of the church and on to the stairs, where she knelt in prayer on her faldstool in front of the chair before the throne. The congregants were silent, waiting for the ceremony of Recognition.

Disraeli looked at Victoria's pale, oval face, her small mouth with the retreating chin, and at her hands crossed over her white robe. And all the pageant dissolved in his mind as he recalled what Lyndhurst had said to him in the coach where Disraeli was waiting outside Kensington Palace after the Privy Council had attended the young Queen on her accession. 'I will always remember,' said Lyndhurst, 'the softness of her hand.'

Disraeli lowered his eyeglass, and the scene in the Abbey became a blur of crimson and gold. Then he raised it again, and he saw Victoria's hands, clearly defined, composed, the hand that he resolved in that moment one day to kiss as her Minister, as her confidant, as her servant. Fector muttered to him, and he didn't hear. He imagined the scene. He would arrive with the Administration to be sworn in at Windsor Castle. The Blue Closet? The Pink Room? He couldn't tell. He would be second – perhaps third or even fourth – behind Sir Robert Peel. He would already be known to the Queen as the devoted upholder of the monarchy against all who threatened it, a defender of tradition though a champion of progress, as a political philosopher whose *Vindication of the English Constitution* had won a tribute from Sir Robert. And as he knelt in front of Victoria and took her hand, she would speak to him. What she would say, he didn't know. All he imagined was that it would be gracious and gentle and private, that she would single him out for her favour, that he would enter her confidence and serve her.

'Getting damn hot!' said Fector.

Disraeli ignored him.

The golden crown, the orb, the Sword of State, the court and aristocracy in their ranks, the Church in its dignity, the gentlemen-at-arms, the Members of Parliament – the Peers and the Commoners of the Realm – this was England, the England which had lived a thousand years, the England of order and authority that he loved and had sworn his dedication to.

The Archbishop of Canterbury, accompanied by the Lord Chancellor, the Lord High Constable and the Garter King of Arms, declared in his loud, orotund voice,

'Sirs, I here present unto you Queen Victoria, the undoubted Queen of this realm . . .'

And when he had done so four times – east, south, west and north – there was a tremendous shout, in which Disraeli joined at the top of his voice.

'God save Queen Victoria!'

In the throng on the pavement outside the Abbey after the service, there was a great jostling as husbands and wives and daughters tried to become reunited and find their grooms and equipages. Disraeli stood alone, greeting Lady Londonderry with a bow that he thought was neither too much nor too little, raising his hat with the appropriate amount of demonstrative enthusiasm to the Duke departing in his coach, and leaning on his cane as if he were waiting for his carriage.

He had already decided to walk through the Park to the Carlton Club when he saw Mrs Edmonds standing in front of the Norman Porch. He approached her, and said, 'My dear Mrs Edmonds, I'm delighted to see you. Do I find you well?'

'You find me exhausted.'

She was wearing a rose-coloured crêpe-de-chine pelisse with a matching bonnet that made her look younger than thirty.

'Happily,' he said, 'no one could tell. What a perfect robe, if you'll permit me to say so.'

'I do permit you to say so,' she said in a sulky voice. 'What a tiresome occasion! Why didn't the Archbishop put the crown on her head and have done with it? Eight hours!'

She pouted, and her blue eyes behind her dark lashes were mocking.

'Ah, dear lady,' said Disraeli, 'you are making fun of me. Time is an ingredient. How can you make a soufflé without – '

She interrupted him.

'My carriage is in Parliament Square, Ben.' She caught his quick glance as he looked around him at her familiar use of his name. 'Pray escort me there.'

'I – I fear, Clarissa, I'm expected at the Carlton.'

'Nevertheless,' she said, 'I would ask you to escort me to my carriage.'

'Of course,' he said.

He walked with her from the shadow of the Abbey into the sunlit square, and as they walked she took his arm.

'It's three weeks,' she said, 'since you've called at Bryanston House.'

He raised his hat to Lady Jersey as she leaned from her open carriage, and tried too late to remove his arm from Mrs Edmonds' hand. She flushed, and said, 'Do I embarrass you?'

'No – of course not.'

'Do you fear to be seen with me in public?'

'My dear Clarissa – ' He looked around, apprehensive that they might be overheard.

'Then why don't you see me in private?' she said.

'I'm sorry,' he replied. 'The demands on my time in the House and the constituency have been very great.'

'You always found time in the past.'

'These are exceptional days.'

'I want you to call tonight.'

For the first time her imperious tone had changed into an enquiry.

He hesitated and said, 'Tonight's impossible. I've been taken for over a week.'

Her groom had jumped from the carriage and was holding open the door. She stood for a moment looking down at her lilac parasol.

'Oh, Ben,' she said. 'I've missed you. Please – I can't bear it. How often did you say – so many things about love? Didn't you mean any of it? Please come and see me this evening.'

He took her hand and bowed over it. Then, seeing her eyes,

tear-filled and outraged, he said, 'Soon. Please be patient. I'll come and see you – soon.'

He walked into St James's Park reflecting on the deputation of Maidstone constituents who the previous day had visited him to demand payment of some debts outstanding from the last Election. Sustenance, costs, legal expenses, bribes! What did it matter how they were called? No one had petitioned to upset the result. It was only the lawyers and the bailiffs who disturbed him, lurking behind his creditors.

D'Orsay was right. He'd have to get married. But to whom? He drew up in his imagination a platoon of eligible heiresses, the left-overs of three seasons. Too fat, too thin, too talkative, too stupid.

He groaned, and swung his cane. The sunshine lay on the roses by the lake, and the willows were brushing the water. In his mind, he still heard the exalted, rolling anthem, and the thought of the Queen on the threshold of a new age where he too would start his own new life. Clarissa? Ah, Clarissa. He had already said goodbye.

As he crossed the ornamental bridge and looked towards the Horse Guards, he calculated that all he needed immediately was £2000, a modest sum. But where could he get it?

D'Orsay was right. He'd have to get married.

Chapter Two

After dinner at Mrs Wyndham Lewis's house in Grosvenor Gate, Mr George Beauclerk, formerly of the Royal Welch Fusiliers, sat facing Disraeli with a baleful expression on his face.

At the age of sixty or so he still retained the traces of numismatic good looks which made many compare him with the Waterloo medal struck of the Duke. Indeed, his victories in other fields were almost as famous as Wellington's. He had wooed several widows, acquired a few legacies, and had now decided that Mary Anne might crown his fortunes and end his celibacy. The only obstacle, he felt, to his success was the cold-mannered, buckish Disraeli, who made his own traditionally cut clothes seem old-fashioned and his whole person slow.

'Would Mrs Wyndham Lewis care to join me in a duet?' Beauclerk asked Mrs Yate, Mary Anne's aged mother, who was sitting in a brooding silence like a stone buddha with her beringed hands clasped over her corsage. He was proud of his baritone voice, which had subdued many a soprano.

'I think not,' said Mrs Yate, suddenly becoming flesh. 'I cannot think that Mrs Wyndham Lewis would care to sing after only three months of mourning.'

Mary Anne paused in making a petit-point sampler, but didn't speak, since although she was a 'rattle' on most other occasions, she always felt subdued in her mother's presence.

'I had merely thought,' said Beauclerk apologetically. 'I – '

Mary Anne's brother, Major Evans, still in uniform as his regiment was taking part in the guard at the Palace, looked at Beauclerk with an adjutant's scowl.

'I had merely thought,' Beauclerk went on, 'something in keeping. Like "Yesteryear the Springtime".'

When he was agitated he pronounced his 'Rs' like 'Ws'.

Dismissing him, Mrs Yate turned to Mrs Bulwer, Mary

Anne's particular friend, wearing a new buttercup silk dress, somewhat lost against the yellow damasks of the drawing-room. Rosina Bulwer had failed to get a seat in the Abbey, and her conversation during dinner had been a lament about the crowds and the heat, overturned carriages and the recent death of her lap-dog, Fairy.

'I trust, Mrs Bulwer,' said Mrs Yate, 'your return to Taunton won't be too sad a one.'

'I have nothing to return to,' said Rosina in a melancholy voice. 'Mr Bulwer is – in Cheltenham.'

A glance passed round the circle at the mention of her husband.

'And Fairy – ' She reached for her handkerchief and wiped her eyes. Simultaneously Mary Anne and Mrs Yate imitated her action.

'Fairy is gone. You've no idea, Mary Anne, what it is to be deprived of the one being you love without reserve. Fairy's the only *faithful*, true and disinterested heart I ever owned. I am still prostrate.'

She waved, and a manservant brought her another brandy and water. Mary Anne lowered her sampler, and he poured a brandy for her too.

'Why the devil can't she get another dog?' the Major asked Mrs Yate in loud tones.

Mrs Bulwer affected not to hear him, although this was difficult since she was only two paces away.

'The heart you have lost is irreplaceable,' said Mary Anne in her Welsh voice, putting her cambric handkerchief to one eye and watching the effect of her words.

Disraeli echoed, 'Irreplaceable.'

He had to admit to himself that he'd heard better conversation in other drawing-rooms, but his purpose today was to please Mrs Lewis.

'My poor Fairy!' said Mrs Bulwer, bursting into loud sobs as she hurried in an access of grief from the drawing-room, followed by Beauclerk, who indicated with a gesture to Disraeli that he needed no assistance in dealing with the situation.

'Very human – dogs,' said the Major apologetically, pouring himself another glass of port.

His military collar was sawing at his neck; the malaria he'd contracted in Madagascar was disturbing his circulation; his face was flushed; and he wanted to go to bed. Disraeli wanted to turn the conversation from dogs, but Mrs Yate hadn't finished.

'Mrs Bulwer has commissioned a beautiful memorial stone for Fairy,' she said.

'A monument to her poodle?' said Disraeli. 'I'm surprised Mrs Bulwer isn't wearing mourning.'

Mrs Yate looked at him sharply. She had warned Mary Anne not to be taken in by a young adventurer who everybody knew had already ruined at least two married women, Mrs Bolton and the unhappy Lady Sykes. To make it worse, Mary Anne was smiling appreciatively at Disraeli's ill-natured sarcasm.

'Grief has many garbs,' said Mrs Yate. 'Mrs B needs no instruction in propriety.'

Mrs Bulwer returned on Beauclerk's arm, obviously comforted by him, and the conversation soon became lively. Disraeli would have liked to talk about the coronation, but Mary Anne and Mrs Bulwer, under Mrs Yate's approving glance, chose to talk about Taunton. Then for a quarter of an hour they played riddles, a game in which the Major, after nearly two bottles of port, wasn't greatly successful.

'Well, let's tell fortunes,' said Mary Anne. 'Mr Beauclerk is very good at reading palms.' She dropped her voice. 'He foretold the death of the King.'

Considering that the old Lion had been dying for a year this didn't seem remarkable, Disraeli thought, but he preserved a morose silence.

Beauclerk took Mary Anne's hand and gazed at it reflectively under Mrs Yate's benevolent eye, which was also observing with relish Disraeli's discomfiture.

'I foresee,' said Beauclerk, tracing with his forefinger a line in the palm of her hand, 'a long and happy life in the serene companionship of one to whom your heart will always be a treasure.'

He raised his eyes from her palm, and she flushed and turned her head to her brother. Beauclerk peered again into her palm, till she could feel his breath on it.

'Ah – yes, there'll be someone who'll seek to divert you from your happy destiny. Look – a serpent in your Eden.'

Mary Anne gazed at him in alarm.

'But have no fear,' said Beauclerk, bringing into play the bourdon of his baritone. 'The serpent will be scotched.'

'Bravo!' said Disraeli, applauding languidly. 'A soothsayer with good news!'

'Shall Mr Beauclerk tell your fortune?' said Mary Anne, dimpling.

'I think not,' said Disraeli. 'I've already settled it.'

The Major was the first to rise. There had been a disturbance outside the Palace, and an orderly brought him a summons from his Colonel to come at once to the Horse Guards. Mrs Yate embraced her son as if he were going into battle, and overcome with emotion retired to bed as soon as he left.

Beauclerk continued to face Disraeli, determined to outsit him. Though for the blink of an eyelid Disraeli fell asleep twice, he was equally determined that Beauclerk should leave before him. Both of them affected to be absorbed by Mrs Bulwer's anecdotes, between sips of brandy, of her girlhood in Ireland.

'Very wearying – a Coronation,' Beauclerk broke in as she burst into a spasm of coughing.

'For the Queen?' asked Disraeli.

'No – the spectators. You look tired out, Disraeli.' His 'R' had become a pronounced 'W'.

'Not at all. Perfectly fresh.'

'Very white, if I may say so.'

'Mr Disraeli has a delicate complexion,' said Mary Anne.

'And how was the Queen?' she asked, turning the subject. 'I've been waiting all the evening for you to tell us. Is it true the Archbishop squeezed the ring on the wrong finger?'

'No, the finger was all right. It was the ring that was wrong.'

'How terrible!' said Mary Anne. 'And what about Lord Rolle? They say he fell on his head at the steps of the throne. I can t imagine anything more dreadful.'

'I suppose he could have dropped dead,' said Mrs Bulwer.

'Nothing so final,' said Disraeli. 'I witnessed it all. He made too deep a bow, and arthritis locked his joints and prevented him unfolding.'

To Beauclerk's displeasure, Mary Anne tittered.

Disraeli continued impassively.

'The Queen rose from her throne and helped him.'

'What graciousness!' said Mary Anne, clasping her hands together. 'You must tell us more, Mr Disraeli – no, everything. Oh, how poor Wyndham would have enjoyed it! . . . The whole ceremony from beginning to end.'

Beauclerk began to admit defeat. He longed to retire and smoke, and he sank back into his chair.

'From the beginning to the end, it took eight hours. Even a summary, madam, would need at least two.'

'Oh, that's too short,' said Mary Anne. 'Begin with the ladies. Who were the most beautiful?'

'In your absence, dear Mrs Lewis, Lady Londonderry and Lady Jersey were the two Junos. They outblazed even the Queen, who started, of course, at a certain disadvantage.'

'How so?'

'She began in a linen shift. It was only at four o'clock or so that she was fully dressed in her regalia.'

'Long may she reign over us,' said Beauclerk stoutly.

'Amen,' said Mrs Bulwer.

'And then, of course,' said Disraeli, 'there was the Countess Sablonowska and Mrs Edmonds – '

'Oh!' said Mary Anne. 'Everyone's talking of her.'

' – this season's beauty.'

Mary Anne became thoughtful and changed the subject.

'The peers must have looked glorious in their robes and miniver and coronets.'

'Glorious but at times somewhat bizarre,' said Disraeli. 'Especially in the retiring rooms. I saw Lord Ward drinking champagne from a pewter pot – his dress *rather* disordered.'

Mary Anne laughed; Beauclerk frowned; and Mrs Bulwer sniffed.

'Oh, tell us more,' said Mary Anne.

After Disraeli had spent twenty minutes describing the Coronation, a snore interrupted him. Beauclerk had fallen asleep, and Mrs Bulwer dozed, her glass in her hand.

'I fear,' said Disraeli to Beauclerk, who awoke with a start, 'I've only reached the Recognition.'

'It's enough,' said Beauclerk sourly. 'I can't help feeling you've exhausted the subject. If Mrs Bulwer will permit me, I will escort her home.'

In Park Lane a vast murmuring crowd was waiting for the Hyde Park fireworks. As if lit by bonfires, the western night sky glowed yellow and red with patriotic illuminations outside the shops and houses. The air was filled with jumbled tunes; bands, singing, and far-off cries that rose in a bizarre clamour to the balcony of Grosvenor Gate, where Mary Anne, wearing a shawl and bonnet, and Disraeli, bareheaded and without his cloak, stood looking down on the celebrations.

'You must take care, Mr Disraeli,' said Mary Anne. 'The night air is deceptive.'

He liked her solicitude, and was about to comment on it when there was the sudden hiss of a firework, and a cheer came from the Park. A huge girandole burst in the sky, crackling and twisting and finally cascading in a series of chandeliers over the roofs of the surrounding houses.

With each explosion, a great Ah! rose from the crowd, as if they felt the release within themselves. The Park below became dappled with Bengal lights and Roman candles, earthbound salutes to the rockets that shot through the sky, one after another in changing polychrome.

'We must drink a toast to the Queen,' said Mary Anne breathlessly. 'While the fireworks are still bursting. Oh, I love fireworks. They fizz right inside me!'

She was excited by the colour and volleys, and looked especially youthful with her eyes brightened by the lights. Even her black and white and violet mourning dress was redeemed from melancholy by her naked shoulders and her corsage with its deep V.

Disraeli brought a bottle of champagne and filled two

28

glasses, and said, 'To your very good health, madam.'

'To yours, sir, but you must leave, Mr Disraeli, when the fête ends,' said Mary Anne. 'I – I am in seclusion. What would people say if they saw me entertaining a handsome young man with black curls? It wouldn't be suitable.'

She drank, and Disraeli filled her glass again.

'Not suitable? Have you forgotten, Mrs Wyndham Lewis, you once called me your Parliamentary protégé?'

She giggled slightly. 'Parliamentary, yes – but – '

'Could there be anything more suitable on the night of the Coronation that marks a turning-point in England's history – could there be anything more suitable than for us to be joined in celebration?'

He was indignant, and Mary Anne faltered.

'Perhaps I should leave,' said Disraeli, turning away with a wounded expression.

'Oh, no – no – not yet.'

'I must go. I see you don't want me to stay.'

She put her arm in his, and he came back to the wrought-iron parapet, his face still hurt.

'Perhaps,' she said meekly, 'another toast to the Queen. In memory of my husband – dear Wyndham.'

'In memory of dear – in memory of Wyndham,' said Disraeli, raising his glass.

Lack of sleep and the champagne made him feel that he was floating, serenely remote from the infernal orchestra below.

'The best of friends – of colleagues – to us both.'

'How we both miss him!' said Mary Anne.

'How sad that I can't stay at Maidstone,' said Disraeli.

'But why?'

'I fear – no, not now. Wyndham's gone, and this is a night when I can't talk to you of material things – the expenses – election expenses I incurred with your late husband. My difficulties – my debts – were happily incurred, yes, happily for more reasons than one.' He looked at her closely. 'But difficulties all the same.'

'Oh, you mustn't suffer for your sacrifices. Indeed not. You must allow me to help you.'

'No – I couldn't allow you to do so. Besides, if I were to tell you that the sum is trivial – '

'But if it's trivial, all the more so.'

'It is trivial. A mere thousand pounds.'

'Oh, Mr Disraeli, let's not talk of money,' said Mary Anne, standing close to him and holding her glass. 'You must treat me – as if I were a loving sister.'

'What would Mr Beauclerk say?'

'I hate him,' said Mary Anne defiantly. 'He is too old.'

Disraeli's face was close to her. Her nose was perhaps rather long. Her mouth somewhat small. On the other hand, her eyes were alert and encouraging.

Disraeli said, 'Let's drink a toast to youth.'

As they raised their glasses a rocket burst made the windows rattle. Her hand shook, and she spilled the champagne on her bodice.

'I'm so silly,' she said falteringly.

'Never mind,' said Disraeli. He drew Mary Anne into the shadows of the cornice and undid her bonnet and laid it on the wrought-iron table. She looked up at him in silence. Then he took her handkerchief and wiped the edge of her shawl.

'I am obliged,' she said.

'Permit me,' he said, and passed the handkerchief lightly over the lace at her waist and over the front of her neck.

She didn't move, and he put his left hand behind her head.

'Oh no,' she said.

He continued to wipe the champagne as it trickled between her breasts.

'No,' Mary Anne murmured. 'Not here. We must go inside.'

'Yes,' said Disraeli, acquiescing.

He followed her contemplatively as she walked with her head lowered into the saloon. The maidservant was extinguishing the candles, and Disraeli looked enquiringly at Mary Anne.

'You can leave the lights, Emily,' Mary Anne said. The maid curtseyed and withdrew. 'She's to leave next week,' Mary Anne whispered.

They waited a few minutes, and neither spoke, but at the

entrance to the hall she paused for a moment and put her finger to her lip, then pointed upwards.

Disraeli inclined his head. Earlier in the evening, Mrs Yate had spent some time telling Mrs Bulwer that she never slept a wink, and although Mary Anne had tentatively disputed the point, her mother had declared emphatically that at night she could hear a fly walking.

They climbed the marble staircase, halting after every three or four steps. In Disraeli's ears, her footsteps were like the clicking of the castanets he had so much liked on his travels in Spain some years before, the accompaniment to a slow mating dance. Mary Anne's solitary candle threw shadows over the grim family portraits on the staircase, and although Disraeli had been a frequent visitor to Grosvenor Gate when Wyndham Lewis was alive, he now felt like an explorer entering the blank areas of his map.

Mrs Yate's room, as he already knew, led from the landing at the top of the stairs, and when Mary Anne gestured to him, he understood her purpose. Carefully, he removed his shoes and trod soundlessly behind her till she reached her own bedroom and opened the heavy mahogany door that squealed gently on its hinges. Disraeli closed it behind him, and turned the key.

Mary Anne had placed the candlestick on her dressing-table, and Disraeli took it and lit the sconces by the looking-glass. For a few seconds he stood behind her with his hands clasped under her breasts, contemplating their faces in the mirror, hers pert and excited, his own saturnine and solemn.

'You look like Lucifer,' she said, and she panted a little.

'He was the bearer of light,' said Disraeli, and he lit another sconce.

'Do we need so much light?' she asked.

'Most certainly,' said Disraeli gravely. 'Your beauty needs to be observed.'

He turned her towards him, and as he kissed her and felt the thudding of her heart, he glanced at the reflections in the looking-glass – the great four-poster bed hewn, no doubt, from the oaks of the Gower peninsula, the paintings of

Carnarvon Castle and kine drinking at a brook, and the portrait of Mr Wyndham Lewis, presented by his grateful constituents, with his high forehead, his mutton-chop whiskers and his steady eyes under his thick eyebrows, fixed on him with a severe expression. Disraeli revolved Mary Anne, whose eyes were tightly shut, till they had reversed their positions. But now he found himself looking directly at the picture itself. Feeling his arms slacken, Mary Anne opened her eyes, stared at Wyndham Lewis in the looking-glass, and said with a deep sigh,

'Such a good man! Such a very good man! For so many years we were but friends.'

'In that case,' said Disraeli, 'he will welcome his widow's new happiness.'

He began to undo her dress, and she said, 'Dear Ben – please wait.'

She was trembling, and went into her dressing-room, and while she was gone Disraeli took off his jacket and hung it carefully on a wooden dumb-valet that had belonged, he supposed, to Wyndham Lewis. Then he took off his chains and his waistcoat, and finally his linen and trousers. He studied his tall, pale body in the glass for a few minutes, and was satisfied that it still had the line of youth. 'A pot-belly,' he had once written, 'is a foretaste of death;' but he felt eager and alive. How strange it was that after listening for so long to Mrs Lewis prattling away, he was about to share her bed. The relict of the late Mr Wyndham Lewis. He shrugged his shoulders. The night was warm, but his skin had begun to horripilate. He was impatient for her to return. At the same time, there was an important question he had to put to her.

She came back from her dressing-room in a peignoir with her dark hair flowing over her shoulders, her eyes still bright from the champagne.

'You look like a bride,' said Disraeli.

'Oh, Ben, Ben,' she said, and her peignoir opened against his chest. She was confused, guilty, ecstatic.

'Dear Ben – so long – '

She clung to him.

'So long – such a long time – '

He drew her on to the bed, and she clung to him in a frenzy, kissing him and biting his lips.

'So long – oh, Ben – '

She lay with her eyes clenched, her mouth open beneath his. He stroked her hair and her brow and kissed her hands. Then slowly she opened her eyes, and looked up at his face, mournful in the candlelight.

'What is it, my dearest?' she asked. 'What is it? Do I displease you?'

He leaned on his elbow, and looked down at her.

'No, Mary Anne – you please and delight me. It isn't that. But there is something that lies between us.'

'What is it? Please tell me. There must never be anything that comes between us.'

He hesitated, and she pressed her face against his arm.

'Tell me, Ben. I must know.'

He kissed her again, and said, 'Very well, Mary Anne. I will tell you, but this must make an end of it. I told you I have to leave Maidstone – perhaps London too.'

'Oh no.'

'Alas, yes. The expense of the election was beyond my means. Mr Lewis – Wyndham – I hesitate to say this since he is now departed – he undertook to reimburse me for my outlay. Unhappily, his faculties failing at the last, he left no record.'

'He was a shadow of himself.'

She clung to him more tightly.

'Yes,' said Disraeli. 'His memory – but what does it matter now? My honour requires that I should sell my library, renounce – '

'No. You mustn't. If Wyndham gave you such undertakings, I must discharge them. How much is it?'

He laid her head gently on the pillow.

'Two thousand pounds.'

She half-closed her eyes, and her face was flushed.

'Two – two thousand pounds?' She was panting again. 'You said – oh, Ben – darling Ben – you said a *thousand* on the balcony.'

'But the legal fees,' Disraeli said in a whisper.

'Ah yes – the legal fees – dear Ben – the legal fees – so long – such a long time – dear Ben – you mustn't have worries – the legal fees – the legal fees – two thousand pounds – for Maidstone!'

The last word was a shriek, and Disraeli, covering her mouth with kisses, wondered if her cry would raise the household. He also asked himself later as she slept on his shoulder whether he had advanced or retarded his matrimonial prospects by his impetuous wooing.

Chapter Three

In the valley below the Manor House of Bradenham, the corn was stacked and the autumn sun lay hot on the fissured earth of the lawns where Sarah Disraeli was walking with George Inglefield, a wealthy farmer of the neighbourhood who two years earlier, at the age of thirty-four, had unexpectedly taken Holy Orders.

'Are you well acquainted with your diocese?' she asked.

'I've visited it twice and met the Bishop,' said Inglefield awkwardly. 'The church in my parish is Saxon with Norman additions. Lord Ashley has assured me of a devout congregation.'

'It will be a great contrast with your former life. Ralph and Jem will miss their riding master.'

'Your brothers,' he said, 'will do very well without me. And then again, even as a parson, I'll keep my interest in the land. I hope that in time we'll all renew our friendship when you visit Dorset.'

'But I still don't understand why you decided to leave Buckinghamshire. I remember so clearly the day you told me of your intention to go to Oxford to read theology.'

She twirled her parasol behind her shoulder.

'Ben said he thought you the last person to confine yourself in a parish.'

'Why should he have thought that?'

'Well, to begin with, you were such a hunting enthusiast.'

'There's many a hunting parson in Dorset, Miss Disraeli. My purpose, though, isn't just to look for new coverts.'

'What is it then?'

'I wanted to follow my vocation – to serve the poor – '

'That's a very worthy purpose. You could have done so at High Wycombe. Why exile yourself to Dorset?'

'I wanted to remove myself as far as I could from Bucking-hamshire.'

They had reached the birch copse out of sight of the white manor house, and Inglefield paused. Sarah hesitated. She didn't want to pursue the subject.

'Shall we return?'

'A few moments longer,' he replied. 'I left Bradenham – '

He was confused, and tugged a leaf from a tree.

'I left,' he went on, 'because it had become painful for me to be in your presence.'

'That isn't very kind.'

'No – you must let me explain.'

In the chestnut tree the rooks were cawing to each other, and Inglefield waited to make himself heard.

'You see, when Ben brought Lord Lyndhurst to Braden-ham, I felt I could have no place in the future you fore-saw.'

She stiffened at the mention of Lyndhurst, and looked hostilely at the sinewy hand holding the leaf.

'How could you know what future I foresaw?'

She had indeed foreseen that Lyndhurst might have offered to marry her, but instead he had spoken to her of his engage-ment to a French heiress.

'I've been inept,' said Inglefield.

He threw the leaf to the ground.

'No, I'm glad you spoke. You see, whatever might have been – I always had the duty to care for my father – my mother too – as long as they needed me.'

'But forgive me if I persist. You were betrothed to Mr Meredith when I first knew you, and only his tragic death in the Near East – '

She shook her head slowly.

'It was a long time ago – seven years. Yes, I would have married him . . . But you see, Mr Inglefield, sometimes one discovers one's vocation late in life. Sometimes one's vocation is to renounce.'

'Why should you make that sacrifice? Why should you deny yourself your own happiness?'

'I said "renunciation", not sacrifice. There are many kinds of happiness.'

'I had hoped that one day I might return,' Inglefield began, but he was interrupted by voices and the sound of a carriage arriving at the gates.

'Our guests,' said Sarah.

'My hope is that you'll stay with us as long as you can,' she said, and ran to the carriage where Baum, Disraeli's valet, wearing his best black suit, and Tita, her father's major-domo in his oriental dress with daggers at his waist, were disputing the luggage, and Disraeli himself was helping Mary Anne and Mrs Yate, groaning and complaining, to descend.

'Hello, Inglefield,' Disraeli said. 'Delighted to see you.'

Inglefield shook his hand, noting how time had faded their intimacy. The Radical Disraeli was now, he knew, a fully-fledged Tory, a member of the Carlton Club and a social figure in London. He wondered how, in the drive from Wycombe, Disraeli had managed to preserve his coat uncreased. Disraeli looked back at him, observing that Inglefield's fair hair seemed to have become thinner and his face more lined in keeping with his gravity and his clerical status.

Before dinner, Disraeli and Sarah strolled together in the walled garden.

'A widow, Ben?'

'A second marriage,' he said, 'helps one avoid the errors of a first.'

She smiled, and said, 'In that case, we both have much to experience. Do you love her?'

'Love?' said Disraeli. 'I've always felt that if you love before marriage, you squander an inheritance before you get it.'

She ignored his teasing as they stood by an old yew tree calcified in a rockery at the centre of the garden.

'But the difference in age? You realize Mrs Lewis is some years older than you.'

'Ten, eleven, twelve – perhaps more. I don't know. There's a plateau in human experience where age is irrelevant.'

'She'll bear you no children.'

'Malthus would have approved. Besides, she'll give me all the more of her attention. I couldn't possibly compete with a nursery.'

'But a younger woman – '

'Too exhausting.'

'And in fifteen years' time?'

'Fifteen years' time is still an eternity away. I have to think of this week and next week. . . You too should marry.'

'I have to think of our parents,' she said.

She turned away.

'I try not to think about it, Ben. You know I'll never abandon them.'

He took her hand and looked at her face, shadowed by her bonnet.

'Of course you won't abandon them, but why shouldn't you have your own home?'

'I have. It's here.'

He shook his head.

'In every dutiful family there's always one victim – the one who takes on the duties of the others. Why don't you accept George Inglefield? Everyone in the county – '

'I'm perfectly content,' Sarah interrupted. 'I dislike change. I only wish everything could always be as it was in that summer when we first came here from Bloomsbury. Do you remember the courtyard and the white magnolias? Do you remember that July?'

'Oh yes, very well,' said Disraeli. 'I'd just lost a lot of money in South American mines.'

She smiled and kissed his cheek, and surrounded by the scent of privet and honeysuckle and thyme, they walked happily past the church towards the broad stairway leading to the house.

Although during the Parliamentary session Disraeli hadn't been to Bradenham, Sarah's letters had kept him informed of its day-to-day affairs, such as the trouble about Mrs Fawcett the housekeeper and Tita because of their cheerful anticipation of matrimony, and the discovery of the priest-hole in the

Jacobean wine-cellar. Disraeli in turn had written to her regularly about politics and the London season and his social success at a splendid dinner with the élite of the town that included the Duke in his Garter, Riband, and Golden Fleece; and his introduction to the Lansdownes and the Salisburys and the Rothschilds, whose women, he wrote, looked like Murillos. And then there was the Parliamentary gossip about the Whigs and the Tories and the Speaker in his tricorne hat reprimanding Daniel O'Connell for calling the Tories 'perjured'; and the account of his own speeches in favour of the Corn Laws that had won him praise in the Chamber and popularity in the Smoking Room.

Despite this correspondence, Bradenham in Disraeli's absence had begun to seem more and more remote. He liked to think that among the beechwoods of Buckinghamshire and the farms in the valley, the seasons revolved with only the fall and renewal of the leaves and the growth and harvest of crops to mark change. Far away in Mayfair, he usually thought of his family, his reserved but intimidating mother, his gentle father, his devoted and self-effacing sister and his turbulent brothers, as a community that defied all the temporal accidents that befell other people; even when he acknowledged the contrary to Sarah, he still refused to experience what he admitted. Yet now when he saw his father standing in his library he was suddenly aware of change. In the light of the two candles on Isaac's desk, he saw his white hair falling in strands from under his embroidered skull-cap over the collar of a brown velvet banyan, and his thin gold glasses slipping on his nose.

'Father!' Disraeli said quietly.

His father turned and his face became lively at the sound of his son's voice. Disraeli stretched out his hand, and Isaac rose and took a step to meet him, but faltered before embracing him.

'Pray sit, Ben,' said Isaac, and he groped his way towards his armchair. Disraeli touched his elbow to help him, but his father said amiably, 'Thank you. No, I don't need help. It's merely a temporary clouding of my vision that will soon get better. At least, Dr Moberley says so.'

Disraeli sat, and looked at the almost sightless eyes of his scholarly old father, his teacher and preceptor whose library had been his university.

'I hope, sir, that while I'm here you'll allow me to read to you.'

'No, Ben, I'm like Milton. My daughter is my eyes. Sarah won't let anyone take her place – no one at all.'

Disraeli acquiesced.

'Our life in Bradenham is very tranquil,' said the old man. 'Unlike Milton, I'm happy to say I'm not involved in polemics. Remember, Ben, how his critic Salmasius described our countrymen in *Defensio Regia*? "Englishmen," he said, "toss the heads of their kings like tennis balls!" Sport and regicide! Ah yes! It provokes a laugh . . . Political antipathies are really the worst of passions.'

'Perhaps not the worst, Father,' said Disraeli, 'but among the more interesting.'

He looked at the manuscript in Sarah's hand on his father's table.

'I see you're revising, sir, your *Life of King Charles*.'

'At my age everything is revision. I've tried in this book to present the monarchy as our central institution which can only be shaken at the nation's peril. No state can exist without a framework of institutions to which the generality subscribe. Without them, there's nothing but flux and civil strife. I'm happy to have lived to see a young Queen on the throne . . . Come, Ben! Let's prepare for dinner.'

'There's a matter, Father, I'd like to talk to you about,' said Disraeli, delaying him.

'Ah yes, your novel *Venetia*. Yes, I promised to write to you. A work of the utmost talent.'

'Thank you, Father.'

Isaac groped for his snuff-box, and Disraeli handed it to him.

'There's some other matter I wanted to discuss with you, sir. I felt I should tell you as soon as possible of my wish to get married.'

His father was silent for a few moments.

'Married – yes,' he said at last. 'I would be happy to see my children settled. Take Sarah. She has every quality. Why doesn't she get married? A pleasing lady in every way. She's the soul of the household. I would have been very happy for her to have married Lord Lyndhurst after his lamented wife died.'

'Lyndhurst, sir, was already pledged to Miss Goldsmith.'

Isaac brushed the difficulty away.

'And then there's Inglefield. He was a very good farmer.'

'He will be, I'm sure, a very good clergyman. For the time being, Sarah feels it her – is happy to be at home. It is I who want to get married.'

'Not Lady Sykes, I trust. I'm under the apprehension that she's still married.'

'She is,' said Disraeli.

'Then there's another lady who, I am informed, is an intimate of yours. Mrs Edmonds, I think.'

The name in his father's mouth startled Disraeli, and he cast his mind over those who might have told him – or perhaps Sarah – of his relationship with her. Mrs Austen? He remembered seeing Mrs Austen in an adjacent box at the King's Theatre one night when he was escorting Mrs Edmonds.

'I must tell you, Ben, with the privilege bestowed on me by our connection, that it would be unwise of you to think of matrimony with Mrs Edmonds.'

'But, sir – '

'To begin with, it's uncertain that the lady is in fact a widow. It is thought that she has a husband living on the Continent. She is, I gather, possessed of many external charms. Yet I have to tell you, Ben, that according to my reliable information, she has already enjoyed the protection of a certain peer, and a Mr Hudson who may be known to you.'

'I would hesitate, sir, to challenge your opinion, even if it came from a tainted source – perhaps some rival of Mrs Edmonds moved by jealousy. I can only say that to my knowledge Mrs Edmonds is merely an unfortunate lady whose husband fought very gallantly in the Polish War of Liberation, and died under Cossack sabres. That, at any rate, is what she told me. With the considerable competence he left her, she has already established herself at the heart of London as an outstanding hostess.'

'Does she receive – ladies?' asked the old man.

'Naturally,' said Disraeli. 'Lady Blessington – '

'Who else, Ben?'

'There are prejudices and jealousies, sir. The fact that every man in London is in love with Mrs Edmonds is enough for her to incur the censure of the drawing-rooms. But I assure you, Mrs Edmonds is a lady of the highest virtue.'

'Who are her family?'

'I – I believe they had something to do with India – but our discussion of Mrs Edmonds's merits is academic. She isn't the lady I have in mind.'

'My dear boy,' his father grumbled, 'you should have said so at once.'

'The lady I have in mind is Mrs Wyndham Lewis – the widow of my former colleague at Maidstone.'

'Mrs Lewis? Yes – yes. A very lively lady, as I recall. Of mature years, I believe.'

'Isn't that more gratifying than frivolous immaturity?'

Isaac pondered again, and Disraeli waited anxiously for his comment.

'Frivolous immaturity!' Isaac repeated after his son, echoing the words with relish. 'I don't think that's necessarily the antithesis of maturity. Shouldn't you marry a young and sober woman by whom you will have children and rear a dynasty?'

'Sir,' said Disraeli stiffly, 'I'm a literary man – a politician if you like – not a stock breeder. James is the farmer. He goes to Aylesbury market. Let him raise a brood if he cares to.'

Isaac tapped with his spectacles on the table.

'But it's still true, Ben, that if you marry in your youth a middle-aged lady, you will be married to an old woman in your prime . . . Is that wise?' he added mildly.

'How can I peer so far into the future?' said Disraeli. 'All I am sure of, Father, is that for my present needs I must get married.'

'Must?'

'Yes ... Besides, I have a further and most compelling reason to marry my colleague's widow.'

Disraeli's eye had caught sight in his father's bookcase of *The Genius of Judaism*, a study Isaac had written early in the century.

'I have always thought, sir, that one of the most moving precepts in the Pentateuch is the injunction on the Israelite to marry the widow of a deceased brother.'

'That is true,' Isaac said in a sing-song tone. 'According to the Rabbis, it's the duty of a man to marry the widow of a deceased brother. Why is that? It's because in Biblical times there would have been no one else to provide for the sustenance of the widow, and though Mrs Lewis, I take it, is a lady of means, humanity requires that she should be morally supported.'

'Mr Lewis was very close to me. In many respects, no brother could have been closer.'

Isaac raised his dimmed eyes, and on his mouth was an ironic smile.

'You mean you will find every reason to marry Mrs Lewis?'

'Yes, Father.'

'Come near, Ben,' said Isaac. 'You have my blessing in good measure.' Then he said in Hebrew, 'May the Lord bless and keep you ...'

Disraeli bowed his head. It was time, he felt, for Mary Anne to know of his intention to marry her.

After dinner Mrs Yate sat asleep in her chair in the drawing-room, Mrs Disraeli was sewing, Isaac was indulgently playing riddles with Mary Anne, and Disraeli, his brothers and Inglefield were examining a gun that James had bought from a farmer in Missenden.

'Now, Mr Isaac,' Mary Anne said in her lilting voice, 'I think this time I'm going to catch you – it's a riddle about Sir Robert Peel.'

'Yes, of course,' said Isaac abstractedly. 'That's very interesting indeed . . . Sir Robert Peel . . . excellent . . . yes, yes, it provokes a laugh. Pray join us, Mr Inglefield. We were discussing Sir Robert Peel. I don't know him personally, but I esteem him highly. He has seven children . . .' He peered at Inglefield. 'You are looking well, sir. I imagine as a clergyman you'll now remove yourself from public affairs.'

'On the contrary, sir,' said Inglefield, 'I don't believe the Church should be remote from secular responsibilities. We live, after all, at a great crisis in our nation's history. Everywhere there's a stirring.'

'Yes,' said Isaac. 'Railways – railways! Everything's in movement.'

'More than that – I'm thinking of popular protest – the resentments of the poor.'

'Goodness,' said Mary Anne. 'You do sound like a Jacobin, Mr Inglefield.'

'There's a certain Jacobinism of *events*, Mrs Lewis, that makes one sound a Jacobin merely to relate them. Look at what's happening – Bristol and Nottingham looted – riots in Spitalfields – bloodshed in Manchester!'

'And what's the reason for this upsurge?' Disraeli asked, leaning against the fireplace.

'Hunger,' said Inglefield.

'Not agitation? Subversion? What about the Political Unions, the London Working Men's Associations – the Roebucks, the O'Conners, the Places?'

'If you mean the Chartists – '

'Yes, the Chartists – the secret societies.'

'The secret societies are proof that we need more reform. Where there's no representation, you'll always have con-spiracy,' said Inglefield. 'As for the Chartists, what's their offence? They believe in universal suffrage and annual Parliaments, and say so. It's the natural demand of a self-reliant people. The danger of our times, in my view, lies in our institutions divorcing themselves from the popular interest. It's the precondition of rebellion.'

His voice rose, and James sneezed loudly and woke Mrs Yate.

'Bless you!' said Mrs Disraeli.

Everyone except Isaac Disraeli laughed.

44

'The custom of saluting after sneezing,' he declared, 'is a very old one, especially when the sneeze comes from the right-hand side of an assembly. Petrarch says in his *Life of Themistocles* that before a naval battle it was an omen of victory.'

'James,' said Mary Anne cheerfully, 'you must join the Navy. My father, you know, was a naval officer.'

Isaac tried to rise and Disraeli hurried to help him to his feet. Leaning on Sarah's arm, he went over to Mary Anne, and took her hand.

'I thank you, Mrs Lewis,' he said, 'for joining us at Braden-ham. I'm afraid you didn't complete your riddle, but you've brightened our day.'

She looked from Isaac to Disraeli, and said, 'My own even more.'

After the others had taken their candles from the sideboard and retired, Disraeli invited Inglefield to smoke in the library.

'You were saying,' he said, filling his *narguilah*, 'that the aristocracy is remote from the people. But is that really so? In Buckinghamshire, the peasant has his cottage. His needs are simple. His pleasures are his family and his festivals. When he's ill, the Church or the Manor cares for him. Take my sister. Each week of her life she calls on the poor in the parish.'

'Does she visit the Aylesbury workhouse?'

'No – I dissuaded her because I oppose the new Poor Law and the social mathematics that measures to a spoonful what the poor need to keep alive before they fall into self-indulgence. Our workhouse system degrades the overseers as well as the paupers.'

The moon had risen, and through the open window they could see the valley and the village lapped in its delicate light.

'What about the degradation you can't see?'

Inglefield pointed to a group of cottages sheltering in the lee of a wood.

'The county wage is eight shillings a week, and you know, Disraeli, that when I tried to raise it I was denounced by all the gentlemen of the neighbourhood. Our agricultural situation is shameful, and our towns are even worse. We are entering on a new feudal age. The whole of the labouring class is being pauperized by landowners and industrialists alike.'

Disraeli puffed his *narguilah* calmly. As a Member of Parliament with responsibility, he felt he could be indulgent to the clergyman.

'And what would you do, Inglefield?'

'Oh, for a start I want to see a cheap food policy. I'm for a total repeal of the Corn Laws. To tax imported grain is to tax the labourer's bread.'

'But by ruining our own grain growers, how will you help the farm labourer?'

'That isn't the alternative. If the workers in the towns and on the land have cheap food, trade will grow. The producer and the consumer will both enjoy the benefit.'

Disraeli watched the smoke from the long pipe curl in the air.

'Cheap imported grain, Inglefield, and starvation wages to go with it. Take away the duty on corn and you'll destroy our farmers and leave the country to the mercy of the manufacturers – the most rapacious the world has ever seen.'

'I can't believe that cheap food necessarily means low wages. Nor do the operatives of Manchester or the unemployed or even the farm labourers believe it. What they demand is a voice in their own affairs.'

'Demand. That's the new cry. It's the euphemism for violence. As a clergyman who believes in moral not physical force, how can you support this "demand"?'

'I don't accept that a rational demand is the equivalent of violence. To begin with we – the Chartists – would support our petition by proclaiming a national holiday.'

'A national holiday? You mean a general strike.'

'Oh, not a bit. A general strike would be seditious. A national holiday is a right.'

'Sophistic, my dear fellow! And what then?'

'We'll demonstrate to the nation the enormous numbers supporting our cause. We'll advance in a great procession on the Commons, bearing our petition, and Parliament will yield.'

'I don't think that will happen,' said Disraeli. 'When you

46

get to Parliament Street, you'll be stopped by a platoon of soldiers and a few police. "Kindly may we proceed?" your Mr O'Connor and Mr Hetherington will say. "No, gentlemen," the Commissioner of Police will reply. "But two of you may take your petition to the House if the main body stays behind. I have a cab at your disposal." "Thank you very much, sir," your leaders will say. And they'll climb in. And that'll be the end of it.'

Disraeli puffed a mouthful of smoke towards the ceiling.

'You don't think much of our spirit,' said Inglefield stiffly.

'Oh, I think a great deal of your spirit,' said Disraeli. 'But more of the nation's common sense. The English don't like revolutions.'

The moon had gone behind a cloud, the candles were guttering, and Inglefield, who was staying overnight, shook hands with Disraeli and went to bed.

Disraeli heard his father's clock chime two, and rose from the uncomfortable position in which he had fallen asleep in the studded armchair. His world encircled him – his books, his family, and now Mrs Wyndham Lewis. Mary Anne. He didn't love her as he had loved others in the past. That was true. But what did the word 'love' mean that his sister kept advancing as the criterion for marriage? Mary Anne was affectionate, eager, anxious to please, indiscreet, a gossip, imperfectly educated but warm-hearted and grateful. D'Orsay had been right. Gratitude was a form of love; and why should she not be grateful, even though she could find many suitors like Beauclerk; why shouldn't she be grateful to have found so unexpectedly a young and determined lover?

And if gratitude was a form of love, then he too could feel conjugal love in the security that Mary Anne could give him when otherwise, as D'Orsay had foreseen, he might have become one of those ageing and ill-provisioned bachelors, dyed and omnipresent, contemptuously used by hostesses as table-companions for widows and aged spinsters. This wasn't the love that had blazed through his life during that ardent year when Lady Sykes was his mistress. Nor could it even be com-

47

pared with his feeling for Mrs Edmonds. The thought of Clarissa Edmonds made him uneasy. Whatever the consequences, the time had come at last for him to call on her and tell her his intentions. The decision soothed him, and he looked towards the sky above the tree-tops, flushed with delicate pink over Squire Lowther's land, and that too was a counterpart to his serene mood that had quickly returned.

He smiled at his recollection of the old Squire, who had examined him during his first election when he had stood as a candidate for Wycombe. 'Do you support the agricultural interest, Mr Disraeli?' 'I do, sir.' 'Then, God's firkins, I will support you,' the Squire had said, and so he had done.

A bitter scent of tobacco hung in the air, and Disraeli breathed deeply. Then he breathed again, and the scent was acrid.

He looked through the window and saw that behind the screen of trees a hayrick was burning, and already the whole of the western sky was leaping with turbulent shadows and reflections of flames, illuminating the farms in the valley with an evil light. The smoke made Disraeli cough, and he knocked over the armchair as he rushed to waken his brothers and Inglefield.

Within a few minutes they were dressed and running across the fields in the direction of the blaze. Every now and again shreds of burnt straw drifted like black snowflakes in the night breeze and settled on the hedgerows. Guided by the shouts and the neighing of horses, Disraeli brushed the branches aside as he went through a defile he'd known as a boy to reach the farm ahead of the others.

Old Squire Lowther, wearing leggings, a nightshirt and a nightcap, was giving orders to about twenty farm-workers and villagers who had formed a chain to pass buckets from the well.

'Hang 'em!' he was shouting in an incantation. 'I'd hang 'em! Hang 'em and damn 'em! Ah, Mr Disraeli, a year's work – up in flames – ' His face was streaming with sweat, as the pyre that had seemed to be settling suddenly flared up again. 'A year's work – oh, damn them! Burnt my ricks – them rick-burners.'

While Ralph and James took off their jackets and joined the farm-workers who were beating out the sparks that were spreading to the barley-fields, Disraeli and Inglefield went to the nearby stables where the farmhands were leading the horses, kicking in terror, from their stalls. A neighbouring farmer joined them.

'I knew it,' he said. 'I knew it would happen when the Squire spoke about the Chartists at the Bucks Farmers' dinner. "The hulks ain't enough," he says. "Give 'em the gallows." This is their answer.'

'Not the Chartists,' Inglefield muttered. 'They'd never do it.'

'They're all the same – rick-burners, Chartists, trade unions – all the same,' said the farmer.

He went into the stables to quieten a cart-horse, and tugged it out by its halter.

Disraeli and Inglefield walked over a sodden path leading from the pond to the almost burnt-out ricks and the nearby copse where the leaves were black in the dying light. Apart from the occasional crackle of a twig there were only whispers. The farm labourers with their hats off stood with their heads lowered as if at a funeral, and a cottager brought a blanket and laid it over the shoulders of Squire Lowther, now sitting on a tree stump with James and Ralph at his side. The old man looked up, his face suffused, and Disraeli couldn't tell whether he was sweating or crying.

'Oh, damn them Chartists,' he kept saying. 'All that toil. All that toil. They burnt me ricks.'

Inglefield, Disraeli and his brothers returned in silence to Bradenham.

'There must be change,' said Inglefield.

'Change, perhaps,' said Disraeli. 'But we must protect our institutions.'

The household had been awakened by the alarm, and Sarah was waiting with the servants on the landing for news. Disraeli reassured her, and gradually the manor fell into silence.

Disraeli went out again with Inglefield to stand at the gate, looking down over the valley to the hamlet of Bradenham. The sky had become dark, and only a faint smell of burnt straw lingering among the freshness of the beech woods recalled the fire.

Though he had only just arrived, Disraeli already wanted to return to Westminster. It was only there, he said to Inglefield, that the fires of the rick-burners would be finally extinguished. He would speak in Parliament of the plight of the agricultural labourers and demand that they be helped. The answer to revolution wasn't counter-revolution but reform.

'Reform . . .' he said.

But Inglefield had already gone into the manor, and Disraeli, wide-awake, walked up and down the lawns, rehearsing a speech on agricultural reform and wondering what to do next in his wooing of Mary Anne.

Chapter Four

Leaning out of the window, Baum said, 'I see him, sir. He's coming.'

'Very well,' said Disraeli. 'Let us receive him hospitably.'

'The Amontillado sherry?' asked the valet.

'I think not,' said Disraeli. 'The inferior one. We don't want to encourage him unduly.'

He sat himself in an armchair in his rooms in Park Street and took up *The Times*. He had no wish to show Mr Lawson that he was in any way discomfited by his call.

'Ah, my dear Disraeli,' said his visitor, stretching out his hand as he entered. 'Delighted to catch you in. Left my card three or four times. Very happy to see you.'

He sat, and took off his gold spectacles and wiped his forehead.

'How, sir, did you know where I was staying?' asked Disraeli.

'Well,' said Lawson, 'the House is in session, so I assumed you'd be in London. Then again I met our friend Mr Huffam, who told me exactly where you might be.' He looked around him appraisingly. 'Good address – Park Street. I always think there's cash value and credit in a good address – even if you can't afford it.'

Disraeli waved Baum, who had brought the sherry decanter, into the next room.

'As you see,' he said loftily, 'I can afford it.'

'You may be able to, sir,' said Lawson, 'but I'm not so sure your creditors can. I've come to tell you, Mr Disraeli, that I ain't going to renew your bills.'

Disraeli didn't answer, but poured him a glassful of sherry.

'I hope you'll try a glass of this,' he said. 'I have it specially brought in. I doubt if you've ever tasted anything like it.'

Lawson sipped it, and said, 'It's fair.'

'There are tastes, Lawson, that have to be acquired. What were you saying about my bills?'

'I said I ain't going to renew them. There's that bill of D'Orsay's I bought from Crocky.'

'My dear fellow,' said Disraeli, 'if you were to refuse to renew the D'Orsay bill, you'd make yourself a laughing-stock in the City of London. There's a lot of paper circulating in the discount houses that takes its origin among D'Orsay's set.'

'Too much of it,' said Lawson doggedly. 'I've renewed that bill twice, and I'm not doing it again. I wouldn't have done it last time except for my respect for your father – a very nice old gentleman I used to know at Bevis Marks. The bill's due next Friday, and I expect you to pay.'

'I naturally will pay,' said Disraeli, standing. He tugged at his waistcoat. 'No one can ever say that I have defaulted on a debt. Postponed payment – yes, when circumstances have obliged me to change my arrangements. You understand, Lawson, that's a different matter. What I don't grasp, though, is why you have changed your disposition in so – you'll forgive the term – in so brutal a manner.'

Lawson turned his broad-brimmed hat in his hand, and the large diamond on his second finger glittered in the lamplight.

'Well, I'll be frank with you, Mr Disraeli. You came to me a few weeks ago, and I examined you as to your financial prospects.'

'That is so. I laid bare to you my expectations and my resources.'

'Quite right. Your resources were nil, and your expectations an advance from your publishers – '

'That is true.'

' – and the prospect of an advantageous marriage.'

Disraeli was silent.

'Nothing wrong with that,' said Lawson, raising his hand. 'God forbid that I should think ill of a man who borrows against a marriage settlement! The only trouble is that word has come to my ear – ' he lowered his voice as if imparting a confidence – 'that your prospects with a certain party have substantially diminished, and it was against such prospects that me an' me partner, Mr Nathan, was prepared to extend your bill.'

'And what has led you to the conclusion, Lawson, that my matrimonial plans have altered since I described them to you?'

'I shouldn't tell you, but I will. Your friend, Mr Huffam, informs me, having heard it from Lady Morgan, that Mrs Lewis has declined your offer of marriage.'

Lawson ended his statement in a voice of triumph tinged with regret. He had hoped that Disraeli, for whom he had been for many years a banker, as he described himself, and a money-lender, as others described him, would have proved after his marriage to be an even better client than before. Now he saw him receding into the ruck of all the other men-about-town with high hopes but small means whose accounts he'd had to close with bailiffs and orders of distraint.

'Mr Huffam,' said Disraeli, 'is no more than a tale-bearer, a sort of masculine bawd who lives off the meaner satisfactions of the malicious and frustrated. It would give my enemies great pleasure, Lawson, to think I'd been rejected. Nothing is farther from the truth. Believe me, my dear fellow – ' he put his hands on the squat shoulders of the shorter man, and Lawson looked up at him with caution – 'there's not a word of truth in what Huffam has told you. Huffam was my political agent at Wycombe. He regarded it as his task to promote rumour, and he did it very well. Unhappily, it's a habit he can't shake off. Take my word for it; but I beg you to be discreet since Mrs Lewis, so recently widowed, is reluctant for it to be known. We will be wed later this year.'

Lawson looked dubious.

'You are sure, sir?'

'Who could be more sure?'

'When will it be?'

'The exact time is, of course, the prerogative of the lady.'

'In that case,' said Lawson, observing Disraeli carefully, 'let me be the first to congratulate you.'

'You may indeed,' said Disraeli. 'And if you really wish it, I'm prepared to settle the bill on the due date.'

'As you wish,' Lawson murmured.

'But it would be a convenience if you extended it,' Disraeli added quickly.

'If you prefer it,' said Lawson, still hesitating.

Disraeli smiled graciously.

'A little more sherry?'

'I think not,' said Lawson, retiring backwards through the door that Baum, who had been listening outside, now held open. 'It sits rather heavy on the chest.'

After Lawson left, Disraeli stood at the window, watching the rain dappling the pavements and the roofs of the carriages splashing through the February night. Mr Huffam's embarrassing account had been right. Mary Anne had indeed rejected his offer of marriage the previous day, when in an angry, recriminatory scene she had suddenly accused him of seeking to marry her only for her fortune. Her wholly unexpected refusal had left him bewildered and hopeless. Lawson had merely deepened his worries.

In the months that had passed since Mary Anne's visit to Bradenham, Disraeli, after being a faithful attendant at Grosvenor Gate, had at last insisted that she must make up her mind about marriage. She had answered by quoting Mrs Bulwer and Lady Morgan, harpies he knew well, who had warned her against him. Mrs Bulwer, having failed in marriage herself, couldn't bear the sight of anyone else's happiness; the raddled Lady Morgan considered a day ill-spent if she didn't implant an anxiety in the mind of a friend.

Over the fireplace were the familiar cards. 'Lady Londonderry requests the honour of the company of Mr Benjamin Disraeli . . .' 'Lady Jersey At Home . . .' An invitation to breakfast from Sir Robert Peel. A water-party at Twickenham. Three dinners on three successive days . . . But what did his place in society add up to? In the lamplight Disraeli studied the gilt looking-glass that reflected the silver daggers, the oriental tapestries on the walls and the *narguilahs* that he had brought back from the Near East. They were his, but for the rest, it was a roomful of his landlord's possessions.

His hair was abundant and dark, but he detected a number

of grey hairs which he was sure had grown since his rebuff of the night before. However carefully he had tried to conceal it from Lawson, Mrs Lewis's snub would be the talk of society within days. He'd be known as an unscrupulous usurper of his colleague's place, an adventurer who had scarcely waited a few months before trying to win both the widow and her legacy. Mrs Wyndham Lewis herself would be regarded by her enemies as reckless and by her friends as fortunate. What chance would he now have of making a desirable marriage?

Lawson was a leech who never left him, but another even more monstrous thought had begun to obsess him. What if Mary Anne herself, with the mathematical glint in her eye that he now knew well, were to insist on prompt repayment of her Maidstone 'loan'? His father had already advanced him his second quarter's allowance. His brothers were penniless. The friends like D'Orsay from whom he could borrow in the past owed him money which they couldn't find. For all her shortcomings Mrs Lewis, the chatterbox forever recalling the Service traditions of her family, was his best guarantee of security and respectability, his bulwark against a total insolvency.

The previous evening he had demanded that Mary Anne should decide at once. She had replied, 'Pray don't demand, sir. If you persist, I'll ask you to leave my house forever.' He had bowed and turned his back, hoping that she would follow him to the door. Instead, the manservant had seen him out. Twenty-four hours later he'd heard nothing from her. Disraeli sighed, and sat himself at the secretaire to write her a letter.

'My dear Mrs Wyndham Lewis,' he began. 'As a woman of the world . . .' He stopped, wondering how she would react to the description. 'As a woman of the world' – that was the essence of the matter in his connection with a woman twelve years older than himself, a woman of experience who could have no illusions about the way people would regard their liaison.

As a woman of the world, you can't be unacquainted with the difference in our relative positions. The continuation of the present state of affairs can only harm your reputation and injure my own name. There's only one construction which Society justly puts on a connection between a rich woman and a man she avowedly loves but doesn't marry. In England especially there is no stigma more damning.

He paused. Perhaps there were stigmas more damning, and they recurred to him despite his unwillingness to think about them. There was the stigma of being the dependent lover of a rich married woman; there was the stigma of being the paramour of a patron's mistress. And both had attached themselves to him when he had lived with Lady Sykes.

But that was another matter.

The situation at present is that I must choose between being ridiculous or being contemptible. If you jilt me, I become ridiculous; but if I sink into what Lady Morgan has already called me, 'Mrs Lewis's *de novo*', I become contemptible.

May I now turn to a matter I would have preferred to leave untouched? In justice to both of us, I must refer to it candidly.

He began to write hurriedly.

I must admit that when I made my first advances to you, I wasn't influenced by romantic feelings. My father had long wished me to marry; my settling down was the implied condition of a disposition of his property which would have been convenient to me. I myself, about to begin my career, wanted the solace of a home, and shrank from the torturing passions of intrigue. I wasn't blind to worldly advantages in such an alliance; but I had already proved that my heart was not to be bought.

I found you in sorrow as a widow, and I was touched. I found you, as I thought, amiable, tender, and yet acute and gifted with no ordinary mind – one whom I could look upon with pride as the partner of my life, who could sympathize with all my projects and feelings, console me in moments of depression, share my hour of triumph, and work with me for our happiness.

He stopped, and re-read the paragraph. Yes, it was all true. He no longer wanted intrigue. His liaison with Henrietta had almost destroyed him. His affair with Mrs Edmonds was behind him, he hoped. And as for saying his heart wasn't for sale, that was true too. A Miss Wardle, a thirty-three-year-old heiress with £10,000 a year had been introduced to him by Lady Cork with a view to marriage, but she had been of such invincible ugliness and insuperable stupidity that he had jibbed. His heart could certainly not be bought. Not at that price.

Yet he didn't want Mary Anne to misunderstand. He had to make it clear that money, unimportant as it was in principle, needn't be a barrier to marriage, since in any case her resources were only a moderate inducement.

As far as your fortune is concerned, I will be equally frank. It proved much less than I, or anyone else, imagined.

He introduced a careless tone.

It was in fact a fortune which couldn't benefit me in the slightest degree; it was merely a jointure, enough to maintain your establishment and gratify your private tastes.

To eat and sleep in your house and nominally call it mine – these could only be objects for a penniless adventurer. Was this a reason for me to sacrifice my liberty, and that indefinite future which is one of the charms of existence? No. When I told you on the night of the Coronation that there was only one link between us, I felt my heart inextricably engaged to you. From that moment I devoted to you all the passion of my being. Alas! I poured it on sand.

Disraeli paused again. There was one important matter he had to dispose of. She had agreed to make him her 'Maidstone loan' at a moment in their relationship which he felt it hardly gentlemanly to remember.

He had looked down at her tightly closed eyes and her small

eager mouth, kissing and talking and talking, the Phryne of Grosvenor Gate.

'*Oh, Ben – you shall have it.*'

'*No – I – I can't take it.*'

'*A thousand pounds – a thousand pounds – two thousand pounds – it's so little – you must take it . . . Oh, Ben – Ben – Ben!*'

And so he had borrowed £2000, and this was the sum that the previous day she suddenly accused him of taking under the blanket of love.

He would deal with that too.

'Little did I think when I wept – ' it was a familiar catharsis – 'when you poured upon me in a manner so unexpected and so irresistible the pent-up savings of your affection – ' she had certainly been enthusiastic – 'that I was receiving the wages of my degradation.'

He liked the phrase and repeated it aloud.

Weak, wretched fool! I accepted your loan, and was only waiting for my agent to give me the account and the bill when you were at Bradenham for me to repay it to your bankers. Didn't you realize it?

As he wrote, he felt a surge of resentment. What right had she to question his motives? Of course he intended to repay the loan. It was merely a coincidence that just at the moment he had run out of funds. He would no longer defend himself. It was time to attack.

I wouldn't condescend [he wrote] to be the minion of a princess. Not all the gold in Ophir could lead me to the altar. Far different are the qualities I require in the partner of my existence. My nature demands that my life should be perpetual love.

Perpetual love. That was true. He couldn't be happy unless he was in the state of excitement, anxiety and expectation that he called love.

Now for a few reproaches to Mary Anne. He had reached the end, and felt it time for pathos.

You have done what my enemies have failed to do – you

have broken my spirit. From the highest to the humblest scene of my life, from the brilliant world of fame to my own domestic hearth, you have poisoned all. I have no place of refuge; home is odious, the world oppressive.

Tears started to his eyes at the description of his unhappy condition, but catching sight of the cards on the mantelpiece, he reminded himself that he had yet to answer Lady Jersey's invitation, and should do so without further delay.

Farewell! [he concluded]. I won't wish you happiness, for it is not in your nature to obtain it. For a few years you may flutter in some frivolous circle. But the time will come when you will sigh for any heart that could love, and despair of one that could be faithful. *Then* will be the penal hour of retribution; *then* you will recall to your memory the passionate heart you have forfeited and the genius you have betrayed.

He sealed the letter and rang for Baum. The Swiss valet came limping in, and Disraeli said, 'Take this to Mrs Wyndham Lewis.'

Baum looked out at the rainy street, and said, 'Now – at this time of night, sir?'

'Now,' said Disraeli solemnly. 'It's a letter I have written – perhaps on the eve of my execution.'

Baum said, 'What will you be wearing tomorrow, sir?'

'My darkest clothes,' said Disraeli.

Chapter Five

Mrs Edmonds's house in George Street, Westminster, situated as it was between two aristocratic mansions, was at once obscure and prominent. It was obscure because its façade was overshadowed by the porte-cochères and the Corinthian pillars on each side; prominent because of the distinguished callers who daily tugged its bell. Some were men of letters, others statesmen and soldiers; many were members of famous families, and there were also one or two lawyers; no one had actually seen a clergyman at Mrs Edmonds's, though it was widely held that she herself belonged to an ecclesiastical family that included a Bishop of Cawnpore; but gaiters *had* been seen to enter.

She was, in fact, an Irishwoman, the daughter of a Newry cattle-dealer and sutler to the Indian Army. When her father died in India, she was brought up with the daughter of the household in a regimental establishment, but at the age of seventeen, following a contretemps with the adjutant's wife who returned prematurely from a stay in the hills, she found herself returned to England, where with the graces she had acquired she became for a short period a governess to the children of an exiled Polish prince. It was here that she met and married Count Bronislaus in a short but happy marriage that ended with his death in the Polish uprisings and left her with a posthumous daughter.

In Paris, where the enterprise against the Russians was prepared, she rapidly became the centre and inspiration of the Polish exiles, and even after the failure and death of her husband, she still remained in an intimacy with the revolutionaries which was the subject of Russian representations not only to the court of Louis Philippe where she had been welcomed, but also by Count Pozzo di Borgo to Lord Melbourne and later to Sir Robert Peel when she returned to London under her maiden name of Edmonds.

In George Street Mrs Edmonds never seemed to lack money. There were undoubtedly more gentleman than lady callers at the house, but no one felt this an impropriety. According to reports, the Duke had known her family in India; some said she was related to the Wellesleys. However that might be, the Duke had certainly called on her when she first arrived at George Street, and with that cachet she had become a hostess, not so grand as Lady Londonderry or Lady Jersey, but certainly less aloof than either, at once the pet and the ruler of a brilliant coterie which rivalled Lady Blessington's at Gore House.

She wasn't well educated, but she listened attentively and overheard a great deal of what was said by the writers and artists and politicians of her salon. Through her correspondence with the exiled Polish landowners in Paris, she was always ready to offer a piece of gossip about France to her guests, thus enhancing her reputation for intelligence and sophistication. Apart from all this, she was an exceptionally pretty woman whose menus when the House was in session were carefully composed to attract the maximum of enthusiasm from gourmets.

Apart from a few favourite and ever-present guests like Colonel Tankerton and Mr Hudson, the railway magnate as he was always called, Mrs Edmonds chose her guests like a mason composing a mosaic. This one wouldn't fit; that one didn't have the right tone. If anyone ever behaved the least bit unsuitably, he was never asked again. And so within three seasons Mrs Edmonds had become one of the famous and sought-after hostesses of London; it was regarded in the clubs as a social accolade to be asked to call on her, and a mark of fashionable acceptance to be invited to one of her small dinner-parties.

It was nearly six o'clock, and her afternoon guests were leaving. As usual, Colonel Tankerton, haranguing, and Mr Hudson, silent, stayed to the last. There were few subjects on which

Tankerton didn't claim to be an expert. Having served in an Indian cavalry regiment, he regarded himself as not inferior to any provincial governor in his knowledge of Indian affairs; and having inherited a substantial fortune from his father, a clerk in the East India Company's office who had made his money in peculation, he felt qualified to out-talk even the Chancellor of the Exchequer on the subject of private finance or public expenditure. He had acquired a large estate in Ireland, owned a number of racehorses, was a successful gambler, and would have been completely happy if only, at the age of forty-four, he had a seat in Parliament and a baronetcy to match his wealth and self-esteem.

'I hear there's a seat going at Shrewsbury,' he said to Mrs Edmonds. There wasn't a borough she wasn't familiar with, whether Whig or Tory or Radical. Perhaps especially Radical, since Lord Melbourne himself had made the observation, relayed to her by a friend, that Mrs Edmonds would be much more visitable if she gave up her association with 'those damned Irish rads', whom he bracketed with the Polish insurgents.

'They've been talking about it at the Carlton,' said Tankerton.

'So I hear,' she said. 'But I doubt if the seat's for you.'

She had known Tankerton in India, and had once met his father, the East India Company clerk. Even in her charitable memory she recalled him as a small, deferential man in a counting-house, acquiring his fortune by stealth rather than by obvious pillage, quite different from the heavy, swaggering cavalryman that Tankerton turned out to be. For his standing in Mayfair, Tankerton could have wished that no one could recall his derivation, but since Mrs Edmonds did so, he had decided that his best course was to enter into an understanding with her to refer as little as possible to the past. He was helped in this by her own shamefaced recollection of meeting Tankerton at a horse-sale conducted by her father when Tankerton was a remount officer, and her father was drunk. But that was a long time ago, and when they had met again after several years, they were different people, linked by discretion and social self-interest.

'Why shouldn't I get Shrewsbury?' Tankerton asked, lounging against the piano. She played a phrase of a Chopin mazurka, and stopped.

'Do please continue,' said Mr Hudson, content to sit in the shadows of the room and to admire her.

'No,' she said, closing the piano. 'Not now – another time. You won't get Shrewsbury, Colonel, because I happen to know it's already pledged. They want someone young – ' Tankerton scowled – 'someone dedicated to the agricultural interest. If there's to be an Election – '

'Not yet, I think,' said Mr Hudson, and Mrs Edmonds listened to him respectfully because, emerging from obscurity, Hudson, through his operations in building railways, had quickly obtained the confidence of politicians and courtiers, all eager to take part in one way or another in the booming enterprise that enriched the speculators even as it mutilated the land.

'You see, madam,' said Tankerton in his resounding voice, 'there *is* time. I have, for your information, already met some Shrewsbury gentlemen at the Carlton Club.'

'You still won't get it,' said Mrs Edmonds. 'For *your* information, Colonel, Shrewsbury's already been promised to Mr Disraeli.'

'Disraeli?' said Tankerton, unbelieving. 'But that's impossible. The fellow doesn't know a dray-horse from a cow. What's he got to do with farming? He only pushed himself into Maidstone on the back of that old dodderer Mr Wyndham Lewis. Besides, he's a – '

'Yes, I know,' said Mrs Edmonds. 'But you see, Colonel, he's got something else. Has he not, Mr Hudson?'

'Yes,' said Hudson gloomily. 'He's got something else.'

'Well, that's very mysterious,' said Tankerton. 'But I propose to go for Shrewsbury all the same. Matter of fact, I'm running down there next week to meet His Lordship and several gentlemen anxious to nominate me.'

'In that case,' said Mrs Edmonds, laughing, 'you'd better be quick. Quick, quick!'

She pulled the bell, and a servant entered to usher her two

visitors out. Colonel Tankerton inclined his head with an angry expression. Mr Hudson took her hand.

'Tomorrow?' he said.

'Tomorrow,' she answered.

She watched him leave, thinking of his patience and determination, wishing that she could feel something for this wealthy and assiduous attendant who only the week before had given her five thousand pounds for the relief of expatriates and the widows of the Polish nobility.

After her visitors had gone, she returned to the piano and played the Chopin mazurka to the end. As she did so, her daughter Elizabeth came from the nursery and stood at her side.

'Do you like it?' she asked her child.

'Yes, Mama,' said Elizabeth. 'Will you play me some more?'

'Of course,' said Mrs Edmonds. She kissed her daughter, who at that moment with her broad cheekbones and pale eyes reminded her of the Count, and she again played a few bars of the mazurka he had loved.

'Play me a waltz. Look, Mama, I can waltz,' said Elizabeth. She turned in her long dress with its lace petticoat showing above her shoes.

'Mr Disraeli!' the manservant announced, and Mrs Edmonds ended her playing with a flourish and a discord while the child still turned and turned.

'Oh, Mama, don't stop,' said Elizabeth. 'You mustn't stop.'

But her mother was already standing with her hand outstretched to Disraeli.

'You've been too long a stranger,' she said.

Disraeli glanced quickly from her to Elizabeth, and Elizabeth gave him a rapid and sulky glance in return while her eyes filled with tears. It recalled his first visit to Henrietta Sykes in Upper Grosvenor Street and his first glimpse of her little girl happily playing with her dog. But Elizabeth was different, cold and suspicious, mistrustful of the strange men who surrounded her mother and spoiled her fun.

'Forgive me!' said Disraeli. 'I've interrupted your playing.'

'It doesn't matter,' said Mrs Edmonds.

'That waltz. Just once more.'

She began to play, and Disraeli gravely invited Elizabeth to dance. Solemnly she accepted his invitation, and he encircled her waist as they waltzed together between the wine-tables till at last they reached the double door where, detaching herself, Elizabeth made a quick curtsy and fled.

Mrs Edmonds rose.

'You see, Diz, you're very frightening to young ladies. It's that dangerous curl.'

He had started at the nickname which the Carlton Club had attached to him, but there was something about its familiarity which he welcomed. Beneath Clarissa Edmonds's delicate elegance there was a robustness which derived, he suspected, from a more plebeian background than that of her late husband.

'I'm not made to dance in public. Your daughter abandoned me, I fear, because I tripped over her at the twirl.'

'That's a very good reason,' said Mrs Edmonds. 'Do please be seated.'

He sat on the sofa opposite her as she poured for him a hock and seltzer.

'Ah, Clarissa,' he said, accepting the glass. 'You have the great virtue of anticipating a man's desires, and being right. The great vice is to anticipate and be wrong. Had you offered me champagne or madeira, I would have left at once.'

'Does that mean,' she said, 'you've come to stay?'

'No – not really to stay. I just wanted to see you, Clarissa – to explain something.'

He stood, and walked over to the fireplace, and she rose and followed him.

'What is it, Ben?' she asked, and her tone was unlike the mocking voice that she had used when she had addressed him before by his Carlton nickname. He took her face in his hands, and she looked up at him trustingly as if she was sure that whatever he was about to tell her would at last be truthful and for her best interest.

'I've decided to leave Maidstone.'

'You told me you might,' she said, and leaned her forehead against his cravat. 'Is there something new?'

He kissed the parting of her hair, and inhaled its scent. Then he said,

'Nothing new. On the contrary, it's something old. The haberdashers and the butchers and a variety of other burgesses still expect to be paid for their votes as in the past. And my agent is still demanding payment for some old bribes incurred by Mr Wyndham Lewis. And I rashly put my signature to D'Orsay's bill for three thousand pounds. I have concluded that I've neither the means to pay the bribes nor the time to spend in resisting these exactions.'

She smiled up at him, and said,

'But that's very satisfactory. You'll make a new start.'

'In a sense,' said Disraeli. 'In a sense. I am still waiting for news of Shrewsbury.'

'You have a rival,' she said.

'Who?'

'Colonel Tankerton.'

She gave him the information because she wanted to help and please him.

Disraeli became thoughtful.

'Yes,' she went on. 'He's going to Shrewsbury next week. When are you going, Ben?'

'Tomorrow.'

She clung to his arm and led him back to the sofa.

'Dear Ben,' she said. 'I've missed you so much. You were so cruel to me at the Abbey. Why have you kept away so long?'

He looked down at the striped brocade, and said,

'Clarissa, I have something to tell you.'

She waited.

'I'm going to get married.'

She leaned back against a cushion and he noticed that a light moisture glistened on her forehead.

'Then it's very proper of you to tell me so. May I ask whom you have honoured in this way?'

Her voice was restrained as if the words she used were blocked at the epiglottis.

'It is I who am being honoured.'

'Who is she?'

Mrs Edmonds's voice had become sharper, more defined.

'I fear it might perhaps be premature – '

'Premature? What do you mean?'

'I have no personal precedent, Clarissa. I understand the lady in question would have to make the announcement.'

'Announcement?' she said. She screamed at him. 'What announcement? Who the devil do you think I am to be treated like this?'

This, thought Disraeli, as he looked at her flushed face, is the sutler's daughter.

'My dear Clarissa,' he said, crossing his legs, 'it isn't my wish to treat you with anything but the most complete respect. You surely don't imagine I'd dedicate myself to a lifelong celibacy. You must have realized the time would come when I'd have to get married.'

'Not yet,' she said, turning her back on him. Her voice was controlled again. 'Not yet. Who is she?'

'I can't tell you.'

'Why not?'

'She hasn't yet accepted me.'

'In that case,' said Mrs Edmonds triumphantly, 'there's no announcement to make. So you can tell me. You must tell me.'

Once again she sat at his side on the sofa, and began to undo the buttons of his shirt.

'No, Clarissa,' he said, putting his hand over hers. 'No.'

She withdrew from him, and said,

'Are you pledged to fidelity?'

He did the buttons up slowly, and said,

'Only to myself . . . You mustn't be displeased with me. I'm weary of intrigue and deception and exhausting passions. I have an idea of the life I want to lead. I want serenity. I want to apply myself to my work with a secure domestic background.'

'And me? What about me?'

'You already have everything you need for happiness – an establishment, devoted friends, a pretty daughter, your own person. Everything a woman could desire.'

'Who is she, Ben? I must know.'

He picked up a French flowered paper-weight and studied it thoughtfully, rolling its smooth surface in his palm. Then he said slowly, 'Mrs Wyndham Lewis.'

She looked at him for a second, unbelieving. Then she said, defining each syllable,

'Mrs Wyndham Lewis?'

'Yes,' he said curtly.

'But – but, my dear Ben, is she going to marry you or adopt you? She must be years older than you are.'

'There's a small difference in our ages – an irrelevance.'

He was feeling sorry he'd confided his intentions to her and he rose.

'Mrs Wyndham Lewis,' she repeated. 'Poor Ben! Would you like another hock and seltzer?'

'I think not,' he answered stiffly.

On his way to his rooms, his relief at having ended a connection which had become a habit rather than a joy was tempered by the thought that his disclosure of Mary Anne's name to Mrs Edmonds might prove a double embarrassment. If Mary Anne refused him, he'd be accused of having compromised her name by bandying it about in Mrs Edmonds's presence. If she accepted him, the premature disclosure from George Street might so distress Mary Anne that she could have second thoughts about the whole affair. Quite apart from that, he had received no word from her. The previous evening he had walked past Grosvenor Gate, and the blinds of her bedroom were drawn. A caller or two had been admitted, and had left within seconds as if only for the space of time to leave a card. She seemed to have retired into a total seclusion.

Baum was waiting for him on the steps at Park Street.

'It's here, sir, it's here,' he said in his solid Teutonic voice. He was holding a sealed letter in his hand, and Disraeli's finger fumbled as he tore the flap of the envelope, wet from the rain.

Dearest Ben [he read], for God's sake come to me. I am ill

68

and almost distracted. I will answer all you wish. I never asked you to leave my house, or implied or thought a *word* about money.

You must remember I've been widowed less than a year. I am devoted to you.

For God's sake come to me.

Mary Anne

'Sir?' asked Baum.

'Reprieve, Baum, reprieve.'

He took a sovereign from his fob pocket and gave it to his valet. Then he rushed up the sunlit stairs two at a time to prepare his toilette before calling on Mary Anne.

Only one thought shadowed his happiness – the expression on Mrs Edmonds's face as she offered him the second hock and seltzer.

Chapter Six

Before leaving Grosvenor Gate for the Carlton Club, Disraeli stood in front of Mary Anne for a final inspection.

Two years had passed since their quiet, almost secret marriage had made the tongues of the gossips wag, and closed, for a month at least, the doors of the fashionable drawing-rooms previously open and welcoming to the bachelor novelist. Lady Londonderry and Lady Jersey both struck him off their lists till they learned that Lord Lyndhurst himself had been a witness at the wedding.

Now the rickety Whig Government had been defeated and Lord Melbourne had resigned. The young Queen had sent for Sir Robert Peel, and from all parts of the country Members of Parliament were converging on the headquarters of the Tory Party, in the hope of reminding their leaders while the new Government was being formed that they were available for office.

Mary Anne approved of her husband's well-cut coat and cravat, kissed him affectionately on the cheek, and said, 'You look wonderful. You'll come back a Minister of the Crown.'

He kissed her in return, and set off into the sunshine of Park Lane.

As he walked, he reflected how with the passing of time Mary Anne's talents as a hostess had overcome the hesitations of those who regarded the match as premature, not to say strange. She entertained generously, and since few politicians could resist a dinner, almost the whole of the Tory Party in the House had eventually become guests at Grosvenor Gate.

True, he himself had arrived on the Parliamentary stage like an actor who trips over a loose board at his entrance. True that four years earlier his maiden speech had been a catastrophe, and that he still woke in the night from dreams in which the

Irish Members were bellowing and clucking, in which his lines were forgotten, and the misery of his disaster left him with his heart thudding in the blackness. But all that was over. He had fought his way back, remembering his father's precept – 'Knowledge is the foundation of eloquence'; he had made himself a 'master of facts and figures, dates and calculations', as the Irish Member Mr Sheil had advised him; he had attended the House diligently, sat late into the night, lacerated the Whigs in his constituency speeches, and after his disagreement at Maidstone over election expenses had been welcomed to Shrewsbury at the General Election on the invitation of the country gentlemen and in the face of a virulent campaign waged by a Colonel Tankerton whom he scarcely knew.

He was a Tory, but he had preserved his habit of independence. To Peel's displeasure and the Radicals' delight he had opposed the harsh treatment of the Chartist leaders in their cholera-stricken gaol. He had attacked the new Poor Law and the inhumanity of the workhouse system. Indeed, encouraged by a letter from Mr Inglefield, he had voted against his leaders who favoured a measure to set up a riot police force for Birmingham where the Chartist Convention was sitting. Yet in other respects he had been a good Party man who had cast off in the House the stigma of 'dilettante' fixed on the author of *Vivian Grey* and *The Young Duke* by his enemies on *Fraser's Magazine*.

There was no reason, he felt, as he walked along Park Lane towards the Carlton Club, why he couldn't fulfil a ministerial appointment with the same Parliamentary and social competence as anyone in the Tory Party.

Only two or three of the places had been announced. The rest was rumour. It was certain, though, that the first news of the new jobs would come to the Carlton, which was already simmering with excited talk when he took a seat in the library.

'He's in!'

'No – I assure you – Ashley's out. I've seen the Cabinet List. Refused the Prince's Household. Said he wanted guarantees from the Prime Minister about factory reform.'

'Who's got Ireland?'

'Lord Eliot. Not so fastidious about rotten potatoes as Ashley is about decayed spinners.'

From the other end of the library came a surge of voices, and the speakers behind the pillars where Disraeli was sitting rose and hurried towards the cluster of members surrounding Lord Lyndhurst, the newly appointed Lord Chancellor.

In an ormolu looking-glass framed in the wall opposite, Disraeli observed the attendants gathered around his friend and former patron. Like a funeral or a marriage, an administration in the making created disparate relationships and revived forgotten alliances. Men who hadn't spoken to each other for years suddenly found a common interest. The aspiring condescended to the failed while sharing their fears of mortality. The young sought to look graver, the reverend to look younger. And everyone attending Lyndhurst had an eye on the messenger at the door who might bring a happy summons from the Prime Minister to join his administration.

As in a saraband, the groups formed and re-formed, those advancing bringing with them a murmuring train of sycophants, those retreating bowing their heads, a scene enhanced for the spectators by the bright sunlight that lit the faces nearest the mullioned windows. For the performers, each whisper was an alarm, each partner a competitor, another's smile a personal setback. They eyed each other with mistrust, observing each departure from the salon with suspicion, and sometimes with pain.

Disraeli sat alone. If there had been anything for him to hope through Lyndhurst, the tall, elegant lawyer with the Roman head, the thick eyebrows that had intimidated so many litigants, and the soft, self-indulgent mouth, it had already been realized or destroyed. During the years when Lady Sykes had been his mistress and Lyndhurst their companion, sometimes in circumstances like their visits to Bradenham which had shocked the county, Lyndhurst at her prompting had given him political instructions and the promise of advancement. It was a relationship that now belonged to a past which he no longer wanted to remember.

And yet his recollection persisted. He had loved Henrietta

till the attachment became a yoke. All that survived in the last year was the encumbrance of a complaisant husband calling him to responsibilities he wanted to discard and an establishment he couldn't afford.

Then Henrietta had become Daniel Maclise's mistress and his own unintended part in it had been that he had commissioned the artist to paint her portrait. Disraeli remembered the notice in the *Berkshire Chronicle*: 'Whereas Henrietta Sykes, the wife of me, Sir Francis Sykes, Baronet, hath committed adultery with Daniel Maclise, Portrait and Picture Painter (with whom she was found in bed at my house, No. 29 Park Lane . . .). This is to give notice that hereafter I shall not be answerable for any debts she may contract . . .'

Sir Francis Sykes, the *cocu* who had tolerated a Lord Chancellor and a political novelist as his wife's lovers, had jibbed at a picture painter.

In the end, though, Sykes had taken her back, and despite everything, Disraeli thought with an ache, he could understand why. But there were more immediate questions to be attended to.

Who was in? Who was out? The Club was steadily becoming more crowded as its members stood discussing names. Another two voices, assertive but unidentifiable, came from the armchairs beneath the portrait of Lord Bolingbroke on the other side of the pillar.

'No,' said the first. 'Wharncliffe and Knatchbull are certainly in. Murray's got the Ordnance, Buckingham the Privy Seal. We are, after all, a conservative party. I can't see there'll be change.'

'Perhaps some of the younger men,' the second speaker murmured. He added a name, and Disraeli leaned his head back to hear.

'Who? Who?'

Again the whispered name.

'Heavens, no! He may be one of the Chosen – certainly not one of the Called.'

Disraeli couldn't see the speaker, but the one who had suggested his name, he saw when he turned his head, was Lord

73

George Bentinck, a man he knew better for the value of his stud than for his political distinction, a nephew of the late Prime Minister, Canning, and an almost silent Member of Parliament for over twenty years.

Angrily, Disraeli turned to *The Times*.

'Royal Surrey Theatre,' he read. 'Last week of *Mazeppa*. Tuesday, August 31, 1841.

'This evening we present Lord Byron's *Mazeppa* with Mr Ducrow's magnificent stud of forty horses, highly trained palfreys, fairy pygmy ponies and equestrian troupe . . .'

His mood changed at once. In an election speech at Wycombe he had used Mr Ducrow and his act as a simile for Lord Grey, the former Whig Prime Minister, and his Cabinet, but it was a simile that could equally well apply to his leader, Peel, and some of the mediocrities he relied on.

'Mr Ducrow, that celebrated gentleman,' he had said to an overflowing audience at the Red Lion Hotel, 'rides six horses! What a prodigious achievement! You fly to witness it; unfortunately one of the horses is ill. He substitutes a donkey . . . No matter! Ducrow is still admirable, bounding along in a spangled jacket . . . Now two more of the steeds get the staggers and lo! He puts three jackasses in their stead!'

The farmers and squires had roared their approval. Mr Disraeli might be a novelist, a dandy in purple velvet with more chains than the Lord Mayor of London. But as Mr Huffam, his former agent, said, 'He knows a horse from an ass.'

He wasn't quite so sure about Peel. Like the Whigs, Grey, Melbourne and Lord John Russell before him, Peel would no doubt have to ride some of the titled aristocratic donkeys who had surrounded him in Opposition. But would there – could there – be a place for a charger like himself?

Cautiously he began to walk towards the billiard room. For a second he caught Lyndhurst's eye, but then the Lord Chancellor turned his face towards the cheerful group near him, Sir Edward Sugden, Lord Granville Somerset and Sir William Webb-Follett, all with a distressing air of plotters, strengthened by Sugden's sympathetic but casual nod in passing before he returned to his absorbed conversation. Reading faces was like reading entrails; an inexact art. But an averted eye was a discouraging augury. Perhaps after all *The Times* was wrong in saying that the Ministry was incomplete, and Peel *had* completed his Ministry. Perhaps after all his own exclusion was a fact that explained Lyndhurst's uneasiness as he passed.

On his way to the door, Disraeli was stopped by George Smythe, the son of Lord Strangford, his proposer at the Carlton. Smythe had just been elected to the House of Commons, and was the centre of a cheerful group of young men, friends from Eton and Cambridge, whom he was eager to introduce to Disraeli.

'This is Lord John Manners – and Mr Baillie-Cochrane.'

Disraeli bowed gravely. He was ten years older than either, and their respectful manner in counterpart to the irreverence of Smythe made him feel older still. Smythe's good looks, his indifference to the opinion of his elders, his contempt for mediocrity, were echoes of his younger self, while at the same time he admired the easy grace with which Smythe and his friends, assuming their new estate before the old proprietors moved out, occupied the centre of the room, their voices unsubdued by the presence of their seniors.

'Well, Disraeli,' said Smythe, 'what's new from the New Court?'

'Rothschild's or Windsor?' Disraeli said nonchalantly.

'Whitehall Gardens,' said Smythe. 'The only matters of importance are the Household Appointments.'

'Especially the Buckhounds,' said Manners.

His handsome face was serious, and Disraeli realized that Manners, a mediævalist, was genuinely concerned lest the Mastership of the archaic Buckhounds should pass into profane hands.

He looked at him coolly.

'As in all good households,' he said, 'it will end with the appropriate compromise. Sir Robert will recommend. The Queen will appoint.'

'Curious hybrid,' said Manners.

'Sir Robert's test,' said Smythe confidently, 'is *cui bono?*'

'It's an English settlement,' said Disraeli.

'I detest utilitarian judgments,' said Manners.

Smythe looked at Disraeli. Too polite to ask him directly, he was interested to know if he had received a call to Whitehall Gardens. Disraeli read his glance and turned away. Manners and Baillie-Cochrane followed him with an assessing look as he took his hat and went into the Mall. They weren't sure that they liked him.

After his unavailing wait at the Club, Disraeli decided to return to Grosvenor Gate in the hope that a message might be waiting for him there. As he walked, he began to compose a letter.

'Dear Sir Robert Peel . . . My dear Sir Robert Peel . . . My dear Sir . . .' The form was important. Even though his hopes of office were dwindling, he wouldn't genuflect.

'Dear Sir Robert, I have shrunk from intruding – ' no, that would be too deferential. 'I have shrunk from *obtruding* myself upon you at this moment . . .'

That would do for a start. He would ask, not beg. He would state his credentials and claim his entitlement.

'. . . I have had to struggle against a storm of political hate and malice which few men have ever experienced from the moment that, at the instigation of a member of your Cabinet – ' he'd bring in a reference to Lord Lyndhurst – 'I enrolled myself under your banner . . .' That sounded right. Five elections – the immense cost – why not remind the Prime Minister of those energetic and extravagant years?

But was it enough? Behind him he heard footsteps, and turned to find that Mr Huffam had caught up with him.

'Well, Mr Disraeli,' said Huffam, 'I trust that I may soon be privileged to congratulate you.'

Disraeli examined the short-winded figure beside him, as the sweating face looked up with a private irony. Huffam was now the Duke of Buckingham's man of affairs and a prospective candidate, and he had no wish to offend him.

'I'm content to wait,' he said wryly.

'Very galling – inactivity – for a spirited man.'

Disraeli waved his afternoon cane, and the sunlight glittered on its silver ferrule.

'I think not,' he said. 'I've always regarded patience as a form of action. Besides, I hear there are many posts to fill.'

Forti nihil difficile was the motto Disraeli had adopted. Determination, eloquence, courage were important, and nothing was difficult for the strong. But patronage was decisive. To seek a place in a ministry when patronage had asserted its power was like arriving at a theatre when all the seats were taken.

'Maybe so,' said Huffam. 'Maybe so.'

He nudged Disraeli confidentially as they walked.

'Goulburn's got the Treasury, you know.'

'Indeed,' said Disraeli, shrinking from the familiarity of his former agent's elbow.

'Yes,' said Huffam, ' 'tis certain. I heard it from our friend the Duke of Buckingham.'

'Indeed,' Disraeli repeated, reminding himself that in the light of Huffam's connections he should treat him cautiously.

'Yes,' said Huffam complacently. 'The Duke has the Privy Seal. It's now confirmed.'

Disraeli's spirits rose. Years before, the Duke of Buckingham had encouraged his Parliamentary ambitions in Wycombe, and remained his friend.

'And then,' added Huffam, 'there's Mr Gladstone. A young man of great talent. Of considerable religious dedication.'

'Yes,' said Disraeli, anxious to get rid of the uninvited companion whose disclosures he had ceased to relish. 'I shall bid you goodbye, Mr Huffam, as I am making for Park Lane.'

'Exactly my way.' Huffam spoke in short bursts, Disraeli thought, like a barking dog. 'Yes – Gladstone. Set his mind on the Chief Secretaryship for Ireland. Not a chance, of course . . . not a chance. Peel told him so. The Ulster Protestants couldn't swallow a High Church Puseyite . . . Didn't want the Vice-Presidency – absolutely refused it.'

'The Vice-Presidency?'

'Trade, sir, Trade. No, he didn't want it. Said the business of politics was to govern men, not deliver parcels.'

77

'A fine distinction,' Disraeli said. 'So he refused.'

He felt as if he had been given a reprieve.

'Yes,' said Huffam, and they walked on a few paces. 'But the matter's still open. Sir Robert will contrive to persuade him 'tis his duty. Besides, it's not nothing to be second to Lord Ripon – President of the Board, you know.'

'No,' said Disraeli, thinking of the Minister, once Prime Minister for a few months, whom he had described as 'an embarrassed and transient phantom'. 'It's next to nothing.'

Then he added quickly, unwilling to detract from Gladstone's merit, 'I'm sure the pupil will teach the master.'

They walked on without speaking till Huffam said,

'By the way, Mr Disraeli, I met Mrs Edmonds in Paris the other day.'

'How is she?' Disraeli asked eagerly.

'She is well – courted by all, and she moves much in society.'

'Ah!'

'She asked to be remembered to you.'

'I am much obliged,' said Disraeli. 'I trust she'll enjoy her stay there.'

Huffam smiled without comment and raised his hat, and they parted.

During each of the four days that followed, Disraeli rose early while Mary Anne was asleep and looked out of the window in the direction of Whitehall Gardens, still hoping that a messenger from Peel, a clerk, a secretary, might arrive on foot, by carriage, by cab. Each time an equipage stopped in Grosvenor Gate and he heard the shouts of the grooms, the harness clinking and the clop of iron-shod hooves, he peered through the window. The very force of his hopes made it seem impossible that Peel wouldn't gratify them in some way, till at last he decided that he must know his fate, come what may, and decided to call on Lord Lyndhurst.

For the visit to George Street he discarded the subfusc frock-coat and plain white shirt that he had taken to wearing in the weeks before the Dissolution. As the likelihood of office receded, so he asked Baum to be more enterprising, more defiant in the dress that he laid out for him. Now he wore a bottle-green coat, a silk shirt with three rows of frills, a cinnamon velvet waistcoat with three gold chains given to him by Mary Anne, and a pair of tight white trousers.

Arriving on foot at Lyndhurst's front door, he tapped with his cane and an apologetic footman quickly received him. Lord Lyndhurst had left for Sussex that very morning. Lady Lyndhurst was still in Paris. Was there something he wished to leave? Disraeli hesitated. Only, he wanted to say, his despair.

'No,' he said instead. 'Say simply that Mr Disraeli called to present his compliments and congratulations to the Lord Chancellor.'

He summoned a cab and hurried back to the Carlton. The solemn doorkeeper saluted him, and anticipated his question.

'No, sir – nothing – no messages – nothing.'

In the vestibule he passed Lord Stanley, the new Colonial Secretary, who affected not to see him. Milner Gibson, old Lord Fitzgerald, preoccupied, greeted him, their eyes lowered as if to ignore his disability. Now that most of the posts were filled, the library was almost empty, and after twenty minutes Disraeli drove gloomily back to Grosvenor Gate.

Mary Anne met him in the drawing-room where the blinds shadowed the Aubusson carpet, and he stood in silence waiting for her to speak, but she shook her head. Then he put his arms around her, and she said, 'I'm very sorry, dearest.'

He didn't answer, but clung to her, and after the buffeting and rejections he had endured she seemed to him like a secure and sheltering anchorage. She had no ambition for him except that he should be happy in the fulfilment of his own ambitions. She sought nothing from him except his presence. There was nothing she had concealed from him when she agreed to marry him, and nothing that she had exacted of him as a condition of their relationship. In the two years that had passed, she had shown him only devotion and attention, and his gratitude had grown into a loving dependence within their domestic life that both soothed and surprised him.

'They mustn't hurt you,' she said. 'I do hate them all.'

He stroked her face beneath the ringlets at the side of her cheeks, and said,

'Don't worry, Mary Anne . . . While you're at my side, I'm invulnerable.'

He released her, and went to the window and once again looked down the empty street.

Chapter Seven

In his Palladian mansion at Whitehall Gardens Sir Robert Peel, attended by his secretary Mr Edward Drummond, was taking leave of his guests after the first Cabinet dinner since his appointment as Prime Minister. During his earlier administration he had decided to use his house as the real centre of government, though he still maintained No. 10 Downing Street for day-to-day work, and he felt a special pride that in the splendour of his rooms, the umbered magnificence of his paintings by Rembrandt and the quality of his chef, he, the son of a cotton manufacturer, could match the aristocrats Lord Haddington, Lord Wharncliffe, Lord Aberdeen, the Duke of Buckingham and the others who filed past him as he stood at the top of the broad staircase lined with liveried footmen.

Peel had given his colleagues a survey of the problems which the new government had to face. There was the war in China, a 'wrestle with a barrelful of treacle' he called it, where every victory was a new involvement and peace like a shadow marched always one step ahead. There was the army in Afghanistan, isolated and vulnerable. Between Canada and the United States lay the disputed North-East frontier, the dangerous site of a threatened eruption.

But it was at home, Peel had emphasized to his attentive colleagues, that the greatest danger lay. The falling revenue, Chartist agitators, and stagnant industry had produced a national malaise. Towns like Bolton and Paisley were living on charity. The Anti-Corn Law League had excited an attack on landlords and aristocrats every bit as violent as the Chartist onslaught against the mill-owners. The aim of the administration, the new Prime Minister said, would be to increase the mutually dependent prosperity of town and countryside.

At the end of his statement Mr Henry Goulburn, the

Chancellor of the Exchequer, led the applause, and the dinner broke up in good humour as the Ministers began to leave for the relaxations of Apsley House. But the Duke of Buckingham held back.

'We count on you, Sir Robert,' he said, 'to look after the agricultural interest.'

'That,' said Peel, 'will be my general purpose.'

'No – particular purpose. Particular,' Buckingham said, moving reluctantly towards the stairs. 'You've got to watch out for those Leaguers. They spent ninety thousand pounds last year feeding sedition. Magistrates among them . . . endangered the public peace . . . excited the mob . . . promised them immunity. That villain Cobden's a demagogue!'

Limping with sciatica, Peel took Buckingham's arm, accompanying him to the hall. He was anxious not to offend the Duke, whom the Protectionists regarded as their chief patron.

'Yes,' he said, 'we're in danger from the demagogues. Cobden calls the Corn Laws a bread tax. It's a dangerous cry. We must refute him.'

'Damn Cobden!' said Buckingham, shaking with rage. 'The Leaguers want to abolish the tax so they can reduce the wages of their mill-workers and bring ruin to the farmer. We can't have it. What do you say, Peel?'

'I say,' said Peel, 'that only if the domestic distress I spoke about could be directly attributed to the Corn Laws – only then would I favour repeal.'

'Ah!' said Buckingham with a frown.

'But,' Peel went on rapidly, 'since nothing at present can convince me of that, I'm induced to maintain the Corn Laws as they stand.'

'Ah!' said Buckingham a second time, now smiling. He took his hat from the footman, and said to Peel, 'You've summed it up. Protection, Sir Robert! We must protect the agricultural interest.'

The last to leave was Mr William Ewart Gladstone, the son of Sir John Gladstone, an old friend of Peel. As a Christian responsibility, Gladstone had wanted to be Chief Secretary of

Ireland, but Peel had persuaded him he had other outlets for his religious zeal. And so, after a profound self-examination and a long discussion with his wife, Gladstone had agreed as an alternative moral duty to become Vice-President at the Board of Trade, where he could resist the sale of Indian opium to the Chinese and the import into England of slave-grown sugar from Brazil. Peel was delighted to have in his government the tall, powerfully built young man whose gravity would counterbalance the frivolity of some members of the Party, the clubmen, the ageing dandies and the gamesters, always ready to join in a mischievous cabal.

'I'm happy, Gladstone,' he said, 'that you came. I'm looking forward to reading your *Church Principles* when I return to Drayton. I've already heard high opinions of it.'

'I trust, Sir Robert, you'll find my book elevating,' said Gladstone.

Peel shook his hand affectionately.

When Peel and Drummond were alone, they walked to the Prime Minister's closet, where the red box with his correspondence and despatches lay open on a secretaire.

'I think that went very well, Drummond.'

'Admirably,' said Drummond. 'Provided it lasts.'

Peel smiled, and turned his attention to a tabbed pile of letters.

'I don't imagine,' he said, 'there'll be any trouble with our supporters as long as I have a few jobs left. The problem is, for every job I fill, there are ten men discontented. And the one who gets it is usually ungrateful.'

He riffled through the letters.

'What a disagreeable task! Office, pensions, honours. You know, Drummond, I sometimes feel there's a rare and valuable distinction in being without an honour. We shouldn't let it become extinct – what sort of honour is there when everyone has it?'

Drummond said nothing. Between him and Peel there was not only a physical resemblance, emphasized by their auburn hair, but also an understanding that needed little verbal communication. He handed Peel the office-seeking applications, one by one, and the Prime Minister commented.

'Attwood – no. Deverell – no. Herries – well, he'll have to find a seat – lay it on one side. Here's Sugden. Good God, the man's insatiable!'

'The position, Prime Minister, is that following his appointment as Lord Chancellor in Ireland, he feels a peerage would be a fitting addition.'

'No,' said Peel firmly, his hair prickling. 'No. Sugden's got a pension as a judge. Why the devil should he have a peerage? No . . . no.'

'Perhaps,' said Drummond soothingly, 'we can keep this for tomorrow.'

'Yes – tomorrow, tomorrow.'

The Prime Minister's elated mood following the dinner was subsiding, and he rose and limped towards a globe of the world and turned it with his fingers.

'How different,' he said as if to himself, 'is a public servant from a public man! Some of our friends boast of being public men when their only thought is to add to the public dead-weight. Pensions, jobs, patronage – uncles, cousins, nephews, old retainers – I'm surrounded by parasites, all stretching out their hands. When I read these applications for office, I have a sense of profound disgust.'

'But it's reasonable, Prime Minister, that those who engage in political affairs should seek power.'

'This isn't a question of power. These people are only looking for doles.'

Shortly before midnight, Mary Anne went into her bedroom at Grosvenor Gate and, in the light of the flambeaux from the street, studied the pale, sleeping face of Disraeli, who had gone to bed early after taking a draught of laudanum. For a moment she hesitated, listening to the thin drift of music from London-derry House where the new ministry was being celebrated.

Hurriedly choosing a flowered bonnet, she put on a velvet mantle and, glancing at herself in the looking-glass, decided that she was suitably dressed for a call.

During the previous few days she had been thinking, sometimes with hope, sometimes with terror, of her plan, a secret that every now and again she'd wanted to confess to her husband. But then she had shrunk from its enormity. To tell him might be to frustrate her own purpose. Yet not to tell him, if the plan went wrong, could be for him to forfeit his faith in her. On the other hand, how could she endure any longer his anguished hopes, his hourly disappointments, his stricken expression which the defiant posture of his head couldn't hide? If she'd had a child and someone had mistreated it she could scarcely have felt a deeper sense of outrage, a greater anger, than she felt about the Prime Minister's injustice to her husband.

Earlier in the day she had warned Blagden, the groom, that she would require the carriage, their wedding present from Isaac d'Israeli, to be waiting at midnight outside Grosvenor Gate. Blagden's eyelid had drooped in a wink, but when she frowned he pretended that he had a piece of grit in it. Once conceived, her project had developed an independent and compelling logic not to be disturbed by a groom's familiarity. Was she wise? She no longer knew. All she was conscious of was that she had committed herself to a hazardous and irrevocable enterprise.

'St James's Street,' she ordered.

They drove past Londonderry House, and its yard had the usual commotion of jostling horses and swearing coachmen. A fiery light from the linkmen's torches lay over buildings and trees, and the scene seemed to her like a classical canvas portraying a great despot entering Sardanapolis in triumph while the conquered begged for mercy. Outside Apsley House, where another reception in honour of the new ministry was being held, the gas-jets roared and statuesque dragoons with glittering helmets nonchalantly held their mounts in rein. The festivities made her feel resentful and excluded. But after her carriage left St James's Street and the roads returned to their normal starlit darkness, she became convinced that she was embarking on a terrible course, a descent into a Hades where she could only meet disaster for herself and her husband.

'Where now, ma'am?' asked Blagden.

'Whitehall,' she whispered.

Every now and again she looked out into the Park and saw the huddled shape of one of the homeless who preferred the warmth of the summer night beneath the elms to the stench of the rookeries, and she shrank into the corner of her carriage. She wanted to order the driver to turn back, but the horse snorted and began a gentle trot on the downhill slope as far as the Thames embankment, where the river's blackness was pricked by the lamps of moored barges, and the silence was total except for an occasional cry from the lookouts on the craft and a splash of oars.

The horse and coachman were indecisive.

'Where to, ma'am?' asked Blagden again.

She didn't answer, and Blagden sat holding his whip like a sceptre as Mary Anne assembled her courage. After a few minutes the horse shook itself, and Blagden asked, 'Where now, ma'am?'

'To Whitehall Gardens,' said Mary Anne. Then she added in a firm voice, 'To Sir Robert Peel's house.'

'Sir Robert's,' Blagden echoed in his hoarse voice. 'Sir Robert Peel's house.'

He flicked his whip, and the grey picked itself from its lethargy and trotted cheerfully on.

'Yes – yes. Pray be seated, Mrs Disraeli,' said Peel, adjusting the bow of his white neck-tie as she entered. 'Mr Drummond –' he waved to Drummond ' – my unfortunate secretary – has several hours of labour before him.'

'I trust you'll forgive me for arriving unannounced at such an hour. I'm reluctant to disturb you,' said Mary Anne.

'Disturb?' said Peel. 'You release me, madam. Pray be seated. I've often said to Lady Peel how wearisome it is to return in her absence from the House, only to find nothing but sleeping servants and empty rooms. Isn't that so, Mr Drummond?'

Drummond bowed, and Mary Anne looked at him, hoping that he would leave so that she could talk alone to the Prime Minister.

Peel caught her glance, and said, 'You will no doubt excuse Mr Drummond. Never a moment's leisure, not even at midnight.'

Drummond smiled faintly, and withdrew. Mary Anne smiled gratefully. Peel was making her visit less difficult than she had feared.

'A glass of madeira, madam?'

She thanked him, and Peel rose and poured her the wine from a decanter.

'There's little respite,' he said, 'in London. I have a passion for music that I can rarely indulge. But when the government's complete, I hope to get some leisure to enjoy the opera. Do I not see you sometimes at the King's Theatre?'

'We have our box.'

'Ah, yes, indeed. I much enjoyed the Auber the other night.'

'*Les Diamants de la Couronne.*'

'And yet, I prefer Rossini.'

He began a detailed comparison of Rossini and Auber that went on for several minutes. Mary Anne fretted. She hadn't come to talk to him about the opera. What did Rossini matter? What did Auber mean to either of them? She tried to interrupt the Prime Minister, but he pursued his theme inexorably, and she drank the rest of the madeira fast to mark the limits of her interest in his lecture. Her neck became flushed with the wine and her indignation.

'Sir Robert,' she broke in. 'I mustn't encroach unduly on your time.'

He waited for her to continue, examining an official document that he took from the table. Her mind went blank, and she began to talk more quickly, searching for the sentence to make her meaning explicit.

'I came here – I fear my arrival at this hour is unconventional – you see, Sir Robert, only the most compelling reasons could have made me – how can I say this? – present myself unattended in this way. I have a request to you which I have formulated in this letter . . .'

She took a letter from a fold in her mantle and laid it on the table in front of him. He went to open it, but she said,

'No – please – not yet. I must explain if you will be good enough to bear with me.'

He put his fingers together and looked at her with composure.

'This is very difficult for me,' she said, squeezing her handkerchief between her fingers. 'You may have guessed my object in visiting you at such an hour.'

Peel said, 'I can only imagine, madam, that you are prompted by altruism.'

'No, selfishness. My husband is unhappy, and I suffer.' She began to speak rapidly. 'Please, Sir Robert, I beg you. Don't be angry with me for my intrusion . . . You must know how Mr Disraeli has exerted himself in your cause. You must know that all he has ever asked of you is your approbation. He has never hesitated to make enemies – the most vindictive enemies – of *your* enemies.'

She paused, and her eyes filled with tears. Peel looked away.

'He – he is one to whom literature meant so much. Yet he gave it all up for politics – to serve your party – our party – at the side of my late husband, Mr Wyndham Lewis. I must tell you, Sir Robert, that if you fail to recognize his abilities – '

'If I fail to recognize his abilities – ?'

Peel echoed her words, and waited for the conclusion.

' – then he will feel,' she faltered, 'his whole life was a mistake – a failure – '

Peel was silent and she swallowed, searching for some additional argument to reinforce her case.

'And for myself – I can only say that through my influence alone – forty thousand pounds was spent at Maidstone in the Tory cause.'

The Welsh cadence in her voice became more emphatic.

Peel's expression hardened, and he said, 'Do you suggest, madam, that forty thousand pounds is the price of office?'

'Oh, no – no. My dear Sir Robert – ' she clutched her mantle – 'that wasn't my thought or suggestion. I mention the figure merely to show the exertions – the sacrifice – '

The Prime Minister rose.

'I am sorry that Mr Disraeli should have sacrificed so much

to no apparent purpose – except perhaps the victory of our cause . . .' He picked up a folio and laid it down again. 'His sacrifice, I'm obliged to say, was unsolicited. No one has been press-ganged into our ranks. If Mr Disraeli gave us his support, he shouldn't have done so in the expectation of preferment. No one's entitled to such an expectation.'

Peel didn't look her in the face that became pale as he went on.

'You must understand, madam, that the offices at my disposal fall far short of the claimants. Some have served our party loyally for many years.'

She interrupted, and Peel stopped so that she might continue.

'He was encouraged to hope,' she said defiantly. 'Yes, he was – he was encouraged to hope.'

'Indeed? By whom, madam?'

'By Lord Lyndhurst.'

Peel restrained the words that came to his mind.

'Everyone is entitled to hope. But Lord Lyndhurst is Lord Chancellor, not Prime Minister.'

His mouth had become set, a little twisted.

Mary Anne stood. Now she realized that there was nothing she could gain from the tall, cold-eyed statesman.

'I am grateful to you, Sir Robert, for receiving me,' she said, 'though I've been at a disadvantage.'

'I'm obliged to you,' said Peel, 'for having taken the trouble to allow me to explain what might easily have been misunderstood.'

He bowed to her, and escorted her towards the door. There she stopped, and said,

'I've one thing to ask of you, sir.'

'By all means.'

'It is that no one – neither my husband nor anyone else – should *ever* know of my mortification.'

The Prime Minister, followed by a footman, led her to the steps of her carriage.

'I'd never consider it a mortification for a wife to seek to promote her husband's interests. On the contrary, I would regard it as a great merit.'

He handed her into the carriage, and Blagden, whistling cheerfully, whipped up the horse as Mary Anne pressed herself into the cushions, wiping her eyes.

When Peel returned to his bureau, Drummond was waiting for him. They didn't speak, and Peel sat at his desk that looked over the river.

'It's intolerable,' he said at last.

Drummond untied the tape from another batch of letters.

'He has talent,' he said.

'A talent for mischief,' said Peel. 'He brought Lady Sykes to ruin.'

'Perhaps she herself – ' Drummond began.

'No,' said Peel. 'She had the misfortune to have a complaisant husband.'

'Was he more culpable than Lyndhurst?' Drummond asked.

'Not more culpable but equally foolish. Disraeli made use of them both.'

He sighed, and rose. Then he shook his head, and returned to the subject as if his doubts were still unresolved.

'Despite all that,' he said, 'I might have considered him for some office in trade or finance. He's a man of ability. That can't be denied. But when it came to a job, it was Lord Stanley who decided me to the contrary. "I'd never serve in an administration with that rascal Disraeli" were his words. Something to do with Stanley's younger brother, I believe. He says Disraeli enticed the young man into a gambling hell in St James's, and got some payments from the Bonds. Very nasty affair!'

'I doubt, Prime Minister, if Henry Stanley needed much enticing. You'll find him every night gambling at one of the clubs.'

'Yes – but Graham as Home Secretary drew my attention to another objection. I gather Disraeli frequents Mrs Edmonds.'

'Only before his marriage. She entertained very widely.'

'Her associations have been indiscreet.'

'The Duke visited her.'

'He was always trusting.'

'Perhaps Disraeli was too.'

'She's a woman with dangerous connections, the Home Secretary tells me.'

'As far as I know,' said Drummond, 'Disraeli hasn't been in communication with her for the last two years.'

'How do you know?'

'I enquired. It occurred to me you might consider Mr Disraeli for preferment, and I wanted to give you the information you sought.'

The Prime Minister smiled slowly.

'Drummond, you are undoubtedly a perfect secretary.'

Drummond said modestly, 'Well, you see, Prime Minister, I had already read Mr Disraeli's own application for office.'

'Curious!' said Peel. 'Very curious! How strange that Mrs Disraeli should have come here to reinforce his letter! What remarkable things a proud woman will do for a man which she would never do for herself!'

'I doubt if Mrs Disraeli knew her husband had already written to you,' said Drummond.

Peel picked up Disraeli's letter from the table.

' "To be unrecognized by you at this moment," ' he read aloud, ' "appears to me to be overwhelming, and I appeal to your own heart – to that justice and that magnanimity which I feel sure are your characteristics – to save me from an intolerable situation." That is Disraeli himself.'

'These literary men – ' Drummond began.

'Literary or not, I think, Drummond, it's a letter worth keeping.'

Half an hour later, Mary Anne cautiously closed the door at Grosvenor Gate, and took a candle to light herself to bed. At the top of the stairs Disraeli, wearing a smoking cap and a green velvet banyan, opened the door leading from his study.

'The time is nearly one o'clock in the morning. I have the right to ask, madam, where you've been.'

She lowered her head, and without speaking hurried past him through their bedroom into her boudoir, where she locked the door.

In the hall below, Disraeli could hear a manservant shuffling about, and he waited until there was silence. Then he knocked at the door of the boudoir.

Silence.

He knocked more loudly, and said, 'Mary Anne – it's essential that I talk to you.'

Still silence.

'Mary Anne,' he said sharply, rattling the door-knob. 'I demand that you come out at once. Otherwise, I will – ' His voice trailed away.

He had wanted to say that he'd leave the house, perhaps never to return, but how could he do so? Amid all his other anxieties, the thought that he might be obliged to leave Grosvenor Gate with its warmth and security because of some squalid domestic disruption appalled him. She had been a gentle, acquiescent wife, uniquely devoted to him as he thought, only differing from him from time to time about their financial affairs which she insisted on controlling as *she* thought. Every now and again a past debt or a bill, forgotten or at least suppressed from mind, would be presented at Grosvenor Gate by a clerk, and once by a bailiff. He usually managed to intercept them, but twice Mary Anne had received the creditors, and the result had been their only disputes, followed by tears and desperate and amorous reconciliation.

'Otherwise I will – I will – '

What use was a threat? It was late, and he was wearing carpet slippers and he had no desire to displace himself, and besides there was the matter of D'Orsay's accursed bill, well-thumbed and regularly renewed, on which he was now paying forty per cent interest to Mr Lawson. Forty per cent! Only the previous day he had confessed his debt to Mary Anne, and she with a gentle chiding, restrained because of his political disappointments, had at last promised to pay off the outstanding interest.

But forty per cent! Even standing outside Mary Anne's locked door, the enormity of the interest rate took precedence over his parallel thoughts of her friends and former suitors; Augustus Fitzhardinge Berkeley – asinine name – the odious George Beauclerk – the idiotic Stapleton – that damned Captain

Neil! Forty per cent. Where had she been? Which of her friends had she been visiting at midnight? What an absurdity that he should be standing outside her door like the Emperor Henry in the snow at Canossa waiting on the papal pleasure. She had urged him to his bed, and then left for a rendezvous. Berkeley? Beauclerk – that notorious legacy-hunter? The same ignoble rabble of hangers-on who presented themselves at Grosvenor Gate when his colleague Wyndham Lewis was alive; and afterwards as well? He had begun to doubt.

He turned the handle again, and this time the door was unlocked. Mary Anne was sitting at her dressing-table.

Disraeli stood over her with an impassive expression, though he felt as if every part of him, his heart, his entrails and his lungs, had turned as pale as his face.

'Well, madam?' he said.

Slowly she turned her face upwards, her eyes reddened with weeping, her face blotched with red patches.

'Oh, Ben,' she said. 'Ben!'

He waited for her to continue.

'I've done something – something terrible.'

Again she burst into sobbing, and said, 'You'll never forgive me – never.'

She took his hand to kiss it, but he drew it away.

'You had better tell me everything,' he said, his face composed. Neil? Beauclerk? Berkeley? Infidelity was like death. It was the first that mattered, and to know the first was to have knowledge of them all.

'Who was it?' he asked in a controlled voice. She was silent, and he stroked her hair, her side curls wet with tears, his compassion giving him a sense of nobility that he enjoyed even as he felt within him the knife of betrayal.

'The Prime Minister,' she muttered. 'Sir Robert Peel.'

'Peel! *Peel?*'

Disraeli took a step back, and looked at her incredulously.

'You've visited Sir Robert Peel? Good God, madam, you've had an assignation with Peel?'

'Oh, no, Ben,' she said with a shocked expression. 'I called on him unannounced.'

Disraeli walked to the window, and spoke with his back to her so that she could not see his angered face.

'Why?'

'Please forgive me,' Mary Anne whispered. 'I called on him – I asked him – not to forget you – in these last days – in completing his administration.'

She had stopped crying, and sat with her head lowered, the shadows from the guttering candles flickering over her face. He looked at her in a confusion of shame and rage. She had doubled his humiliation and deepened his mortification, and if her visit to Peel became known, he would become the laughing-stock of London.

'Dear Ben,' she said, 'I don't want to live.'

As she spoke he approached her slowly, his anger ebbing away, and he knelt at her feet and took her hands in his.

Of Peel's final rejection he was now sure. But Mary Anne's tears were the tears of fidelity, not betrayal. And as he looked up into her face, they slowly smiled at each other.

'Dearest,' she said, stroking his hair, 'did you know that Peel has two glass eyes?'

When she awoke in the night, Disraeli was sitting by the window, looking out over the moonlit Hyde Park. She felt the warmth he had left, and called out in alarm,

'Ben! Ben!'

He came back and sat on the bedside.

'Why aren't you asleep, my darling?' she asked.

'I was thinking of Peel.'

'You mustn't.'

'He made you weep.'

'I wept for my failure.'

'He made you weep. And he will regret it. But first we will go away – abroad – to Paris!'

'Yes – to Paris – I am very stupid . . . Come back to bed, dearest. I knew so little before we met. You must educate me, Ben.'

'Have I not?' he asked.

'Yes,' she said. 'But more!'

94

Chapter Eight

The snow over the Tuileries Gardens left the tree-trunks beneath the whitened branches in a dark, criss-crossed pattern stretching from the Palace to the Louvre. The sky was a cold and brilliant blue, and Mary Anne stood with her husband watching the skaters moving over the frozen lake to the music of a Meyerbeer waltz played by the cuirassier band. A child fell and burst into tears. A dog barked and slithered on the ice. Everywhere else there was laughter as the skaters, singly and in pairs, glided in time to the music.

Mary Anne clung to Disraeli's arm. They had only been at the Hotel de l'Europe a few weeks, but already they were established as members of Parisian society. Lyndhurst and his father-in-law, M. Goldsmith, had given them introductions, and the console table in the vestibule leading to their apartment was covered with invitations from the Duc de Gramont, the Rothschilds, the Comtesse de Castellane, Countess Apponyi, and the English wintering in Paris. That same evening Disraeli was due to be received by King Louis Philippe at the Tuileries Palace, near their hotel.

Gradually the disappointments of the previous year had faded, even though the resentments persisted. While in Opposition, Disraeli had felt an equal among men without place, but on the government back benches he was an outsider, excluded from the circle of those who had arrived, a supernumerary with a vote but no real part in decision, frustrated and resentful each time he saw Ministers of inferior ability acting as spokesmen at Sir Robert Peel's side.

But he had made his mind up never again to risk for himself the affront that the Prime Minister had given him directly and through Mary Anne, nor ever to complain even in the face of the well-meant condolences of his friends. He had no intention of being crushed by Peel's rejection or of being isolated from the Tory Party. Let the ministerial mediocrities have their day; they'd be forgotten when their role was over. If for the time being he was denied his proper part at Westminster, he would find a wider scene for his talents.

His young acquaintances George Smythe and Baillie-Cochrane had written to him from Geneva proposing a meeting in Paris to discuss their plans for the new session, and the prospect stimulated him. In the crisp winter air, far from the fug and counter-cries of Westminster, surrounded by happy and welcoming faces, he felt his vigour return. Here in Paris, the city of light and intellect, the city of Lamartine and Hugo, where history was made by historians like Guizot and Thiers, here in Paris they would understand him. What did it matter that he was unknown at the court of Windsor? He was already acquainted with Louis Philippe from the days of the King's exile at Twickenham. As for Peel and his spavined asses, they might hate him, but one day they'd fear him.

He was happy. One-two-three. One-two-three. Mary Anne's booted foot tapped the rhythm of the waltz. The windows of the Palace glittered in the sun. Beyond lay the broad-flowing Seine. The rococo fountains were festooned with stalactites. Stone Apollos, rimed with frost, embraced naked nymphs, and skaters danced with their arms around each other's waists. Tonight he had an audience with the King, tomorrow a ball at Rothschild's in the Faubourg St Honoré. Disraeli thought of Peel's frigid and disapproving eyes, and the thought left him indifferent.

'What a lovely child!' he exclaimed as a girl wrapped in furs skated past them, hand in hand with a woman of about thirty, fashionably dressed in black.

'All children are lovely,' said Mary Anne.

She held his arm more closely as if to compensate herself for her own deprivation. Disraeli took her gloved hand in his, and raised his eyeglass to the flowing corn-coloured hair of the girl, moving gracefully with her taller companion.

'Do you recognize her?' asked Mary Anne.

'Yes,' he said. 'That's Mrs Edmonds and her daughter.'

He stood straighter, and raised the beaver collar of his coat. 'Shall we perhaps return? It's getting rather cold.'

'I didn't know she was in Paris,' said Mary Anne.

'Is there any reason why we should?' asked Disraeli. 'You should keep your hands within your fur.'

The faint warmth of the winter sun dissolved the snow on the branches, and Mary Anne clutched her husband as a white shower hissed on to their shoulders.

'Do you know her very well?' she asked casually.

'As one knows people in town,' said Disraeli. 'She was a widow, married at one time to a Polish count when he was killed in their war of liberation against the Russians. She had a house in George Street, I believe.'

He raised his tall hat ceremoniously as Mrs Edmonds and her daughter, after circling the lake, drew near.

'Mr Disraeli!' she said. Her face was bright from exercise, her eyes shone in the sunlight, and she looked enquiringly at Mary Anne.

'May I present my wife,' said Disraeli, and Mrs Edmonds, hesitating between a bow to an older woman and a handshake, scrutinized Mary Anne for a fraction of a second and inclined her head before her eyes returned to Disraeli.

'What a very great pleasure to meet you both in Paris! *Dis bonjour*, Elizabeth.' The little girl scowled and curtsied. 'I hope you're here for a long time?'

'It will be too short,' said Disraeli, taking her hand and bowing over it.

Mrs Edmonds smiled at Mary Anne.

'We must see each other often,' she said. 'We are at the Hotel de Rivoli.' Then with a quick au revoir, she and her daughter skated towards the fountains.

'Shall we return?' said Mary Anne. 'It is getting cold after all.'

They walked over the crunching snow towards the hotel.

'She's very beautiful – your Mrs Edmonds,' said Mary Anne.

'I believe she is generally thought so,' said Disraeli.

The *chasseurs* at the entrance to the Hotel de l'Europe leapt to

97

their feet and flung open the double doors leading to the lobby, where a blazing fire greeted them.

'Good morning, madame. Good morning, Excellency. Good morning, milord.'

The doormen and ushers weren't sure of Disraeli's exact title, but his consequence had been firmly established the previous day by a letter, embossed with the royal arms, delivered to him at the hotel by a court messenger. One of the pages led the way respectfully to their large suite on the first floor. In the vestibule a group of visitors rose, and Disraeli greeted them as Mary Anne went through to her room, and Baum helped him off with his coat.

'And who are these gentlemen?' he asked.

His valet, happily restored to the opportunity of speaking his native Swiss-French, said confidentially, 'From the press – *La France, L'Indépendant, La Nation* – several others.'

'In that case,' said Disraeli, 'we mustn't keep them waiting. You must be kind to the press, Baum. It's a golden rule.'

'But in the drawing-room,' Baum said, turning to a guttural English, 'are Mr Smythe and Mr Cochrane.'

'That's another matter,' said Disraeli.

He excused himself to the journalists, and hurried to meet the Members of Parliament who had arrived the previous day from Geneva. Cochrane had grown a short beard which fringed his jaw, but Smythe had the unchanged, insolent air of youth that always pleased Disraeli.

Smythe took his hand affectionately; Cochrane, more reserved, waited for Disraeli to greet him.

'Wintering in Paris is a form of English madness,' said Smythe. 'Rather like the Laplanders going south in search of the sun – to St Petersburg.'

He huddled with his back against the porcelain-tiled stove.

'You've been frozen by the Swiss Calvinists,' said Disraeli.

'No,' said Smythe. 'I escaped. They wanted to roast me in hell-fire. Almost made me a Voltairean.'

The three men moved to the double-glazed windows, looking out at the snow that had turned to a delicate blue under the changing sky.

'Such an extraordinary light,' said Disraeli. 'When I was in Jerusalem they said its air made men wise. But Zion is built on hills. What do you say of Paris, Cochrane?'

'That it makes men mad,' said Cochrane. 'Paris is a whore of a city – all beautiful on the surface, corrupt within. Undoubtedly a city of the plains.'

'You can't know virtue till you know vice. The Manichaeans . . .'

'A heresy,' said Cochrane glumly.

All the way from Switzerland he had lectured Smythe on the need for a revival of Christian faith in daily life. Newman and the Oxford Movement had ushered in an ecclesiastical renaissance. What was now required, he urged, was the restoration to politics of religious principle.

'The Manichaeans,' Cochrane went on, 'gave equal weight to good and evil. It's our Christian duty to affirm the supremacy of the good.'

'A Cambridge Movement,' said Smythe.

He walked round the room restlessly, explaining to Disraeli the theme of a spiritual revival in politics that he and Cochrane had elaborated in Geneva.

'You must stop prowling, George,' said Cochrane. 'You're swishing your tail.'

'It's my way of ruminating,' said Smythe. 'Did I say a Cambridge Movement? . . . No, not a Cambridge Movement – an England Movement! A Young England Movement!'

He halted.

'That's it, Diz. A Young England Movement – a movement of youth to restore our old institutions, to revive our ancient customs – '

'The maypole?' Disraeli asked.

'Why not? There was a time when our peasantry danced. We had Holy Days. Why not revive them?'

'By all means, but you're in error about the people. You assume they'll always love the noblest when they see it. They don't.'

'It's Rousseau's fallacy,' said Cochrane. 'But what d'you expect of a country that prides itself on being ruled by a citizen

99

king? You'd think the son of Philippe Egalité would remember what the rabble did to his father.'

'What the mob gives, the mob takes away,' said Smythe. 'It took the father's head and gave the son a crown. That's only fair. One each!'

Disraeli's expression didn't change.

'Louis Philippe's task,' he said, 'is to reconcile. He has had to shake hands with murder. Like Charles II.'

'Quite right,' said Smythe. 'Why shouldn't he give everything the royal touch? Everyone hand in hand! More folk-dancing – more festivals – it's a good party cry. Long live festivals!'

'But not in England,' said Disraeli.

'Why not in England?' asked Cochrane.

'Well,' said Disraeli, 'just remember the Eglinton Tournament. The flower of our aristocracy turned out their attics and rummaged their cellars. Armour, standards, embroidered coats.'

He shrugged his shoulders.

'Then it rained,' he went on. 'Lord Eglinton had defied the gods of Manchester.'

Cochrane protested.

'Our folk festivals have gone on for centuries, notwithstanding.'

'No doubt,' said Disraeli. 'No doubt. It's not our destiny always to be washed out by rain. I'm only saying that any party which depends on our weather will lack a sound foundation.'

Suddenly he changed his manner, and said, 'Our national greatness can't be restored by circuses. We must have a real alliance between the people and their leaders – throne, Church and Parliament. The danger comes from the Whigs and their manufacturer friends. They're trying to turn the people into helots under an oligarchy. They want a confrontation between the classes. And they've found their ally in Peel!'

Cochrane sat watchfully while Smythe, lounging by the window, turned his face from the Tuileries towards Disraeli.

'In the next two or three years,' said Disraeli, 'Peel – mark my words – will abandon our Tory prescription. He'll turn from protection to free trade.'

'Abandon his own party?' asked Smythe.

'No,' said Disraeli. 'His own principles. And our task – the task of Young England – must be to resist him.'

They spoke for almost an hour till Baum reappeared.

'The gentlemen in the ante-chamber,' he said. 'They're getting impatient.'

'It's all right,' said Disraeli. 'In Paris I receive each day between eleven and one. They can come another time.'

Smythe raised his eyebrows to Cochrane. 'Diz in glory,' he murmured. Then there was silence.

'You all look very quiet,' said Mary Anne, entering the room. 'As if you're conspiring.'

'We are, madam,' said Smythe. 'We're conspiring to visit Manchester.'

'In that case,' said Mary Anne, 'you must take me with you.'

The same night Disraeli, in court dress, watched the King, preceded by his chamberlain and his gentlemen-in-waiting, move slowly and with a benevolent and grandfatherly air around the circle of his guests at the Palace. A few words here about the early snow; a few words there about La Grisi's latest appearance at the Opéra. The men bowed; the ladies in their grandes toilettes curtsied like a flower-walk swept by a breeze. General Baudrand, his aide-de-camp, selected those to be distinguished by presentation.

As the King paused to talk to the tall English Ambassador, Lord Cowley, brother of the Duke of Wellington, Mary Anne leaned forward, peering over the shoulders of the royal entourage to see them better. Disraeli restrained her with a light touch on her elbow.

'Is it true,' she asked in a loud whisper, 'that they call him Mr Pear?'

Disraeli gave her a chilly look, and she took a quick half-step behind him. It was true, all the same, that the satirists called the King M. Poire; Louis Philippe, spreading outwards from his shining dewlaps to his wide belly, did look like a pear.

Even the Grand Cross of the Legion of Honour and its sash failed somehow to give him distinction. At any moment Disraeli expected him to produce a cigar and bite off the end, like one of those Americans he'd sojourned with in exile. And yet, there was a certain grandeur about him. He had crossed the Alps on foot, wandered penniless in the New World, lived humbly in England, still took pride in his skill at slicing ham, an art he proudly claimed to have learned from a waiter at Twickenham, where he used to eat the ninepenny 'ordinary', and had at last won a throne and survived more than one attempt on his life.

Who was there among the King's detractors to equal him in courage and determination – and high romance?

The King bowed to Mary Anne, and she made a new deep curtsy.

'My dear sir,' he said, turning to Disraeli, 'I'm delighted to see you again.'

From the corner of his eye Disraeli observed the effect of the word 'again' on the English Ambassador. Lord Cowley, who had given him an unenthusiastic, though courteous, welcome to Paris, affected not to have heard.

'Mr Disraeli,' the King said, in English tinged with a light American accent, 'always recalls to me my happy days in Twickenham. Dear old Twick – the river, the villas! Was it always sunny in Twickenham, Mr Disraeli?'

'When you were there, sir,' said Disraeli, 'always.'

The Ambassador blanched. The King smiled affably and said, 'We must have some further talk.'

General Baudrand was already guiding him towards the next of his visitors, and Disraeli withdrew into the circle. He could see from the admiring expressions of the women on-lookers that the King's 'again' had established him in a single word as a courtier. His face was impassive as the circle dissolved, and he walked with Mary Anne through a crush of royal guests. Men he didn't know greeted him. Ladies-in-waiting looked at him with curiosity from behind their fans. And Baron James de Rothschild from his settee asked a by-stander to introduce the Disraelis to him.

'You know my nephew in London, do you not?' said the Baron, rising with the help of his cane to greet Mary Anne. 'We will meet at my ball.'

It was as if Disraeli's passport had now been stamped.

General Baudrand was standing at his elbow.

'His Majesty the King presents his compliments to Mr Disraeli, and would welcome his attendance.'

Disraeli detected a flicker of appreciation in Rothschild's heavy eyes, and excused himself. Madame Baudrand, an Englishwoman, offered to look after Mary Anne, and Disraeli, followed by the Ambassador's disapproving glance, accompanied Baudrand to the King's retiring room. From his sofa the King, patting a nearby cushion, called Disraeli to join him at his side. His gentleman-in-waiting withdrew a few steps, and the King said comfortably, 'I'm delighted with the Anglo-Saxon invasion of Paris.'

'We're still in your debt for the Norman Conquest, Your Majesty,' said Disraeli.

'The best of *revanches*,' said the King, heaving himself a little higher. 'You've changed, I see, since you wrote *Gallomania?*'

'Yes, sire,' said Disraeli simply. 'Lord Palmerston has made my views outdated. I once accused him of an exaggerated passion for France. Now he has transferred his affections to Russia – at least for the time being. It's the kind of elderly infatuation for which he's notorious.'

'They can be deep and poignant,' said the King ruminatively. 'What's the mood in the House of Commons?'

'It's hard to say. In these last twelve months we've been preoccupied with home affairs. Not a single debate on foreign policy.'

'But our own relations – how do you think these matters might improve? There's so much room for misunderstanding. Syria – Egypt – ah!'

'We need new minds, Your Majesty,' said Disraeli. 'It so happens our young Members of Parliament are looking for leadership – turning to men with novel ideas.'

Louis Philippe took a grape from a bowl of fruit and examined it carefully before eating it.

'Well, tell me, Mr Disraeli, how you'd translate these ideas into action?'

Disraeli felt a rush of enthusiasm.

'Let us imagine the situation, Your Majesty. On the very day our Parliament reassembles, an influential Member – ' he raised his chin – 'takes up the question of Anglo-French relations. He asks the Foreign Secretary whether he will seek a new *entente*.'

'And the Foreign Secretary?'

'The Foreign Secretary answers, "Yes, sir." It's a "yes" that reverberates through the Cabinets of Europe.'

Louis Philippe asked through a mush of grapes, 'And who would the gentleman be whose genius produces that welcome answer?'

'Your Majesty,' said Disraeli, holding his gaze for a second, 'I can only say he's a gentleman who has already been solicited to put himself at the head of a party of the youth of England for precisely this purpose.'

'But what would your Palmerston – what would Sir Robert Peel have to say to this? They would, I assume, say something.'

'They might protest, but they'd have to acquiesce.'

'And public opinion? All this needs money – no doubt a newspaper.'

'I've thought of all those things, Your Majesty,' said Disraeli. 'Certainly the cost would be great.'

The British Ambassador, waiting under the arch, turned his good ear to the audience chamber.

'The cost would be great?'

'I mean, in time and energy,' Disraeli corrected himself quickly, seeing the King's suspicious look. 'But it would be worthwhile. We'd have to wean the press from its pro-Russian position. I'm not saying, mind you, our press is corrupt; but it *can* be organized.'

Disraeli's excitement brought a flush to his pale face, and he was still developing his theme when the Buhl clock struck eleven.

Baudrand approached.

'Your Majesty – the English Ambassador.'

'Soon – soon,' said Louis Philippe impatiently. 'Pray continue, Mr Disraeli. Your presentation is worthy of one of your books. What are you writing now?'

'A new novel, Your Majesty, dealing with the condition of England. I'm hoping it will say something political speeches can't explain.'

He stopped. The King seemed to have fallen asleep, and Disraeli waited in anguish for him to snore.

'Very interesting,' said the King, opening one eye.

Disraeli rose. The laconic comment left him with a sense of failure.

'Very interesting,' the King repeated in his rumbling voice. 'Kindly come and see me, sir, at St Cloud next week. My aide-de-camp will arrange the time.'

Disraeli bowed, and withdrew three steps before turning. The English Ambassador was waiting outside the chamber, and greeted the smiling Disraeli with the tremor of an unfriendly lip.

Because the Court was in mourning for the Prince Royal, killed in a riding accident, there was no dancing, and the courtiers moved from room to room in a pavan without music.

'No pâté de foie gras, I'm sorry to say, Mrs Disraeli,' said Smythe, returning from the buffet. 'Only salmon mousse or terrine. Mourning here is a matter of menus rather than toilettes.'

'Oh, how well I understand,' said Mary Anne. 'My poor brother – my poor mother – both gone in one year! I could eat nothing, let alone wear pretty clothes. But mauve is very unbecoming for most people . . . What can be keeping Ben? Did you see how the King drew him aside? How warm it is here! Don't you think gas-lamps should be reserved for public lighting? Such an uncomplimentary light.'

She fluttered her fan and looked around for Disraeli.

'Shall we perhaps study the Fragonard paintings?' asked Smythe.

'Oh, no, indeed not,' said Mary Anne. 'I can't really approve of the libertine school of painting. On our honeymoon, Mr Smythe, I do assure you, I had to sit up half the night so that Dizzy shouldn't look at the nude ladies in the Rubens engravings.'

'You must have been very occupied,' said Smythe. 'I'll find him and lead him from temptation.'

After leaving Louis Philippe, Disraeli, bestowing salutes and exchanging conversation, moved through the red silk state rooms towards the Orangery. Ahead of him, in the wake of a Hungarian officer begalloned in a close-fitting uniform, the shoulders of Mrs Edmonds appeared and disappeared like a white boat in a wine-coloured sea. Disraeli's greetings and pauses became shorter. At the Orangery he moved quickly around a luxuriant palm-tree and came face to face with her.

'A happy coincidence,' he said.

She introduced him to the captain, and said, 'Count Zichy was about to bring me a sherbet.'

The captain raised his finely pointed eyebrows in surprise, and withdrew through the press of the crowd and the interconnecting rooms that seemed multiplied to infinity by the looking-glasses.

'State rooms upon state rooms! Mirrors and illusions!' Mrs Edmonds said wistfully. 'Oh, Ben, what illusions you created in me!'

'You can't have a palace without illusions. What are you doing in Paris?' he asked.

She turned to acknowledge a greeting.

'I'm here for the winter season,' she answered lightly. 'I like distractions. Should I have any other purpose?'

He hesitated.

'No,' he said. 'But London has missed you.'

The King appeared in the Gallery of Diana and his guests, like a river changing course, flowed in his direction. Disraeli and Mrs Edmonds remained alone by a huge azalea warmed into a precocious bloom.

'I've missed London,' she said. She looked at him with

eyes that seemed green in the candlelight. Then she said, 'I missed you. Why did you never return? You were very cruel.'

Disraeli shook his head.

'It was impossible – it is impossible.'

'But why?'

He looked at her steadily.

'I had made a decision and a resolution. I couldn't return to George Street, Clarissa, without resuming our connection as it had been.'

'Would that have been so intolerable?'

She smiled, and he observed her tongue half-mocking between her small teeth.

'Alas,' he said, 'all-too-tolerable.'

Standing close to her, he observed that already around her eyes there was a faint network of lines. Her delicate complexion too had a hectic flush he hadn't noticed in London.

'What has happened to you in the last two years?'

She paused and smiled, and he thought her face and her gestures were all composed so that neither he nor anyone who passed by would know what she really felt.

'I thought of you, Ben.'

'And what else?'

'I travelled with Mr Hudson.'

The name of the railway magnate was a pang, and he said languidly, 'By rail, of course.'

'Mostly by carriage,' she said without changing her expression. 'In Italy – among the myrtles and the mimosa – I thought of you very much. Will you come and see me in London?'

'No – it's impossible.'

'Why?' she asked a second time, but this time sharply.

'My life, Clarissa – you must know this – was a turbulent one till my marriage. Then, for the first time – '

'Poor Ben!' she said. It was the ghost of an echo of what she had said to him on parting in George Street.

He was displeased with her commiseration.

'In what respect?' he asked.

She looked at him straight in the eyes, and said,

'You've impoverished yourself. No, I don't mean – no, not in connection with myself. You were once a radical . . .'

He murmured an agreement.

'Yes, you believed in generous causes – you befriended the disadvantaged. You spoke up for the Chartists – you cared about the exiles. And now?'

'I'm unchanged.'

'I think not. Your greatest passion is to have the ear of a Prince.'

'You're unkind.'

'Truthfull'

His shoulders touched her bare arm as she musingly stroked the tassel at the end of a plaited cord of the striped yellow curtains. Then they heard voices approaching, and drew apart.

'Ah, Ben,' said Mary Anne brightly, appearing with Smythe. 'We've been looking for you everywhere. They're all asking me to tell them what the King told you, and I have to say I don't know. It's very embarrassing keeping secrets when one doesn't have any. Don't you think so, Mrs Edmonds?'

Mary Anne took Disraeli's arm, and it seemed to him that with her rouged cheeks she looked more than ever like a shepherdess at a fancy dress ball.

'I offered to invent some,' said Smythe apologetically, 'but Mrs Disraeli felt they'd lack authenticity.'

'Come along,' said Mary Anne. 'M. Guizot – or is it M. Thiers? – I always confuse them – at any rate one or the other – is anxious to meet you.'

Disraeli turned to Mrs Edmonds. In his eyes was an enquiry. Her face was pale, grave, beautiful and, he suspected, contemptuous. She fingered her ruby pendant, smiled to Mary Anne, and didn't look at him again.

The captain was approaching with the sherbet. Mrs Edmonds greeted him with a deliberate absorption, and they went and sat on two gilt chairs overhung by a violet jacaranda.

Chapter Nine

At the Athenæum meeting of the Manchester Artisans' Literary Society the faces looked up at Disraeli as if expecting a great revelation, a disclosure that would explain the mystery of their transformed world in which the open countryside had been changed into the brick enclosures of factories and mills; row upon row of faces rising in tiers to the balcony and from there to the roof, where the silhouettes of those standing against the arched windows behind the seats showed that the great hall was packed out; pallid, earnest faces in the gaslight of the young working men who had come together, as the articles of their society prescribed, for their 'improvement and betterment', and to hear the spokesmen of Young England, Disraeli, Smythe, and Lord John Manners.

After their meeting in Paris, the Young England Members had become an informal Parliamentary group led by Disraeli, and the words 'Dare to be great!' which he had written in his novel *Coningsby*, had become their blazon. Without a settled programme except for a general concern about the condition of England, their unity lay in their attachment to their chief, their captain, their *caïd*, as Smythe called Disraeli. Like acolytes, they walked with him in the corridors of Westminster; sat in a circle around him in the Smoking Room; and joined him at his table in Bellamy's, still the spokesman of youth against the arid elders of the Front Bench, Sir Robert Peel among them.

Indifference galled Disraeli more than hostility, and Peel had proved himself a master of the calculated slight. Never did he turn his head or offer encouragement when Disraeli spoke in the Chamber. In the lobbies he contrived to avert his face, not so ostentatiously that Disraeli could think himself insulted, but with sufficient effect for him to realize that he was being deliberately ignored.

In compensation, Disraeli enjoyed the admiration of the aristocratic and dashing young men, recent recruits to Parliament from the universities, who, the glummer the faces of the Front Bench when Disraeli uttered his irreverences, became all the more unrestrained in their cheers. Disraeli's reputation as an orator had grown rapidly since the arrival of Peel's administration. When the ushers shouted 'Mr Disraeli on his legs' into the Smoking Room or the refreshment rooms, there would be an immediate rising and trooping into the Chamber. Cigars would be left unfinished, steaks would be allowed to go cold; and a litter of half-full glasses in the Smoking Room was the regular tribute to 'Mr Disraeli on his legs'.

Since he had written *Coningsby*, his fame had grown, for it was more than a novel; it was a manifesto. He had called for a return to 'political fidelity', by which he meant faith in institutions and principles as distinct from the arbitrary pragmatism that he attributed to his leaders. Despite the frowns of the older Members of Parliament, Young England had become a Westminster fashion. In Manchester, Disraeli wanted to submit it to a more popular test.

He looked down at the faces over the lamp by his lectern, and at the beginning of his speech paid his audience a collective compliment.

'Manchester,' he said, 'is the Athens of the North, a triumph of genius.'

He paused, and watched the stir of pleasure beneath him. The firm-set mouths opened slightly as if in a sigh. It was the moment for further flattery. He quoted Virgil in the original Latin. The words hung incomprehensible but pleasing as Disraeli prepared to offer his listeners yet another compliment. Only a few weeks earlier, Manchester had been the scene of rioting and clashes with the police. Now Disraeli blandly congratulated the townsmen on their rejection of violence as a means of political change.

'How happy I am,' he said, 'to find myself here in Manchester, a city that has dethroned force and placed instead on the high seat – intelligence!'

The image appealed to the radical mood of the workmen,

and they cheered his concept of despotism overthrown, of reason, the mother of revolution, installed in its place, and order and change synthesized into something higher and nobler through intellect.

Disraeli stood on the rostrum waiting for silence. Then he said in his melodious and at the same time resonant voice, raising his heavily-lidded eyes slowly to the hall's glass dome, 'Knowledge is like the patriarch's dream. Its base rests on primeval earth – its crest is lost in the shadowy splendour of the stars.'

Every one of the two thousand faces looked upwards as if expecting to see the ladder materialize.

'It is the great authors who for ages have held the chain of science and philosophy, of poetry and erudition; they are the angels ascending and descending on the sacred scale, sustaining the communication between man and heaven.'

He paused again, and there was a sigh from the audience as if for a few moments they too had caught a glimpse of the heavenly traffic.

Disraeli glanced at Mary Anne's enraptured face and returned to his notes, satisfied with the effect of the image. After speaking for over an hour and a half, he came to his peroration.

'The youth of a nation,' he declaimed, 'are the trustees of posterity . . . And I give you this counsel, which I have ever given to youth.' He raised his voice to a shout. 'I tell you to *aspire!*'

After a moment of total silence, the whole audience in a sudden awakening from a spell rose to its feet, with boots resounding on the wooden floor as they clapped and cheered for over a minute, till Disraeli himself stood, bowing to the audience and to Smythe and to Lord John Manners applauding on each side. His face was solemn but triumphant. Young England, he felt, could speak to the people.

The following morning Mr Inglefield, who had travelled from Dorset to attend a Chartist meeting in Manchester, called on Disraeli and Mary Anne at their hotel. He was more stately than Disraeli remembered him in the days when he was wooing

Sarah, perhaps more self-conscious as the agent of Lord Ashley's philanthropic works than he had seemed when he gave up farming to be a clergyman.

'A felicitous coincidence brings me here,' he said. 'As I mentioned in my letter, Lord Ashley has asked me to collate some further statistics on the employment of children in the mills. I'd like to offer you my congratulations on your very talented speech at the Artisans' Literary Society.'

'Not talent – genius,' said Mary Anne. 'Did you see how they shouted and wept when Mr Disraeli spoke?'

'Not wept, surely,' said Mr Inglefield primly.

Since he had become a clergyman his appearance had somewhat altered, and not only in respect of his garb. His sinewy hands, accustomed to work on his father's farm, had become white, and his fingers soft; his face, given an added dignity by long side-whiskers, still wore its serious, enquiring expression, but it had become less intense and his voice had become indulgent, as if to balm the sinner even while reprehending his sin. And though his hair was thinner, his figure was stouter.

'Your friend Mr Ferrand has already been good enough to introduce me to some parts of the city you might like to see. I'm at your disposal should you wish to do so.'

Disraeli thanked him and said, 'Let us leave forthwith.'

Mary Anne said, 'You must wear a coat, Ben. This October air is very treacherous. With your bronchitis!'

He submitted to her demand patiently, and Baum, whom Mary Anne had summoned, helped him on with his coat. Inglefield proposed that they should take a cab to the factory districts in Pendleton or Chorlton or Deansgate.

'You see, it's possible to pass over the heights of the city and imagine Manchester as merely a place of pleasant villas.'

'Pray guide me,' said Disraeli.

'I'll take you to the Irk, a district of the poor,' said Inglefield. He summoned a cab in the street, and said, 'The Irk!'

'The Irk?' said the cabman. 'What'd two gentlemen want there?'

Climbing into the cab, they drove through streets of prosperous-looking villas to Long Millgate, the entrance to the mill area lining the canals and the River Irk. A thin rain had begun to fall, and from the high ground Disraeli saw spread before them an endless pattern of black slated rooftops, interspersed with small courtyards descending to the river where the tanneries gave off a stench of putrefaction, blown in gusts that made Disraeli put his handkerchief to his face.

'Drive on, sir?' shouted the cabman.

'Yes, drive on,' said Disraeli.

They were passing close to the parapet lining the riverbank, and below they could see the slime and refuse from the factories rotting behind the weirs and adding another foulness to the air.

'Up there,' said Mr Inglefield, pleased at the effect of the scene on Disraeli, whose frown had steadily deepened, 'is the workhouse.'

Disraeli looked up at the workhouse, beetling from behind its parapets on to the back-to-back houses below.

'Ain't going no further,' said the cab-driver as they reached the station of the Liverpool and Leeds Railway.

'Why not?' asked Inglefield.

'Ain't going no further,' the driver repeated.

Seeing that it was useless to argue, Inglefield said, 'Wait for us at the station, my man, and you'll be rewarded with a guinea.'

The cab-driver touched his hat with his whip, and Disraeli set off on foot with the clergyman to explore the quarter leading to Brown and Thilwell's mills. Gingerly treading their way past puddles in the unpaved alleys and courts where pigs, fattened by the offal and refuse piled and strewn on all sides, huddled near bare-footed women and children, they ignored the curiosity and hostility of onlookers from the doors of the ramshackle, decaying terraces. Inglefield wanted to lead his companion across the railway line, but at every turn they came to a cul-de-sac.

'On a day like this, even Theseus in his labyrinth would have given up,' said Disraeli.

'We've hardly started,' said Inglefield, and they trudged on.

He enquired after Sarah circumspectly, and asked if she still visited the poor in the village.

'Yes,' said Disraeli. 'She's an angel of compassion.'

'But this,' said Inglefield with a wave at the befouled alleys, 'would have defeated even the angels.'

From a side street someone threw a turnip that missed, and outside one of the gin-shops a drunken woman in a patched shawl screamed 'Bugger you, mister!' at Disraeli. Mr Inglefield walked over to her, and she said contritely, 'I'm sorry, Holy Father.'

Instead of disclaiming the title as he intended, he asked the way to Brown and Thilwell's. Immediately a group of ragged children, several beggars and some old men formed around them, and with contradictory instructions escorted them to the main road where, seeing two policemen, they disappeared.

From Mr Ferrand, one of the Young England group, and Government Blue Books, Disraeli had already formed an idea of how the factory workers lived. Whereas in London poverty in the back streets was masked by fashionable façades and concealed like a disease under the gaudy metropolitan exterior, in the industrial towns it lay exposed in the shadow of the factory with no relief but the gin-shop, no ceremony except the ritual of the Church, and no concept of beauty except for family memories of the open fields before the sulphurous chimneys polluted them.

Disraeli wanted to see for himself what the factory system had done to a peasantry without land, sucked into the towns together with the Irish immigrants on the fourpenny steamship crossings to Liverpool, who had exchanged famine and servitude in the countryside for the hunger and squalor of English urban life. It wasn't enough for the Tory Party to champion the agricultural interest. Those he had come to see in Manchester were the children of the villages and the farms. Until Young England could become the champion of both town and countryside, it could scarcely claim to be the spokesman of the nation or of the Tory Party it sought to inspire.

Mr Thilwell, a tall and friendly man in his middle fifties who had known Robert Owen and had been recommended to

Disraeli by Mr Ferrand, regarded himself as an enlightened employer, and explained to Inglefield and Disraeli as they walked through rows of women operatives and the children darting between the machines with their cleaning utensils, the principles on which he ran his factory. The frames of the looms shuddered and clattered, and he had to shout his comments. Disraeli interrupted him.

'These children, sir – '

'They're the doffers – their work is light – they mount and take down the bobbins.'

'Yes – and their wages?'

Disraeli made an entry in pencil in his notebook.

'Those under thirteen earn about five shillings a week – the young girls from sixteen to twenty earn ten to twelve shillings. That's rather better than an agricultural labourer in Dorset, eh, Mr Inglefield?'

'And does this kind of female labour have any ill-effect on domestic life?'

Thilwell considered the matter.

'I wouldn't deny that the absence of the mother from the hearth could injure the family. That's true. But you'll see – I have tried to work my looms by family labour – I encourage the women to bring their children.'

'I see,' said Disraeli. 'I observe that unmarried females in the factory – '

'Ah, yes,' said Thilwell, 'there is, unhappily, a certain amount of immorality – the late nights, the early mornings – the total of illegitimate children is high. I must add, though, that this year the Evangelical Union has considerably increased the number of tracts in order to offset the temptation to forni-cation.'

They walked on to another large workshop, where for a few moments Disraeli could see nothing because of the hissing steam.

'In this part – the dyeing and bleaching,' said Thilwell, 'the work is arduous – the constant damp, I fear – but if I may say so, it's well paid. We choose strong, unmarried women.'

Disraeli coughed, and peered through the billowing steam

at the women working at troughs with their sleeves rolled up and their dresses clinging damply to their breasts. His cough was echoed; and then it was as if the whole room was filled with a hoarse, tubercular coughing that made Disraeli recoil.

'Unhealthy work, I imagine.'

'It has to be done,' said Thilwell. 'They get four shillings extra each week for their labours. In the machine age we must adapt ourselves to the processes of the machine.'

'Why, sir, can't we adapt the machine to our physical capacities?'

'Because our competitors won't do so. Look at Europe. Look at America. We have set off before them in the industrial race, but if we lag they'll catch us – perhaps surpass us. As it is, our commerce leads the world.'

Disraeli looked again at the children with faces like adults', and made no comment.

They had reached the door of the factory, and Inglefield was preparing to take his leave.

'My dear Mr Disraeli,' said Thilwell in a soothing tone, 'wages must be competitive. I will tell you how you can help to improve the lot of these operatives as I see you wish to do. Enable us to produce more cheaply.'

'How?'

'By abolishing the Corn Taxes. Give the people cheap bread, sir. Then you'll see a surge of prosperity and energy such as the country has never known. You'll see workers with sturdy bodies and children with straight legs and plump cheeks.'

Mr Inglefield said, 'How right! How true!'

'Could it be,' said Disraeli, 'that the manufacturers will insist on lower wages as a counterpart to cheap bread?'

Thilwell shrugged his shoulders.

'We must compete, sir. We must compete.'

The rain had stopped, but the sky was still livid, leaning over the Irk and its environs as if to smother it. With Inglefield, who had arranged the itinerary in advance, Disraeli had already visited three mills, his head full of a din that he had never heard before, and of Breughelish images of crippled and stunted men and women such as he had never seen even in medieval paintings. He had a vertigo from the incessant movement of the machines, hour after hour, with the workers, nominally their masters, attached to them in fact like Mazeppas to their horses.

'They are victims of their labour,' said Inglefield. 'A generation that has grown up in darkness.'

'Perhaps we should return to the hotel,' said Disraeli.

'I thought perhaps you'd like to see a school.'

Disraeli acquiesced, but reluctantly. He was thinking of hot water, and a cognac to ease the chill in his feet.

The school was a Church of England school, and Inglefield was greeted by the master, Mr Dodds, with deference.

'Everything is taught here – we have single classes,' he said in a nervous, panting voice. 'Sums and reading and writing – and religion. The four R's. But religion's the most important, sir. You see, sir, they come and go, and their parents take them off to the factory. We have one big class of sixty-three, and naturally I give the better ones some extra tuition.'

'Can they read?' asked Disraeli.

'Some can,' said Mr Dodds, 'but mostly we teach by rote.'

'May we ask your boys a few questions?' asked Inglefield.

'By all means, sir, by all means. This way, sir.'

He led them into a large, sombre room, overheated by a stove, where large numbers of boys were throwing books at one another or wrestling.

Dodds smacked his cane on the desk and shouted, 'Quiet!'

Immediately there was a silence.

'These gentlemen have come to examine you . . . You, boy!' he said in a thunderous voice that neither Disraeli nor Inglefield had attributed to him. The boy, undersized and large-eyed, with a shaven head, looked at him in terror.

'What's four and two, boy?'

The boy was silent. Mr Dodds waited, gently swishing his cane against his leg.

'Well, boy?'

There was a susurration around him, a hissing of the word 'six'.

'Six, please, sir,' said the boy.

Mr Dodds pursed his lips and turned to the next boy, who had been picking his nose reflectively.

'What's four and three?'

'Seven,' said the boy, undistracted from his exploration.

'Sir!' said the teacher.

'Sir,' said the boy limply.

'Could you perhaps tell me what three and four make?' asked Disraeli.

'Dunno,' said the boy conclusively.

'What is two and two?' Inglefield asked the class.

Every hand went up.

'Four, sir – four.'

'And what is two and one? You, boy.'

'Two and one makes three,' chanted the boy, who looked older than the rest of the class.

'And what does two and two and seven make?' asked Disraeli.

The boy looked blank.

'We have limited ourselves,' said the teacher, as if he felt Disraeli had offered a criticism, 'to simple propositions.'

'Shall we perhaps try Scripture?' Disraeli asked. 'How many boys go to Sunday School?'

Every hand was raised.

'Who was Adam?' Disraeli asked.

The class looked bewildered.

'I know, sir,' said the first boy, straining to catch Disraeli's attention with his uplifted hand.

'Well?'

'Please, sir, he was Jesus Christ.'

Disraeli turned to Inglefield.

'An interesting heresy, but a profound insight. Perhaps someone can tell me who were the Apostles.'

'The Apostles.'

The word was lisped through the classroom, while the children stared at the blackboard as if expecting to see its meaning inscribed there. Suddenly a dark-haired boy in the back row put up his hand.

'Please, teacher, I knows it,' he said.

Dodds smiled amiably. The manner of Mr Disraeli's questioning confused him. He wasn't sure if he was pleased or displeased with the answers.

'Well, boy, who were the Apostles?'

'Please, sir,' said the boy in a fluting voice, 'they're the lepers.'

Disraeli put on his hat.

'It's true,' he said. 'They were the insulted and the injured and the excluded . . . The lepers – that's very good. Thank you, Mr Dodds, for receiving us. You have our best wishes in your arduous task.'

'Permit me, sir, to make an observation,' said Mr Dodds nervously.

'By all means,' said Disraeli.

'I was present at your oration yesterday, which I heard, I may be permitted to say, with great pleasure. You spoke, sir, of the "shadowy splendour of the empyrean". It was a beautiful phrase, sir – beautiful.' He became bolder. 'Swep' us away.'

Disraeli looked pleased.

'But here – in this class – it means little . . . Tom, come here.'

The boy who had described Adam as Jesus Christ came forward timidly and stood with his head bowed. Disraeli noticed that it was covered with sores, and he took a step back.

'What did you have for breakfast, Tom?' he asked.

'Bit o' bread,' said the boy.

Mr Dodds patted the boy on the shoulder and sent him back to the bench.

'You'll understand, sir,' he said to Disraeli, 'the difficulty of teaching hungry children.'

He had exhausted his temerity, and bowed profoundly to his two visitors as they left.

The cabman was waiting for them at the station, and they drove in silence through the drizzle that had started again.

'Well, Ben,' said Mr Inglefield at last, 'you've seen something of the condition of England. What is your view?'

They had left the working-class districts and had reached the colonnade of villas on the heights. The sun came out as they left the belt of rain lying beneath them over the Irk.

'I think,' said Disraeli, 'that those we saw today – our fellow-countrymen – have too little part in their heritage – too little reward for their labour – too little experience of joy. I have never believed that the benefits of the next world can compensate for deprivation in this one. We must speak for them.'

'When, sir?'

'At once.'

Suddenly Disraeli seemed to rid himself of his exhaustion.

'Yes,' he said, and his somnolent eyes became brilliant with elation. 'I will speak for them. I will write about them. I will speak about them, sir, because I have seen what no one speaks of though it lies in front of our eyes. I will speak of the Two Englands – the England of the rich and the England of the poor. I will speak of it so that there will be first shame, and then deeds to end their division.'

'Can that division ever be ended?' asked Inglefield.

'Yes,' said Disraeli. 'That must be our task. To create One England, whole and united.'

They had reached the mill-owners' villas, and the sun, breaking through the tumbled clouds, lay in bright shafts over the stucco façades.

Chapter Ten

'Shall I see you at dinner tonight, Drummond?'

'Yes, Prime Minister,' said his secretary. 'But I have an important engagement before then.'

The Prime Minister watched tolerantly from his window as Drummond went into the garden to play ball with the children of the household. After a quarter of an hour he heard Drummond say, 'That will be enough.'

The children danced around the secretary in protest, and he conceded good-humouredly, 'All right – one more game.'

In the middle of the lawn behind No. 10 Downing Street, the youngest threw the ball to the others, laughing and shouting in the winter sun brightening their faces. Though a bachelor, Drummond was always at ease with children, and he decided that he still had time to play a little longer and then walk down Whitehall to the family bank before taking tea with his sister in Lower Grosvenor Street.

'That will do,' a governess said sharply with an authority that Drummond envied.

'One more game,' clamoured a five-year-old girl, a friend of the Peel children.

'No,' said the governess. 'Mr Drummond has better things to deal with.'

'Nothing better,' Drummond said. 'This is my only exercise. I'll tell you what – let's play another time.'

'Tomorrow?'

'Yes, tomorrow.'

'You promise?'

'I promise.'

The little girl surveyed him.

'Are you a hundred?' she asked.

'Only half of that. Fifty.'

She continued to contemplate him.

'That's very old. Will you die soon?'

'Not very soon,' he reassured her.

'Come on, miss,' said the governess, 'or I'll have to tie your tongue up.'

Drummond waved goodbye to them and they waved back, sorry to see him go because there was no father, no uncle in Whitehall who had more time for playing games or could tell better stories, especially about the Queen, than Mr Drummond.

Lord Haddington, First Lord of the Admiralty, was waiting for him as he passed through the vestibule into the street, and they sauntered together towards the Admiralty under a sky that had become swollen and uddered with rain clouds.

'Well, Mr Drummond,' said the First Lord, 'how d'you see the new session?'

'Like the old one,' said Drummond cautiously. 'Like the one before it! There's never any real change. I serve my masters and believe that somehow or other England must always win.'

'It's a comforting philosophy for the Navy. But as I told the Prime Minister, we need four new frigates. We can't allow the French to outbuild us. Then again, there's the West Indies trade route, less and less protected. Great anxiety among the Admirals!'

'Of course,' said Drummond, knowing better than to contradict a naval minister intent on enlarging the Fleet.

'You'll mention it?'

'Certainly,' said Drummond. 'I'll mention it.'

His principle with Ministers was always to 'mention it'.

Near the Admiralty the two men shook hands and parted, and Drummond, walking on the almost empty road towards Charing Cross, felt elated and, for the first time in many days, free from responsibility. His career had been spent in the intimacy of four Prime Ministers – Ripon, Canning, Wellington, and now Sir Robert Peel. Ripon, he reflected, was an accident; Canning a poet in action; Wellington a parliamentary amateur; but Peel the statesman he most admired. The previous summer he had accompanied him to Scotland during the royal visit, staying in the great houses at Dalkeith, Scone and Tay-mouth, derelict mansions, chill and sparsely furnished. The journey and the royal progress had been intended to rouse enthusiasm for the Queen and the dynasty, but what he remembered most was the lack of organization, the unruly crowds, Peel's distaste for those who shook his hands till his knuckles were swollen, and his own drive through Edinburgh in the Prime Minister's carriage, when the spectators cheered him in the belief that he was Sir Robert Peel himself. But there had also been abuse and threats from demonstrators chasing the Queen's coach.

In a way he'd expected it, for the previous summer there had been riots in the countryside and the Home Secretary had sent him a report of an intended Chartist attack on Peel's own home at Drayton. Policemen had been killed in Manchester, rioters sabred by dragoons at Preston and Burslem, railways torn up near Birmingham. With the onset of winter the fury had died out. It was just as well, Drummond thought. In his public as in his private life, the Prime Minister wasn't a man who looked for violent confrontations. Years before, he had declined a challenge from Daniel O'Connell, on the grounds that duelling was a medieval absurdity. Drummond was glad that, like the Prime Minister, the Queen disapproved of a practice that had cost the country too many of its best young officers.

As the sun sank, leaving a tracery of scarlet clouds over St James's Park, he quickened his pace, intending before nightfall to buy his sister the gloves he'd seen in a window at Booth's, and the thought of the hot buttery muffins in Grosvenor Street made him feel hungry. He smiled at a woman street-crier's wail, 'Fresh-catched larks! Titlarks! Mudlarks! Fresh-catched larks!'

At that moment he felt a blow in his back like a punch, and he stumbled a step and sank to his knees. As he looked up he saw an unknown face, enquiring but detached; and close to his eyes a pointing pistol. Above the black cravat the face was pale, with a nose that seemed too small for it and eyes like those of the dead. Drummond wanted to speak, but the face and the cries and the buildings moved farther and farther away. Then he felt tired, and could no longer see, though there were voices he could still hear. He had no pain. Everything was well, except for the weariness that made him want to lie on the Whitehall pavement and sleep.

A few seconds earlier he had been thinking of mauve gloves and muffin-bells and children playing ball. Where was Lord Haddington? How could he tell the Prime Minister about this absurd mishap in Whitehall that kept him from dinner? Who was the stranger? The voices approached and receded. He was being raised and carried. Who were these unfamiliar people who laid their hands on him?

Dusk had fallen, and standing in the thin rain the apprentice with the blood-smeared smock was telling Groves the fishmonger and the spectators what had happened.

'Well, there's this gentleman walking along, very happy. He's tapping the railings with his cane, and smiling to himself. Then this other man comes along.'

'A footpad?'

'No, well dressed, like. And he lifts his pistol and shouts, "You'll trouble me no more," or some such words. And then there's a bang and this gentleman begins to slip on his knees – surprised – and his coat is burning – smoking – and just then the murderer – ' He began to cry.

'Stop snivelling, boy. Go on!' said Groves, wiping his hands on his striped apron.

'Well, the murderer takes another pistol from his coat pocket and is going to shoot him again, sir, as the gentleman is lying on the ground.'

They waited.

'But the policeman comes up and knocks his arm down and the pistol goes off and misses. Then I runs over, and while the policeman's holding the man on the road, I try and pick up the gentleman, and he just lies there in my arms and says, "Let me rest a bit, please. I just want to rest." '

The boy began to cry again, and his audience turned away

to look at the rain-washed brown sacks covering the blood-stains on the pavement.

'They say he's dead . . .'

'He's an Irishman. They took him in a cab to the Bridewell.'

'Sir Robert Peel – recognized his red hair.'

'Very gallant constable . . .'

'Mr Drummond, they say – mistook him for the Prime Minister.'

'No – it's Sir Robert himself.'

The constable, now joined by several others, dispersed the crowd and returned to the sacking, where the blood had seeped from beneath, congealing in a spidery pattern that reached the gutter.

Towards five o'clock a breathless Mr Huffam reported in the Carlton that the Prime Minister had been assassinated, and that, passing through Whitehall, he himself had observed the criminal being taken away under arrest by the police. He hadn't actually seen the body of Sir Robert, but he gathered from someone in the crowd that it had been removed and would be transferred to Drayton. Within a few minutes an MP confirmed Mr Huffam's story. He had been at the Central Criminal Court and heard it stated that the assassin was an aggrieved Irishman called Daniel Macnaghten, some said a Protestant, while others said he was an O'Connellite demanding repeal of the Act of Union. It was all part of a revolutionary plot, Huffam said, compared with which the Cato Street conspiracy to murder the Cabinet some years earlier was a mere game.

'In this state of affairs,' said Mr Huffam, already composing a new administration for the benefit of the members around him, 'the Queen will have to turn to Johnny Russell. A strong hand and placatory measures! Lyndhurst would never do. Failing Johnny, the Duke – '

'By no means sure,' said Lord Alvanley, who had been reading in a deep leather armchair. 'Must have a leader we can trust. Mind you, I never thought Peel would die a natural death.'

There was a mutter of disapproval from his neighbours, and Alvanley's suffused face became darker.

'Too many lies,' he said in a rumbling voice as if to himself. 'Too many lies.'

'Sir Robert was our greatest parliamentarian,' said another member elegiacally. 'His fame is secure.'

Alvanley said, 'Better get down to the House. Can't tell what the others will be up to.'

'His unhappy family!' sighed an elderly peer, waking from a doze. 'The Queen will be very upset. She'd only just got used to him!'

With each new arrival the account of the assassination became more elaborate, and soon the club was thronged with groups discussing its significance. The rumour quickly spread that not one but several murders had taken place, and that the Commissioner of Police on the Home Secretary's order had arrested dozens of Irishmen at Seven Dials, where a plot had been hatched to burn down the House of Commons. Various foreign revolutionaries, it was stated in the library, had landed secretly in Essex in order to link up with the Irish secessionists. The Duke had already roused the militia, and Sir James Graham was going to call up the reserve police after advising the Queen against returning to London. Mr Huffam, wearing his gravest expression, said that in his view every manor should become a fortress in readiness for an insurrection signalled by the murder, and several members confirmed that even before this terrible event they had laid in water and ammunition.

At the height of the excited discussion, the Prime Minister, accompanied by the Home Secretary and two members of the Cabinet Office, entered the saloon. There was at once an astonished and embarrassed hush, as if the legatees at the reading of a will had been interrupted by the entry of the corpse.

'An appalling tragedy,' said the Prime Minister to the members who, quickly recovering themselves, gathered round him. He shook his head in incomprehension.

'Drummond was the kindest – the best of men . . . Why

should anyone have wanted to kill him? I've just been to the House and shown myself and made a statement. In times like this rumour is dangerous. The whole object of political assassination is to destroy faith in authority and make authority itself cringe in fear.'

'The assassin, sir?' asked a voice. 'Is it a plot?'

'It's too early to say, sir,' said Peel. 'All we know is that a noble character had been foully destroyed.'

He took a glass of brandy and water brought to him by a waiter, and began to raise it to his mouth, but his hand shook and he spilled it. He replaced the glass on the table. The others looked away.

The following day at Windsor, the Prime Minister, summoned to report on the assassination, stood with his head bowed in front of the Queen in the Blue Closet.

The Queen looked at him sulkily. She had disliked Peel ever since he had usurped, as she felt, the position of Lord Melbourne, her guide, instructor and familiar. Whereas Melbourne had every courtly grace, Peel shifted from one foot to another when he spoke to her. He never looked her in the eye, unlike the former Whig Prime Minister who, to her delight, teased and flirted with her, old though he was. Beside, Melbourne was handsome, with regular open features that contrasted with Peel's long upper lip and shifting gaze.

'Most deplorable,' she said in her high girlish voice. 'I can't understand why my Ministers permit such fanatics to roam at large in London.'

'There's no doubt, ma'am,' he said, 'but that Macnaghten, a turner by trade though not without financial resources which are now being investigated, is a fanatic. The doctors believe him to be a madman. He certainly lived alone in squalor despite his means. What happened was that he saw Mr Drummond driving in my carriage through Edinburgh and, mistaking him for myself – perhaps through the similarity of our stature – followed him to London. There he lay in wait – lurking near Downing Street – and finally, as Your Majesty knows, he shot him in the street. Whether he acted in isolation or in concert with others we can't yet know. The Home Secretary is carrying out an exhaustive investigation together with the Commissioner of Police. The doctors may decide he's insane, but, of course, a man may be a madman and a conspirator at the same time.'

'He must be executed,' said Victoria. She was pregnant again, and felt uncomfortable and disturbed by incoherent and menacing images that peopled her imagination since the two attempts on her own life and the murder of Drummond.

'The courts, ma'am, must decide, especially in face of a novel doctrine that insanity, however criminal the act, absolves the perpetrator from responsibility.'

'But that's absurd – absurd,' said the Queen in her high voice, with a glance at Prince Albert who had just entered the room. 'What has justice to do with medical diagnosis? Justice is a matter for judges. Murder's always an act of madness. Shall it henceforward be without retribution? Poor Mr Drummond! Such a good, kind man! So colourless! To be shot down like an animal in a battue! And to think he was murdered in error – that it might have been yourself – or myself – or my own husband!'

Albert moved to her side and placed himself in a composed and protective posture, his hand on her shoulder, while she looked up at him fondly. Suddenly she frowned, as if she had a new thought.

'And what about your New Police, Mr Prime Minister? What were they doing when this outrage was being committed?'

Peel looked at the polished floor, and shifted his weight from one foot to another.

'The police, ma'am, arrived very rapidly, in time to prevent a second shot being fired.'

'Too late,' said the Queen crisply. 'It's the first that counts.' She put her hand over Prince Albert's.

'I've spoken to the Home Secretary,' said the Prime Minister. 'He has undertaken to provide increased measures for the protection of Your Gracious Majesty and the royal family. Yet I'm obliged to say, ma'am, that public persons must always be at some risk. That, I fear, is our destiny.'

'You must minimize the risk. That, I think, is your duty. And Lady Peel – what must she be thinking?'

'She's distraught, ma'am, prostrate with grief and anxiety.'

'I understand her fears.'

She didn't take her eyes from Albert's smooth features as she spoke.

'Poor Mr Drummond!' she said. 'He's universally regretted. Since yesterday, people can scarcely think or speak of anything else. To destroy so noble a life with a few shillings' worth of metal!'

'A few shillings' worth of metal,' Albert echoed in his guttural voice.

'I trust,' she went on, 'the judges will inflict the death penalty on the murderer. How else are traitors to be deterred? Pray, Sir Robert, offer our sympathy to Lady Peel. What a gloomy day!'

She glanced at the windows, where a torrential rain was hammering at the panes.

Peel muttered his agreement, bowed, and retreated. The audience was over. On the way through the private apartments with the escort of a gentleman usher he met a nurse carrying Edward, the two-year-old Prince of Wales. The two men stood aside, and together made an obeisance to the child.

For several days, whenever Peel rose to speak in the House or walked to Whitehall Gardens, he felt as if an assassin's pistol was pointed at him as surely as the pistol aimed at Drummond and at his own predecessor, Mr Perceval, who had been assassinated in the Central Hall of the House of Commons. Drummond's body lay at Lower Grosvenor Street, a surprised and querying expression on his face; and, looking at it when he went to pay homage before the private burial, Peel felt a distaste for politics. Why, he asked himself, should he expose himself any longer to the abuse, the danger, the malignancy of parliamentary feuds, the long servitude of attendance and debate, the demands of the dissatisfied and the aggrieved that gnawed away his life? Why shouldn't he retire peacefully with his collection of pictures to his country pursuits at Drayton, in the happy company of his wife Julia and their children? It was a beckoning prospect, a comfort amid the evil dreams he had endured since Drummond's death.

On the night of the murder, his young assistant secretary brought him a sealed envelope, delivered by a man in a cloak who had handed it to a manservant without leaving his name. Peel, sitting at his desk, asked the secretary to open it. The letter read:

> Mr Drummond was an error. You, sir, are next.
>
> Captain Swing.

Revolted, Peel took the letter between his fingertips, holding the obscenity as far from himself as possible. He wanted to tear it up so that he could imagine it had never been written, but the secretary said, 'Forgive me, Prime Minister. Perhaps the Home Secretary should see it.'

'Yes,' said Peel sombrely. 'Captain Swing in England – this is a sad development. Send it at once to Sir James Graham.'

The secretary left the room, and the Prime Minister leaned his forehead on the cool mahogany of his desk to ease the pain. Captain Swing's guns behind the Irish hedgerows were pointing at him in Whitehall. It was like being told by his physician that he was suffering from a fatal disease. A day's, a month's delay? A year's reprieve from death? Never to stand or walk without fear of a nameless and faceless assassin. To be condemned to an incurable malady while others were healthy and free. To have to walk or ride with a disguised policeman at his side or behind him. Always to be observed – never more to respond to a glance without suspicion or apprehension. So his life would henceforward have to be.

He sat in Cabinet at the centre of the long table, his fingers pressed together as Sir James Graham reported on Drummond's murder, the general issue of public order, and the continuing violence in Ireland that had caused the Government to bring in a Coercion Bill.

'It's clear,' said the Home Secretary, 'that the spread of violence to England has some connection with the domestic condition of Ireland. With your permission, Prime Minister, I've asked the scientists to report.'

Peel nodded, and a secretary went to bring them from an ante-room.

The news had just reached London of the appearance of potato blight in Ireland, heightening the danger already pointed out by the Devon Commission that a failure of the potato crop in the light of the Irish system of land tenure and the endemic poverty and unemployment could be fatal to the peasantry. The Prime Minister had sent a new commission, led by Dr John Lindley and Dr Lyon Playfair, to make a further investigation, and they had returned to London with a preliminary report on the day of Drummond's death.

Professor Lindley, a heavily built man of about fifty, with a number of specimens of diseased potatoes in glass containers in his hands, bowed clumsily to the Prime Minister, who waved both scientists to their chairs.

'Thank you, gentlemen. It was good of you to come. Perhaps you'll tell us your observations – we've had to rely so far on partial reports from the Deputy Lieutenants. Who will begin?'

Lindley stroked his mutton-chop whiskers and said in a thin voice that contrasted with his powerful frame, 'Perhaps I may, Mr Prime Minister. I'm sure you want no preamble. I must simply report that Ireland is on the edge of a great catastrophe.'

The Prime Minister looked at him gravely, and Lindley stood and pointed with a thick finger to the markings on the potatoes in the containers.

'Here, sir, you see those purplish brown patches – they're the early symptoms of the blight – and there you see the groups of spores, thousands of them clustered together. They're the source of the infection.'

The Ministers peered together at the ugly mould.

'The spores become airborne – they float – they swim in rain droplets – they settle on leaves, and when, Prime Minister, you get muggy weather – rain, the prevailing western wind –

you have the ideal condition for spreading the disease. This summer has been no more than a continuation of a very wet winter – rain and squalls all the time.'

'How much of the crop is infected?' asked Peel, passing his finger through his hair.

'About half, sir.'

'What about last year's stocks?'

'There are none left.'

'None?'

'None. They've been eaten.'

'What about next season's crop?' asked the Home Secretary.

'I'm afraid the soil itself has become infected.'

'But surely,' said the Lord Privy Seal, himself a landowner, 'the potatoes – or at least the plants – can be treated?'

'Our botanists and chemists are engaged without respite in studying the matter. The difficulty is the potatoes putrefy in the damp.'

'What about the residue – the healthy part of the potatoes?' the Lord Privy Seal insisted.

Lindley shrugged his shoulders and answered unemotionally, 'You can extract the starch, Your Lordship, but it won't support the human frame. Sir John Murray has suggested boiling the residue into a mash with bran and salt. That might perhaps nourish pigs and cattle. But in human beings it causes vomiting. With great respect, Prime Minister, though I recognize the duty of scientists to identify and remedy the disease, the immediate problem – ' he bowed – 'is to deal with its present consequences.'

The Prime Minister turned to Playfair, the younger of the two scientists, who had been waiting impatiently to intervene.

'Have you anything to say, Dr Playfair?'

'By your leave, sir,' said Playfair, 'I'd like to tell you exactly my observations. A month ago I was in Clontarf. That very first day I rode out at dawn to inspect the crop. It was one of those days, you know, when the sun appears at intervals and the woodlands steam with a grey miasma. I remember observing, sir, how it magnified the peasants and their barefooted children into strange inhuman shapes. I suppose it's why the Irish believe in giants.'

'Yes, yes,' said Peel. He wasn't interested in poetic fancy, and wanted the young scientist to tell him the facts.

'I got off my cob because it shied away when we got to the potato fields – the stench, you see, sir – it was like a newly covered charnel pit.'

The Home Secretary wiped his face with his handkerchief as if he could smell the foul potatoes.

'I wanted to make a test, so I squelched my way through the furrows – you understand, they were sodden – and I scooped up some plants. At first sight the tubers looked white, but in a second you could see the black decay. I went from patch to patch – the same. Some of the potatoes had already been pulled. They'd turned into a stinking mould.'

There was a silence.

'Mr Prime Minister,' Playfair went on, 'I saw a whole village, a ragged starving company, assembled outside the manor house, asking for relief. And when the noble proprietor appeared on the steps, they went down on their knees and begged – begged for a morsel of bread!'

The Cabinet was listening attentively, and Playfair became bolder.

'Gentlemen, I can't divorce my observations as a scientist from my human involvement. Famine turns men into animals. There've been atrocious murders – householders maimed and mutilated in front of their wives and children – death threats from the Molly McGuire Society and assassinations by Captain Rock and Captain Swing. And all this because of the terrible struggle for a few strips of earth held by a pauper and starving peasantry.'

'What about the landlords?' Graham asked curtly. 'If they don't get rents, how can they pay their rates? The rates, you know, are a cumulative charge on their estates.'

'Mr Home Secretary,' said Playfair, 'if I may say so with respect, you speak of the Irish peasantry as if they're the labourers of Suffolk. The Irish have no property except their rags. When they're evicted, they live literally in holes dug in the bog. If men are reduced to the level of beasts, you must expect them to live and die like beasts. What's happening in Ireland is the worst of civil wars. It's what Mr Disraeli has called a war of the "poor against the poor".'

The mention of Disraeli's name produced a wave of visible displeasure on the faces around the table. Peel turned to Lindley.

'And what is your prescription, sir, for the present problem in Ireland?'

'The immediate problem is food,' said Lindley, affirming his authority as the senior member of the Commission. 'I suggest we send into Ireland, as a measure of famine relief, a massive supply of Indian corn. Without it, there'll be a million dead next year.'

'And after it's been eaten?' said Peel.

'The problem of Ireland will still be there. The need of Ireland is land reform and the untaxed import of corn,' Lindley said boldly. Playfair nodded his head energetically.

The Prime Minister didn't reply.

When the scientists had gone, Graham said, 'D'you think he exaggerates, Prime Minister?'

'No,' said Peel gloomily. 'The Irish are an exhausted people. They depend on a single crop. They're doomed to live on prayer and charity. They must have cheap food if their problems are ever to be solved, and the curse of violence ended.'

Despite the report on the origins of violence, Minister after Minister, as the meeting continued, expressed the fear that the present disorder, supported as it was by some English radicals, might be contagious at home unless it was sternly repressed in Ireland. At his place behind the long table, Peel listened in silence.

Then, after he had heard the Cabinet's views, he said, 'I am obliged to you, gentlemen. The bitterness we're dealing with affects every class. You saw what happened yesterday with Hawick's Motion. All he purported to ask was for a committee to investigate the distress of the nation.'

A bird settled on the window-sill overlooking the garden,

and Peel watched it pensively until it flew away with a ruffle of its wings.

'There was no dissent. We all agreed about the committee. Yet Mr Cobden used the debate as an occasion for malevolence to hold me personally responsible for the country's sufferings.'

'You disposed of him, Prime Minister,' said the Home Secretary gruffly.

'Not entirely,' said Peel with a wave of his hand. 'When an agitator like Cobden drops his poison, it remains. It's an incitement to assassination, Home Secretary.'

The Ministers had already discussed among themselves Cobden's venomous jibe at Peel for his fears about his own life after Drummond's murder, but no one spoke. The Prime Minister was absorbed, tapping with his fingers on the table, till at last he stood, and the others immediately rose.

'No,' said Peel, pursuing a private train of thought, his back to the huge gilt looking-glass. 'I'll never be intimidated. Never! But we must be careful that the secessionists find no comfort in our ranks.'

There was a murmur of agreement.

'I shall be taking a chop at Bellamy's. I trust I shan't be without company.'

Lord Aberdeen said, 'Indeed not,' and he and Graham walked across Whitehall with Peel to the dining-room in the House of Commons.

As they arrived, they saw Disraeli, Cochrane, Smythe and Lord John Manners sitting at their regular table in the corner, and Peel pointed them out to the Home Secretary in a deprecatory gesture which he didn't try to hide.

'There's our Mr Disraeli, surrounded as usual by his ephebes.'

'What's the fashion today?' asked the Home Secretary.

'Decorum and self-importance, I suspect,' said Aberdeen. 'The age of the dandies is over. You know, we had a remarkable report on Disraeli from Paris.'

'You must tell us all about it,' said the Prime Minister.

'I gather he tried to cut a great dash there,' said the Home

Secretary. 'Took a suite – received delegations – called on the notables – gave audiences.'

'The Ambassador complained,' said Aberdeen, 'that everyone thought Disraeli the new ambassador. I gather he almost hoodwinked the King as well.'

'In what way?' asked Peel, taking a glass of claret.

'Oh, on the principle that every domestic poodle becomes a St Bernard abroad, he insinuated himself into the Court – St Cloud, the Tuileries. Described himself as the leader of the Young England party, Cowley tells me. Young England!'

He spoke the last two words with distaste at the presumption of those who now used it as their label.

'What a world of *arrivistes* we live in!' said Graham, the words rumbling through his heavy frame. 'I'm a man of the eighteenth century – a boy when the new century began. But I remember it well. We had our nabobs, but they are exemplars of modesty and distinction compared with these new men of the counting-houses and their families and their penniless apers. Disraeli's a master at using his connections with the Rothschilds. In Paris especially, Rothschild's an Open Sesame.'

'It must help,' said Aberdeen, 'to belong to their clan.'

'Not so much in England,' said Graham. 'Having failed with his own fraternity, the fellow had the impudence to ask me to get a government job for his brother. I refused, of course, bearing in mind his speech on the Irish Arms Bill – his abstentions – his general behaviour – his – !'

Words failed him.

'He'll overlook any snub if it suits him,' said Aberdeen. 'Disraeli has the chameleon quality of assimilating himself to any advantageous background. Just look how he's taken on the style of his Ganymedes!'

Except for his curling hair, Disraeli, seen from behind, was indistinguishable in his dark coat from the young aristocrats listening to him attentively.

'Remarkable how the fellow moves on,' said Graham with a growl as he plunged his fork into the pie which the waiter had hurriedly brought him. 'I remember him hanging on to

D'Orsay and his set at Gore House. That was before the Count ran into his money troubles.'

'And poor Lady Blessington turned to literature,' said Aberdeen. 'Heath's Book of Beauty. The gentlewoman's recompense.'

'Nowadays,' said Graham, 'the fellow's all piety, incense and mischief with his lordlings. Clever, too!'

'There's no question,' Peel said, 'about his cleverness. He stands head and shoulders above the rest. But he's quite exceptionally insolent.'

'You'd hardly credit it, but he wrote Louis Philippe a memorandum,' said Aberdeen wryly, 'about my "mystical hallucinations".'

He laughed, but Peel frowned.

'There's disloyalty for you. Very characteristic. Are you sure, though?'

'Oh, yes. Graham intercepted the note, and sent me a copy.'

Peel raised his eyebrows.

'Intercepted it? Isn't that rather dangerous, Graham?'

Graham said, 'It's only dangerous if it comes to light. *Salus reipublicae suprema lex.*'

'A nice point. What else did it contain?'

The Prime Minister's curiosity rose above his sense of propriety.

'Disraeli suggested to the King that he could "organize" the British press in a pro-French sense.'

Peel slowly shook his head as if baffled by Disraeli's extravagances.

'There's another point,' said Graham. 'We've received reports from the Ambassador that Disraeli met Mrs Edmonds a number of times.'

'Mrs Edmonds, as I recall her, was a superior strumpet. I'm not surprised that Disraeli frequented her before he became, so to speak, respectable. But what is she up to in Paris?'

'She's the friend and consort of every revolutionary in Europe.'

'Curious that Louis Philippe tolerates her.'

'She's a useful source of information.'

137

'A dangerous liaison for a British MP. The man's totally unprincipled,' said the Prime Minister. 'In life as in politics. After all, he began as a radical, and was never quite sure if he was a Whig or a Tory.'

The Home Secretary put his table-napkin to his lips, and then said, 'We'd be better off without him. We can't trust him. It's far better to have an open enemy than a hypocritical traitor. We must get rid of him.'

Peel was about to reply, but he was interrupted by the arrival of the chops, and they returned to the question of law and order in Ireland.

Shortly afterwards, Peel sat in the half-empty Chamber of the House of Commons, listening to a long and bitter speech by one of Cobden's supporters opposing the enlistment of army pensioners as an anti-riot reserve. He was thinking of his land in Staffordshire where the dark clouds would be scudding over the stubbled fields; of a hare running zigzag in front of him; and the echo of guns overlaying the tinnitus in his head that was like a secret conversation with an ever-present hobgoblin perched on his shoulder. Only in the country, far from the engloomed and airless Chamber where he had been sitting day and night with only a few hours' intermission for breakfast or a change of linen, was there a respite with his dogs barking and scrambling, the game spread out on the ground, the friendly servants, his wife and children, the happy exhaustion.

After twenty-three years of marriage, he still felt a pang of exile when his wife was at their home in Drayton Manor and he at Westminster. The question recurred. Why did he endure the argument, the abuse, the misrepresentation, the gross raillery of the Commons, the threat of assassination? Was it to serve the Queen? He detested the trivial talk at Windsor.

'*Did you ride today?*'

'*No, ma'am.*'

'*It was very cold.*'

'*Yes, ma'am.*'

'*I think it will be cold again tomorrow.*'

'*Yes, indeed, ma'am.*'

But he was a servant of the Crown and the people; that was the duty which he sought to fulfil both in private and in public.

'Will this man go on for long?' he asked Thomas Fremantle, the Whip, who was sitting next to him.

'For ever,' said Fremantle gloomily. 'If he can't talk the Bill out, he'll try to get a "count" when he's driven enough of us to suicide.'

He glanced anxiously around to see whether the quorum of the House could be maintained.

'Ah, well!' said Peel with resignation. 'We'll have to keep a House.'

'Luckily,' said Fremantle, 'there's been a frost. No racing today, and our men will soon be arriving.'

Peel smiled and, placing his writing tablet on his knees, wrote to his wife.

My own dearest love,
    I again write to you from this odious place where I spend the greater part of the day.

From below the gangway came a mutter of conversation, an *obbligato* to the keening theme of the orator, and Peel wrote on as if he were taking notes of the debate.

I left here this morning at two and am here again at twelve. The only news is that Macnaghten is being tried at the Old Bailey, and his counsel pleads 'Not Guilty' on the grounds of his insanity. On the other hand, everyone here is convinced that he was the centre of an Irish conspiracy involving many others. There is a great feeling against the judges, including Sir Wm Follett who seems to sympathize with the plea, and the Queen has written to me to say '*everybody* is morally *convinced* that the malefactor is perfectly conscious of what he did!'

In the meantime, the murders in Ireland continue. The other day a private on parade stepped out of his rank and shot dead the adjutant of his regiment. The way things are going, Ireland may destroy us yet.

I can hardly see to write to you, although it is noon –

everything is gloomy and dark, and I see there are candles in the Lobby of the House.

Forgive this melancholy script. I feel very solitary without you.

Believe me, my own dearest love,

Your tired but affectionate husband,

Robert Peel.

He finished the letter, sighed, and looked around for a messenger. The thought of Drummond, his dead secretary, persisted in his mind as vividly as when he was alive. Like the Queen, he wanted the death penalty for Macnaghten, not merely because he himself had been intended as the victim, but because he believed that the assassin's act would be imitated by other lunatics, revolutionaries and conspirators. At night as by day, he went on foot from the House of Commons to Whitehall Gardens so that he could reassure himself of his personal courage. Superstitious in certain matters, though devout, he lived with a presentiment of disaster. Alvanley's remark at the Carlton Club that he wouldn't die a natural death had been reported to him, and the thought of the malevolence that surrounded him kept him awake.

He handed the letter to a messenger and shut his eyes, his hat tipped over his face. After a few moments he opened them and saw Disraeli walking up the gangway to his usual place behind him. Peel slid lower into his seat and put his legs on the despatch-box table. When Disraeli passed him he felt the same tremor of apprehension as when he had learned of Drummond's murder. Disraeli – Mrs Edmonds – the murder – they fused in his weary mind.

To achieve power a man had to be tireless, unrelenting, possessed of a single purpose to which all else was subordinate. So it had been with himself. He had led the Tory Party with dedication; he had learnt everything there was to know about procedure and Members of Parliament.

But Disraeli was different from himself and from any other he'd known in the House. However often Disraeli was felled, he rose like Mendoza, the Hebrew bare-knuckle fighter, to carry on the fight. An insult rebounded from him like a pea catapulted against a muscled chest. And the race that exhausted others only seemed to stimulate and excite him. Disraeli's goal was power, and nothing could divert him from the pursuit of it.

Very slowly Peel turned his head to look at Disraeli's ivory-pale face, so different from the robust, florid, open-air faces of his own supporters, bench upon bench of them, reaching as far as the Serjeant at Arms at the Bar. No. Disraeli didn't matter. But Sir James Graham was right. The party would be better off with Disraeli as an identified and isolated enemy rather than a false friend. The Young Englanders themselves weren't a problem. They were eager for office. He knew from Lord Strangford, Smythe's father, that they could be detached from their captain by a *pourboire*. But Disraeli was different from the young aristocrats. He was a man with a different background. He couldn't be bought with a tip.

The Prime Minister heard his own name mentioned, and instinctively took off his tall hat and rose to his feet to contradict an observation by Mr Cobden.

'The honourable gentleman,' he said, 'is mistaken – though that is not unusual.'

A great roar of approval rose behind him.

Peel turned his head, and glanced with satisfaction at the faces on his side of the House. All were enthusiastic except for Disraeli, who had covered his mouth to conceal a yawn.

Chapter Eleven

Lord George Bentinck reined in the horse, and from the driving seat of his open carriage greeted Disraeli.

'Do you choose to be alone?' he asked, 'or would you care, sir, to drive with me?'

They were both guests of Mr Hope, the wealthiest of the Young England group, in a large house-party at Deepdene in Gloucestershire.

Disraeli and Mary Anne, who had been staying at the castle for several weeks, felt in their cantonment like soldiers on a campaign where calm was intermittently broken by bursts of fury. During the week, everything was tranquil; but the week-end was heralded by scouts and cornets dashing from one wing to another, organizing billets, ensuring that those estranged weren't placed too close to each other, and those in search of each other's company at night had no problem of successful access, especially in view of Lord Palmerston's much discussed mishap at Windsor, when he had blundered into the bedroom of the wrong lady-in-waiting.

On Thursdays the *fourgons* arrived with their brass-bound boxes containing the ammunition of the *toilettes* that blazed at each other across the dinner table, the changes of dress that alternated with the changes of menu, till on the Monday the post-horn and the railway whistle announced that the skirmishes and the flirtations were over. At this point Mr Hope, having said farewell to most of his guests, would retire for two or three days to recuperate for his next visitors, while Disraeli resumed work on his new novel.

For his own part, he often wished as he stood bidding his fellow-guests goodbye it could have been on the steps of his own estate rather than his host's. His father's house at Bradenham was all very well, but there too he was in a sense a guest.

Always to meet his London friends at other people's country houses was embarrassing, and he had recently discussed with Mary Anne the possibility of acquiring a house and land in Buckinghamshire.

But Mary Anne had told him, prudently he had to admit, about the expense of their London house. And of course there were other debts, including the one that irked him most, the debt he had contracted on D'Orsay's behalf, a bill that had long since left the hand of Crockford and been sold by Lawson and discounted and resold; but, ever more crumpled, soiled and over-written, it always came back to him for payment or renewal, its exorbitant compound interest accumulating to heights far beyond its original value. Nor was there any hope of getting anything back from his old friend. Despite his elegant house, D'Orsay was virtually bankrupt, and Lady Blessington's mediocre authorship was poorly rewarded. Four thousand three hundred pounds! The debt continued to grow. What did it profit Disraeli to be a friend of the Rothschilds if he couldn't release himself from a bill of a paltry few thousand pounds?

For the time being, though, he didn't feel any great pressure from his creditors, since he had lately fed them with some of Mary Anne's income. In addition he had planned two more novels, each of them to bring him perhaps another thousand pounds or so, the same amount as he had been paid for *Coningsby*. It would be enough to tide him over into the year 1845. And then? He was a fatalist. 'If it's the will of Allah – !' As a young man he had returned with that talismanic phrase from Palestine, and astonished the drawing-rooms with his exotic invocation. He was now over forty, but it was still true. With God's will, he would triumph.

'Would you care, sir, to drive?'

Disraeli looked up at Bentinck, who was wearing a light blue Newmarket mackintosh with a blue velvet collar and cuffs, and breeches of white cord. In his walking cloak, he felt at a disadvantage. Although he saw Bentinck regularly at the House and sometimes at the Carlton Club, they had never engaged in conversation. Bentinck was known as an outstanding sportsman and a friend of Lord Stanley. There wasn't a ball-game in which he hadn't excelled. As a patron of the turf he was unequalled. In the smoking-rooms, sometimes still in 'pink' and covered by a coat after a hurried arrival from some not-too-distant run, he would sit surrounded by cronies whose talk would be all of horses. Disraeli was uneasy in the presence of Bentinck's handsome but plethoric face, his commanding voice, his aggressive demeanour of a wealthy country gentleman. True, he had been secretary to the former Prime Minister, his uncle Canning, and had also served in the army. Yet he had always seemed without a true interest in public affairs.

At Bentinck's invitation, Disraeli hesitated. Then he observed that in his expression there was something mild and friendly. In the corridors of the House of Commons, Members of Parliament passed each other constantly without greeting, their brows knitted, their eyes preoccupied even when they knew each other well. They allowed heavy doors, reinforced with brass, to swing in each other's faces when they could have held them. But when they met outside in some other setting it was as if they'd never really seen each other. The hostile repartee, the competing stance, the disdainful look, the negligent style, vanished in a neutral, social air.

'I'd be delighted,' said Disraeli, 'provided I can send a messenger to the house to announce that I've vanished.'

Bentinck called a gamekeeper, and Disraeli scribbled a note for Mary Anne.

'Where are we going?' he asked.

'To the races,' said Bentinck.

'How excellent!' said Disraeli, lying back in the racing *britzka*. 'It was always my ambition to be driven to the races by Lord George Bentinck.'

Bentinck laughed loudly, flicked his whip, and the glossy black horse jerked forward into a trot.

'You must explain to me,' said Disraeli as the summery pink and white hedgerows sped past them, 'how it is that when you drive you always seem to be going downhill.'

At the approaches to the race-course the copses and lanes gave way to the low walls of Gloucestershire stone, and on the main road Bentinck outpaced the carts and wains and carriages that drew aside to let him pass. Ahead of them they could see a coach, its four horses throwing up clouds of dust on the straight road leading to Povney Manor. Bentinck touched his horse lightly with his whip, urging it nearer the heavy coach, now swaying towards the ditch by the jagged wall. On the outside, a boy with a crushed tall hat looked down scornfully at the light *britzka* which had the impertinence to try to pass. The postilion blew his horn, a blast of derision and a warning to the chickens that scattered with a squawk, leaving two feathers drifting in the air. When Bentinck went to pass, the coach lurched towards the right, rumbling in a rut till the coachman pulled it out. The postilion gave a celebratory blast, the *britzka* rattled in sympathy with the coach as if it were a partner in a dance, and Disraeli surreptitiously gripped the side of the light carriage.

'God damn him!' said Bentinck. He put the nose of his horse ahead of the rear wheels of the coach, indifferent to the discomfort of his companion, his only wish to pass the obstructive coach. A light foam lay on the horse's mouth, and Bentinck leaned forward in his seat, easing the reins and urging the animal on. Two women looked in alarm from the window, and one of them screamed as the rear shaft swung towards the harness of the coach. The black horse began to pant in great sighing groans, and its flanks, tendrilled with sweat, laboured under the strain of the race. Its mouth suddenly became flecked with pink, and Disraeli looked at Bentinck.

Bentinck swore, tightened the reins and held back the horse till the coach drew away with the postilion blowing another blast. The boy waved his hat, and Bentinck grumbled.

'We are entitled to kill ourselves, Mr Disraeli, but not our horses.'

As if in acknowledgement, the horse swept up its head and swished its tail, and the *britzka* slowed to an easy pace.

'If there's one thing I understand,' said Bentinck with some self-satisfaction, 'it's men and horses.'

'That's more than enough,' said Disraeli.

Near the Heath the traffic grew thicker, coaches interspersed with families on foot out for the day, percherons pulling drays loaded with tuns of ale, char-à-bancs, and gipsy women with children at their breasts begging from shrinking ladies and offering to tell their fortunes. Disraeli expected Bentinck to drive straight to the ring, but instead he guided his horse at a trot to some high ground overlooking the course.

'You know,' he said, 'I've given my life to racing – with the passion that other men give to women.'

'I'm aware,' said Disraeli, 'of the debt the Turf owes you. The Running Rein case – '

'Ah, yes,' said Bentinck, pleased that Disraeli had referred to his long and strenuous battle in the law courts to prove that a four-year-old horse had been substituted for a three-year-old in the Derby. 'Racing is a noble sport with many opportunities for dishonour. I've tried to change it. What I learnt very young, Mr Disraeli, is that if someone cheats you once, never trust him again. Never! Never trust a man who doesn't pay his bets, or refuses to acknowledge his debts.'

'Most certainly,' Disraeli murmured.

Bentinck lowered his powerful form to the ground, and they walked together to a stile and leaned over it, looking down on the stand, the harlequin pattern of the race-course, and the tents around it.

'When I was a young man,' said Bentinck, 'I fell into debt. They were heavy debts, but I acknowledged them. My father always said, "Get into debt if you must. But never deny it!" '

'Excellent advice,' said Disraeli. He had never denied his debts. That would have been as great a betrayal as to deny his origins, but he wondered to himself why Bentinck had chosen to offer him this homily. Everyone knew that Bentinck, with a hundred horses in his stables and forty in training, was obsessively attached to the Turf. He had a passion for organization, and in slacker days had insisted on strict punctuality for stewards, trainers and jockeys. It was he who had introduced the practice of saddling and parading before the stands. Through his exertions, despite the old Act of Parliament which said that no stake should exceed one hundred pounds, the prize-money had been steadily raised. Bentinck had never hesitated to sue in order to test the law; nor had he shrunk from a challenge when it came to giving the lie to anyone who disputed a bet.

'It's not an accident,' he said to Disraeli, 'that I asked you to drive with me.'

'That increases my pleasure.'

Bentinck looked towards the race-course, and a slight impatience entered his features as if he was eager to dispose of a matter that troubled him.

'I've listened to you in the House with attention, and I've long admired your eloquence, your independence and your courage. I heard you speak the other day on Ireland. That was very good. Mind you, it all boils down to railways.'

'Railways?'

'Yes – give the Irish railways. They'll have work. The land will rise in value. And there's your Irish question solved.'

'Ah,' said Disraeli. 'You must first define the Irish question. One day it's the Pope, the next day potatoes. At one moment it's the lack of an aristocracy; the next, as you say, a lack of railways. In my view, Lord George, the problem is absenteeism. You have in Ireland a starving population with a territorial aristocracy that lives in England or Scotland; you have an established church that's not their church. And in addition you have the weakest executive in the world. *That's* the Irish question.'

'But the executive is our own Government, is it not? Mustn't we take responsibility for failure?'

'Most certainly.'

'And Peel?'

The two men faced each other for a second without speaking. Then Disraeli said, 'There's nothing I'd say to you in private about the Prime Minister that I wouldn't say to his face – indeed have already said. I believe he's a weak man who makes strong gestures, but as long as he upholds our party's traditional principles he'll have my support – and, I can say, the support of my friends.'

'Too vague!' said Bentinck abruptly. 'What are you referring to, sir?'

'I refer in particular to his attitude towards the agricultural interest. If Peel now somersaults and turns against the Corn Laws that protect that interest in favour of Free Trade, he'll be in the position of your man who repudiates his debts.'

Disraeli watched Bentinck's face carefully. He could see he had used a comparison that touched him.

'By God, you're right! My uncle Canning never trusted him. Couldn't trust him on Catholic Emancipation. A twister!'

He was becoming angry at his memories, and smacked his whip against the stile.

'If I didn't have the stable – '

'With your talents, Lord George,' said Disraeli blandly, 'perhaps – '

'Dammit, I might,' said Bentinck. 'Look here, Disraeli. We must have more talk about this. D'you know, only the other day I thought of getting that fellow – what's his name? – Martin – the Queen's Counsel – to come into the House and speak for the agricultural interest.'

He studied Disraeli.

'I think you could do it for me yourself – yes, even better.'

Disraeli smiled faintly. If he had his own talents and Bentinck's wealth, there'd be no problem.

'Lord George,' he said courteously, 'I am obliged to you. In politics, I am my own man.'

He turned to go, but Bentinck put his hand on his arm.

'I'm sorry, Mr Disraeli. Maybe I gave you a wrong impression. I wanted to talk to you precisely because you're your own man. I'm sick of the tired hacks of our party.'

Disraeli bowed. 'In that case, he said, 'I should be happy to be your ally. The agricultural interest has always been my concern. I need little prompting.'

They talked in friendly terms for another five minutes, and at last, seeing the race signalled, Bentinck took Disraeli's arm and began to tell him as they returned to the *britzka* about his mare Crucifix, by Priam, which a few years before had won the Oaks.

Outside the saddling enclosure the crowds made way for Bentinck as for an emperor. Two stable lads stopped fighting. Trainers raised their hats. The shouting of tipsters faded away, and jockeys already mounted touched caps with their whips as their horses clopped past in the sudden silence.

Disraeli followed in Bentinck's wake, delighted with the new experience of being an intimate of the leading member of the Jockey Club. Colonel Tankerton, Mr O'Mahey, Mr Lowndes-Guinness, Major-General Sir Edward Oving, Lord Fermor, Baron Hochleitner – from the corner of his eye he could see the glances, at once deferential and curious, directed by some of the owners at Bentinck and his unfamiliar colleague.

Disraeli knew the points of a horse. But although from time to time he attended race-meetings as a social obligation, he disliked the preoccupation of owners and jockeys with withers and rumps and weights and irons, and the parading and assessing and saddling always tired him. Hitherto he would have liked all race-meetings to be races without intervals.

Now he began to see some merit in the interminable preparations. A gourmet needed an interval between courses.

When Bentinck entered the changing-room, the jockeys, some of them half-naked, immediately rose. Disraeli put a cambric handkerchief to his face as if to blow his nose, but in reality to shield it from the stale, sweaty smells. Bentinck's response was different.

'Well, Lobb,' he said to a thin sixteen-year-old jockey who was standing with one boot on, 'are you on a winner today?'

'Dunno, me lord,' said the boy. ' 'E's a puller.'

'Well, don't pull him back too hard,' said Bentinck, moving on. 'And what about you, Grimes?'

Grimes, a forty-year-old veteran with the body of a youth, said, 'Good chance today, my lord. Givin' 'em pounds, but Retarius likes a strong wind.'

'Well, good luck to you all, lads,' said Bentinck.

'Thank you, sir,' said the jockeys in an uneven chorus, and Bentinck and Disraeli moved off towards the enclosure. A breeze had blown up over the Heath, and Disraeli inhaled deeply. The scent of grass mingled with the ammoniacal smell of horses, and the restrained yet excited conversation around the rails was a counterpoint to the dignified stroll and prance of the mounts. The ladies with their parasols spoke in squeals never heard in their drawing-rooms. The value of racing, Disraeli decided, was that it gave a reserved people, governed by predictable social rules, the chance to scream and enjoy the unpredictable.

'Well,' said Bentinck to Colonel Tankerton, 'have you a winner, Colonel? . . . This is Mr Disraeli.'

As if he'd never met him before, Tankerton gave Disraeli a limp greeting, and Disraeli, who had prepared a friendly response, nodded in return.

'D'you fancy Priam?' Bentinck asked.

'I fancy the horse,' said Tankerton, 'but not the odds – two to one.'

He preened himself in his dark green riding coat and doe-skin breeches, and kicked the grass with a hessian boot. His face had the same flush as Lord George's; it was an outdoor face that enjoyed the self-inflicted anxieties of the hunt and the race-course.

'What d'you think of Retarius?'

'Nothing,' said Tankerton. 'Charles always puts the wrong horse in the wrong race. Retarius is a cart-horse.'

He half-turned his back on Disraeli, excluding him from the topic, and went on to give Bentinck the history of Retarius's failures and how it had only won the previous season through a series of accidents.

'What'll you give us on Retarius?' Bentinck asked, reintroducing Disraeli into the conversation.

'Eights,' Tankerton said at once. 'Against!'

'Good God,' said Bentinck. 'Eights? After what you've just told us?'

'I'll make it nines,' said Tankerton. 'How much?'

'Five hundred,' said Bentinck. 'Will you join me, Disraeli?'

Tankerton surveyed him, and Disraeli hesitated. Since that evening at Crockford's on the night of the Coronation, he'd given up gambling and had no wish to begin again. He had seen too many young men ruined at the tables. But he wouldn't show fear in the face of Bentinck, still less of Tankerton, and he said idly, 'Two fifty will suit me.'

They turned towards the course, where the horses, to the din of the crowd, were cantering up in a long procession.

Disraeli held tightly to his hat. The breeze had turned into a powerful wind that was making the tents flap. In his mind he had already said farewell to his stake, but the gesture was worthwhile. Tankerton was known to him as an Irish land-owner who spent almost all his time in England, and had engaged in violent but unsuccessful competition for the Shrewsbury seat, a bigot with an obscure past whose prejudices were more passionate than those of the most intransigent Tories in the House, a dubious figure of Mrs Edmonds's entourage. The two hundred and fifty pounds he had wagered were well lost if only as a retort to Tankerton's insolence.

The flags at the starting post were cracking, whip-like, and the horses were wheeling and rearing as their jockeys man-œuvred them into position. Then, before Disraeli realized the signal had been given, he saw that the horses were off, settling down easily to the three-mile race. He raised his glass to his eyes, and the horses, strung out along the inside rail, became clearly visible. Leading the fifteen runners was Priam, its jockey all in red, moving in what seemed no more than an easy gallop. Sixth from the end Retarius, which he recognized from the black and white quarterings of its rider, was steadily losing ground to the rest of the field.

'I'm afraid our horse is lagging,' he said.

'Give it a chance, my dear sir,' Bentinck answered. 'They've a long way to go. It's the last lap that counts. Just wait and see what happens when they come round again.'

The spectators in the stand watched the first lap idly.

'Galcador – Priam – Rosario – Alcazar – Flying Fox – Felton – Surprise – Barley Mow.' Tankerton called the order of the field, his voice emphatic in controlling his excitement. He had given Bentinck long odds, but he hadn't been sure that his judgment would have been vindicated so contemptuously by events. Retarius was now lying fourteenth and seemed to be ambling, as if his rider had no wish to exert his mount unduly in a forlorn enterprise. A waiter passed, and Bentinck offered his neighbours champagne. He himself took a cognac.

Retarius had moved up one place and was lying equal third from last, and Disraeli eyed its hindquarters with enmity. Retarius had betrayed him. Now the spectators were beginning to shout encouragement, and they shouted at the tops of their voices; pretty women screamed, showing their teeth and their gullets and stamping their parasols on the wooden boards of the stands. Disraeli looked at them mournfully. 'Come on, Rosario – Priam, Priam – come on Felton – Rosario – Barley Mow!' They were all enemies who wanted the horse he hadn't backed to win. Tankerton, standing with his hands clutching a rail, had taken off his hat, and his hair fell over his forehead in the sharp gusts of wind that threatened to drag the ropes of the tents from their pins. It gave him a simian appearance.

'Now,' said Bentinck as the horses came around a third time, 'now you'll see.'

The drumming of hooves reached their ears before they could identify the jockeys' silks. This time some of the leading horses had changed places, and Rosario and Felton had fallen back.

'Too much weight,' said Bentinck. 'They're carrying nine stone six. Grimes is eight stone. They're running into the wind for half the time.'

Retarius had moved up, still with the same labouring gait, and was lying sixth, but Priam, which had been second almost the whole way, stretched itself apparently without effort and moved two lengths ahead of Galcador.

Another circuit, and the crowd was shouting in a baying duet, 'Priam – Gal-ca-dor – Priam – Galcador!'

Tankerton looked over his shoulder at Bentinck and said, 'Like tens?'

'Yes,' said Bentinck. 'Two-fifty – and a hundred for Mr Disraeli.'

Tankerton smiled, and returned to his position. The horses had disappeared on the other side of the course, and the cheers were carried from there in a tribal wail.

'In racing,' said Bentinck, 'you need two qualities – patience and stamina.'

'Skill, perhaps?'

'That's it,' said Bentinck. 'The best mount won't win unless you ride it properly. Grimes is a good 'un. The others are getting tired.'

'Priam – Priam!' It was a cry of despair. The favourite was slipping back, and new names were being shouted. 'Rosario – Flying Fox – Retarius!'

A bell rang.

'God blast me!' said Bentinck, his voice rising to a shout. 'He's going to do it! Retarius – Retarius! Give him your whip, boy. Retarius!'

And Disraeli joined in. 'Retarius! Retarius!' His voice sounded through the uproar.

'No – come on, Priam! Priam!'

'Retarius! Retarius!'

'Galcador – Rosario!' Tankerton was shouting. Anything but Retarius. He looked as if he would himself lash the grunting horses to the finishing post. But Grimes, riding in his curious posture with his short stirrup leathers and his body crouched over Retarius's withers, seemed as fresh in the last furlong as he had at the start.

'He'll do it! He'll do it!' Bentinck shouted.

At the touch of Grimes's whip, Retarius thrust himself between the leaders, Galcador and Rosario, and rode in comfortably to the finishing post, two lengths ahead of the field.

Disraeli put his hands in his pockets. He was trembling, but he wasn't sure whether it was from the unseasonably glacial wind or from excitement. He had won two thousand pounds on his first bet and a thousand on his second, and he owed his sudden affluence to Bentinck, who was standing there as if nothing unusual had happened.

'Your man rides like a crab,' said Tankerton.

'Have you any objection?' asked Bentinck.

Tankerton hesitated.

'No,' he said. 'I merely dislike it as a style.'

'Don't worry,' said Bentinck good-humouredly. 'You

won't see its like in your lifetime. We'll take your bills, sir.'

Mary Anne stood waiting at the entrance to the drive as the *britzka*, now covered with its *calèche* hood, drew up.

'My dear Mrs Disraeli!' said Bentinck apologetically.

'How could you have taken Mr Disraeli off like that?' she said. 'In that thin cloak – he could have caught the influenza. He is very susceptible to the cold, Lord George. Come, Ben. You will have a rapid walk to restore your circulation.'

'May I drive you, madam?' Bentinck asked good-humouredly.

'No, thank you,' said Mary Anne. 'I never drive without my husband.'

Bentinck bowed gravely, and said, 'I look forward to the pleasure of dining with you tonight.'

In their bedroom, Mary Anne was still reproachful. Although the wind had fallen and dusk had settled velvety over the Italian gardens, she still felt cold from her long wait.

'Look,' she said, 'my fingers are icicles.'

Patiently, Disraeli put her hands to his mouth and kissed them.

Mary Anne sat on the bed and dangled her foot. He unlaced her satin boot and took it off.

'You see,' she said, 'my feet are chilled as well.'

She unfurled her stocking, and Disraeli held her foot between his hands.

'You have a very beautiful foot,' he said. 'More beautiful than any sculptured cast.'

'Have I?' she asked, and looked at him to see if his eyes wore the delicate expression of mockery that she had learned to see in him when he paid an extravagant compliment. His face was solemn, and he touched her toes with his lips.

'You made me very anxious, my dearest,' she said, passing her fingers over his thick, curling hair.

'I'm sorry,' Disraeli said, kissing her ankle. 'Bentinck insisted on staying for the last race.' He wanted to tell her about his winnings, but decided that on the whole reticence was wiser.

'If you were happy – ' she began indulgently.

'Never *entirely* happy without Mary Anne,' he replied, and he thought with a sudden surprise that this was the truth. At the beginning of their marriage, especially when he felt that he had married not only Mary Anne but her mother and brother as well, he had sometimes experienced a despair, as if he had surrendered everything that was free and gracious in his life. But after the deaths of his mother-in-law and her brother, Mary Anne, who had provided a shelter for all of them, seemed herself to be in need of protection. Isolated and childless, they had turned to each other in mutual dependence.

'When will your maid come to dress you?' he said.

'Not yet,' said Mary Anne. 'Not till I ring the bell. Our baths are drawn.'

'I'll help you,' said Disraeli.

'Do you like Lord George Bentinck?' she asked, standing in front of the looking-glass.

'Very much,' said Disraeli, unbuttoning the back of her redingote.

'But he is so unlike your Young England friends.'

'He's approximately my own age – perhaps a couple of years older.'

'He's very serious.'

'These are serious days.'

Her skirt fell to the ground, and he began to unlace her stays. She watched the whalebones loosen till he swept her corset off with his left hand.

'And Mr Smythe,' she said with her eyes shut. 'What does Bentinck think of George Smythe?'

'He doesn't care for him,' said Disraeli, kissing her beneath the long curls on her neck. He observed her pale body in the light of the sconces.

'Are you twenty-two?' he asked, folding his arms around her.

She opened her eyes and smiled to him in the glass.

'No – twenty-one.'

During dinner, Disraeli found himself next to Lady Dorothy Anstey, a pretty young woman who had been at Court, knew

Baroness Lehzen, the Queen's former governess, and had recently returned with her parents from a tour of the Rhineland.

'I sat on the deck of the steamer for a whole summer's day,' she said, 'and read *Coningsby*. I've read all your novels, Mr Disraeli, and loved them all. But *Coningsby*'s the one I loved best. I'll always think of it with sunlight glittering on the water and music and young people singing, and castles on high rocks. And the wonderful contrast between old Lord Monmouth and his grandson. What was his name?'

'Harry.'

'Yes – and that terrible woman – that rouged demi-mondaine – what was her name?'

'Mrs Guy Flouncey.'

'Yes – of course. Mrs Flouncey. How suitable!'

A footman removed the Limoges plate from in front of him, and interrupted their conversation. He caught Mary Anne's eye from the other side of the table, and gave her an encouraging smile. Her two neighbours had been diverted by their younger companions, and she seemed lost.

'And what didn't you like in my novel?'

'The politics – I hate politics – all that passage about how the parties – the Whigs and the Tories – came into being. Am I silly?'

'My dear child,' said a bishop on the other side of her, tucking his napkin under his chin, 'the ancient Greeks called the private citizens who took no part in politics – idiots!'

He addressed himself to the fish, and said no more to her. In confusion she turned back to Disraeli.

'Oh, I hope you don't misunderstand me,' she said. 'Everyone's talking about *Coningsby*. Papa says it's the most important book of our times.'

'It's a judgment my father shares,' said Disraeli. He studied her delicate profile, and said, 'Have you read Heine?'

'No,' she said, 'but I have read Goethe – the *Elective Affinities*. Do you believe in elective affinities, Mr Disraeli?'

He was about to answer when from the other side of the

table came Mary Anne's plangent and lilting voice, addressing
Beresford Hope.

'. . . so beautiful at Stowe. You've no idea – do pass me the
salt – but it was so cold – freezing. We were all waiting in the
vestibule for the Queen – an hour – you've no idea – I was
wearing black velvet – do you like black velvet? – yes, most
men do – I had hanging sleeves like these – but knotted with
blue velvet bows, and diamonds, of course.'

'Yes – yes,' said Beresford Hope. Mary Anne didn't pause.

'But poor Dizzy was shivering, actually shivering – his teeth
were chattering like castanets – you see, the floor was marble
and there was a freezing wind. And then we were presented
to Her Majesty and the Prince, with the Duke and Duchess
standing behind.'

'Really!' said Beresford Hope glumly.

'And do you know,' said Mary Anne triumphantly as some
of her neighbours fell silent to hear the rest of the anecdote of
the visit to the Duke and Duchess of Buckingham, 'the
Duchess told me later that the Queen said, "Look, there's Mr
Disraeli!" Can you imagine it?'

'How fascinating to be singled out like that,' said Lady
Dorothy.

'The trout,' said Disraeli, 'is exceptional.'

Mary Anne had begun a new anecdote about their visit to
Stowe, and Disraeli, in mid-flirtation, decided that she needed
all his attention.

'Madame Disraeli is indeed *en grande beauté*,' said Baron Eschen-
bach in the salon, with a devouring look at her bodice, cut
low over her shoulders and bordered with a bertha of lace
frills and ribbons.

Mary Anne looked upwards to Disraeli for his approval of
the diplomat's compliment. It delighted him. All around were
groups and couples, the women sitting, the men courteously
dispersed, but most of them longing for the moment when
their companions would take their candles and retire, so that
they themselves could go to the smoking room and play
billiards. Henry Hope stood quietly by the piano, waiting for

Miss Thomas, a soprano from the King's Theatre, to sing an aria from *Damon and Pythias*. He had the hospitable quality, Disraeli observed, shared by Lionel Rothschild, of always submerging himself among his guests, so that while ever-present he was also detached. Sitting on a sofa nearby was his brother, Beresford Hope, and Lady Elizabeth Spencer-Stanhope. For a second Disraeli caught his eye, but Beresford Hope's glance fluttered over his shoulder.

'You know,' Disraeli said in an aside as Smythe joined them, 'I have a talent for drawing the enmity of elder brothers – Beresford Hope, Edward Stanley, and Lord Titchfield.'

'Curious trinity!' said Smythe. 'Titchfield once told me that he'd like to live in a grotto and speak to no one . . . Don't worry, Diz, about Beresford. His only fear is that you'll make off with his brother's millions.'

'And Stanley?'

'He's different. If I had to be anyone else, I'd want to be Stanley.'

'Why not Dizzy?' asked Mary Anne.

'Ah,' said Smythe. 'It would mean, Mrs Disraeli, I'd be married to you – and that would be too much honour.'

She smacked his wrist with her fan, and Smythe showed an exaggerated contrition before he moved away.

There was a whisper for silence, and the voice of Miss Thomas filled the room, a bland pleasure added to the warm contentments already induced by Henry Hope's Rhine wines and clarets and cognacs and flambés and soufflés and a day of idleness, gossip and sport.

After the ladies had been conducted to their rooms the men returned, some in tasselled smoking caps, making for the billiard room that Hope had built below the level of the terrace, and that could only be reached by a broad and slippery marble stair.

'*Difficilis est descensus Averni*,' said Smythe. 'But after dinner it's almost impossible. This is the case against the third bottle.'

He groped for a sunken rail in the wall as the throng of cheerful men, talking loudly and without restraint since they had been released from their womenfolk, clattered or felt their way down the staircase. Disraeli made no comment. Out of regard for his host and as a mark of his 'clubbability', the fashionable term at White's, he was taking part in a ritual which inwardly he shrank from.

The relaxed hours in the billiard room at house-parties when the civilizing effect of women was removed always reminded him of Tacitus's description of the Germanic tribes at their ease, swigging and boasting. To absent himself would have invited a charge of arrogance or nonconformity. He sighed, and followed Smythe into the room, where some were already smoking cigars or long pipes, while others, with their jackets removed, were arranging the balls on the billiard-tables or chalking cues. Colonel Tankerton, he noticed, was lounging against a pillar near the first billiard-table, talking to Beresford Hope and tapping a cue impatiently against his right thigh.

Before Bentinck and Disraeli left the racecourse, Tankerton had handed each of them a note-of-hand. When he had given Disraeli his note he had turned his head away as Disraeli went to thank him, and during dinner he had hardly spoken, eating little and concentrating on the claret.

Tankerton said something to Beresford Hope, and they both stared at Disraeli for a few seconds. Disraeli couldn't see them very clearly, and raised his eyeglass to study them. Tankerton muttered something, and they both turned their backs. Disraeli drew down his white waistcoat and inspected his cuffs. His coat sat easily on his hips, and he felt elated. Hostility never gave him the clutch of fear that others sometimes spoke about. It excited him. If Tankerton wanted an enemy, he was ready.

At that moment he saw Bentinck enter the room, and felt a quick affection for this large-boned sportsman who earlier in the day had so ingenuously offered him his friendship. In the company sprawling in armchairs, drinking brandy and floating in smoke, there was no one else he could count on, not even the socially promiscuous Smythe, who went from group to group leaving a trail of laughter.

Seeing Disraeli standing alone, Bentinck came over and said, 'Care for a game? You can give me fifty start.'

'I'd give you a hundred if only I knew how to play. The ball and I have a long-standing feud. We go different ways.'

Bentinck laughed.

'In that case, you must be my marker. Come on, Mr Culver – I'll play you two hundred up.'

'Very well,' said Mr Culver, one of the largest landowners in Gloucestershire. 'Ten guineas a point.'

They began to play, and a small group gathered to watch Culver's small, delicate hands which contrasted with his robust face, as he made a break that went on to thirty-seven till he found himself with his ball at the centre of the table while red and white spot were pressed against the cushions at each end.

Around the table there was a hush, and Culver chalked his cue carefully. He was hesitating between using a cue-rest and leaning over the table. A manservant handed him a glass of brandy which he sipped. There was a titter from the shadows, then a new hush.

Culver addressed the ball, and as he went to strike it, Tankerton, still leaning against the pillar, called out, 'For God's sake, man, get on with it!'

Culver mis-cued, and the ball slewed away from the red, hit the cushion, and dribbled back to where it had started. There was a groan from the spectators, and Culver straightened himself with a smile. Bentinck scowled into the shadows.

'I'm sorry, Culver. He put you off. Let's have it again.'

'Not a bit,' said Culver. 'I'd already hit it.'

Bentinck made a cannon, then potted the red and quickly caught up with Culver's score.

'Jolly well done,' said Tankerton drunkenly.

Bentinck laid down his cue and again glanced at the pillar. His lips had tightened.

'Thirty-nine,' said Culver.

Disraeli marked the score.

In the background the conversation mounted and the on-lookers began to move away to the second table, where Henry Hope himself was playing. Bentinck, squinting down the cue, addressed the ball.

'No,' said Tankerton loudly to another guest as they turned towards the chairs at the end of the room, 'it was a rotten day. Had to pay out, dear boy.'

Bentinck paused.

'The outsiders were running well.' Tankerton lowered his voice confidentially, but the voices around him had fallen too. 'George's Jew-boy, you know. Culver had better watch the marker.'

Bentinck laid down his cue, and simultaneously Disraeli turned, his face white. The metal tag that he had pushed along the scoreboard rattled gently in the sudden silence.

'Mr Tankerton!' Disraeli called, and his voice was constricted.

'No, my bird, I think,' Bentinck said, interposing himself between Disraeli and Tankerton.

Around them was a surge, a mingling of anxiety and excitement, and a few guests rose from their armchairs to see what was happening in the knot that had formed close to Tankerton.

He had turned when Disraeli called his name, and approached the table with a malign expression.

'Can I be of service to you, sir?' he asked Disraeli.

Before Disraeli could answer, Bentinck said with an amiable air, 'No, to me, Tankerton.'

'Delighted,' said Tankerton, and a smile passed around the group. Tankerton had the satisfied manner of one who had taken a risk and succeeded. 'I am always ready to be of service.'

'Well – I took some money off you today.'

'That's so.'

Tankerton straightened himself. The recollection was disagreeable, and he noticed that Bentinck was frowning. The cheerful mood around them had fallen.

'I wonder, sir,' said Bentinck, 'if you'd help me to improve my winnings still further.'

'What's the bet, Lord George?' said Tankerton.

Bentinck took a step forward till he stood less than half a pace from Tankerton.

'I'm betting my friend Disraeli a thousand guineas to a

shilling that you'll have left Deepdene by tomorrow morning –
at eight o'clock.'

Tankerton looked quickly at the faces around him. One or
two drew away as if they wished to have no part in the scene.
Henry Hope stood quiet and watchful. The others examined
with curiosity Bentinck's casual stance.

'My dear Bentinck,' said Tankerton, forming his lips and
teeth into a smile, 'I wouldn't encourage you to bet on a
certainty. I've already arranged for my carriage at seven.'

He half-turned, as if the matter was triumphantly disposed
of.

'One moment, sir,' said Bentinck. 'I have a side bet with Mr
Disraeli. It's for two thousand guineas to a shilling. I've bet
him that if by chance you intended to leave tomorrow, you'd
now anticipate your departure by six hours.'

'George!' Hope intervened feebly. Tankerton lowered his
glance.

'If I have unwittingly offended you, Lord George – '

'If you are still here within an hour, Tankerton . . .' He turned
to Culver. 'We'll postpone our game till tomorrow. Come, Mr
Disraeli.'

He took Disraeli's arm, and the group surrounding them
parted as they went out together on to the moonlit terrace.
The night was warmer than the day, the air was heavy with
the scent of honeysuckle and privet; and they walked for a few
minutes in silence.

'I think you'll owe me a shilling,' said Bentinck.

'More than that,' Disraeli answered. 'Infinite riches.'

Chapter Twelve

For several weeks there had been rumours in the clubs, hints in the *Morning Chronicle* and *Fraser's Magazine*, and gossip at Almack's that the Tory leadership had decided to rid the party of Disraeli. Before that, Sir James Graham and the Whips had tried to organize a form of boycott when Disraeli rose to speak. The Government Front Bench would begin to drift to the exits after his first sentences, with a file of Parliamentary Secretaries and their lesser followers behind them. Yet the curiosity of Members and Disraeli's own magnetism always ensured a steady movement from the committee rooms and refreshment rooms back to the Chamber. The enemies of Disraeli left with an ostentatious indifference; but the friends of Bentinck hurried in with a loud tugging of the heavy doors, filling the back benches and congregating at the Bar in an excited clamour till the Chamber was packed and, at last, fell to listening to the familiar voice, sarcastic, challenging, provoking, interrupted only by laughter and cheers. Despite the official disapproval, even Disraeli's opponents had begun to regard his speeches as *bravura* performances in a style they had never heard in Parliament, let alone in the counties or boroughs.

Some of the Tory leadership, Peel among them, had wanted to treat Disraeli as an eccentric and isolated back-bencher. But by his alliance with Bentinck, Disraeli had become a spokesman of a powerful party within the Tory Party, the party of the country gentlemen, the squires, the farmers. The Whips might sneer at the idea of a lackland novelist speaking for the landed gentry. Yet in the time that had passed since his return from Paris and the beginning of his friendship with Bentinck, he had not only succeeded in becoming the spokesman of the agricultural interest but he had also given that interest a view of politics which raised the subject into an act of faith. In his novel *Coningsby*, he had called it 'fidelity'. Faith in institutions –

the monarchy, the Church and the people assembled in Parliament.

Political philosophy had long been out of fashion. But Disraeli's analytical speeches and his appeal from the scepticism and materialism of an industrial age to principles and inherited ideas had imposed on Members of Parliament a respect which no amount of sneers or ostracism by the Whips could will away.

For the Tory leader, too long the subject of his taunts and criticism for their pragmatic policies, the time had come to destroy Disraeli's privileged sanctuary in the heart of the party by a dramatic rejection. Disraeli had put down a question to Peel by Private Notice about the opening of Mazzini's private letters by the Home Secretary. It was a matter on which he was especially sensitive, since he was sure that his own correspondence with Louis Philippe was intercepted and examined on Graham's orders. Reluctantly, Peel had agreed to use the occasion for the parliamentary annihilation of Disraeli. His purpose was a well-kept secret, but notice of the question had been posted in the lobbies, and the House was full when Disraeli rose.

'Mr Speaker, sir, I rise to ask the Prime Minister a question of which I have given him private notice.'

The Chamber fell silent.

'Sir,' said Disraeli, 'I hesitate to raise a matter which I feel may be the subject of an inaccurate and perhaps hostile report. Yet I think the Prime Minister will acquit me of any personal hostility and recognize that I ask this question in a friendly spirit.'

There was a mutter from Peel's neighbours of 'Get on with it.'

'The subject,' said Disraeli in a level tone, 'affects two great English principles, the right of privacy and the right of political asylum.'

A loud 'Hear, hear' came from the Whigs.

'It has been reported, though I am unwilling to believe it, that the Home Secretary has intercepted – if that is the right

164

word – private letters sent by Signor Mazzini, the Italian patriot to whom we have given sanctuary in London. They were addressed to a gentleman named Signor Bandiera in Italy. This would, of course, have been an intolerable abuse, were it true – which I can scarcely credit.'

'It is true,' a Radical called out from across the Chamber.

'But worse than that is the allegation that copies of these letters were sent by the Home Secretary to the Naples Government.'

The whole Chamber seemed to sigh with a collective 'Ah!'

Peel gazed at the chandelier.

'There's a further report,' said Disraeli, 'that following this action, Signor Bandiera has been summarily tried and executed.

'Shame!' 'Disgraceful!' came a chorus of Whig voices.

Disraeli resumed his seat and folded his arms as the Prime Minister rose to reply. Peel began in a restrained voice.

'Mr Speaker, sir,' he said, 'there is to be a debate on this subject initiated as a vote of censure by honourable Gentlemen opposite. I will not, therefore, anticipate my speech on that occasion, when I will certainly deal with the question raised by the honourable Gentleman. I only regret that he's so eager – so precipitate in wishing to discharge the office of the opponents of the administration.'

He looked contemptuously over his shoulder at Disraeli.

'Mark you, sir, the honourable Gentleman has a perfect right to support a hostile Motion; but don't let him say he does it in a friendly spirit.' He coughed. 'Perhaps I can remind him of the verse of a great statesman, the late Mr Canning, whom he claims to admire.'

He glanced quickly at a note.

'Here is what Mr Canning had to say.

> *'Give me the avowed, the erect, the manly foe:*
> *Bold, I can meet, perhaps may turn the blow.'*

He paused, and looking Disraeli straight in the face, gave him the *coup de grâce*.

> '*But of all plagues, good Heaven, thy wrath can send,*
> *Save, save, O save me from the* candid friend!'

A roar of triumph came from Peel's supporters, and the derision at his taunt sounded in Disraeli's ears like the clamour of a yelping pack that renewed itself as grinning Members repeated the words to the deaf and passed them on to those in the shadow of the Gallery beyond the Bar, moving even his own friends to join in with a reluctant relish. Only Lord George Bentinck sitting next to him was grim and unsmiling. He revered his uncle Canning, and believed he'd been driven to a premature death by the treachery and defection of his fellow-Minister Peel on the question of Catholic Emancipation. And Peel had now dared to call the shade of Canning to his assistance!

'First he betrays him; then he plunders him,' he said with a scowl.

Disraeli didn't answer. Peel and Graham were laughing together, the Clerk of the House stood and called 'Order, I say,' and the House was moving on to its next business.

As Disraeli made his way with Bentinck through the crowd into the Members' Lobby, a group of Peel's supporters who earlier had been drinking steadily in the Smoking Room and were now congregated at the foot of a statue of Pitt, chanted *sotto voce*, 'Save, save, O save us from our candid friend!'

Bentinck turned angrily towards them, but Disraeli said calmly, 'Not now, Lord George. I'll have something to say later.'

In the days that followed the Prime Minister's snub, Disraeli noticed that he often had empty places at his side in the Carlton dining-room. The party leaders set the example by passing him in the corridors at Westminster with an ostentatious indifference that sprang from their knowledge that the Young England group was moribund if not dead, and the feeling that Peel had finally crushed Disraeli's chances with the country gentlemen by his magisterial snub. Lord John Manners was lost in a chivalric mist of versifying, George Smythe was travelling abroad in search of pleasure, and the more ambitious young men were unwilling to compromise themselves by too close an association with Disraeli. The ostracism was completed by the Whigs, since a politician descending is of little concern even to opponents.

For his part, Disraeli affected not to notice. In the days that followed, he continued to attend the debates regularly, taking his usual place behind Sir Robert Peel and sitting gravely for hours listening to the stumbling speeches of the country gentlemen, bewildered by renewed rumours that the Prime Minister intended to abolish the Corn Laws and, in particular, provide cheap foreign grain for Ireland.

As he left St Stephen's Hall, he heard his name called from an open carriage in Parliament Square.

'Why so gloomy, Mr Disraeli?'

'My dear Lady Jersey,' he said, acting a smile, 'I've been listening to Mr Lucas – a *lucus a non lucendo*, so to speak.'

'You mustn't talk Latin to me. I'm a very simple person.'

Disraeli looked at the graceful figure and the armorial bearings on the carriage door, and said, 'But I always think of you as Juno.'

She preened herself a little, and invited him to drive with her across the Park. Happy to be diverted from his obsessive thoughts of Peel's jeer, he accepted. In the late summer afternoon the trees were turning russet, and Disraeli at Lady Jersey's side felt pleased by the obsequious salutes from other carriages and riders.

'What's this I hear about you quarrelling with Sir Robert?'

'We have a well-established lack of sympathy.'

'But that's no way to make progress in the Party. I hear your friends behave very insolently towards him.'

'If disagreement is insolence, yes. The Prime Minister will tolerate anything except dissent.'

'But your intellect?'

'He mistrusts it. He regards it as an impropriety.'

'How very sad!' said Lady Jersey. 'You would greatly improve the Front Bench. They're all so dismal. Plain, too.'

The horses trotted on until she said,

'Do tell me, Mr Disraeli. Do you know a person called Mrs Edmonds – Mrs Clarissa Edmonds?'

Surprised by the mention of her name, Disraeli hesitated before he answered.

'Yes – she had a house in George Street and she's been living in France, I believe.'

'She has returned to England,' said Lady Jersey, looking straight ahead.

'Ah, yes,' said Disraeli noncommittally. The news made him feel uncomfortable, and his delight in the drive began to fade. From time to time he had heard reports that Mrs Edmonds and Mr Hudson had been travelling in Italy, and one curious reference to her in connection with the trial of Daniel Macnaghten, the assassin of Mr Drummond. Apparently a considerable sum of money in his possession had come from some source abroad whose funds derived from Mrs Edmonds.

No one suggested that she had been party to a conspiracy to attack the Prime Minister. In any case, the court's findings that Macnaghten was insane precluded any further probing of how Mrs Edmonds's philanthropic and political financing in Paris had reached Macnaghten's pocket. So pretty a woman, it was felt, couldn't possibly have any connection with so dastardly a crime.

But there was no doubt that the rumours tainted her reputation. Disraeli would have liked to have turned to some other topic.

'Yes,' said Lady Jersey. 'Mrs Edmonds is back. Faster!' she said to the coachman, tapping him on the shoulder with her parasol. The horse quickened its pace, and the clatter of its hooves overlaid their conversation. 'What do you know of her, Mr Disraeli?'

Disraeli reflected.

'She's a very handsome woman.'

'So I understand.'

'She's very spirited – she has a great enthusiasm for romantic causes like the liberation of Poland.'

'You mean she's a revolutionary.'

'In some respects – in some respects. I don't think her

revolutionary fervour is such that it would induce her to renounce society.'

'And she has means?'

As a great heiress herself, Lady Jersey was quick to apply a sumptuary criterion to the subject.

'I would doubt if she still had personal resources.'

Disraeli turned his face fully to Lady Jersey and recognized that her enquiries were leading towards a deeper question which she was reluctant to put.

'How, then, is she able to entertain on so lavish a scale – to dress as she does – to maintain a carriage like the one she's got? Heavens, she behaves like a Duchess of the blood!'

'I'm not qualified to say,' said Disraeli with restraint. He wanted to leave the matter, but Lady Jersey persisted.

'It's my impression that Mrs Edmonds is experienced in dealing with gentlemen. Perhaps she has ties with men of means.'

'No doubt!' Disraeli murmured. He raised his hat to Lady Somers who was driving past, and he was grateful for the distraction.

'They say she's the mistress of Mr Hudson,' said Lady Jersey.

'So I hear. It's generally accepted.'

Lady Jersey stamped her parasol on the carriage floor.

'What concerns me is that she's been developing an intimacy with my younger son Francis. I am deeply worried. You know what Francis is like. He's generous, weak, easily manipulated. I'm very afraid for him.'

Disraeli put his hand on her glove, and said, 'I doubt if you have reason for anxiety. Mrs Edmonds's chief joy is to be the centre of flattery. She has need of audiences – I mean, male audiences. I've known her for several years, and I've observed that this year's friends are rarely last year's friends. She has a few cavaliers in attendance, but that's all. She's capable of being foolish in her enthusiasm, but I've never known her to be wicked.'

She frowned slightly.

'If you see her, would you perhaps tell her to leave Francis alone?'

'If I saw her, that might be the best way to excite her interest in him further. Pray don't worry, Lady Jersey. I will inform you if there's any danger.'

'Dear Mr Disraeli,' she said. 'Tell me about your quarrel with Sir Robert Peel.'

'I will shortly reply to him,' said Disraeli broodingly.

'I see you've found a new ally.'

'George Bentinck?'

'Yes. I know he's an expert on horses. Can he help you in the House? He's so ebullient and angry, and I do wish he wouldn't talk at the top of his voice all the time, and throw his arms about when he speaks. Why don't you talk to him, and calm him down a little?'

'Oh, that would be a great mistake. This is a time for vehemence. Lord George is trying to say what all the country gentlemen want to hear. He wants the government to pledge itself not to betray the farmers.'

'But can he say it effectively? It's one thing to bark at the government in a country house, but quite different, surely, in Parliament?'

'Not if we bark in unison.'

They had reached Park Lane, and Disraeli said, 'Allow me to escort you to the Square.'

She thanked him, and they drove on without speaking.

'If you hear anything, Mr Disraeli, about Francis – ' she said at last, her queenly air momentarily subdued.

'Have no fear!' he said confidently.

He helped her to descend at her town house, and declined her offer to return in the carriage. The news about Mrs Edmonds troubled him, and he wanted to walk back to Park Lane, and reflect.

Three days later, shortly before seven o'clock, Disraeli rose in a Chamber crowded with government supporters, Ministers, junior Ministers and their dependants, waiting to hear the speech in which, Disraeli had let it be known in the Carlton, he intended to reply to Peel on the subject of political consistency. The Whigs had heard the news at the Reform and, led by Lord John Russell, gnome-like and acid, they too had turned up in force to enjoy their opponents' fratricide.

As Disraeli stood, a faint groan came from the government benches. A 'Hear! hear!' from Bentinck, picked up by some of the Tory squires, urged him on.

'Mr Speaker, sir,' he said, putting his thumbs under the lapels of his coat in the nonchalant gesture that always enraged his critics. 'Mr Speaker, I have lately been charged by some of my right honourable friends with a certain fidelity to those principles I was sent by my constituents to maintain in this House. They sent me, mark you, to sit on *this* side of the House, their object being to seek a Tory majority and support a Tory ministry. Some on the government benches may disagree with me in upholding those principles. In that case, it seems to me, it's for them, not for myself as they suggest, to cross the floor of the House.'

There was a murmur of approval.

'Who, after all, is the turncoat? It's the Prime Minister, not myself. He caught the Whigs bathing, and walked away with their clothes.'

There was loud laughter, and even the Speaker smiled. The only faces that remained unmoved were Peel's and Disraeli's.

'He left them in full possession of their liberal position – and he himself is a strict conservative of their garments.'

The laughter rolled over the benches.

'Mark you,' he went on, 'the Prime Minister always likes in his strictures to appeal to an eminent authority. He knows what the introduction of a great name does in debate – how important is its effect and occasionally how electrical. The Prime Minister never refers to any author who isn't great or loved. Canning, for example.

'We all admire his genius. We all – ' he paused and looked at Peel – 'we all, at least *most* of us, deplore his untimely end . . . And we all sympathize with the late Mr Canning in his fierce struggle in his day with supreme prejudice and sublime mediocrity.'

The allusion to Peel was clear, and the cheering began even before he ended the sentence.

'The Prime Minister may be sure that a quotation from such an authority will always have a telling effect – like the lines, for example, on friendship, written by Mr Canning and quoted by the Rt. Hon. Gentleman the other day.'

He lowered his voice to an ironic, conversational level, and Members strained to hear it.

'The theme, the poet, the speaker – what a felicitous combination! Its effect in debate must surely be overwhelming.'

Disraeli stopped, and his audience waited, the smiling faces of his supporters turned towards him.

'But if the quotation is addressed to me – as I feel was the intention – all that remains is for me publicly to congratulate the Prime Minister not only on his ready memory – but on his courageous conscience!'

The cheers became a roar that swelled till it filled the Chamber. Everyone in the House recalled Sir Robert Peel's treatment of Canning over the question of Catholic Emancipation, on which he had first deserted him and then adopted his policy. The Prime Minister sat with his chin sunk in his chest, turning his papers in his hand.

When Disraeli left the Chamber, Bentinck was the first to congratulate him, and Disraeli advanced to the Smoking Room like a leader, with a retinue that included Bentinck himself. The new grouping was a reality, more solidly based than Young England, more powerful in the country, the collective interest of the farmers, backed and organized by Lord George Bentinck, who at last had found an orator capable of resisting the parliamentary mastery that Sir Robert Peel had exercised over the Tory Party for so many years. Disraeli took his favourite armchair, and noticed that several of his former critics smiled at him benevolently.

On the way home after the House rose, Bentinck said, 'It's all settled. Corn Law repeal is to be brought in this session.'

He was excited by the challenge and took Disraeli's arm confidentially.

'Yes. I heard it from one of Graham's friends. The issue has become clear. Think of it – no more "yes, buts" and "no, buts". It's either "yes" or "no".'

Disraeli invited him to his study and went to take one of his *narguilahs*; but looking at Bentinck's robust countryman's face, he changed his mind. Instead, he took a short briarwood pipe and began to fill it.

At that moment he saw on a salver on the study table a letter franked in Paris at the Hotel Bristol. It was marked 'Urgent', and he recognized George Smythe's handwriting. Excusing himself to Bentinck, he opened the letter happily.

My dear Diz [he read],

I hear from my father that Lord Aberdeen has invited me to serve as his Under-Secretary. I am in despair. How can I accept? How can I refuse? I can't reject an offer transmitted with such insistence by my father.

Disraeli's mouth set.

I don't know which eye to weep with.

Politics apart, I've been devilishly involved with Mrs Edmonds, whom I met on my travels with an attendant hussar, Mr Francis Villiers, and her exquisite daughter, alternately denouncing the British Government, protesting her feelings for you which are of an obsessive kind, and urging us to join her in purchasing annuities for the refugee nobility and reconstituting Poland. She is returning or has returned to England. I felt you should know.

To revert to my sad choice, I recognize that for me to become a Peelite, as I must, will pain you, and that is most painful of all. Be that as it may, *caro* Diz, I want you to know that I remain eternally bound to you for all that you did for me in my fledgling years. You have not only the affection but also the profound gratitude of your friend,

George Smythe.

Disraeli put the letter back on the salver.

Bentinck, seeing his subdued expression, said, 'Not bad news, I trust?'

'An obituary notice, I fear. George Smythe has taken a job

173

in the administration. Young England's *nunc dimittis*.'

'Damn his eyes!' said Bentinck. 'I knew he would. Where the devil is he?'

'Travelling in Europe.'

'Smythe always lacked something.'

'I will tell you what he lacked. He lacked something very useful in a man. He lacked gratitude – a word he often used but never understood.'

'By God, you're right! Gratitude! That's a great quality. Not much of that in Westminster. No gratitude! Just hopes of favours to come!'

Disraeli crossed the room to where Bentinck was looking out at the trees of Hyde Park, and stood at his side. Gratitude, he had often thought, was a form of love. In the mirror he caught a glimpse of his own face, dark and saturnine, next to Bentinck's open countryman's features, and recalled their strange and felicitous meeting.

'No,' Bentinck repeated. 'There's not much gratitude at Westminster.'

Disraeli glanced at him, and was silent. When he had first met Bentinck, he had found an ally against Peel. At Deepdene, the ally had become a friend and protector against his enemies. And now? He looked affectionately at Bentinck's heavy, self-absorbed face. Yes – gratitude was a form of love.

Chapter Thirteen

The railway carriage rolled along comfortably on the way to Aylesbury, where Disraeli, Mary Anne and Bentinck were due to be met by the groom from Bradenham. Despite his wife's protests at the extravagance, Disraeli had hired the Duke of Buckingham's velvet-lined drawing-room, while Bentinck had a more modest drawing-room to himself in an adjacent carriage.

From the sofa, with his head on Mary Anne's lap, Disraeli glanced through the wide windows at the landscape of early spring, the umbered furrows, the first sprinkle of green on the skeletal trees, the cold blue patches in the opalescent sky.

'D'you think we're going too fast?' Mary Anne said. 'One of these days, Ben, you must explain to me what makes a steam engine move.'

'I think,' said Disraeli idly, 'it's got something to do with the steam kettle, but bigger.'

The train stopped with a lurch, and Disraeli got to his feet and opened the window.

'What is it?' Mary Anne asked anxiously.

'There seems to be a herd of cows pasturing on the line.'

Mary Anne stood behind him, clinging to his waist in case he fell out.

'Put your head in,' she said. 'You know what happened to Mr Huskisson. He was killed by an up-train – or was it a down-train? – poor soul! Trains are very dangerous.'

'It isn't trains that are dangerous,' Disraeli replied. 'It's passengers. All would have been well if the late Member for Liverpool hadn't rushed across the line to greet the Duke.'

'It should teach us to be more circumspect in crossing lines.'

'Or less precipitate in greeting dukes. This is the decade of the people. Don't you recall, Mary Anne?'

He pointed to the copy of *Sybil*, his novel on the state of the people that he had written the previous year.

'There are two nations,' he had written, 'between whom there is no intercourse, no sympathy, who are fed by a different food, ordered by different manners, and governed by different laws – the England of the Rich and the Poor.'

The description had already become a byword at Westminster and in Fleet Street. Some of the reviewers felt that the existence of the two nations was obvious; others said that it was only obvious as the law of gravity, once discovered, was obvious. The politicians thought it surprising no one had thought of it before. But everyone accepted that Disraeli had told in his novel a solemn truth that henceforward couldn't be ignored.

No Member of Parliament identified himself with the less pleasing characters in the novel, but all recognized in them their enemies. And everyone knew whom Disraeli meant when he wrote satirically of a 'gentleman in Downing Street'. Peel, it was true, didn't read novels, and, indeed, it might have escaped him had not Mr Huffam written to bring the passage to his attention.

The leather-bound copy of *Sybil* was Mary Anne's gift to Isaac, and she caressed the binding proudly.

'Whenever you're severe with me, Ben,' she said, 'I'll read you the dedication aloud.'

'I'm being severe with you,' said Disraeli.

'Very well! "I would inscribe this work to one whose noble spirit and gentle nature ever prompt her to sympathize with the suffering; to one whose sweet voice has often encouraged, and whose taste and judgment have ever guided its pages: the most severe of critics, but – a perfect wife!" Oh, Ben,' she said, looking up at him, her eyes filled with tears, 'why do I cry whenever I read this?'

'You have weak lachrymal glands,' he said, kissing her forehead.

'I haven't.'

'Well, then, you're touched by my devotion.'

'How can you say that?' she said. 'You know you married me for money.'

Disraeli took her hand and fondled it.

'So they say,' he said. 'So they say.'

The train started up again, and they sat abruptly on the sofa.

'I do so wish I'd met you twenty years ago,' said Mary Anne. When she spoke of the difference in their ages Disraeli usually discouraged her, but as the train trundled between the darkening fields and the sun disappeared in a red afterglow, she put her head on his shoulder and he listened to her.

'I was pretty – so much prettier than today. And I would have had twenty more years with you. Do you know, my dearest, I feel that any moment I spend away from you is wasted. I want to be with you every moment of my life.'

Too much, thought Disraeli. Far too much.

'Companionship is heightened by occasional separation,' he said aloud.

'Ours doesn't need heightening,' said Mary Anne firmly. 'I need to see you all the time.'

'I feel,' said Disraeli, 'that you do.'

She looked up at him with a quick glance, but he had already composed his features in his Pharaonic manner, and they sat in silence till the train passed Beaconsfield and was approaching Aylesbury, when Mary Anne rose cheerfully to assemble the hat boxes, the wines and fondants, the family gifts and the small portmanteaux.

The train jolted to a stop and the bearded station-master advanced to greet the party with his silk hat doffed, followed by a porter carrying a footstool for Mary Anne.

When they arrived at Bradenham the lamps were already lit and the beech fires crackling, but the house was unusually quiet. Disraeli had left Baum in London, and the groom who met them with Isaac's carriage helped Mary Anne to descend. The main door was open and Disraeli followed her into the hall with Bentinck, puzzled by the absence of Sarah.

His mother, pouter-bosomed, came to meet him, and he kissed the broad golden wedding ring on her hand and presented Lord George Bentinck to her. She asked him about the journey, and Bentinck, always ill-at-ease with women, replied that he hadn't noticed it since he had slept. A servant took him to his room, and Disraeli, left alone with his mother and troubled by her unusually withdrawn manner, said, 'Is anything wrong?'

'No,' she said, 'everything is well. But your father is resting in his room, and Sarah has driven to Marlow to bring Mr and Mrs Inglefield to stay with us.'

'I see,' he replied. 'I would willingly have gone in her place, had I known.'

'Your times of arrival didn't coincide,' said Mrs Disraeli stiffly. 'In any case, Sarah was anxious to greet Mrs Inglefield personally to show she had no reserve about the marriage.'

'Poor Sarah!' said Disraeli.

'Why poor Sarah?' his mother asked, moving towards the drawing-room.

He shrugged his shoulders. 'She seems to be destined for disappointment. Why does she have to choose doomed or unattainable men?'

'Your notions are absurd, Ben,' his mother said in her imperious voice. 'Mr Meredith wasn't foredoomed. He was a very pleasant, plodding young man who had the misfortune to be stricken by smallpox. He is not the first nor will he be the last.'

Disraeli looked into the blazing log fire, remembering how his sister's fiancé had died, not exactly in his arms as he wrote at the time, but in a miserable bed in a hostelry in Alexandria. His mother was observing him with the faintly mocking air that intimidated him, now as when he was a child. He could stand face to face with kings without lowering his eyes, but in his mother's presence he felt a resentful humility. 'My Arabian son,' she had called him as a boy when he had said the Arabs were Jews on horseback. She had disliked her own Jewish origin, and was displeased to find its traits reproduced in her eldest son's features. Ralph and James fitted better into the Buckinghamshire environment. Once when as a child he was dangerously ill with a fever at the house his father rented at Hyde Heath, his mother had come to his room to comfort him, and he remembered the fall of her hair over his face with

178

an obsessional longing for a tenderness and a protection that she had never repeated. When he had approached her in search of affection, she had rejected him. 'Dear child, go away.' It was the alienating command that had sounded in his ears till he was a grown man. 'Dear child, go away.'

Sometimes he felt that the only intimacy she could express towards him was on behalf of his brothers. She would lay a hand on his arm and say, 'Ben, you must see that James becomes a Justice of the Peace . . . Ben, you must get Ralph a clerkship.'

And there was nothing she asked that he wouldn't seek to perform, though as in the case of Ralph it meant a rejection by the Home Secretary, and in the case of James a rebuff because the Lord Lieutenant wouldn't give a magistracy to a tenant farmer, even if he was the son of the respected Mr Isaac D'Israeli.

'Well,' she said, 'what other setbacks d'you fear for Sarah?'

'Only that she may find her life has disappeared without her noticing. At one time I felt that Lyndhurst – '

'Lord Lyndhurst was in search of a dowry or a mistress. Sarah could be neither.'

'And then I'd hoped that Inglefield – ' Disraeli murmured.

'Mr Inglefield I found excessively radical,' she replied. 'I could never see, Ben, how you could ever consort with a clergyman who spent so much of his time advocating Chartism and other forms of revolution masquerading as reform. I want you to make it clear to him that he's not to be radical in front of the other guests. What a magnificent bearing Lord George has! You should model yourself on him, Ben.'

She had already turned to the housekeeper and Disraeli, indignant but docile, hurried up the stairs to his father's bedroom.

The old man was pretending to be asleep, and Disraeli went quietly to the side of his bed and stood looking at his white hair, the red nightcap, and the freckled hands spread over the counterpane.

'Father,' he said.

179

' "The theme, the poet, the speaker," ' said Isaac, as to himself, quoting *The Times*'s report of Disraeli's taunting apostrophe of Peel during their clash. Disraeli smiled when he saw that his father was awake, and then he noticed the colour of his pupils and his smile faded.

' "The theme, the poet, the speaker," ' the old man repeated. 'That was splendid! Come and sit next to me for a few minutes – just a few.'

'As long as you wish, Father.'

'Well, first of all, bid Lord George welcome and offer him my apologies. My constitution, I fear, *don't* allow me to take part in late dinners. Tell me if you and your wife are well. You mustn't overtax your system. Health is most important.'

'I am well, sir.'

Isaac fumbled for his son's hand and held it.

'You must work with less concentration. Even genius can over-exert itself. Take a seat. Tell me all the news from Westminster. Tell me about the debates. What's the problem of England?'

'Is that a riddle?'

'No – a question.'

'Well, I'll tell you, Father. It's Ireland.'

'Perhaps the problem of Ireland is the English. Sir Robert, perhaps!'

'In some measure.'

'There's talk of famine in Ireland. Cheap corn would be a help – is that not so?'

'There's three times as much corn in bond as there was last year. What Ireland needs isn't the crumbs of charity. It needs a revolution in its agriculture and industry. It's the only way to end the civil war.'

'And what has Mr O'Connell to say about Sir Robert's plans?'

'He calls Sir Robert "Orange Peel", and claims he's always hated Catholics. Even his grant to the Maynooth Seminary was just a sop.'

'But won't the grant help?' the old man continued in his gentle voice.

'No, sir. There's nothing like a grant to antagonize its recipients.'

'Ah, Ben, Ben! You mustn't be cynical . . .' The old man had become tired. 'When I was a young man – I was travelling in France . . . Yes, it provokes a laugh . . .'

Isaac had shut his eyes again. Disraeli waited. His father had released his hand and fallen asleep, expelling his breath in little puffs.

Disraeli was about to walk quietly away when his father woke and said, 'And what is your problem, Ben?'

Disraeli hesitated, not wishing to burden his father with the truth, yet aware that if he dismissed the question his father would feel rejected.

'I suppose, sir,' he said reflectively, 'my most considerable problem is that I speak for a party of landowners and have no part in what I represent. I feel I am no more than an advocate in a cause which isn't my own. Demosthenes himself would be an outsider in such a situation. At the same time, I attract every enmity from the Peelites. They want to get rid of me. There's never a day without someone coming up to me in the lobby and whispering of some plot to oust me.'

The old man was silent, his fingers moving slowly over the counterpane, his striped red nightcap falling over the pillow.

'You must be sublime,' he said at last in a whisper. 'While you fulfil your duty, Ben, never complain. Be sublime. Never complain – never explain. They'll only distort what you say.'

In the bedroom, Sarah was brushing her hair and wishing that she didn't have to go down to dinner but could instead stay looking into the darkness and repeating the same action till everything that oppressed her disappeared; the burden of the long years of seeing her mother and father decline, her loneliness, the confusion that Mary Anne had brought into her spirit, the change in her loving intimacy with her brother whose letters seemed to have become briefer and colder.

Through the half-open door she could see Mary Anne talking to Lord George Bentinck and Mr Inglefield. Inglefield's hair had become grey in the past six or seven years, but he had the same expression – or was it the same expression? She didn't know. She brushed her hair more firmly. And his wife was a ninny, a silly, pretty girl with a dimple who said 'yes' and 'no' and looked at her husband before she could say even that. And their infant had cried all the way from Marlow, and been sick in its swaddling clothes. And the nurse had been argumentative.

But the child was beautiful. She stroked her hair more slowly, and stopped.

'Oh no,' came the voice of Mary Anne from below. 'Every day is a miracle. I never know what excitement my husband will bring into my life.'

Sarah began to brush her hair fiercely as the clear voice went on.

'We do everything together if we possibly can. If I had my way, I'd never let him out of my sight.'

And then Mr Inglefield's voice, more assertive than she'd known it. She wasn't listening to the words. The sound alone made her want to cry. If only she had been free from the responsibility of caring for her parents, if only she could have *experienced* joy without learning of it at second hand, if only James Meredith hadn't died and Lord Lyndhurst hadn't pursued the bullion of Mr Goldsmith, and Mr Inglefield hadn't arrived too late – perhaps if Ben had been more thoughtful! But that was a treacherous thought. He was an Alexander with a world to conquer. She loved him for his struggles, and shared in his triumphs, and he had sheltered her from the pain of his wounds.

She loved Ben, and she coiled her hair around her ears. She was glad that Lord George was his friend. And Mr Inglefield – yes, but all that had to belong to the past. She examined her cheeks in the looking-glass and wished she could add some rouge, like Mary Anne.

Then she patted the lace of her blue dress and advanced to the door.

'Oh no, Lord George! I should never want to live in Swansea again. *Shrewsbury* is *quite* far enough from London,' came Mary Anne's voice in a shriek.

Sarah wondered how Ben could endure it. She practised her smile, and closed the door carefully behind her.

Disraeli was waiting for her on the landing, and her rigid smile became transformed into a smile of happiness as he gave her his arm and led her down the wide stairs to join the cheerful guests below.

Chapter Fourteen

'Heard the news?' asked Mr Huffam with the impatience of a bearer of ill-tidings as he hurried into White's. A few members raised their heads from their newspapers, since although Mr Huffam's gossip was usually wrong, it was often interesting; and when he came straight from the Carlton, scandalous.

'Lord George Bentinck,' said Mr Huffam portentously, standing with his legs apart in front of the fire and addressing himself to the oil painting of Coronation, the Derby winner, on the opposite wall, 'is selling his stud!'

'Ridiculous!' said Sir William Jolliffe, resuming his introspection. The others affected not to have heard. Huffam was too extravagant. He'd be saying next that the Prince Consort had sold the Crown Jewels.

'I assure you it's true,' said Mr Huffam, displeased by their ungrateful reception of his startling revelation. 'I assure you he's selling all his racing interests lock, stock and barrel. He's giving up the Turf entirely to devote himself to politics. It's all over the Carlton, you know. They're talking of nothing else.'

'He's probably joking,' said a voice.

'He'd never joke about anything so serious,' said Mr Huffam. 'You know how he's been going on – never eats till the House rises – he's like a man possessed.'

'Malign influences!' came Beresford Hope's deep voice from the embossed armchair. 'Malign influences! They should be exorcised. It's uncanny nowadays when you go into the Smoking Room. Even the tables have gone Free Trade and Protectionist.'

'Heaven help us,' said Mr Huffam piously. 'It's a sad business. Families are divided – abuse is the order of the day! It will be a happy moment for England when these questions are resolved.'

George Smythe joined them, and said in his drawl, 'Quite right, Huffam! Bentinck's using the most distressing language. I don't mind him calling me a flunkey, but when he describes the parliamentary secretaries as janissaries, he's really going too far. Forty paid janissaries!' He spoke the words with distaste. 'Incidentally, Hope, were the Sultan's janissaries eunuchs?'

Hope laughed. 'I'm sure he had that in mind even if they weren't. He'll probably repeat it in the House. You can ask him then what he meant.'

'It's typical of him,' said Smythe in an equable tone. 'Always ready for public brawls. Forty janissaries – forty Ministers – the Forty Thieves. He misses the days of duelling. D'you remember when he called Squire Osbaldeston out?'

'Indeed I do,' said Mr Huffam officiously. 'They found some quarrel over a bet, and George took the first shot on the Heath. Missed the Squire by a mile.'

'Perhaps he didn't want to hit him,' said Smythe. 'George loves a fight, but he's the most generous man I've known.'

Mr Huffam was impatient of these niceties, and wanted to complete his story.

'Well, the Squire took aim at George, and George just stood there, cool as you like. "Two to one in your favour, Squire," George calls out. "In hundreds." At that, the Squire lowers his pistol and says, "Odds are too short! Bet's off!" And they both shake hands, and leave.'

They laughed again, and Mr Huffam went on maliciously. 'But forty paid janissaries! I can't believe George thought up that phrase all on his own. I should imagine Disraeli invented it for him. George has become like one of those ventriloquist's dummies on Dizzy's knee.'

'He's a malign influence,' Beresford Hope repeated. 'By God, that fellow Disraeli plays Bentinck the way Paganini played the fiddle. Come to think of it, he looks like Paganini disinterred.'

There was another guffaw.

'Why the deuce don't Bentinck write his own speeches?' Hope went on.

'Oh, he's had a go at it,' said Mr Huffam. 'They're not exactly Ciceronian. I'd say more the Racing Calendar than the Orations. Nothing but facts and figures. Then when he delivers them, he waves his arms about like a race-course tout, and bellows at the top of his voice.'

'The trouble with our squires, alas,' said Smythe, 'is that they talk best over their brandy and port. If only they could drink in the Chamber, we'd have several hundred orators. Why should they exert themselves, though, when Disraeli does it so much better for them?'

Without commenting, Mr Huffam looked at his fob watch and said, 'Ah, well – I must be off. Good afternoon, gentlemen. Good afternoon, Colonel' – to Tankerton who had just come in – 'I'm off to hear your friend Disraeli.'

Tankerton looked balefully after him as he hurried out into the May afternoon, bursting to tell everyone he met about Lord George Bentinck's sacrifice for the nation.

'Huffam always reminds me of a horsefly,' said Hope.

'A bluebottle on a compost heap,' said Smythe.

'Heard about Bentinck?' Hope asked Tankerton.

'Yes – we were talking about him this morning. I think he's gone mad. I do believe he's been mesmerized by Disraeli. Still, I'd like to get down to the sale. Wouldn't mind bidding for Surplice myself. I think there'll be some bargains.'

They became thoughtful as they dismissed Bentinck's politics from their minds, giving their undivided attention to his stable, which they continued to discuss when they walked down St James's to the House of Commons where the Third Reading of the Bill to repeal the Corn Laws was due to take place.

The Corn Law debates had dragged on throughout the spring of 1846, passion mingling with boredom as words, constantly repeated, began to lose their meaning, and arguments turned into exhausted party cries, with the Prime Minister, now in alliance with the liberal Free Traders, stubbornly urging the need for change, while the Protectionists replied with statistical arguments and quotations from past debates to refute him in his own words.

In the general tedium, everyone began to wish that the great disagreement might come to an end and that old friendships, interrupted for too long by partisan anger, could be resumed. Everyone, that is to say, except Lord George Bentinck, who seemed to gain in polemical vigour as he strained his physical energies.

The indolent country gentlemen watched with concern as Bentinck's ruddy complexion turned to a matt pallor in the airless, windowless corridors of the Palace of Westminster; his apparent eccentricity in selling his stud had left them amazed; and as he hurried between the Chamber and the Library carrying books, reports and papers under his arm, they looked at him in wonder. When he stopped to talk to his friends beneath the Gothic arches, they sometimes tried to discuss the prospects at Newmarket, but all he wanted was a promise of attendance for a division. He moved with an aristocratic indifference to their anxieties. He was leader of the Protectionists in the Commons as Lord Stanley was in the Lords; and he deferred to no one but the grand strategist and orator of the opposition, the proconsul of the country gentlemen, the self-styled tribune of the labouring classes, Disraeli himself.

Disraeli looked up at Mary Anne in the Ladies' Gallery, behind the brass rails, and gave her a slight bow. In return, she raised her left hand. It was enough. He was reassured by her presence. A few places away from her was Lady Peel, and next to her Mrs Gladstone, all in black, looking stiffly ahead. Among the subfusc dresses and the dark bonnets in the 'cage', his short-sighted eyes caught a blur of pink, and he raised his eyeglass surreptitiously to see who it was. He lowered his glass almost at once. Mrs Edmonds, serene and strikingly dressed, was sitting in a privileged position in the front row next to the Peers' Gallery. Rapidly the thought crossed his mind that someone of influence must have procured her an admission order. And then he marvelled at the way in which, despite her uneasy status and the talk about some of her connections, she always succeeded in being received even if she wasn't always visited by the leaders of society. And he wondered whom she had come to flatter and goad today. She liked to decorate her salon with fashionable foreign revolutionaries; but she was simultaneously a consort of the aristocratic and the established. Had she come to support Peel? Hudson was there in his inconspicuous place on the back bench, always ready to cheer the government whatever government it might be. Good for railway stocks. Disraeli sat motionless, his fingers tightening slightly on his notes in his left hand. He had long lived down the catastrophe of his Maiden Speech. But he never rose without an initial tremor as he recalled the hostile faces, the cat-calls and finally the moment when, amid the uproar, he had thrown away his notes and shouted in a terrible voice, high above the din, 'I sit down now. But the time will come when you will hear me!'

In the presence of Sir Robert Peel nearby, calm, relaxed and confident, he always felt that he had to vindicate himself again, and he composed his features, waiting for the Speaker to call him. The Peelites, he knew, had mustered their full strength, the place-men in the administration reinforced by their clients and hangers-on. But together with Bentinck, he had organized the tactics of the Protectionists. The alliance of the Peelites and their former opponents, the liberal Free Traders, might enable the Prime Minister to carry the Motion to repeal the Corn Laws. But the Protectionists could, in turn, ally themselves with the Irish Members and the liberals in opposing the Irish Coercion Bill, designed to repress the violence in Ireland which had come in the wake of the failure of the potato crop and the spreading famine. Disraeli had already charged Peel with 'trying to feed a starving people with muskets'. Might not the Protectionists tear down the government in a side-attack on the Irish question, even if they couldn't win on the issue of Protection? An *ad hoc* coalition with the Irish and the radicals was a tactic, however paradoxical, which Bentinck's Tories had decided to keep in reserve.

'Mr Disraeli!' called the Speaker.

Disraeli removed his hat, and paused for a moment to look

around the crowded, oak-lined Chamber at the Whigs and the Tories and the radicals and the Irish and the Serjeant-at-Arms with his sword below the gangway, and the Members hurrying in from the Smoking Room to gather on the green carpet at the Bar of the House, and the clerks at the table and the golden mace and the galleries still rustling with his name, and the opaque windows that cocooned them all.

He began quietly, and someone shouted, 'Speak up!'

'The Prime Minister,' he claimed as Members fell silent to hear him better, 'has not only broken his promises on the Corn Laws, but he has made his party perjure themselves too.

'What a compliment you have paid to the Rt. Hon. Gentleman,' he said, turning to the Peelites. 'Not only do you vote for him, but you vote against your own opinions in support of the policies which in the past he has drilled you to oppose.'

A loud cheer came from behind him, and it was like a following breeze in his sails.

'There's been nothing like it since the conversion of the Saxons by Charlemagne . . . There they were, ranged on the banks of the Rhine to resist the great Emperor. But when he appeared, instead of conquering the Saxons, he converted them.'

He paused, and went on,

'They were converted in battalions and baptized in platoons.'

The laughter rose, and even some Peelites, squirming beneath his irony, joined in.

Disraeli glanced at Peel.

'I acquit the Rt. Hon. Gentleman of premeditated treachery.' It was a repudiation that underlined the charge. 'The Prime Minister's problem is that he always trades on the ideas and intelligence of others. He is, in fact, a burglar of other people's intellects who has committed political petty larceny on a grand scale – but he has the perpetual misfortune to be mistaken.'

'A burglar of other people's intellects.' The phrase was repeated from mouth to mouth, and fed itself into a second wave of renewed laughter so that Disraeli could hardly continue.

As he accumulated his indictment and the first hour of his

speech passed into the second, as his taunts and sarcasms multiplied and the indignation of the squires against the Prime Minister rose, their laughter at Disraeli's jibes fusing with their derision of the government bench, Peel ceased to mutter to his neighbours; he shut his eyes and sank his chin into his collar.

'Our countrymen won't long endure the huckstering tyranny of the government,' Disraeli declared in a firm voice, and the cheers swelled in all parts of the House. 'Those leaders are political pedlars who bought their followers in the cheapest market; and sold *us* in the dearest.'

Now the cheers had become almost continuous. He had cast a net of villainy over the Prime Minister, and over his fellow rebels a cloak of injured virtue. He had only to speak to hear his endorsement in the roar of 'Hear! Hear!'

At last he reached his peroration, and paused to wipe his brow with a cambric handkerchief as he waited for the cheers to subside. Every face except those on his own front bench was turned attentively to him, and he resumed in a great stillness.

'I know, Mr Speaker,' he said, 'there are many who believe the time is gone by when one could appeal to those high and honest impulses that were once the mainstay and the main element of the English character. I know, sir, that we appeal to a people debauched by public gambling, and stimulated and encouraged by an inefficient and shortsighted Prime Minister. I know the public mind is polluted with economic fancies – a depraved desire that the rich may become richer without industry or toil. I know that all faith in public men is lost.

'But, sir,' he went on, 'I have faith in the enduring elements of the English character. It may be in vain now in the midnight of the government's intoxication to tell them that they will wake up to bitterness. It may be idle now, in the springtime of their economic frenzy, to warn them that there may be an ebb of trouble.'

His voice became crepuscular and solemn.

'But the dark and inevitable hour will arrive.'

There was a new silence in the Chamber, as if Members were waiting for that hour to strike.

'Then,' said Disraeli, 'when the government's spirits are softened by misfortune, they will return to those principles that made England great and which, in our belief, will alone keep England great. Then too, sir, perchance they may remember, not with unkindness, those who, though betrayed and deserted, were neither ashamed nor afraid to struggle for the "good old cause" – the cause with which are associated principles the most popular and sentiments the most entirely national – the cause of labour, the cause of the people, the cause of England!'

His voice rose with his last words to a challenge, and as he sat down the benches around him seemed to rise. The 'Hear! Hears!' went on and on in continuous waves of sound from the Members around him, now standing and waving their Order Papers. Bentinck smiled, and patted him on the arm approvingly. Others leaned towards him with their congratulations. The Protectionists cheered him and each other in delight. And still the ovation rolled on, marking his triumph in the very place where, eight years before, they had shouted him down. Now they had heard him. Disraeli sat with his eyes lowered for a few moments while he again wiped his forehead, which was streaming with sweat. Lord John Russell, the Whig leader, was on his feet trying to get a hearing through the din of cheers that hadn't abated.

Then Disraeli looked up towards Mary Anne. She leaned close to the brass rail and raised her fingers almost imperceptibly in a private gesture.

In the government Whips' office the triumphant speech of Disraeli was anxiously discussed. None of the Peelites could deny its impact or that it might have swayed the intended votes of some waverers, and in the hours that followed as the debate went on, Fremantle, the Chief Whip, kept drafting lists in his ledger of the reliable Peelites, a column for the doubtful and one for those who might abstain when the vote came.

In the corridor a group of back bench MPs, summoned by

Fremantle as if to a headmaster's study, was waiting to be questioned about their intentions. The oak door opened, and a young Member who earlier in the day had been seen to be canvassed by Bentinck and Disraeli appeared. He was white-faced and shaken, and the others quickly surrounded him.

'Well?'

'Well, what?'

'What did the Chief have to say?'

'Nothing much – just passed the time of day.'

'Anything else?'

'Not really – asked me if I still wanted the Tory Whip sent to my usual address.'

They looked at the floor as Fremantle's secretary courteously invited the next doubter into the room.

'You must attack Disraeli,' the Chief Whip urged Peel when he reported the result of the interviews to the Prime Minister. He had come to the conclusion that only by discrediting personally the Protectionist spokesman could they be sure of winning the vote. 'Remind him of how he crawled to you for a job. Let the House know the real reason for his venom! You must make it clear, especially to the younger men, that Disraeli has merely been elevating a private grudge into a public cause.'

Peel listened broodingly. Disliking the vindictiveness of others, he had little wish to practise it himself. But he sent his private secretary to Whitehall Gardens to bring him Disraeli's letter of five years before, applying for a post in his administration.

He was dressed for dinner, and wanted to dimiss the disagreeable subject of Disraeli from his mind.

When the Speaker called 'Prime Minister', Peel glanced towards the Chief Whip in expectation of his messenger's return. The Chief Whip shook his head and hurried to the door to send another secretary to make enquiries. Peel decided not to refer to Disraeli until he held the letter in his hand.

'Mr Speaker, sir,' he began, 'my honour and conscience have been called in question.'

Immediately a howl of rage came from the country Members.

'Honour!'

'Conscience!'

They threw the words back with derision. Their faces became inflamed; their jaws opened in a single baying sound. Some waved their arms in contempt and shouted 'Sit down!' Others turned away from him, waving their arms dismissively.

Peel stood amid the uproar, bewildered. This was the place where for years he had known only deference and respect. He tried to speak, but they wouldn't allow him to. The clamour was overwhelming and his mouth twitched.

'Conscience – what do you know about it?'

'Honour – rubbish!'

Disraeli observed Peel impassively. The Prime Minister's eyes seemed filled with tears.

'Order! Order!' said the Speaker in a firm voice, standing to his full height. The tumult slowly died down, and the Speaker said:

'Prime Minister!'

Peel cleared his throat, collected himself and continued, pressing the case for the abolition of the corn taxes with the courteous accumulation of argument that was his custom. The faces around him were stony and unreceptive. Every now and again he was interrupted. He realized that the only way to discredit the oafs who taunted him was to discredit their champion. A contemptuous aside would be enough. He looked again towards the door, hoping the letter would have arrived. But there was no messenger, and he moved on. He would have to deal with the matter by improvising

'May I now turn to the observations of the Hon. Gentleman the Member for Shrewsbury. He has spoken of me in somewhat disparaging terms. I make no complaint of that. The Hon. Gentleman has his own criteria of conduct, his own standards of public debate. They are not necessarily those of the majority of Hon. Gentlemen in this House.'

A stern and reprehending cheer came from around him, and Peel half-turned his head to look directly at Disraeli.

'But I will only say that if the Hon. Gentleman entertains the opinion of me he now puts forward, it's a little surprising that in the spring five years ago, after his long experience of my public career, he should have been prepared to give me his confidence. It's still more surprising that he should have been ready to unite his fortunes with mine in office. It's astonishing that he should have actually *begged* me for a place in my administration!'

There was an exaggerated gasp of surprise from the Chamber and a prolonged 'Oh!' The Home Secretary, the Chancellor and the Chief Whip led the 'Hear! Hear!' amid the jeers of the Peelites.

Disraeli didn't stir, but recalling the long day of waiting at the Carlton and the crushing snub to Mary Anne, he felt the humiliation begin to gnaw again. *Begged.* He sensed the disdain of some of the country Members at being joined, as they felt, in their sincere vehemence against the Free Traders by a place-seeker who'd cloaked his personal disappointments in the martyrdom of an idealist. *Begged.* Peel's counter-attack was offensive, enough to embarrass Disraeli's friends and to isolate him. He knew he would have to reply.

While Peel was speaking, a messenger handed a note to a Member who passed it along the benches to Disraeli. The writing was unfamiliar, half-literate, and he put the letter unread in his pocket. But during a passage of figures read by the Prime Minister he took it out and glanced at it.

'Sir,' it said, 'the news I have to tell you is sudden and lamentable. Her ladyship my lady Lady Sykes died today at home. She always spoke well of you, sir. Yours truly, (Mrs) B. Poulter.'

His hand began to tremble, and he read it again. Suddenly the benches opposite him became a green miasma, Peel's voice a meaningless sound. Henrietta dead. He could see her vibrant and alive, her face as he had seen it at the opera, full of happiness and delight; her face at night in the Grange, when they had loved each other with the sound of the sea to accompany their tranquillity. And that was over, and all that ardent body had lain a corpse while he was speaking.

'If I may have the Honourable Gentleman's attention . . .' said Peel. He waited, and repeated the words. Disraeli started, and acknowledged the Prime Minister's reference to himself.

The letter, he saw, was headed Little Missenden. Henrietta had died only a few miles from Bradenham.

'There is no love but love at first sight. The passions that endure flash like lightning; they scorch the soul, but it is warmed forever.'

So he had described first love after his meeting with Henrietta at the King's Theatre.

The crumpled letter was the epitaph to their season of joy.

At the end of the Prime Minister's speech, after the cheers had ebbed away, Disraeli rose and asked permission of the Speaker to make a personal statement. At once Peel whispered urgently to Graham to make fresh enquiries about Disraeli's letter. He was certain he had entrusted it to Drummond for safe keeping in the files.

Disraeli observed the hurried discussion between the two men, and studied the benches around him. Would Peel still have his letter? Would he read it to the House? He wasn't sure. He glanced at the enquiring faces around him, and then at Mary Anne's anxious expression in the gallery. 'If ever I gamble again,' he had once declared to D'Orsay, 'it will only be in the high game.' And that was how it had to be.

'Mr Speaker, sir,' he said, holding the lapels of his dark green coat, 'I am obliged to you for your permission to comment on the Prime Minister's reference to me. It was wounding and severe. I will only say that if I'd been an applicant for office when the Prime Minister formed his administration, there'd have been nothing dishonourable in it. It might have been in good taste, or not. But there'd have been nothing dishonourable about it . . . There is one thing, however, I flatly deny. I deny that I ever, directly or indirectly, asked or solicited, let alone *begged*, office from the Prime Minister. Such a charge is entirely unfounded.'

He placed his hand on the fob pocket of his waistcoat as if to emphasize his denial, and resumed his place in silence.

At that moment Graham returned and whispered in Peel's ear. Some of Edward Drummond's personal papers, he had learned, had been burnt on the orders of his executor. Disraeli's letter might have been among them. It was certain that it had disappeared.

Peel shrugged his shoulders and looked at Disraeli. This time it was Disraeli who averted his eyes.

Towards four o'clock in the morning there were loud shouts of 'Divide! Divide!' and the Speaker rose to call the Division. The cry 'Division!' was relayed from usher to usher, through the Smoking Room, the Library and Westminster Hall, where some stragglers were returning from the clubs.

On the benches where they had sat cramped, shoulder to shoulder, during the final hours, Members uncurled and stretched themselves, and slowly began to move towards the lobbies.

'Ayes to the right – Noes to the left.'

Peel, flanked by the Home Secretary and Chancellor, looking straight in front of him, awaited the second call for the division. The Chief Whip stood by the entrance to the Aye lobby, counting his followers. The Whigs went in first, buoyant and chattering, confident of a majority that Peel's advocacy now made certain. Some of Sir Robert Peel's supporters advanced more slowly, barely speaking, as if they wanted to delay as long as possible the repugnant and irrevocable decision that had allied them with their enemies.

On their way to the No lobby, the Protectionists, till lately for the most part friends of Peel, converged on the Free Traders like a hostile army behind the Speaker's chair. Sir William Jolliffe, a staunch Tory, passing between the Table and the Front Bench, muttered an apology as Peel greeted him; there had been no more loyal a supporter of the administration than Jolliffe. He bowed, wavered, then resolutely advanced into the No lobby behind Disraeli and Lord George Bentinck.

The voice of the teller in the No lobby was a litany of betrayal to Peel, and he shrugged his shoulders. But at the other end of the Aye lobby the teller was calling in a loud voice, '299 – 300 – 301 . . .'

'It's all right,' the Chief Whip whispered urgently as Peel and the other Ministers entered the lobby. 'We've done it. We've won.'

'Have we?' said Peel.

He was quickly caught up in the press of Whigs and Irish Members, jostling as they swept him on against his own recent followers, the great Tory captain who in the eyes of the country gentlemen had surrendered to the enemy along with his Praetorian Guard.

At five o'clock in the morning, when Disraeli returned from the House, Mary Anne was still waiting, dozing in her chair. As always, the rooms were brilliantly lit, though the sun already shone through the curtains, and a welcoming decanter of claret stood on the table. She rose and embraced him, and drew him sleepily to the sofa.

'Your speech was wonderful – wonderful,' she said. 'They were all talking about you – even Mrs Gladstone, and you know how grudging she is . . . How was the vote, my dearest?'

'They won,' he said. 'But it was a Pyrrhic victory for Peel. He lost his friends – 240 out of 352 – and he was saved by his enemies. But not for long. We'll beat him on the Irish Coercion Bill, that's now certain – absolutely certain.'

He took a glass of wine and said, anxious for reassurance, 'Were you satisfied with me?'

'Proud – the proudest woman in England . . . Why are you looking sombre?'

'I wasn't happy that I had to rebut the Prime Minister about his charge – '

'But what else could you have done, Diz?' she said, quickly comforting him. 'What a blackguardly thing, to taunt you with asking to serve the nation!'

'I was taken aback. I had to brazen it out. I had no option.'

'Of course you hadn't,' she reassured him. 'He should never

197

have referred to the matter. Most ungentlemanly. Besides, he promised me he'd never, never mention my application.'

She looked for other arguments to remove his melancholy.

'But it's all gone, my dearest. You mustn't worry. Tomorrow there'll be a new Tory Party and you and Lord George Bentinck will lead it.'

He raised his head and smiled to her.

'You know, Mary Anne,' he said, looking into her welling eyes, 'you once said I married you for money.'

'Didn't you?' she said, stroking his hair.

'Yes,' said Disraeli. 'But if I were to do it again, it would certainly be for love.'

Chapter Fifteen

In the early morning air at Gunnersbury Park, Baron Lionel de Rothschild was in high spirits. Despite their victorious repeal of the Corn Laws, the Peel government had been defeated on the Irish question, overthrown by a disparate alliance of Lord George Bentinck's Protectionists, the Irish and the Whigs, which had swept Lord John Russell, Rothschild's friend, into power and himself into Parliament as the Junior Member for the City of London. Under the existing law he could not, as a practising Jew, take the Oath of Allegiance on the 'true faith as a Christian', and was therefore debarred from his seat. But that was merely a difficulty to be overcome. The Bill to remove Jewish disabilities would be brought in again. The Lords might again reject what a majority of the Commons had voted for in previous Parliaments. But Rothschild was convinced that the time would inevitably come when Parliament would admit Jews to their full civil rights.

Rothschild had offered himself to the electorate of the City of London not only as a Free Trader but also as a candidate on behalf of religious freedom. 'As your representative,' he said in his election address, 'as the representative of the most wealthy, the most important, the most intelligent constituency in the world, I am confident I shall not be refused admission to Parliament on account of some restrictive form of words in the Oath of Allegiance.'

He had piled flattery on principle, and he had been triumphantly elected. With Russell himself committed to proposing the Motion on the Jewish Disabilities Bill and Peel's undertaking of support, the only question that remained was whether the Protectionist Tories, the conservatives of the realm, would agree to admit an elected candidate to Parliament

199

who couldn't subscribe to the existing formula of a Christian oath. Rothschild had asked Disraeli to advise him about the country gentlemen's attitudes.

Disraeli trod gingerly behind him over the stepping-stones of the Japanese garden.

'I fear I've never excelled in field sports,' he said.

Lionel de Rothschild, four years younger than Disraeli, but plump and several inches shorter, smiled.

'Perhaps it's too early for exertion. Even the water-lilies are asleep. This garden was designed by a Zen philosopher for patience and contemplation. Like the Japanese,' he said as they approached the moon-viewing porch overlooking the lake, 'the Jews combine energy with patience. What do a hundred years matter?'

'Everything,' said Disraeli. 'Neither of us can wait so long.'

'For a people – or even a family – time is less important. Consider our own patent of nobility. I mean the Rothschild's. It took us a century to achieve.'

'If I may say so,' said Disraeli, stepping with relief from the jagged stones of the water-garden on to the grass verge, 'to be a prince in Israel is at least as eminent as being a baron in Austria. What patent of nobility can Metternich offer that's as old as – ' he glanced at Rothschild and thought of the Frankfurt ghetto – 'as the priesthood of a nation of priests?'

'That,' said Rothschild, unruffled, 'is for the world that is gone. For the world as it is, a secular aristocracy must have roots in the land. You can't be a prince or even a baron without land.'

The gardens, designed by artists and trimmed by topiarists, fell away on each side to woods and pastures reaching to the horizon, for although it was only recently that the Rothschilds had obtained the right to own land in Austria, they had long held estates in England, and Lionel de Rothschild had the ease of a country gentleman that Disraeli admired and envied.

'In one sense,' said Rothschild, walking on to the stables, 'God's blessing to the Jews wasn't to choose them but to disperse them.'

Disraeli didn't answer.

'A people dispersed is indestructible. Titus – Haman – Torquemada – they can do their worst. But scatter your seed, and it will always flower somewhere.'

The grooms lined up and the bailiff doffed his hat at Rothschild's approach. Some of the animals were being curried and combed, and Disraeli could see that the sleek horses, stamping, clattering and backing on the cobbled stones, were chosen, like the other objects of art at Gunnersbury Park, to fit into the pattern of eclectic luxury that the Rothschilds had composed for themselves as entrants into the aristocracy.

Of all the great houses where he and Mary Anne had stayed during the past few years, none had given him the same sense of unrestricted opulence as Gunnersbury Park. Knebworth, Hatfield and Harcourt were bigger, older outcrops of history and the landscape. The Rothschilds' reconstructed palace was an artefact, a wilful creation, superimposed on the modest house once occupied by George II's daughters. Lionel's agents had scoured Europe to find the pictures, the brocades, the porcelain, the carpets, the furniture, the mouldings, the curios that composed it. Rococo jostled baroque and Birmingham. Disraeli liked it very much.

As they turned away from the stables, he realized what it was that gave the Rothschilds' house a glow that he missed on his visits to the colder Gothic castles where children were consigned to keeps called nurseries. For running down the path to greet them were four of the Rothschild children, Leonora, the prettiest, Evelina, Nathaniel and Alfred, followed by their mother Charlotte, dark-haired, dark-eyed and solemn, together with a nursemaid carrying the three-year-old Leopold. Lionel raised each of the children in his arms and kissed them. Then he took Charlotte's hand and touched it with his lips, as if he hadn't seen her that day.

'The birds,' screamed the nine-year-old Evelina, 'I want to feed the birds.'

'Look, Father,' said Nathaniel, her younger brother, 'I've found a beetle.'

Leonora, the eldest, clung to her mother's hand, and the

family moved on together, discussing domestic matters energetically as Disraeli withdrew.

The three days he and Mary Anne had already spent at Gunnersbury had been a time of political conspiracy and combination. Disraeli had once written of Jerusalem, 'It's splendid to arrive, but what do you do once you get there?' So it had been with the defeat of Peel. No sooner had Peel been beaten on the Irish question than the alliance for his overthrow dissolved. 'Thou shalt not harness the ox and the ass,' Rothschild said of the ill-mated coalition of Protectionists, Whigs and Irish. Only the Whigs had emerged successful. Their former allies against Peel had still not decided their role.

At Gunnersbury Park, Lord John Russell, the new Prime Minister, appeared for dinner and disappeared – a wraith, Disraeli felt, dissolved in its own acidity. Among the other guests, financiers, ambassadors, and Whig and Tory politicians, it was said that 'Johnny' had simply shown himself in advance of the debate on the Jew Bill in order to endorse Rothschild's right to take his place in the House. Some whispered that he had come to meet a mysterious Frenchman, M. de Hautecloque, an emissary from Prince Louis Napoleon. And this to Disraeli seemed curious, since the Paris Rothschilds were the friends, confidants and bankers of Louis Philippe, the king whom Prince Louis Napoleon was seeking to supplant. The Rothschilds, he suspected, had no political prejudices.

After dinner Rothschild, Disraeli and Bentinck went and sat together, smoking in the private apartments.

Rothschild flicked his cigar ash into an enamelled *cendrier*, and said, 'I have no wish to be a tribune of the people. My simple desire is to establish the principle of religious liberty – the right of every citizen to worship freely.'

Bentinck looked at the painted ceiling.

'But,' Rothschild went on as if with a question, 'I wouldn't wish your generous sympathies to be used against you.'

'Why should that be so?' asked Bentinck laconically.

'I mean, sir,' said Rothschild, ' – and I make no bones about it – your party will take it ill, I am reliably informed, if you vote in support of full civil rights for Jews.'

It was still a question.

Bentinck smiled wearily.

'So I understand,' he said. He was noncommittal, and Disraeli quickly changed the subject. He knew that Bentinck didn't like to be pressed.

'I hear the news from Ireland is bad,' he said.

'Never worse,' said Rothschild gloomily. 'My agents tell me there are half a million Irishmen existing on the Labour Rate Act alone. The ships travelling to America with emigrants are packed and disease-ridden. Thousands die on the voyage.'

'What a mournful spectacle!' said Disraeli. 'Labourers and overseers on a public dole. A population decimated in three years. A nation too weak from hunger even to break stones by the roadside.'

The pineapples, grapes and peaches in the huge Limoges bowl on the marble table drew his attention, and he wondered whether the hot-houses had defied the cycle of nature, or whether they had been transported by couriers from overseas to Gunnersbury Park, to be at the bedside of Rothschild's guests in need of a midnight refreshment. Connemara seemed as remote as the Ganges. The Irish in their bogs were as strange as the Scythians. Yet, since he had read the report on the condition of Ireland by Professors Lindley and Playfair, his thoughts had returned obsessively to the images they had conjured up. He could never see a miller's wagon, laden with sacks of flour, without recalling Playfair's account of the villagers gathered outside the Clontarf manor, kneeling to beg for bread. Together with those who had fled to the teeming rookeries of Holborn, and the clay-faced labourers encamped by the canals near Manchester, they belonged, he felt, to the vast section of mankind who, persecuted and deprived, finally took on the qualities of degradation which their tormentors attributed to them unjustly in the first place.

Bentinck stood by the fireplace, and said bluntly, 'What are your thoughts on Ireland, Rothschild?'

Rothschild didn't answer at once. He wanted to understand the purpose of the question.

'My thought,' he said after a few moments, 'is that when a man – or a nation – is bleeding to death, you give what aid you can – at once. Peel was right to release the Indian corn for Ireland.'

'Unproductive!' said Bentinck.

'But life-saving,' Rothschild went on calmly.

'It benefited the speculators.'

'There'll always be profiteers of misery. But, my dear Bentinck, relief must begin with charity. We've formed the British Association for Famine Relief, and I've arranged for a number of bankers to contribute.'

'I've no wish to be ungracious. It's a pebble in a pool.'

'A large pebble,' said Rothschild good-humouredly. 'It will spread its effect.'

Bentinck returned to his brandy.

'It's still a pebble. Let me tell you about my plan for railways for Ireland.'

While Rothschild assumed an attentive expression, Disraeli, who had heard Bentinck describe his plans for investment in Irish railways a dozen times, excused himself on the grounds that he had to prepare a speech, and withdrew.

He returned first to the drawing-room, where he had left Mary Anne listening with Lord John Russell to the singer La Grisi, imported at great cost from Paris for the Prime Minister's musical entertainment. Russell's congratulations were sufficient endorsement of her merits to make even the most rigid of the ladies accept the performer as a fellow-guest, and to encourage some of the younger men who had applauded her in Paris to surround her with their homage. Disraeli stood at the door with his eyeglass raised, looking short-sightedly for Mary Anne in the group around the singer. She wasn't there, but he saw her at last sitting on the Baroness's sofa, talking animatedly to a number of gentlemen, absorbed, or at least detained, by her enthusiasm.

Many faces turned towards him and he paused, relishing their gaze as an actor might do when he steps on the stage, or as he himself had so often done when he rose to speak in public. His mastery of the House during the Corn Law debates had been widely acclaimed. *Punch* had called him the Pericles of the Protectionists. And even his political parricide could be forgiven for its drama, skill and despatch.

Then he observed that Mrs Edmonds was approaching him. Now in her mid-thirties, her delicate shoulders had become sculptural and her sympathetic glance was emphasized by her black hair, coiled above a pale face. Since her return to London she had achieved a particular success, not merely because of the great wealth of Mr Hudson, now a patron of the arts and as much an intimate of Cobden and Bright as of Peel and Rothschild, but also because of the new direction of her philanthropy. No longer did she support the revolutionary expatriates, unless, of course, connected with someone like Louis Napoleon. Her enthusiasm, it was stated, was now concentrated on religious and social works like the Society for the Redemption of African Slaves and the Society for the Redemption of Fallen Women which Mrs Gladstone had encouraged her to join. Her salon in George Street had been replaced by her salon in Upper Grosvenor Street, where she had developed the art of never making other women jealous. If the husband of her guest or hostess offered her a compliment she would frown and disengage herself, redoubling her attentions to his wife.

About her incomparable wardrobe she was always self-deprecating, so that those ladies who might have been her rivals were moved to sympathy rather than envy. An old rumour that she wasn't really a widow but that a former husband had been bought off on a *pont d'or* to Dieppe was revived, but found little belief. It was also known that even if Lady Londonderry hadn't actually accepted an invitation to Mrs Edmonds's house, she had excused herself very courteously. And anyhow, there was never a shortage of the nobility eager to be guests of Mrs Edmonds.

'You are lost, Mr Disraeli?' she said from behind her ivory fan.

'Irretrievably,' he said. For a second they held each other's glance.

'Can I guide you?'

'Wherever you wish.'

She took his arm and led him to a sofa half-concealed by palm trees.

'You've become such a famous person since we last met. I heard you speak on the Corn Law Bill. You were quite magnificent. You fascinated the whole House, including myself.'

'I can think of no greater compliment.'

'But there was a moment when I feared for you.'

'Indeed?'

'Yes – when Sir Robert charged you with soliciting office.'

She waved her fan as if to wave away a vexatious thought.

'But you disposed of him very firmly. Mr Hudson was greatly impressed by your retort.'

He glanced at her impassive features, wondering what she really thought or knew, and he observed how her face had changed in the time he had known her. Its outline had become severe and disciplined. Though she and Mrs Bulwer shared a similar background, she had a reticence and a restraint which placed the two Irishwomen apart. Their private and happy hours in George Street seemed far away, and Disraeli wondered if perhaps Clarissa in her new manifestation might prove to be less perilous a connection than she had become on the eve of his marriage.

'Ah, well,' she said, smiling, 'I shouldn't tether the lion of the evening.'

'I've roared enough, dear lady, for a whole week. I suppose you'll be in London till Parliament rises.'

'Alas, no. I will probably be going to Yorkshire in a week or two. Mr Hudson dislikes London.'

'I see,' said Disraeli, and looked at her again. She was unequivocal about her attachment, so that it became the premise of their conversation. But she waited for him to continue. She was a woman who understood the value of silence, and used it as a form of pressure. So did Disraeli. He listened to the rustle of her silks, and thought she had everything he liked in a woman, except, as he had seen at a quick glance when she sat down, that her ankles had become pudgy.

She was the first to speak, and in her voice was the remote inflection that he was familiar with in the accents of the Irish Members.

'I'm not accustomed to draw great authors into alcoves.'

The compliment pleased him more than anything she had said about his political achievement.

'What an extraordinary novel *Tancred* is! And Eva – such a marvellous creation! You know, if I had to model myself on a character in fiction, I'd choose to be Eva.'

'But Eva is the spirit of Judaism.'

She shook her head solemnly.

'No – she's Mother Eve – the spirit of all women.'

She stood up, and Disraeli stood too, half-delighted that the most beautiful woman in the room was at his side.

'I think,' she said, 'we should join Mrs Disraeli.'

She had spoken the words loudly, so that those in the neighbourhood could hear, and Disraeli's feeling of gratification turned instantly into one of annoyance that after the agreeable mixture of badinage and gravity of a few seconds earlier, she had created an impression that he was detaining her.

They walked slowly towards the other end of the room, where Mary Anne was declaiming amid ripples of laughter to an attentive audience. Compared with the smooth décolleté, half-exposing the breasts of Mrs Edmonds, the lace flounces around the neck of his wife's dress seemed fussy. Whereas Mrs Edmonds had a calm, enamelled air, the tip of Mary Anne's nose moved with the rhythm of her speech when she became animated.

'No, go away, Ben,' she said teasingly as he approached. 'I'm telling Monsieur Hautecloque and Mr Greville all about the time Prince Louis Napoleon took us rowing and stranded us on a mud-bank, and I told him he was always starting enterprises without thinking – '

The words cascaded and Mr Greville, clerk to the Privy Council and a relation of Bentinck, listened eagerly while the French agent of the Prince smiled diplomatically.

'Go away,' said Mary Anne. 'If you stand there I'll have to be discreet and very boring.'

Disraeli said, 'Very well. We'll take a glass of champagne, and return at once.'

'I don't like Mr Greville,' said Mrs Edmonds, taking his arm as they walked towards the conservatory. 'I'd have doubts, if I were the Queen, about a secretary to the Privy Council who spends so much time at Newmarket.'

'You mean you don't approve of horse-racing?'

'Oh yes. Otherwise, we lead such predetermined lives in society. I can think of nothing less reliable than a horse.'

'Perhaps a politician?'

She laughed as they sat on a *causeuse*.

'I've only known one very unreliable politician – at least, only one I cared about.'

She quickly reverted to Greville.

'I really don't like Mr Greville,' she went on. 'I always feel he's mentally writing down everything one says for his diary. People who keep diaries should be excluded from company.'

She pretended to bite her lower lip in confusion.

'Perhaps you keep a diary, Diz.'

He showed no emotion at the old familiarity.

'Perhaps you've recorded every word I've ever said.'

'Would that embarrass you?'

'Tonight – no. Perhaps tomorrow.'

She lowered her face.

'Have no fear. I stopped writing my diary ten years ago, and destroyed what I wrote. I regard private diaries designed for publication either as an act of betrayal, or if they're not to be published, as a waste of time.'

'I think,' said Mrs Edmonds, 'Mrs Disraeli may have finished her anecdote. Perhaps we should return to her.'

Mrs Edmonds's dress was of rose-pink silk, and it hissed as she moved. She took his arm again.

'Greville is, of course, the greatest gossip in London,' said Disraeli.

Mrs Edmonds was distracted by the French Ambassador who raised her hand to his lips before saluting Disraeli and moving on.

'Yes,' she said absently, gratified by the Ambassador's

attention. 'Greville's a gossip. But I think he's met his match in your Mary Anne.'

Disraeli frowned and detached his arm, and Mrs Edmonds immediately tried to redeem herself.

'I mean, Mrs Disraeli has such eloquence – I could listen to her for hours.'

Disraeli inclined his head frigidly; then turned with an affectionate smile to his wife.

'Why,' said Mary Anne, after the lady's maid had brushed her hair in her bedroom, 'were you so unkind to that pretty Mrs Edmonds? She was so nice when we met her in Paris. She told me she's sending her daughter to school in Switzerland ... I'm going to bounce on my bed and ruffle it so that the servants won't know I didn't use it, and I'm going to sleep in your bed tonight.'

She was wearing a white peignoir, and her hair hanging loose. She brought him a glass of brandy and he drew her towards him and kissed her.

'I'll spill it,' she said, and put the glass down on a side-table.

'Sometimes,' said Disraeli, 'I think you'd make an excellent mistress.'

'I'll keep practising, and you'll tell me if I make progress. But you haven't told me why you were so cold to Mrs Edmonds.'

'Mrs Edmonds,' said Disraeli, 'is one of those people who must always go too far. Her weakness is that she doesn't know how too-far to go.'

'I see. We won't dine with her on Wednesday a week? She asked me, and I said you'd consult your diary.'

'Did you? Well, I think not.'

'Are you sure? Mr Hudson will be there. You said you wanted to know him better.'

'I still think not.'

'In that case, I'll give you some grapes.'

'Are you tired?'

'No.'

'There's something I want to do with you.'

She looked at him expectantly.

'You may not approve.'

'We'll see.'

She lay on the bed propped against the cushions, and waited.

'I want to rehearse my speech for next week, and I want you to listen.'

She picked up her sampler and threw it on to a chair.

'I hate you,' she said. And then added, 'No, I don't, I love you. If ever I get to heaven, I want to hear you making speeches all the time.'

'All the time?'

'Well – half the time.'

Mary Anne sat in a wicker armchair while Disraeli, in his velvet banyan, walked up and down as if talking to himself.

'There'll be Lord Ashley – an evangelist, a philanthropist. He'll oppose the Bill none the less. He'll argue that the Gospel contains all the moral law. *Ergo*, those who reject the moral law have no title to be citizens, still less legislators. Oh yes, he'll emphasize that he regards the Jews with reverence. That's what they all say. Goulburn, Bankes, Sir Thomas Acland – all against the Bill for the same reason. And on our side we'll have Fox, Lord Morpeth, Sir Harry Verney – perhaps a few others.'

Mary Anne interrupted him.

'Do you really have to speak on the Jew Bill, Ben? Isn't it a nuisance, especially at this time? The names you mentioned against it – aren't they all your friends and supporters? What about Mr Gladstone?'

'He'll speak for the Bill – just to spite me – even knowing that the majority of his constituents at the University of Oxford are against it.'

'He's so pig-headed.'

'Yes, always trying to prove that Jesus and the disciples were Greeks, and won't take no for an answer.'

'Do you have to be so obstinate too?'

'My dear Mary Anne – I choose to be.'

He felt exhilarated and awake although the clock was striking two.

'I'll tell the House,' he said, 'that Christianity isn't the contradiction but the *completion* of Judaism. After all, who are those persons professing the Jewish religion? They are persons who acknowledge exactly the same God as the Christians of this realm.'

He took in his hand a copy of *The Genius of Judaism*, written by his father, which he had used as the basis of his speech, and waved it as he walked about, rehearsing.

'The Jews acknowledge the same divine revelation as yourselves. They are, in human terms, the authors of your religion. It's on the ground of religious truth that I'll vote for the Motion, not just on the ground of religious liberty.'

'You must make sure,' said Mary Anne sleepily, 'that when you talk about "your religion" you make it clear that you mean "our religion" – the Christian religion.'

'Yes,' said Disraeli, 'that is, I confess, a slight problem. I'll try to make it clear in the context. What the Bill's opponents are trying to do is to make it seem that the Jews oppose the Christian church. I'll put it to them – hasn't the church of Christ – the Christian church, whether Roman Catholic or Protestant – made the history of the Jews the most celebrated history in the world?'

Once again Disraeli addressed himself to his imaginary parliamentary audience.

'On every sacred day you read to the people the exploits of Jewish heroes, the proofs of Jewish devotion, the brilliant annals of Jewish magnificence in past ages . . . Every Sunday, every Lord's day, if you wish to express feelings of praise and thanksgiving to the Most High, or if you wish to find expressions of solace in grief, you find both in the words of Jewish prophets and the Jewish psalmists. All the early Christians were Jews. The Christian religion was preached by men who were born Jews; every man in the early ages of the church by whose power, or zeal, or genius the Christian faith was propagated, was a Jew.'

Disraeli stopped and waited. Mary Anne said nothing.

'Are you asleep?' he asked.

'No – I'm thinking.'

'What are you thinking?'

'They won't like it.'

'Why not?'

'Christians don't like being preached at about Christianity – especially, darling Diz, by converts. There are bigots among them, and they'll mutter the things they used to say aloud. They won't say them very loud – but they'll say them all the same.'

'In that case,' Disraeli said in a loud voice that made the crystal lustre quiver and Mary Anne put her finger to her lips, 'I'll tell them. I'll tell them that in exact proportion to their Christian faith, they should wish to perform this act of justice. And I'll tell them that whether they know it or not, they're influenced in their opposition by the darkest superstitions of the darkest ages.'

'They'll say you don't speak for the gentlemen of Shrewsbury. That your seat – '

'I'll tell them I couldn't sit in the House with any misconception on this subject. Whatever the consequences to my future, I refuse to vote except for what I believe to be the principles of religion.'

'And if Colonel Tankerton and his friends taunt you? It's been his theme since he got into the House.'

'Let them. I'll tell the House that as a Christian I won't take upon myself the awful responsibility of excluding from the legislature those who are of the religion in whose bosom *my* Lord and Saviour was born.'

There was a silence, and Disraeli, trembling from the passion that the prospect of the debate conjured up in him, said, 'Well?'

'You know,' said Mary Anne, 'I don't understand politics. I just know what people feel. The country gentlemen don't mind Hebrews as long as they're dead like the ancient Romans or the ancient Greeks. It's when they get nearer home that they don't like the Jews.'

'That's a barbaric prejudice,' said Disraeli, affronted. 'The Jews of today aren't a different people. They're of the direct line of the ancient Hebrews. They've outlived Assyrian kings and Egyptian pharaohs, Roman cæsars and Arabian caliphs.'

Mary Anne waited for him to finish, and then put her arms around him.

'You must keep that for Parliament,' she said. 'I only told you what the country gentlemen will say. Will you ride off on your high horse if I tell you I know them better than you do?'

'We'll see – we'll see,' said Disraeli. He felt discouraged. He knew that the course to which he was committed could only bring him disadvantage with his party.

'What about George Bentinck?' Mary Anne asked, removing her peignoir and preparing to climb into the high bed. 'Does he accept your – your theological arguments?'

'He said he couldn't follow them,' said Disraeli glumly.

'Then how will he vote?'

'For the Jews,' said Disraeli. 'Just as he voted for the Catholics. He believes in religious liberty.'

Mary Anne blew out the candles.

'What a kind man he is!' she said.

She soon fell asleep, her head on Disraeli's shoulder, while he lay awake in the darkness, repeating his speech, fearful of its effect on his supporters, regretful of its imprudence, determined in his intention, wondering what mischief Clarissa Edmonds might make, and contemplating the Rothschild family, forever battling to maintain their eminence among rising and falling exchanges, dynasties and the sons of men.

Chapter Sixteen

Though her thoughts were of the *couturière* she had brought to London from Lyons, Mrs Edmonds listened as if entranced to Lord Stanley as they stood on the steps of the entrance to Knowsley Hall. The week she and Mr Hudson had spent there had so far been a success, since her companion had the art of becoming inconspicuous when his invisibility was an advantage to her, and after many years of disengaging herself from the memory of her father's trade as a horse-dealer, she found that her own knowledge of horses was of considerable benefit in absorbing the interest of her host whose chief passion was racing, closely followed by whist and flirtation.

Despite Lady Jersey's disapproval of Mrs Edmonds, her son Mr Francis Villiers had accepted Lord Stanley's invitation to join his house-party, and there to the general amusement and with the tolerance of Mr Hudson, he followed her like a spaniel. His slim, youthful figure was constantly at her heel, except when she dismissed him in order to 'discuss affairs'. As the week progressed, her need to discuss affairs with Lord Stanley increased. On the second day they had strolled down the cypress walk to the Italian garden, and by the third day their meeting had become an institution. At twelve o'clock, it was generally understood that Lord Stanley and Mrs Edmonds would be walking to the Italian garden, and there was agreement to avoid them.

'I doubt she stands fifteen hands,' said Stanley with an earnest expression, offering her his arm.

'Gone in the wind too,' said Mrs Edmonds, 'and liable, if you ask me, to break a blood vessel. They thought it pointless to put her into training. But really, my lord, when she was mated with Tyresias – what happened? She went on to produce the *unbeatable* Carezza.'

'Strange,' said Stanley, drawing his fur-collared coat closer around him, 'Tyresias's dam never won, nor even his grand-dam, nor his great-grand-dam.'

She held his arm tighter when they approached the cypress trees, and said, 'What does that prove, my lord? Does it suggest there's an advantage in being without a pedigree?'

He looked at her teasing face, brightened by the east wind, and said, 'No – it proves there can be exceptions, provided the stuff is there. Will you stay with us a little longer?'

He was looking straight ahead, his burly figure restrained, his expression preoccupied.

'Would you like me to?'

'I would like you to.'

They skirted the fountains where, linked by culverts, the stone heads of sea-monsters gushed their cascades down to the reedy lake. At the verge they stopped, and she said, 'I'm afraid we must return to London.'

The word 'we' was decisive. It included Mr Hudson.

He put both hands on the gold boss of his cane.

'I understand.'

'But of course,' she went on thoughtfully, 'if you were to ask me to come back – '

He looked up, and there was a complicity in their faces. Putting his cane under his arm, he took both her gloved hands and raised them to his lips. A shot came from the nearby woods, and a bird started up in a flurry from the black branches of an oak. She pressed close to Stanley in apprehension, and he put his hands around her shoulders.

'Good morning,' said Mr Villiers, who appeared through a thicket, carrying a gun. 'I'm afraid – '

'I think, sir, your direction lies that way,' said Lord Stanley, pointing to the wood.

'Yes, most certainly – most certainly,' said the young man. He raised his hat to Mrs Edmonds, who gave him a nod, and Stanley watched him till his gaiters disappeared through the dead bracken.

'What an eccentric fellow!' he said.

'Oh, I don't know,' said Mrs Edmonds. 'He entertains me.'

Unaccustomed to contradiction and displeased by her

approval of Mr Villiers, Stanley sulked as they walked back till the house came into sight, and she touched his fingers with hers.

'Why are you displeased with me?' she asked.

'Displeased? Not at all. I only derive pleasure from your company.'

'Well, I am displeased with you, my lord, and for a much more important reason.'

'What might that be?'

'You now have a great Party at your disposal, but you're lazy. It prevents you from becoming the first name in politics. Sir Robert Peel has gone into a decline since he was beat. I hear he spends his time shooting rabbits at Drayton.'

'They're not so fierce as Bentinck.'

'All the more reason for him not to return to political life in any marked degree. Mr Bulwer was saying to me recently that when a man's work is done, his day is over. The House of Commons has finished with Sir Robert – he's finished with politics.'

'What conclusion does that lead you to, madam?' said Lord Stanley, opening a gate for her.

'It leads me to think,' she said boldly, 'that with a little inspiration – '

'From yourself, no doubt.'

'From myself,' she said seriously, 'and some energy on your own part, you could become Prime Minister very soon.'

'What does Mr Hudson say?'

'I haven't found it necessary to consult him.'

'Ah!'

He was gratified, and said, 'You have to remember, though, that there are others – George Bentinck, perhaps even Disraeli – who could lead the party.'

'Lord George has never wanted to be anything but second. He's always scurrying round for somebody to be second to. Now he's found Mr Disraeli, he goes about like a lover mooning with happiness. I should think Mr Disraeli a much greater danger to you than Lord George.'

'Why a danger?' asked Stanley idly. Politicians bored him

almost as much as politics, and he had no social relations with Disraeli.

'Because he's unscrupulous,' said Mrs Edmonds, prodding the lawn with her parasol. 'You know how he mistreated Lady Sykes and abandoned her. Such a bewildered and foolish woman! She had four children, and in the end she lost everything. When she died she had nothing at all – nothing.'

'Very sad!' said Stanley abruptly, disliking gossip.

'But there's something else,' said Mrs Edmonds. 'You remember during the last Corn Law debate how the Prime Minister challenged him about his application for office?'

'I remember it well, and I remember Disraeli's denial. What of it, madam?'

She withdrew her arm from his, and said, 'If you're going to be severe with me, I can't go on. You'll have to woo me for the information. Dear Lady Ballantyne!'

She left him behind to greet the arbiter of the North, the wealthy dowager in the unfashionable clothes who decided the social acceptability of those who came from the South and sought to advance beyond the Border.

Lady Ballantyne kissed her on each cheek, and said, rolling her 'r's', 'She's the prettiest thing here, don't you agree, Lord Stanley?'

She was known for her outspokenness, and Stanley said gallantly, 'Not only here.'

'That's very much better,' said Mrs Edmonds, taking his arm again as they walked on. 'I was telling you about Mr Disraeli. You realize that in fact he really did seek a job in Sir Robert's administration.'

Stanley shrugged his athlete's shoulders. Accustomed to place-seekers and hunters after patronage, he didn't regard it as a serious offence that Disraeli should have asked for office. Mrs Edmonds was irritated by his indifference, and shook his arm.

'Can't you see how important it is?'

'Why shouldn't Disraeli try and get a place? It happens every day.'

'Oh,' she said in annoyance. 'You're stupid, my lord.'

He smiled. He could think of no one except very small children who were permitted to address him like that.

'Can't you see,' she went on, 'that it's one thing to ask for a job – quite another to tell a blatant lie to the Prime Minister in full view of the House? And that is a man who might lead your Party!'

Stanley stood by the steps and engaged her in earnest conversation, so that some of his guests felt it polite to avert their eyes.

'I agree. That is a serious matter. But if there were evidence, Peel, I'm sure, would have produced it. Graham wouldn't have allowed him to carry chivalry so far.'

'There is evidence,' she said, and her face became demure. 'There's a letter.'

'I understood it disappeared after Drummond was murdered by that madman.'

'If it disappeared, it has reappeared. There's a gentleman who in the interests of the Party feels that you should know of it.'

'Have you seen it?'

'No.'

'How d'you know it exists?'

'I trust my informant.'

'May I ask who the gentleman is and how the letter came into his possession?'

'I can't tell you the name of the gentleman yet. All I can say is that he found it with a variety of other papers in an escritoire belonging to Mr Drummond and sold by his executors at Christie's. I can assure you of its authenticity. Disraeli should be driven from the House.'

With a frown, Stanley changed the subject.

'Will you ride tomorrow, Mrs Edmonds?'

'Yes,' she said gaily. 'If you can keep up with me.'

Hudson was waiting for her at the top of the steps. She hurried past him to her rooms, where her maid was waiting to take her outdoor clothes.

'I'm exhausted, Mary,' she said. 'So much exercise!'

The maid helped her to undress, and she lay looking out

over the park from her chaise-longue. After half an hour a manservant brought her a note. She recognized the handwriting, and opened it without interest.

> Madam [she read],
> A combination of urgent business and personal sensibility compels me to return to London. In the conviction that new friendships will replace the old, if they have not done so already, I offer you my warmest good wishes and the enclosure as a token of regard and farewell.
> Believe me to be,
> Your humble servant,
> G. Hudson.

She leapt from the chaise-longue in a fury, and waved the draft for a thousand pounds as if she was going to tear it into a thousand pieces. She looked at the black marble mantel clock that stood at twenty minutes past twelve, and wanted to get dressed and pursue Mr Hudson who had so departed from character as to object to her embryonic relationship with Stanley. Instead, she returned to the sofa and put the draft carefully into her travelling case. By the time Mr Hudson reached London in one of his trains, she had no doubt that he would have repented of his haste and find himself a thousand pounds the poorer.

She lay on the sofa, and thought of Tankerton and the escritoire and her disclosures to Stanley about Disraeli's letter. She shrugged her shoulders. She had no regrets. The very qualities in Disraeli that once had drawn her to him – his pale face, his black curls on his high forehead, his sensual lower lip – now seemed odious to her. She couldn't remember if she had ever loved him. She was satisfied that in exposing his duplicity she was performing a public service as well as enjoying a private revenge. Why, she asked herself, should this *arriviste* who had behaved towards her with such harsh detachment and deserted her with ironic apologies and obvious relief, have the right to lord it in the Party when he had only maintained his position by gambling on a lie? She had heard it. In the last few days she had become certain that her future lay not in the company of an adventurer like Disraeli or even a convenient and wealthy *entrepreneur* like Hudson. She was suddenly glad that he'd taken offence and gone.

She had long decided that she wanted to remarry or find some stable protector, an aristocratic landowner for preference. Hudson was a townsman. Stanley made her think of cornfields and woods.

She had just finished writing a frigid note of acknowledgement to Mr Hudson when there was a knock at the door.

'Yes,' she said, expecting her maid. The door opened and Francis Villiers appeared. He had changed from his shooting clothes, and she looked in surprise at his fresh face with its fuzz of side-whiskers. He in turn stood without speaking, staring at the curve of her breast in the opening of her peignoir.

'Well,' she said calmly, 'you can't stay here. I have to dress. My maid will be here any moment now.'

He didn't speak, but knelt at her feet by the Amboina table and laid his head in her lap.

She put her hand on his hair where it lay over his collar, and said, 'You'd better get up. Whatever's the matter with you?'

He raised his light-coloured eyes to her, and said with a stutter, 'I'm so unhappy.'

She sealed her letter in an envelope, and wrote the address. 'Why?' she asked.

'Because of everything. You – Hudson – Stanley – '

'What d'you mean?' she asked sharply.

'Everything.'

'You shouldn't spy, Francis.'

He again put his forehead in her lap, and said in a smothered voice, 'I have to know.'

She rose brusquely and went to the window, leaving him with his head bent like a penitent. Then she came back to him.

'Would you do something for me?' she asked.

'Anything in the whole world.'

'Well, take this letter and see it's delivered to the post.'

She smiled to him, and he rose slowly to his feet, the knees of his dark trousers smudged with two patches of fluff from the Axminster carpet.

'You look very silly, Francis,' she said.

'Yes,' he said. She waited for him to speak.

'Would you walk with me tomorrow?' he asked.

'No. Tomorrow I'm riding with Lord Stanley.'

He scowled.

'But you can escort me in the train to London on Friday. I have some important business to deal with.'

His face uncreased in joy, and he took the letter from her hand.

'Clarissa!'

She frowned.

'I bought you a small gift – I ventured to – from Garrards.'

She sat at the dressing-table, and he stood behind her.

'What is it?'

She looked up at his reflection in the looking-glass.

'These,' he said.

He opened a jewel-case, and she looked with delight at two diamond pendants in the shape of snakes.

'They're beautiful,' she said turning, and took one with each hand and put them in her ears.

'You're beautiful,' he said sombrely.

'Francis,' said Mrs Edmonds. 'I'd like you to kiss my shoulder.'

Chapter Seventeen

'We regret the differences which have arisen between leading members of the Protectionist Party and Lord George Bentinck, following his vote in favour of the removal of Jewish disabilities. The motives of the noble Lord are well known, and do honour to his consistency in upholding the cause of emancipation. Yet at the same time, we are obliged to say that Lord George Bentinck has seriously imperilled his prospects – '

Disraeli laid down his copy of the *Morning Chronicle* as the manservant ushered Bentinck into the drawing-room of Grosvenor Gate, the first of the guests to arrive for the dinner to discuss the question of the leadership.

'Yes,' said Bentinck with a quick glance at the newspaper, 'I've read it. But they needn't have a care. I've made up my mind. I'd as soon come to dinner uninvited as thrust myself on an unwilling Party.'

He took a glass of champagne from a tray.

'I trust Mrs Disraeli is well?'

'Very well,' said Disraeli, 'though I fear she won't be with us tonight.'

He returned to the subject.

'We expected resentment.'

'But this is distaste. I've no wish to lead a party of bigots, masquerading as defenders of the Church. I'm going to retire to the back benches.'

'Oh no,' said Disraeli, disturbed by Bentinck's angry determination. During the years of their friendship he had often had to humour Bentinck in his sudden rages. It was only a short time ago that Bentinck had become the unchallenged leader of the Protectionists. And now, a few grumbles from the squires that he and Disraeli alone among the Protectionists had voted for the Bill giving Jews the right to sit in Parliament, had been enough to make him want to resign.

'You mustn't misunderstand me,' said Bentinck, reading Disraeli's expression. 'I don't regret what I've done. I'd have felt a lifelong shame if I hadn't gone into the lobby with you. But that isn't my reason for going. The Party needs a new leader in the Commons.'

Disraeli shook his head.

'If you were to go, what would be left? A hack like Lord Granby or an also-ran like Herries. You know what he's like. He lives in the past. Starts every other sentence with "When I was Chancellor of the Exchequer – " ' '

Bentinck sank into an armchair and spread his legs in his 'Newmarket' manner.

'You know as well as I do that there's another alternative. It's you, Disraeli. You – '

Disraeli interrupted him.

'As long as you're here, George, I've no wish to be leader. But even if, Heaven forbid, you did retire, they'd never accept me. Never. As you know, they'd offer a dozen reasons, each more respectable than the last. Take Stanley himself – he'll tell you that once upon a time I encouraged his younger brother to gamble beyond his means. You may believe me – it's a lie. I might gamble beyond my own means – never beyond another's.'

'I've told him so. You must reassure him at dinner tonight.'

'He doesn't want to be reassured. Stanley persists in believing a lie because it gives him an excuse for a prejudice.'

Bentinck compressed his lips.

'Diz,' he began, and Disraeli knew that in addressing him by the familiar name he was about to say something that he found difficult. Disraeli put his hand over the glass dome of wax fruit and examined it closely in order to give Bentinck time to elaborate his thoughts.

'You've raised the matter of Stanley's prejudice against you. I've had a disagreeable communication.'

'I'm sorry. From whom, pray?'

'From Stanley himself. He tells me a certain person has been to see him and spoken of a letter you wrote to Peel some years ago.'

'Which letter? I wrote him several.'

Bentinck hesitated. He disliked the subject.

'This letter concerns your application for office in his administration.'

Disraeli stood by the fireplace, and said,

'That was a long time ago.'

'Not your repudiation. That was recent.'

Bentinck studied Disraeli's face in the hope that he'd contradict him.

'It's true,' Disraeli said sombrely. Then his expression lightened. 'I won't pretend. I did write to him. But I ask you to consider something. Here was an early indiscretion. It was foolish of me to place myself as a hostage in Peel's hands. I admit it. An indiscretion, but scarcely a sin. Would you not agree?'

'Yes, but – '

'Exactly. Certainly not a sin. And then at the very moment when we were about to gain our victory over Peel – a victory for which you even sold your racehorses – at such a moment Peel attempted to blacken my character in front of Parliament with a bitter taunt.'

He walked about the room as he declaimed.

'What was I to do, George? Break faith with our supporters? Forfeit their confidence? Allow Peel to hold a pistol to me? "Your confession or your political life"?'

He paused, but Bentinck merely examined his fingertips.

'I wrote to him as a Protectionist seeking office to serve as a Protectionist. I could truthfully say in the House that I had never sought office except to influence affairs.'

'Ah, Diz – Diz,' said Bentinck, putting his arm on his shoulder affectionately, 'it's ingenious, but it won't do.'

Disraeli watched a log collapse in the fireplace with a splutter of sparks, and said mournfully,

'No – I'm afraid it won't.'

Bentinck laughed aloud. Then he said solemnly,

'We must get the letter back. If Stanley ever forms a government, you ought to be in it. And if the letter is published by some malevolent hand, it's certain you won't be. Even if the Party wanted you, the Queen – well, never mind that. I want you to be in a position to lead the Party.'

'I'm deeply grateful to you – deeply,' said Disraeli. He looked at the clock that stood at three minutes to eight, and waved the subject of the letter away.

'Stanley will be here soon, and there's one other matter I want to discuss with you.' He frowned. 'It's about Hughenden Manor. You see, whatever happens, a country party needs landowners to lead it and a territorial aristocracy to sustain it; otherwise it's nothing. That's why I have wanted to buy Hughenden Manor. When it first came on the market, I felt that with a country estate I could speak as a country gentleman.'

'And now?'

'Now I fear it's hopeless. The truth is, I still need £25,000.' He spoke elegiacally, and Bentinck made no comment.

'When I left Shrewsbury last year to become a Member for Bucks, I still hoped to raise the money. But now – '

He rose and paced the room.

'After our challenge to Peel, I knew at once that the agricultural interest couldn't be represented by intellect alone. For me to speak on its behalf was merely to act as an advocate, however deep my convictions and sentimental involvement. It wasn't enough. Unless I had a stake in what I fought for, my part in the matter would always seem accidental and meretricious. What did the squires cheer in me during our great debates? You know as well as I do. A useful outsider – a runner they could forget about the moment the race was over.'

'They backed you.'

'And they tried to dismiss me. That was why I wanted an estate,' Disraeli went on. 'I realized I needed a stake in the land. My father was willing to help. And when you were generous enough to act as security for £10,000, my hopes rose.'

'I understand your feeling. I understand. All of us – my

brothers included – want nothing more than to ensure you have a landed base. You know very well that if I could command £25,000 at once – '

Disraeli shrugged his shoulders.

'I'm grateful to you – more than I can ever say. Your friendship has been noble and steadfast. But when you ask me to put myself forward as leader of a party of two hundred and fifty Members, you're asking me to take part in a great enterprise, the defence of powerful and legitimate interests. How could I, as leader, represent interests in which I had no part myself? Imagine a hundred Disraelis in the House; we'd merely be a grand committee of clever individuals. Unless I'm in the game as a player, I must withdraw from public affairs. I want to return to literature.'

'No,' said Bentinck, standing. 'No. You still have a great and important part to play. Let me talk again to my brothers – to my father. Did you say twenty-five thousand?'

'At least,' said Disraeli gravely.

They were interrupted by the butler's announcement of Lord Granby, Lord Stanley and a number of other guests. Granby shook Disraeli's hand. Stanley bowed coolly, and immediately turned his heavy head, set tightly on his sportsman's frame, to the others.

It was the first time Stanley had dined as Disraeli's guest at Grosvenor Gate, but he was relaxed and nonchalant. Fifteen banks had recently failed, and when Bentinck spoke of the monetary crisis, Stanley said in his patrician voice, 'It all boils down to the Bank Charter Act. Not enough money about. And, incidentally, too many forged acceptances. I hear it's become an epidemic.'

'Too much speculation in railways,' said Mr Herries. 'Too much unproductive investment. When I was Chancellor of the Exchequer – '

Disraeli led Stanley into the dining-room.

At dinner, Stanley, unwilling to dwell on disagreeable questions, referred in a loud voice to Mr Vavasour, a character in Disraeli's novel *Tancred*.

'He recalls someone I know well,' he said, 'but the name escapes me.'

'The face is familiar,' said Lord Granby, 'a portrait, I take it.'

Disraeli surveyed the table contentedly. Mary Anne and the butler had organized it well.

'Your Mr Vavasour is very much a second-class man, Disraeli,' said Stanley. 'Where did you find him?'

'Our party isn't short of models,' said Disraeli.

Lord Stanley gave his host a rapid glance. He could see that despite the reconciliation Bentinck had sought in proposing the dinner at Grosvenor Gate, he'd have to handle him carefully.

What Stanley had planned with his friends was that if Bentinck couldn't be persuaded to resume the leadership, Granby or Herries should formally succeed him, with Disraeli in charge of day-to-day parliamentary business. But whatever Disraeli's qualifications as an orator, they would never have him as leader; that had been agreed in the Smoking Room, the Whips' Office, the Carlton, the country houses and even at the party meeting, where the call for Lord Granby as leader had already been made.

By the time they reached the port, none of the guests had yet ventured to turn the discussion to Stanley's plan. Disraeli, observing through half-closed eyes the embarrassment of his guests as they skirted the subject of the subordinate role they'd settled for him, was silent.

At last, Stanley said,

'I think, Disraeli, we ought to talk about some contingencies facing the Party.'

'By all means.'

'Well, then, we can claim one great success. We threw Peel out, and for that matter ourselves, but we still preserve our political coherence.'

'The purity of our conscience,' said Granby, his dewlaps rolling at the bottom of his cheeks.

Herries nodded sagely.

'But then– I fear that on the Jew vote – Lord George accepts this – you and he – how can I put this – ?'

'Frankly?' suggested Disraeli.

'Yes, frankly – you both – for reasons of conscience – '

'Conscience,' echoed Granby.

'Conscience is a sentiment. Forgive me if I claim that it was reason, not conscience, that guided us,' said Disraeli. 'We voted for reasons of reason.'

Bentinck growled his agreement.

'Oh, I understand that,' said Stanley. 'Everyone recognizes, Disraeli, why you voted against the Party on the Jew Bill; we all accept your position. I fear, though, it has excluded you from any chance of the leadership in the Commons. I must be blunt. I won't go into the theme – the prejudices – or even the justification. It's a fact.'

Disraeli observed Stanley without emotion.

'What consequences do you draw from it, my lord?'

'We are seeking your help, your understanding, of a difficult situation. Everyone here is of the view that we want George Bentinck to stay as leader of the Party in the Commons if he will.'

There was a clamour of agreement.

'But if he went, you, Disraeli, would have a position of the highest importance, greater perhaps than the leader. You'd be the leader's guide.'

Disraeli remained silent, playing with a petal in his finger-bowl.

'You mean I'm good enough to serve,' he said at last, ' – good enough to speak, perhaps even good enough to be a front runner for a time; but the animal has to be pulled. I'm never to be the winner.'

'It's the view of the Party.'

'Do you dispute it, my lord?'

'I have to take the sense of others. I must add, however, that it's my own view.'

Disraeli looked around the table at the questioning eyes over the candelabra. Only Bentinck sat with his head lowered, uneasy and unhappy, staring at the serpentine foliage winding between the silver pheasants that decorated the table.

'I'm obliged to you,' said Disraeli, 'for making yourself clear. I – '

He was interrupted by the hurried arrival of Baum, who whispered urgently in his ear.

Disraeli puckered his forehead, excused himself, and followed his valet into the drawing-room, where his brother Ralph, wearing a country suit of cord, was leaning against the white marble fireplace near an arrangement of dried flowers.

'I'm sorry to interrupt your dinner, Ben.'

'Baum has told me.'

'Can you leave tonight? I felt you had to know.'

'It's very difficult, as you see. Lord Stanley – Bentinck – how serious is it?'

'Very.'

Disraeli looked at his brother's inflamed eyes.

'Have you a carriage, Ralph?'

'There's an overnight coach to Wycombe from Camberwell.'

'It's very difficult for me to leave – couldn't we perhaps wait a day or two? We could take an early train – '

Ralph shook his head.

'You must decide for yourself. I must tell you, he's dying. He was barely conscious when I left. Dr Boland thought the guv'nor could live only a few days more.'

From the dining-room came a burst of laughter that made the glass dome over the drawing-room carriage-clock tinkle.

'A few days more!' Disraeli echoed, and he felt his arm quivering. A few days more. If he had twenty-four hours he would have time to arrange the Party's affairs. But his father was dying.

Then he saw Herries pass the open door, guided by a man-servant, and he thought in that moment: was it to consort with Herries and Granby and Stanley that he would linger? He made a decision.

'Mary Anne has gone to bed,' he said. 'Have a few hours sleep, Ralph, and we'll leave together early in the morning.'

He tugged at the bell, and Baum came in.

'Make up a bed for Mr Ralph,' he said. 'We're leaving for

Bradenham at six o'clock. Arrange for the carriage. My father, I'm afraid, is extremely ill.'

'He was a nice old gentleman,' said Baum, taking up a candle from a side-table. 'A very kind old gentleman.'

A few days more. But his father had been there all his life. He was a nice old gentleman. Was – was. How dared Baum speak of him as if he were no longer there! His father. The guv'nor. Perhaps Dr Boland was wrong. He'd go to Bradenham with Ralph as soon as it was light. It was impossible to leave his guests. But what did the leadership matter when his father was dying? What did this struggle of phantoms mean? Why were they laughing in the dining-room when the father he loved was dying?

He returned to the dining-room, and listened to the end of an incomprehensible anecdote told by a guest whose name he had forgotten. Everyone chuckled, and Disraeli joined in.

'Capital!' he said.

They were looking at him. Someone had asked him a question. He hadn't heard.

'You will, of course, be at the Jerseys' on Thursday?' Granby repeated.

'Of course,' said Disraeli.

Thursday. At the Jerseys'. To meet the Party again. Some of the Peelites too. Yes, very important. Lady Jersey was trying to achieve a reconciliation within the Party. It was vital that he should be there.

They were rising now. Stanley had to go, and Disraeli shook his hand. The others were smiling at him. On Thursday. Yes, Thursday. What else had been decided? What conclusion had they reached about the junta to lead the Party? He couldn't recall. There was a mingling of anxieties in his mind. His father. Tankerton and his letter. Lies and phantoms and illusions.

When at last he went to bed, he saw that Mary Anne was asleep. She half-awoke and nestled warmly into his arms, and asked, 'Is everything all right?'

'Yes,' he answered.

'Are you all right?'

'Yes,' he responded.

'I'm very glad,' she said, and fell asleep again.

Sarah was the first to greet them when they arrived at Bradenham. With the shutters still drawn, the hall was lit by lamplight, and her eyes as Disraeli kissed her amid the weeping
maidservants were large and shadowed in her pallid face. So it
had been last year when his mother had died; but then it was
April, and the spring sunshine touching the daffodils and
narcissi in the hall had thrown a benevolence over grief. Now
the manor lay in a January gloom; and they had driven from
Aylesbury under a lowering sky, over roads slippery with ice.
  As he held Sarah's tear-stained face against his, he felt her
quivering shoulders beneath her shawl. She was frail and thin,
and said between her sobbing, 'Oh, Ben. It's all over – gone . . .
At five o'clock this morning.'
  He disengaged himself from her arms, and Tita came forward
and shook his hand. Disraeli had never shaken his hand before.
The servant wore his best broadcloth jacket, and for once was
without his daggers.
  'God's will!' said Tita, and crossed himself in the manner of
the Greek Orthodox Church.
  The servants in their white aprons and black dresses curtsied
timidly and withdrew into the shadows, while James sat on a
chair, his head lowered, without stirring.
  'Where is he?' asked Disraeli.
  Sarah went ahead of him, and he followed her slowly with
Ralph to the top of the wide oak staircase, where she opened
the door and stood aside to let him enter.
  The curtains were closed, and a single candle was burning
by the bedside. Isaac D'Israeli lay with his hands at his side, his
face waxen and composed. Ralph knelt and muttered a prayer.
Disraeli stood, contemplating his father. Now Isaac D'Israeli
knew all, and nothing was hidden, the wondering ended, the
arguments decided, nor ever again would he banter with his
son, nor smile, nor praise, nor speak the familiar words, nor
ever say farewell. He lay there, an English worthy; as Disraeli
looked at his father in death he thought of him too, with his
noble, withdrawn face, as a prince in Israel, of the great line

231

of the Villa Reals, the Medinas, the Laras, the Laredos and the da Costas, whose journey through history had brought them to England a hundred years before. Disraeli bent over his father and kissed his forehead. It was glacial and moist. The cast of the patriarchs had returned in death to Isaac's features, and he was like a quiet stone, unstirring.

Disraeli felt his way down the stairs and on to the lawns beyond the silent house. The cold air touched him; and he wanted to reject the destiny that had taken his father away, and was about to disperse his family. The woods glimmered in the winter light, and he said aloud, 'No – no,' and then turned to see Sarah running across the grass carrying his coat. He stopped and passed his fingers over his eyes, and took the coat from her without speaking.

They then walked together to the house, their arms around each other as they used to long ago.

After the funeral service at Bradenham church, the Disraelis returned for a cold collation to the manor, and soon the rooms filled rapidly with notables and neighbours, magistrates, two or three of the Basevis, his mother's relations, the Lord Lieutenant, clergymen, landowners and their wives; the ladies assembled round the tables, the men chattering in knots and drinking brandy and port. As Disraeli passed among them they mumbled their condolences, then quickly resumed their talk on other matters. The funeral was over, and their faces, organized hitherto in an expression of mourning, could now relax.

'Good God,' said old Squire Lowther, 'he asked me eighty shillings a quarter. So I said to him, "Eighty shillings? You're a booby as well as a robber!" ' He roared with laughter, and the others joined in.

Mary Anne sat with Sarah who was receiving condolences, but Disraeli walked away from the din. The funeral feast had become a party.

He entered the library and shut the door behind him. His father's reading desk was as it had always been, tidily ordered, the manuscript notes on his revised *Life of Charles I* lying next to the first edition. He picked up a page, but Sarah's writing was blurred, and he put it down and stared through the window at the woods.

'Mr Disraeli!'

A hunchbacked figure he recognized as Mr Jacobs, his father's friend, the London bookseller who used to visit Bradenham several times a year with his newly bound store, was standing in the shadows near the firescreen.

'Mr Jacobs,' he said.

Mr Jacobs extended his hand and bowed his head. From outside came another burst of laughter.

'I offer you, sir, my regrets,' said Mr Jacobs simply.

Disraeli took his hand, and remembered his father and Mr Jacobs handling their folios, smiling together and inspecting the endpapers. It was all part of his youth, a time that would never come again, and he felt that among all the noisy assembly he only wanted to be with Mr Jacobs, who had come to his father's funeral because he loved him.

The door opened and, talking loudly, Mr Moxon and Mr Layton, each with a glass of brandy in his hand, made an entry.

'Ah!' said Layton.

'Pray come in,' said Disraeli.

'Yes,' said Layton. 'A very sad occasion. A pillar of the county! An ornament of scholarship!'

'Irreparable loss!' said Moxon. 'Yes – must be getting back to London.'

Disraeli turned to look for Mr Jacobs whom the others had ignored, but his father's friend had glided away as imperceptibly as he had appeared, lost among the mourners who filled the rooms with chatter.

'He was happy,' said Sarah to Canon Inglefield who had been visiting his cousins in Buckinghamshire. 'Only two days before he died, my father heard from his publisher that he was bringing out a complete edition of his works.'

'That must have been a great comfort,' said Inglefield ponderously. In the years that had passed since he left Buckinghamshire, he had risen rapidly in the Church and had modified some of his earlier, more radical views. His hair had thinned, leaving him with a monkish pate, while the dinners which he enjoyed both in his canonical and in his county states, since he had taken again to hunting after renouncing his parochial duties, had given him a broad belly. Sarah gazed at him distantly as he ate his ham and tongue and drank claret.

'Yes,' he said in his orotund voice, 'the natural order takes over. Nothing remains still. Isn't that so, Disraeli?'

'Yes,' said Disraeli.

'We look back and realize how everything moves on. *Eheu fugaces* . . . But there's a new era of prosperity – it changes many attitudes. It's taken the thunder from the radicals.'

Squire Lowther grunted. He sat uncomfortably in his chesterfield overcoat, holding his large, old-fashioned top-hat on his knees.

'I doubt, sir, doubt it very much. The Chartists are plotting a new petition. Look at them Frenchmen. I wouldn't give tuppence for Louis Philippe's throne – it's revolution everywhere. Naples, Vienna – everywhere. Look at that Metternich! There ain't a throne that's stable.'

'Not here,' said Inglefield firmly. 'The throne is secure.'

'God's firkins,' said the Squire, standing his ground, 'they've been stoning the police in Trafalgar Square! Call that nothing?'

'Trivial! Trivial!' said Inglefield loftily. 'In our sea-girt isle there's no place for revolution.'

'And the terrible famine in Ireland?' Sarah put in hesitantly.

'Nature finds its own adjustment,' said Inglefield. 'By its inexorable law, death will reduce the population to the level of that unhappy land's ability to feed it. Remember, Miss Disraeli, the words, "By the sweat of thy brow . . ."'

'Were you not yourself a Chartist, Mr Inglefield?' asked Mrs Broome, a neighbour who had known Inglefield as a young man.

He passed his fingers over the crown of his head, not liking to be reminded of his former opinions.

'In my youth, ma'am, all generous young men had sympathy with the Chartists. But it's past – past. The machine has ended

234

all that. We're living in an industrial age. Prosperity is the way to end civil dissension . . . Ah, well! I must leave. My wife . . . Yes. Must leave. Sad occasion, Miss Disraeli. Very sad. I liked your father. Used to tease me about the Athanasian Creed.'

He rose shortly afterwards, and Disraeli and Sarah accompanied him to the door. The winter day was crisp, and Inglefield sniffed the air. Under his cassock he was wearing riding breeches, and Disraeli felt displeased as he saw a groom leading a horse. On this occasion, he had expected Inglefield to arrive in a carriage.

'Any news from Durham, sir?' asked Inglefield casually as he mounted. He was interested in a vacancy at the Cathedral, and had asked Disraeli to enquire further about it.

'None,' said Disraeli. 'But there's talk of Canon Elcho,' he added maliciously.

'Au revoir,' said Inglefield.

'Goodbye,' said Sarah.

She and her brother looked at each other as Inglefield on his broad-haunched hunter trotted off. They smiled faintly. It was another farewell.

At the reception in Berkeley Square, Disraeli approached his hostess and said, 'Has Stanley arrived?'

'No,' said Lady Jersey. 'He's very insouciant about everything but small matters. Is Lord George here?'

'No, Lady Jersey. He has gone to the country.'

Sitting at the head of the broad staircase on an ornate chair under a baldachin, with the statuesque air of the ornamental sculpture that lined the walls, she looked serene. Many Peelites had come at Stanley's invitation so that, as she planned, there might be a reconciliation over the champagne glasses which her footmen in scarlet livery were handing out. She was wearing her favourite collar of diamonds to emphasize the importance of the occasion.

'The sooner you take charge of these matters, Diz, the better,' she went on. 'I must talk to you soon about Francis and that woman Edmonds. I'm very distressed.'

She smiled as if she were discussing some radiant piece of good news, and those queueing behind Disraeli smiled too.

Disraeli bowed, and walked with Mary Anne into the saloon. At every step he was greeted by Members of Parliament and diplomats. Few of them knew of his bereavement; those like Smythe and Lord John Manners, who had learned of it when they called on him, pressed his hand and walked on. The two Whips, Charles Newdigate and William Beresford, deep in conversation, looked up as Disraeli passed.

'Sorry to hear of your father's illness,' said Newdigate.

'Mr Disraeli's father has just passed away,' said Mary Anne protectively.

'Ah!' said Newdigate. 'My condolences.'

He looked from Disraeli to the orchestra, playing waltzes in a bower, and from the musicians to the fashionable guests of Lady Jersey, a polychrome tableau that would change within a few minutes into a wholly different pattern.

Newdigate's 'Ah!' was like a reproach for an unseemliness, a censure of gaiety in the middle of mourning, and Disraeli's face hardened. For him the reception was a duty, not a diversion. Had he stayed away he would have been charged, even by those who knew of his bereavement, with an indifference to his responsibilities. He turned to Lord Manners, and bowed. Sir John and Lady Buller smiled to him and he gave them a nod. Mr Bankes nodded, and he replied with a smile. His task was to display his presence, to establish Lady Jersey's esteem of him, to greet the Peelites and show himself at Lord Stanley's side.

Proceeding through the rooms and listening to the oceanic roar of talk, he became silent. Then Mary Anne suddenly looked at his face, and her own voice faded. Disraeli was thinking of his father, a figure of stone on his death-bed. Amid the laughter he could hear the weeping of women as the bier was carried by farm labourers from the house to the church-yard, and see the distraught expression of James, whom he had never seen in tears since their boyhood.

His father had never been to Lady Jersey's house. He had never heard him speak in the Commons. And now he never would. A grave in Bradenham churchyard would contain his dust.

Mary Anne waved away the champagne offered by a footman.

At the other end of the room there was a stir and a swirl of greeting as Lord Stanley appeared, and simultaneously Disraeli said to his wife, 'My dear, I must leave.'

'Now – without speaking to Lord Stanley?'

'I must leave.'

She took his arm and Disraeli, followed by a number of enquiring glances, went slowly with her down the broad staircase to the *porte-cochère*.

The carriage took them the hundred yards to Grosvenor Gate, and Disraeli helped Mary Anne to the door.

'I'll be back soon,' he said.

'Oh, Diz,' said Mary Anne, 'you're – you're not returning to the reception without me?'

'No,' said Disraeli. 'I am not.'

He opened the carriage door and said to Blagden,

'Take me to Bevis Marks Place.'

'Where, sir?'

Disraeli repeated his instructions.

'Bevis Marks – in Hoxton – where the City ends.'

'The Jews' place, sir?'

'Yes,' said Disraeli. 'The Jews' place.'

Disraeli entered the synagogue, which lay in darkness except for a lamp lit above the Ark. At once the musty smell of velvet and prayer books revived the memories of the synagogue that he had attended as a boy before his father's dispute with the Elders and his own baptism into the Anglican Church in his thirteenth year. He stood looking at the pews, the stained-glass windows and the dimly visible tablets with Hebrew lettering on the walls.

There was the seat where he had sat with his father. And there was the draped gallery where he had looked up at Sarah and his mother.

'Sir?'

He heard the voice behind him, and started.

'Sir?' the voice of the beadle said again. Disraeli turned to see the small, bearded, friendly-eyed man wearing a silk hat and gabardine gown, and said,

'I've come to see your synagogue – and say a prayer for one who was a congregant.'

'He is dead, sir?'

'Yes – he is dead.'

The *shamus* led him to the light near the Ark, and gave him a Hebrew prayer-book, which he opened at the Sanctification.

Disraeli peered at the Hebrew lettering and tried to recall what he had once known, but the words were unfamiliar.

'*Yisgadal*,' said the beadle.

Disraeli repeated, '*Yisgadal* . . .'

'*V'Yiskadash* . . .'

'*V'Yiskadash* . . .'

'*Sh'mai Raboh* . . .'

'*Sh'mai Raboh* . . .'

'May the Lord's name be magnified and sanctified . . .'

In the penumbra of the eternal light, Disraeli and the beadle repeated in an antiphon the ancient prayer for the dead.

Chapter Eighteen

Lord Stanley stood at the window of his London house with his back to Lord George Bentinck. For a few moments he watched a horse caracoling as its rider tried to bring him under control, and then he turned to Bentinck who was sitting gloomily in a tapestried armchair, and said, 'I should have bought Surplice.'

Bentinck made a sound half-way between a groan and a sigh. At the Newmarket sale of his bloodstock, he had felt as if he had children who were being sold, one by one, into bondage.

'I wish you had,' he said. 'Those damned Cambridgeshire horse-thieves. Never mind – it's past.'

He stretched his legs and thrust his fingers stubbornly into his fob-pockets.

'I should have given him back to you, George, and made you start again.'

'Never. When I've made up my mind, I don't go back on it. You've known me long enough. After I decided to fight Peel, there was no more time for racing. And that was the end of it.'

Stanley leaned against the fireplace, and his aristocratic face, fringed with side-whiskers, was like an echo of his friend's.

'Why, then, did you throw it all over? You were the acknowledged leader of our Party in the Commons. Why the devil did you throw it all over by voting for the Jew Bill? You've nothing to do with those City Hebrews. You know very well, George, you've annoyed the country gentlemen – every one of those who went into the lobby with us against Peel. And now – '

He was beginning to get indignant, and the words tripped over each other.

'You've made yourself ridiculous by voting for Rothschild and Johnny. Good God, George, they all think you've gone mad. Forgive me, my dear fellow – to drop your followers and vote for our enemies!'

'Have you done?' asked Bentinck. He had known Stanley for many years and was tolerant of his bluntness, but he felt his own quick anger rising and wanted to dispose of Stanley's charge.

'I've no more to say.'

'Then let me tell you why I voted for the Jew Bill.'

He stood, and faced Stanley at the fireplace.

'You must know, Edward, I didn't go into politics to lead a party. I didn't sell my horses so's I could get cash to buy my votes with. In one sense, I've spent my life in politics – first at Canning's side and then as a silent Member without ambition; finally – well, I wanted to put Peel out.'

He tugged at the lapels of his morning coat.

'I voted with Disraeli, not out of any tenderness for the Jews –'

'Perhaps some commitment to Disraeli?'

'Not in that matter. We all have an obligation to Disraeli, you too.'

Stanley brushed the disagreeable thought away.

'Yes, you too. Without him, we couldn't have beaten Peel. You must acknowledge it. He sits night and day in the Chamber.'

'So do you.'

'I do, because Disraeli gives the example. It's why in the last year a vague opinion became a Party.'

'Then why did you both kick over the pail when it was full?'

Bentinck paused.

'Because – it's unfashionable to say this, Edward, and I intend it as no reproach – because there are principles more important even than a Party. I believe in religious emancipation. And I'm damned if I'll change my mind because of a coalition of bigots.'

Stanley tugged at the bell, and ordered the manservant to bring in the wine. He had observed that Bentinck's already plethoric face had become suffused, and he was anxious to restore their normal friendly mood. Bentinck drank claret and he drank champagne, and for a few minutes they spoke about farming, the early frosts, the prospects of lambing, the shortage of fodder and the benefit of an expanding railway system.

'You know George Hudson?' Stanley asked negligently.

'I've had some discussion with him. He had the foresight to recognize the value of the locomotive. He's a man of vision.'

'And paper.'

'What d'you mean?'

'I mean he's issuing too much paper – too many shares and bonds. There comes a moment when these things turn out to be a South Sea Bubble.'

'Railways?'

Bentinck was contemptuous.

'Railways are there. They enrich the lands they pass through. Hudson's a public benefactor.'

'Ah well, we'll see.'

Stanley poured another glass of claret from the decanter for Bentinck.

'I hear,' he said casually, 'that Hudson and Mrs Edmonds aren't so close as they were.'

'Really?' said Bentinck. 'I'd doubt if she'd let him go. Too much in it for her!'

He hesitated.

'Forgive me, Edward, if I tell you something in friendship.'

Stanley frowned and rose, and took a book from the table.

'No, don't tell me. I know what you have to say. Don't tell me. It would interfere with our friendship. There are times when a man doesn't want to know, or, if he knows, doesn't want to believe.'

'Well, let it be so,' said Bentinck.

As he left, Bentinck met Colonel Tankerton in the hall. The Colonel bowed, but Bentinck ignored him and hurried into the street.

Lord Stanley's relationship with Mrs Edmonds had developed since her visit to Knowsley Hall. He had called at her house in London and had been somewhat antagonized by the court that attended her, consisting of a few men he knew from the clubs, foreign aristocrats, Mr Hudson, a rather lonely and suppliant figure whom Mrs Edmonds seemed to be punishing for some misdemeanour, and Colonel Tankerton, whom he had met both as a not long elected Member of Parliament and as an owner at Newmarket. After the first visit, he decided not to return, and sent her a note saying that the occasions for talk in her drawing-room were so limited that he couldn't endure to be tantalized without being gratified. The reply, delivered by a liveried messenger, came at once. 'Six o'clock tomorrow-a-week.'

He had called, and there was no one present other than Mrs Edmonds. After half an hour, he had put his arm around her waist and she had smiled and rung for the maidservant and asked him to call again. He had returned, and had revelled in her beauty, her insolence, her familiarity with the world, her knowledge of men and politics. She spoke to him of her youth in Ireland and her life in India; of her marriage and life in Paris; she even spoke of her former acquaintance with the Polish revolutionaries; and Stanley listened to her absorbed. She asked nothing of him; their closest contact was when she gave him her fingertips to kiss. Each time he left her, though, he felt a vague dissatisfaction.

It wasn't that she had refused him. After his first call he had been content to enjoy her gaiety, his unfulfilled appetite, and a novel experience of competition. It was just that he felt for her a curious and rather shameful feeling which in other circumstances he would have called love. He knew that she had had protectors; or so it was said. Francis Villiers? She had laughed the idea to scorn when he had suggested it. Colonel Tankerton? 'My honorific manservant,' she had called him. Mr Hudson? A woman alone in the world required a protector. And then, it was rumoured, Disraeli had been her lover. That was the thought that irked Stanley most. Love. What could Disraeli know of love? When Stanley had hinted at it, Mrs Edmonds had denied any connection with him. She had even denounced him. Stanley was pleased, and wanted to please her.

He had gone so far as to agree at her suggestion to put Tankerton up for the Jockey Club.

'Mr Tankerton,' said the manservant, and Stanley looked up to see Tankerton standing in front of him immaculately dressed, his cravat tied with exaggerated care. Stanley wondered whether he should invite him to sit. Overcoming his distaste in his determination to be serviceable to Mrs Edmonds, he indicated a chair, and Tankerton spread his coat-tails over it.

'I'm obliged to you for receiving me, my lord. Mrs Edmonds was good enough to convey to me your very kind message that you would condescend to propose me for membership of the Jockey Club.'

Stanley grunted.

'I have, my lord, forty horses in training and another twenty coming on.'

Stanley grunted again. He was sorry Mrs Edmonds's smile had persuaded him to such an effort.

'I think,' he said, remembering that Tankerton was his guest, 'there's nothing more to add. I'll put your name in the book, sir – claret, brandy?'

'Brandy, my lord. But I fear there's a matter I ought to bring to your attention.'

'Does it affect your character?'

'No, my lord. The character of others who might in turn affect your proposal. You see, a couple of years ago I had some disagreement with Mr Disraeli.'

'I'm not concerned with Mr Disraeli.'

'No, my lord – no, of course not. The truth of the matter is that our falling-out was over a bet.'

'You mean Mr Disraeli refused to pay?'

Tankerton raised his hands helplessly as if to say, 'Naturally. What would you expect?'

'I was prepared to call him out, my lord – the incident happened at Deepdene in full view of a number of gentlemen – but Mr Disraeli was reluctant, and Lord George Bentinck, always chivalrous, intervened to assume his quarrel.'

'I heard something of this, but not in that form,' said Stanley.

'Well, my lord,' Tankerton hurried on. 'I didn't think that

justice or honour would be served by my shooting Lord George. I have been obliged in my life to fight two duels. I am in all modesty an excellent shot. I needn't say more than that I survived both.'

'I survived.' The words were ominous, and he paused.

Stanley disliked his tone, and said, 'What relevance has this, sir, to the Jockey Club?'

He knew the relevance, but wanted Tankerton to say it.

'The relevance, my lord, is that Lord George might seek to blackball me as a – a retort on Disraeli's behalf. Unless, that is to say, he is persuaded to the contrary.'

'What are you asking?' Stanley said, with repugnance at an unsought involvement in a squalid quarrel. He wanted to get rid of Tankerton, and was now doubly sorry that he had ever embarked on his nomination. He walked up and down the room as Tankerton followed him with his gaze.

'I'm asking you, my lord, to inform Lord George of your intention to nominate me and that you require an undertaking from him that he won't resist my application.'

'On what grounds?' asked Stanley, pausing with his mouth set.

'On the grounds,' said Tankerton, standing, 'that I hold here in my hand Mr Disraeli's letter to Sir Robert Peel – the letter he lied about to the House.' He bowed. 'I am prepared, my lord, to hand you this letter for its destruction or preservation as it may suit you, on the understanding that Lord George don't obstruct my candidature for the Jockey Club.'

Lord Stanley reflected briefly. Then he walked slowly towards Tankerton. Thinking that he was going to shake his hand in agreement, Tankerton put out his hand. Stanley ignored it, and rang the bell by the fireplace.

'But my lord – ' Tankerton began.

'Sir, you are not a gentleman,' said Stanley.

The manservant entered and bowed, and Tankerton, after a moment's hesitation, took his hat and stick from him and left rapidly.

Chapter Nineteen

The Duke of Portland sat in front of the fire, his knees covered with a plaid rug, his two spaniels and a red setter nestling against his legs. His sons, Lord George Bentinck, Lord Titchfield and Lord Henry Bentinck, stood around the old man in a subdued manner, waiting to identify his particular humour for the day so that they could adjust themselves to it.

It was unusual for them to present themselves together before the Duke at Welbeck Abbey. George Bentinck had been visiting Lord Manvers not far away at Thoresby, but Lord Henry spent most of his time in London, and Lord Titchfield, the eldest son, had in recent years developed into a recluse, never travelling except with the blinds of his carriage drawn, and constantly absorbed by the belief that if only everyone lived in grottoes, society would be more wholesome. Though he rarely spoke of this obsession, the word 'grotto' sometimes intruded irrelevantly into his conversation, a puzzling verbal surprise to those who didn't know him and felt they'd misheard, an engaging idiosyncrasy to his family and servants, who serenely ignored it.

The Duke dozed for a few moments and then continued with what he had been saying.

'Disraeli – Disraeli – what sort of man is that? He sounds a foreigner, George. Why d'you want to get mixed up with that sort of fellow?'

George Bentinck traced with his forefinger the grapes of the Grinling Gibbons carving on the fireplace. Of the three brothers, he had always been the one most at ease with his father, indulged by him even when in his youth he had raced a variety of horses under an assortment of different names to frustrate his father's ban on his racing at all. But that was long ago, and the Duke had been pleased when George had suddenly become a dedicated House of Commons man. If there was a flaw in the Duke's enthusiasm for his son's attention to politics, it was that from time to time he had received letters, some anonymous, suggesting that Disraeli's influence on his son was malevolent. He had summoned his three sons to Welbeck to discuss George's request that the family should lend or underwrite a loan of £25,000 to Disraeli.

In other circumstances he would have dismissed such an application as grotesque. But George had been insistent, and he wanted to discuss the matter in order to expose Disraeli's presumption.

'He isn't a foreigner,' said George. 'That's a canard put out by his enemies. In fact, his late father was a man of letters descended from a distinguished Spanish family settled in England for a hundred years.'

The Duke brushed the connection aside.

'Put a cuckoo in a nightingale's nest,' he said. 'Doesn't make him a nightingale. You ain't going to convince me, George, that your Disraeli's an Englishman. What's this money for – eh, eh, Titchfield? Some woman behind this? I know. I know. He's in trouble with some woman, I wager.'

His old eyes seemed to be searching into the past for a parallel to his son's request. Titchfield looked on the carpet to right and left of his father as if he was being pressed to find a solution to an irksome problem when he had much more urgent matters to deal with.

'I really don't know, Father. George says it's necessary to pay up to safeguard the farmers. What woman are you talking about, sir?'

He glanced at his father who was stroking the neck of the red setter.

'I wasn't talking of any woman,' said the Duke. 'Was I, Henry?'

Appealed to, Henry answered in his matter-of-fact voice, 'You were asking, sir, if George was being blackmailed, I take it. Are you, George? Or is it your friend who's being blackmailed?'

His brother flushed angrily.

'I am not being blackmailed. I'm not even being altruistic.

I believe Mr Disraeli is the most brilliant political orator in the House of Commons, and we need him as our representative. Damme – if we lose him, our cause will lack a voice.'

'Is it the right voice?' said the Duke. 'Eh? Eh? Is it the right voice?'

'It will be the right voice,' said Bentinck, 'if Mr Disraeli can himself speak as a landed proprietor. He needs the £25,000 to complete the purchase. It will make all the difference to his position in the Party.'

'Why the devil should the man need a thousand acres?'

'Why should we need thirty thousand?'

'Habit,' said Lord Henry. 'It's all a question of habit. We've had our land so long we'd feel lost if we didn't have it. But your Mr Disraeli would do better without it. He's a politician, not a landed proprietor. What's he got to do with Buckinghamshire? I can't bear these city gentry who've been buying up our countryside.'

'Grottoes,' said Titchfield to himself in a sepulchral voice.

'Eh, what's that?' asked the Duke.

'I said nothing,' Titchfield answered in surprise.

Lord Henry ignored him and went on, '£25,000 is an important sum. I don't hear good reports of Mr Disraeli's financial standing. Bills are all over the place – some of them in very strange hands.'

Lord George Bentinck rose to his feet, his moroseness turned to anger.

'I haven't come here to be quizzed, sir,' he said to his father. 'I know Disraeli. He's much abused – ' he shook his head – 'much maligned. If we are unable to accommodate him, then I will seek to do so out of my own means.'

'Oh, stuff!' said the Duke. 'You mustn't be so choleric, George – bad for your health. Order me a hock and seltzer.' He put his hand to his chest. 'Those physicians – ! Ah!'

Lord Henry summoned a servant, and Titchfield walked about the room, surreptitiously feeling the brocade of the curtains to see if someone might be spying on their conversation.

247

'I hear, Father,' he said, 'there've been a number of strangers in this locality.'

'Vagrants,' said the Duke. 'We'll have to get the justices to clear them out. Irishmen, no doubt.'

'The price of corn fell again yesterday,' said Titchfield. 'I see little hope of improvement. Beggary for some, I imagine.'

'I've asked Mr Rose to present a proposal, sir, for the loan,' said Lord George.

'Who the devil's he?' asked the Duke, raising his hock to his lips with both hands.

'Mr Rose of Baxter, Rose and Norton, Mr Disraeli's solicitors – he's waiting outside.'

'The deuce he is,' said the Duke angrily. 'Who asked him?'

'I did,' said Bentinck. 'I thought it right for you to hear the facts. Mr Rose, I ought to tell you, is also solicitor to the Duke of Buckingham.'

'Scarcely a recommendation!' said the Duke. 'If he'd advised him properly, he wouldn't have gone bankrupt. I'm sorry you took it on yourself, sir, to invite a *solicitor* to call.'

He spoke the word 'solicitor' with a slight pause before it to emphasize his low estimate of such a profession.

'Very well,' said his son, standing. 'I will ask him to leave, and I will leave with him.'

'Don't threaten me, sir,' said the Duke. 'Why the devil are you determined to make me ill? Henry, pass me the brandy.'

The Duke drank hurriedly.

'Why should you expect me to approve of giving Mr Disraeli £25,000 without any discussion at all?'

'I'm discussing it with you, sir.'

'No, you're not. You arrive, make a demand, and then you have the outrageous impertinence to threaten me with a Jew-lawyer.'

'I'm not threatening you. Mr Rose is a respected Christian lawyer, a Buckinghamshire gentleman of the same county as Mr Disraeli, acting among his other interests for the Church Commissioners. Not that it makes him a better lawyer. I've come to urge you in the interest of our Party and our class to assist Mr Disraeli to acquire a stake in the land. Don't you agree, Titchfield?'

Lord Titchfield, who had been sitting with his eyes half-closed, said, 'Yes, of course. Most reasonable. Yes,' he added to himself. 'Grottoes.'

The Duke pulled his rug around him, and grunted.

'Don't quarrel with me, George. Bring him in.'

Bentinck went outside and returned with a fat, middle-aged man, bald-headed but with bushy eyebrows and wearing spectacles. He bowed to the Duke and to Bentinck's brothers, and remained standing, holding his folio in his hand.

'Well, sir,' said the Duke, 'I understand you represent Mr Disraeli.'

'I do, Your Grace,' said Rose in his lawyer's voice. 'Perhaps, Your Grace, I may introduce myself and offer you my credentials. I am Mr Philip Rose of Baxter, Rose and Norton.'

The Duke looked into the fireplace and made no comment.

'Perhaps, Your Grace, it might be for your convenience if I sat.'

The Duke motioned with one finger to a chair which Rose took calmly. He felt warm after his journey, but since no one offered him any refreshment, he merely looked at the champagne and the decanters, sighed, and turned to his duties.

'Mr Disraeli, Your Grace, proposes to buy Hughenden Manor, an extensive property of some seven hundred and fifty acres to the north of High Wycombe, belonging to the Norris family and now put on the market by his executor.'

'What are the rents?' asked the Duke grumpily.

'About a pound an acre, Your Grace,' said the solicitor, referring to his papers. 'About seven hundred and fifty pounds per annum . . . If I may be permitted to say so, it is a desirable property, and the going price of £35,000 is by no means excessive.'

'I suppose, sir, your client lacks the cash.'

'That is so.'

'Then how the devil does he expect to buy it?'

Rose wiped his mouth with a large handkerchief that he drew from an inside pocket.

'To answer that question, Your Grace, is the object of my visit. Mr Disraeli has given the executors a deposit of ten thousand. Lord George Bentinck – ' he bowed – 'Lord Titchfield – ' he bowed – 'and Lord Henry Bentinck have agreed in principle, but subject to Your Grace's approval, to provide the balance.'

'Oh – oh! Indeed!'

The Duke's pallid complexion reddened.

'Oh – oh! Indeed!' he repeated. 'Has Mr Disraeli no other resources? Thought he married an heiress. That was the talk.'

'Mrs Disraeli, Your Grace, is, of course, a lady of means. But – ' Rose smiled indulgently – 'there are certain gentlemen who have a rooted and, if I may say so, an honourable objection to a dependance, however willing, on the side of the other party. Mr Disraeli would not wish to borrow from his wife.'

'But is the man reliable?'

The Duke frowned, and Mr Rose bowed stiffly.

'The confidence, Your Grace, of those who recommend him to you is the measure of his reliability.'

'What would you say, Mr Rose, to garnisheeing the rents?' said Lord Henry in a businesslike voice.

Rose shook his head.

'That, Lord Henry, would be like securing a loan to a servant by deducting weekly a portion of his wages. Mr Disraeli would never agree. Mr Disraeli's a very proud man. I believe he will rather resign his seat than agree to so humiliating a procedure – if I may say so with great respect.'

'Well, he can't have the money for nothing. What's the pledge?' the Duke burst in irascibly. 'If we lend him the money, we should have a mortgage on the property.'

'Oh, Heaven forbid, Your Grace,' said Rose. 'Heaven forbid!' It was a theological invocation that made the Duke slump in his chair. 'You see, Mr Disraeli's a very proud man. He would never live in a mortgaged house. It would be rather like expecting him to live in a labourer's cottage tied to an estate from which he could be evicted at will. That would never do. Oh no, Your Grace, with deep respect – ' he bowed again – 'I couldn't even convey such a suggestion to Mr Disraeli. Perhaps I may be excused – '

He stood with a hurt expression on his face.

'Give Mr Rose a glass of port,' said the Duke to Lord Henry. Rose glanced quickly at Lord George, who turned his back and looked out of the window. He was enraged with his father, Disraeli, Rose and himself that he had to take part in such a humiliating business. The effort of self-control distressed him, and he wanted it to be over.

'Very well,' said the Duke suddenly, as if he had made a decision. 'We'll lend Mr Disraeli £25,000. You'll draw up the papers, sir, in conjunction with my lawyers. Mr Disraeli shall have the money – on recall at three months.'

'Six months,' Rose murmured.

'Three months,' said the Duke.

'Six months, Your Grace,' said Rose. 'In the event that Mr Disraeli couldn't repay the sum on call, he would naturally need a little time – '

'A little time not to pay,' said Titchfield in a bright voice. He looked around mysteriously. 'Father, I am required.'

He bowed to the Duke, and retreated through a side door. The Duke engaged his other two sons in conversation, and Rose went to the window and saw Lord Titchfield enter his closed carriage, pull down the blinds with a clack, and depart with his elderly coachman at top speed.

When Lord George Bentinck left his father's house for Knowsley, he decided that he would take the footpath across the fields. It was a sunny day, and he took an ash walking-stick for the two-hour walk. He was glad that the Disraeli business was now settled. It had been hard to explain to his father that the object of helping Disraeli to buy Hughenden Manor was political, but in the end, perhaps through weariness, his father had yielded.

As Bentinck walked, he thought of the curious changes that had changed and might still change his life, of his conflicts and lawsuits on the turf, his first race at Goodwood when he

251

himself had twice ridden a dead heat. The Member for Lynn. All those passive years in Parliament.

A horse in a field trotted away as he approached. The Oaks, the Thousand Guineas, the Two Thousand Guineas. He'd won them all – everything except the Derby. But he had deliberately and consciously thrown that chance away when he sold his stud. £10,000. A fraction of what they were worth.

He panted as he climbed over a stile. He was forty-six. Neither very old nor young. But he had done everything he had wanted to do. He had served in the Hussars, played every game, taken every risk, and as a youth had been in love. But that was long ago. He was shy with women. What he liked was the struggle of men.

When his father died, his brother Titchfield would be the heir. But he in turn was ailing. Grottoes and drawn blinds. Bentinck slashed at the hawthorn with his walking-stick. If his brother died, he would be the Duke of Portland, a prospect that he neither relished nor rejected. He would enter the House of Lords and be separated from his friends in the Commons.

Disraeli. He crossed the stones over a ford at the bottom of the valley, and felt that he wanted to see him as soon as possible. He wrote to him regularly when he was away, long letters about politics that were, in a sense, letters of affection. Three lines of statistics were a declaration of love which he could never express to his friend in any other form. Since they had walked together arm-in-arm from the billiard room at Deepdene after Tankerton's insult to Disraeli, he had felt himself committed to him in friendship. And yet, it was Disraeli who took the initiative in public affairs, Disraeli who made the decisions. 'We've had enough of leaders. I hope to remain the last of the rank and file.' That's what he had said to Stanley, and that's how he felt in relation to Disraeli.

He was sweating, and he removed his hat and put his fingers to his forehead. A light breeze was blowing from the south, and he felt better, but his forehead was cold and he put his hat on again and leant against a tree. He could see the abbey with its crenellated towers, and half-regretted that he hadn't taken the carriage after all. He smiled. Forty-six. Ten years ago he could have run the distance. The sun troubled his vision and he pressed his hat over his eyes as he set off again up the hill rising slowly to Thoresby.

He wished he hadn't drunk champagne at his father's house. He felt a pain like indigestion rising into his chest and running through his mouth into his arm. He paused again, listening to his sullen heartbeat. So he had sometimes felt as a boy after a foot-race, gasping for breath till his heart recovered its rhythm.

But this pain wouldn't go away. It was insistent like a vice clasped around his chest. Perhaps he was ill. That, too, seemed curious, because he had never known illness. He put his hand again to his head, and it was clammy. He looked towards the abbey, and it seemed to have receded. Bentinck dropped his stick and walked as far as a stile. He had spoken harshly to his father. That had upset him. Disraeli would have Hughenden, and he was glad. The pain was unrelenting and would never end.

Bentinck's knees sagged and he clung to the stile till his fingers uncurled and he lay by the footpath as if asleep, while his hat rolled into the thick grass.

Chapter Twenty

Mary Anne held up the embroidery frame to the light and examined the blue D she was stitching on to a footstool cover. Her husband was in his study on the top floor of Grosvenor Gate, and she was glad that she had a few hours of leisure to complete the tapestry she intended to surprise him with.

When the maid announced, 'Mrs Edmonds,' she put her work on the table. It was three o'clock, an hour when she never received visitors, and she looked with a slight displeasure at some tumbled cushions on the sofa. She couldn't understand why Mrs Edmonds was calling. Disraeli, she knew, had some reason for a lack of sympathy towards her. On the other hand, Mrs Edmonds was a friend of Lord Stanley, and she could scarcely refuse to receive her without offending him. If only Diz were there to give her some guidance! The maid waited, and Mary Anne said, 'Show Mrs Edmonds in.'

She went to the drawing-room door, and her chilliness was at once dissolved by Mrs Edmonds's warm smile; the moiré green silk of her dress whispered as she walked, her black curls beneath a fashionable pink bonnet trembled like bells. Mary Anne smiled back at her, almost embraced her, but instead pressed her hand, and invited her to the alcove overlooking Park Lane.

'You must forgive me,' said Mrs Edmonds serenely as she removed her gloves. 'It's such an inopportune time to call.'

'No, no,' said Mary Anne. 'I always feel elated when I see you – the sun always seems to be shining around you. You look so pretty against the red wallpaper.'

'Ah,' said Mrs Edmonds, 'I have known the shadows, alas, too often. When I lost my husband in the Polish rising – they were terrible days. If you only knew, Mrs Disraeli! We were living in Paris at the Hôtel Lambert. Our friends had been scattered in the insurrection. What an eternity! But they came

together in Paris. The rector of Vilna University – Czartorynski
that wonderful man with his white whiskers!'

Her eyes became radiant at the memory.

'He lived at our hotel – Krasninski, Mickiewicz – they were
all there. And then my husband – the Count – volunteered,
three years later, to return. He died gloriously in the uprising –
sabred by the Tsar's Cossacks.'

Mary Anne took her hand.

'Pray don't speak of it. One must try to dedicate one's self
to the future. What a strange, haphazard lottery is life!'

'Death! So indiscriminate!'

Mrs Edmonds's voice fell.

'I felt I had to come and offer you and Mr Disraeli my
condolences on the loss of his friend. Lord George was such a
noble and chivalrous person.'

Mary Anne's eyes filled with tears.

'My poor husband! He was beside himself with grief. You
can't imagine how afflicted he was and still is. Lord George
and he – they were more like brothers. They were like David
and – who was it?'

'Jonathan,' suggested Mrs Edmonds.

'Yes, that's it, David and Jonathan. We were together when
Mr Disraeli received the telegram. I do so detest telegrams,
don't you? Never any good news. At any rate, Diz opened it
and went as white as a sheet. He faltered, and I helped him to
sit. Poor Diz! He wept.'

'Very sad,' said Mrs Edmonds. 'Poor Mr Disraeli! He's very
sensitive. But happily, he recovers quickly. I've no doubt we
will soon see him in society again.'

The maidservant brought in a tray, and Mary Anne poured
out two cups of tea from the elaborate silver teapot.

'Yes, of course,' she said. 'The world must go on. There's
so much for him to do in Parliament. Now that poor Lord
George has gone there'll be much more claim on Diz's time.
And then there's the estate – '

'The estate?'

'Yes, you could scarcely know, dear Mrs Edmonds. Our
new estate, Hughenden Manor. It's in the most beautiful

position in his new constituency in Bucks – quite near his old family home at Bradenham. I trust you'll visit us. I have so many plans. I want to reconstruct the façade, and make it look rather more Gothic. Stucco is too eighteenth-century, don't you think?'

'Yes,' said Mrs Edmonds absently. Her smiling expression had become reflective. 'Yes. Everything's Gothic nowadays. Even our new House of Commons.'

'So much more noble,' said Mary Anne. 'So much more romantic! Dizzy tells me the Stuarts and their ladies used to dance on the lawns beyond the terrace.'

'Most moving!' said Mrs Edmonds. 'I trust that you will be very happy in your new estate. After all, Mr Disraeli is the natural successor to Lord George as the leader of the Party in the Commons. Lord Stanley was saying so only the other day.'

'Yes,' said Mary Anne thoughtfully. She was about to tell Mrs Edmonds that there was to be a further meeting of the Party to discuss the leadership that very day, but an unaccustomed prudence held her back.

'Mind you,' said Mrs Edmonds, 'there's much jealousy of your husband.'

'Yes, yes, much jealousy.'

'When he comes into a room, the others seem to get smaller.'

'So I've often thought.'

'But it isn't always the finest intellect that wins the greatest prizes.'

'That's true.'

Mary Anne was feeling increasingly uneasy, and wished more than ever that Disraeli would join them. Mrs Edmonds seemed to be thinking of something other than the words she spoke.

There was a long silence, and Mary Anne said, 'And how is your daughter – the one we met seven years ago in Paris? She looked so beautiful skating at your side. She must be a young lady by now.'

'Yes,' said Mrs Edmonds. 'She is a young woman. She's at La Roseraie in Switzerland, finishing her education. My dear Mrs Disraeli, you can scarcely imagine the cost of maintaining an establishment in London, providing for a daughter –

ensuring her place in society. It's very hard to be a woman alone.'

'That was my own fate. But briefly. I had the great happiness to meet my Disraeli. Oh, Mrs Edmonds! The happiness it has given me! Ten years of joy. Everyone tried to discourage me. Mrs Bulwer – you know her – she's living in Cheltenham or Taunton, embittered and alone – some people can't endure the spectacle of other people's happiness – she said to me, "My dear Mary Anne, you're twelve years older than Mr Disraeli. It's absurd." And I said to her, "Where love is, Rosina, age is no separation. In the years we'll be together, there'll be nothing but pure joy." And that's how it has been. Will you take more tea, Mrs Edmonds?'

'I think not. I cannot stay long.'

Mary Anne smiled. She liked Mrs Edmonds's pretty, dimpling face even more now that she was leaving.

'Won't you wait to see Mr Disraeli?'

'No. My purpose was to see you. There are matters I wanted to speak to you about.'

Mary Anne picked up her embroidery. Mrs Edmonds's voice suddenly made her feel menaced.

'You see,' said Mrs Edmonds, 'I have your husband's interests greatly at heart. There was a time I knew him very well.'

Mary Anne began to stitch rapidly.

'I shouldn't like to see any obstacle to his leading the Party. Unfortunately – I am sorry to tell you this – his letter to the former Prime Minister has fallen into hostile hands.'

'Which letter?' Mary Anne asked in a weak voice. She felt as if an incubus had suddenly gripped her and destroyed her happiness.

'The letter Mr Disraeli denied in Parliament he ever wrote,' said Mrs Edmonds firmly. 'You must know the one.'

'What – what do you suggest?'

'Nothing at all. I merely felt that I should warn you.'

'In whose hands has it fallen?'

'I fear – I'm sorry – I couldn't betray a confidence – though in friendship I would tell Mr Disraeli if I thought he was in imminent danger.'

'May I not tell him now?'

'Not yet, my dear Mrs Disraeli. I see no point in distressing him prematurely.'

She rose to go, and Mary Anne painfully with her.

'If there were any likelihood of a change of administration,' said Mrs Edmonds, 'Mr Disraeli would have to reclaim the letter. The Queen would scarcely consider a Minister – ah, well, it's not urgent.'

She moved to the door.

'Be sure, Mrs Disraeli – may I address you as Mary Anne? – I fear I've been excessively formal – I will be careful of Mr Disraeli's interests. And by the way, there is one other matter. Some time ago I discounted a bill of Mr Disraeli's which he gave Mr Crockford some years ago. On Count D'Orsay's behalf. Naturally, I wanted to help a friend when his creditors were pressing.'

'Was that your only consideration?' Mary Anne burst out. Now she saw Mrs Edmonds as an enemy, and she threw away her restraint.

Mrs Edmonds's face had flushed a little, and she was feeling triumphant.

'I only want to tell you that Mr Disraeli will by next Tuesday owe me £9,230. I am sure now that Mr Disraeli's a landed proprietor he'll have no difficulty in finding that sum.'

Mary Anne rose and picked up her embroidery in agitation.

'I must tell you,' she said, 'Mr Disraeli isn't in a position to pay that sum. Hughenden is mortgaged.'

'In that case,' said Mrs Edmonds in a clipped voice, 'I must take what action is open to me to recover my debt.'

Mary Anne went over to her quickly and said, 'I beg you, Mrs Edmonds, do not be precipitate. At this moment – you know that this is a vital time in my husband's career. The Party –'

'I am not concerned with the Party,' said Mrs Edmonds. 'Mr Disraeli has incurred a debt. I want it paid.'

'If I myself pay you all the accumulated interest,' said Mary

Anne, 'will you extend the bill for another year – the last quarter day of 1850?'

Mrs Edmonds said, 'What reason have I to do so?'

'The fact,' said Mary Anne simply, 'that you will be paid the money, and you will postpone your other opportunities of – redress.'

Mrs Edmonds hesitated, and then said, 'I need at least three thousand by tomorrow.'

She doubted whether Mary Anne could find the sum.

'I will pay it,' said Mary Anne. She pulled the bell and the maid entered. Mrs Edmonds left with a frou-frou of her skirts. Mary Anne sat herself by the teacups that trembled as a heavy dray passed in the street outside.

As soon as Disraeli entered the room he saw from the way that Mary Anne kept her head lowered that she was distressed. He went over to her and kissed her cheek, but she still didn't look up.

'And how is your embroidery?' he asked.

'My embroidery is excellent,' she said. Then she fell silent again, and Disraeli took up a copy of *The Times*.

'I'd like you to read my article on "The Prospect of Reform",' he said. 'Lord Sutton admired it greatly.'

'I am very pleased,' said Mary Anne. Suddenly she exclaimed, 'Oh, Ben, that woman Mrs Edmonds has been here.'

'Mrs Edmonds!' said Disraeli, startled.

'Yes, she came to express her condolences about Lord George.'

'George detested her. He regarded her as the most dangerous woman in London. What else did she want?'

Mary Anne moved away from him.

'She wanted to ruin my happiness. She spoke of your letter to Peel – '

Disraeli frowned, and said, 'You mustn't be distressed, Mary Anne. There's some sort of intrigue to revive that story. I will deal with it. What else?'

'She says she's bought your bill.'

Disraeli brushed the lock from his forehead with his fingers.

'Which bill?'

'The Crockford bill. The one that Lawson had. It's over nine thousand. Why didn't you tell me, Ben? What relationship did you have with her?'

Mary Anne sat in an armchair, her face set. Disraeli contemplated her for a moment and then walked to her and touched the back of her lace cap.

'She wanted to ruin your happiness,' he said. 'She has been conspiring with Tankerton to injure me. You mustn't permit it, Mary Anne. You mustn't allow her mischief. Hudson has abandoned her. Stanley refuses to see her because she tried to use him to promote Tankerton's interest.'

He sat at her side and took her hands in his.

'You must trust me, Mary Anne.'

'Must I?'

'Yes.'

She smiled to him slowly.

'Oh, Ben! Such a lot of money! Why should she have bought up your bill? Was it because she loved you?'

Disraeli didn't answer for a few moments.

'Dearest Mary Anne,' he said at last. 'I must tell you all.'

'All?' she asked sceptically.

'Yes, all. Clarissa Edmonds and Tankerton have chosen this moment when the leadership of the Party – perhaps the next Ministry – has to be decided in order to seek to destroy me.'

'You must buy back the bill – the letter.'

'I won't yield to extortionists.'

She shook her head.

'Sometimes you must.'

'I never will – never. I will behave as if Mrs Edmonds and Tankerton don't exist.'

'But you'll consult Mr Rose. He understands these things,' she said sagely.

'Naturally,' he said. 'Let's have a game of backgammon.'

'Dear Ben,' said Mary Anne, reaching out for the table. 'You always count on something turning up.'

The Party meeting wasn't due to begin till six o'clock, and

Disraeli decided to go to the House of Commons on foot, taking his favourite route through St James's Park, where he liked during the session to watch the changing of the seasons as the bare trees budded, blossomed, greened, and at last became russet. He walked with his hat well over his eyes, unwilling to be recognized.

After a long period without a formal leader, the Protectionist Tories were now determined to find a successor to Lord George. Even Stanley had been obliged to swallow his objections to him. There are some insults which lose their impact with time, simply because, like an often repeated jest, they become a bore. So it had been with the litany of abuse Disraeli had endured since he first appeared in London society. Jew-boy, *arriviste*, coxcomb, plagiarist, adventurer – he had survived them all by patience and endurance. Early in his parliamentary life he had vindicated his courage by challenging Daniel O'Connell and his son Morgan to a duel when the father had described him as a 'lineal descendant of the thief on the Cross'. Yes, it had been a gross affront that only a challenge to fight could ease. Since that time his enemies had been careful. They said the same things, but in whispers. Even Tankerton at Deepdene hadn't thought himself overheard. In debate, Disraeli now had no peer unless it was Gladstone, the sombre but eloquent Peelite who seemed to recoil from everything that Disraeli represented and enjoyed. But he was a determined Free Trader and certainly no threat to Disraeli in the Tory Party.

Leaning on his cane, Disraeli paused to look at a strutting mallard. The proud walk, the upright stance, the sharp quack, the darting eye reminded him of Mr Herries, and he smiled to himself. How many men were ornamented by office? How many brought their own decoration? How familiar his own alien name had become in the mouths of the squires and the Whig and Tory aristocrats! His title of aristocracy was longer and in some respects more legitimate than theirs. Yet his struggle to affirm it was a daily one that didn't rely on letters patent or investiture. If he and Mary Anne had had children! – he tapped his stick against the railings lining the path. Perhaps

261

it was well that they hadn't. All his life had been a dedication to the romance of his own life. Was that a selfish pursuit? He had to admit that it was. Was it an unworthy one? Most certainly not. He saw his face and figure reflected in the quiet lake, saturnine and slim. The image pleased him, and he stood regarding himself till a light breeze ruffled his forehead into a frown.

Tankerton and Mrs Edmonds. He would have to deal with them both in time, but for the moment he had to face the Party. A clock at the Horse Guards chimed the half-hour, and he moved across the grass under the elm trees in the direction of Parliament Square.

A policeman in New Palace Yard saluted him, and Disraeli raised his cane in greeting. Already the carriages and cabs were queueing, some to deposit Members, others to await them. A groom at the mounting-block was helping an elderly Member from his horse, and there was a festival air of coming and going which Disraeli always associated with great events in Parliament.

He was hot from his walk, and was preparing to slip quietly into the cathedral-like loneliness of Westminster Hall on his way to Committee Room 14 when he heard his name called by Mr Huffam. At any other time he would have wanted to hurry on, but Mr Huffam could be a nuisance or an advantage at the Party meeting, and Disraeli decided to suppress his ill-humour.

'So we're going to have a new leader,' said Mr Huffam, wiping the sweat from his hat-band.

'No doubt,' said Disraeli. 'In the course of time.'

'It's a happy arrangement in our Party,' said Huffam, trotting at Disraeli's side, 'that our men emerge and are not chosen.'

'Indeed,' said Disraeli.

'Lord Stanley has, no doubt, taken soundings?'

'Do you ask me, Mr Huffam?'

'Yes and no,' said Huffam. 'His lordship has canvassed opinion among the country gentlemen and has, I believe, come to a conclusion. May I congratulate you, sir?'

Disraeli didn't answer. Huffam looked cunning.

'We still need our cry,' he went on. 'Protection is still the soundest cry of all.'

'Protection, sir, is dead and damned,' said Disraeli in a conversational tone. 'Killed by our mid-century prosperity.'

'I beg your pardon,' said Huffam, pausing on the flagstones at the steps facing the great stained-glass window. It was as if someone had uttered a blasphemy at Mass. 'Did I hear you aright, sir?'

Disraeli turned to three young Tory Members following behind him, and raised his hat. They greeted him deferentially.

'On these stairs,' he said, 'King Charles I stood trial and was condemned to death. How fortunate we had our revolution and civil war two hundred years ago!'

They smiled, and escorted him to the Committee Room floor.

Mr Huffam, shaking his head, went before them, spreading the story that Disraeli had said Protection was 'dead and damned'. No one in the already packed Committee Room believed him, and when Disraeli entered with his phalanx, which had steadily grown during his progress through the nave of St Stephen's Hall and over the tessellated floor of the Central Lobby, the applause that greeted him was an acclamation for the man who, everyone already felt, must one day become Leader of the Party.

Chapter Twenty-one

From Benjamin Disraeli, Esq., to Miss Sarah Disraeli.
Hughenden Manor,
October 10, 1849

Dearest Sa,

I am happy that you are established in Twickenham. I only wish you'd visit us more often at Grosvenor Gate, where your welcome is assured by Mary Anne, despite your misunderstanding with her last summer about her flowered bonnet.

To turn from bonnets to more cosmic matters, we are only now beginning to see the shape of a new era that began last year. The guv'nor dead! Bentinck so soon to follow!

But in public as in private affairs, the law is 'Change'. Last year's masters of Europe have been packed out of their palaces and despatched to the boarding-houses of Kensington. M. Guizot, once ablaze with decorations, turns up in Pimlico or some such place. M. Metternich, who made Europe tremble, sits meekly in Mayfair, talking with me as one political philosopher to another.

I went to see King Louis Philippe at Claremont, and his misfortunes are a moral tale which in a Biblical age might well have been included in the canon next to the Book of Job. Imagine a monarch expelled by a mob from the Tuileries, escaping in the humiliating disguise of an English tourist, and finally held semi-incommunicado by Lord Palmerston. (Our Foreign Secretary, who interferes with everyone else abroad, is terrified of interference at home!)

But we can only live as we know how, and Louis Philippe has now made some sort of a court at Claremont. At any rate, he greeted me in the usual circle of his courtiers-in-exile as an old friend. Then he took me into an ill-furnished bedroom, sat me down, and for an hour told me the whole story of his downfall. It was the story of Philippe Égalité, once again destroyed in the person of his son by the *canaille*. At the end of the audience, the poor old man went into positive hysterics, and I had to send for sal volatile to revive him. I'm told the Queen and the Prince Consort have seen him, but secretly in order not to offend Palmerston.

After I left, I heard him giving orders to a chamberlain with no means of carrying them out, and sending for papers he couldn't possibly get since they were burnt in the Tuileries.

The Paris Rothschilds, I hear from Baron Lionel, got a fright over his downfall, but with characteristic prudence Baron James hedged his bets. While other bankers were being ushered to the lamp-posts, Baron James wisely made a substantial distribution for the relief of the victims of the insurrection and escaped the fate of his confrères. He also, I gather, now serves Prince Louis Napoleon with the same diligence as he did the luckless king.

You asked me about Count D'Orsay. Our friend has been living in Paris for some time. After the glory of Gore House ended, the Count, with the pack of creditors at his heels, took refuge there in some *mansarde* he calls his studio. Since Lady B. died he has been ill and almost destitute, and I hear reports that he's sadly changed. Alcibiades has, alas, turned into Hephaistos. The gout, or some still more painful disease, confines him to his couch. But in all that sorrow, Prince Louis Napoleon has given him – or is about to give him – a well-rewarded post at the Beaux-Arts. That is both justice and gratitude, and almost restores my faith in princes.

Unintentionally, poor D'Orsay has left me with a heavy burden. A bill I signed for him ten years ago or more to pay some of his gaming debts at Crockford's still hangs from my neck like a bloated albatross that swells with each quarter's interest. Distressingly, it has fallen into the hands of an unscrupulous blackmailer. All that by the way!

Now let me turn to happier times. As *de facto* leader of

the Party in the Commons, I am like the rider of a restive horse being prepared for a race. The horse doesn't want him. The owner doesn't want him. The trouble is no one else can ride the beast. Tho' from time to time in the last year or so I've offered to dismount and unsaddle, there's always an immediate outcry when I do so. You would think that never has a party leader been so needed as your humble servant.

Most ambiguous of all the protesters when it comes to resignation is our Zeus in the Lords. You'll recall, dear Sarah, how reluctantly Stanley embraced the first proposals after Bentinck resigned that I shd lead the Party in the Commons; and how he offered me the humiliating alternative of becoming a sort of valet to Granby. Now he regards me as the leader *sans pareil*.

I can't say his intimacy with me has grown in the meantime. Our relations are correct and formal. But times have changed, and me with them. He knows it, especially since the death of the ever-lamented George Bentinck, whose biography, incidentally, I am now engaged in writing. Contrary to what I believed when we fought Peel on the issue of Protection, our agriculture has been bruised but certainly not ruined by the end of the Corn Laws. Free trade has unquestionably profited the manufacturers. For us, the Tories, to seek the suffrage of the country with the cry of 'Protection!' would be to court an electoral disaster.

And so I am at present engaged in a battle on two fronts – against the Liberals and Whigs and Rads with their pernicious policies that are dragging us into war with Russia and all sorts of anti-Popery nonsense; and against those in our own Party who want to tie us to the mouldering corpse of Protection.

In case you think I have deserted my friends, let me tell you that what I now want for the agricultural interest is compensation, a subsidy or some tax relief for what Free Trade may have cost them.

I do not doubt that before long – a year, eighteen months,

two years – the Queen will have to send for Stanley to ask him to put our fortunes to the trial. Johnny has had too many close shaves in the lobbies lately. Unhappily our leader lacks confidence in himself as well as in his troops. If there's a change of government, would you like your brother to be Foreign Secretary or Home Secretary? A word from you, dearest Sa, will decide the composition of the next Tory Government, whose potential members have dwelt too long in the tents of the Philistines!

Your most devoted and affectionate,

Ben

From Miss Sarah Disraeli to Benjamin Disraeli, Esq.

The Villa,
Twickenham
November 1, 1849

Dearest Ben,

Your letter, after a long silence which I understand, gave me great pleasure. You have so many obligations, so many correspondents in connection with your duties, that I can only express my joy at what must be a self-denial in my interest. I thought many sad and happy thoughts in reading your letter. How I wish that our parents were still alive to acclaim the position you now command!

Envy, malice and prejudice were the wicked fairies at your political birth. But your own genius has defied and cowed them. Whether you in time to come are Home Secretary or Foreign Secretary in a new administration, I'm sure that thereafter nothing will content you till you are Prime Minister. Do I sound like Lady Macbeth? I hasten to add that I wish no ill to your leader in the Lords, even if he spends more time with horses, billiards and whist than with politics.

Mary Anne, you may know, was good enough to write to me separately. She also offered to introduce me to a milliner so that I could be suitably hatted. I can understand her interest in bonnets, but I trust she won't take it amiss if I tell you I lack the *occasion* for wearing fashionable hats, and therefore, while thanking her for her kindness, must decline.

I subscribe this letter,
Your ever loving sister,
Sa

Post-Scriptum. If there's a new administration, I think you should be Foreign Secretary rather than Home Secretary.

S.

Chapter Twenty-two

As Disraeli drove through the Regent's Park in his open carriage, he observed with pleasure the crowds strolling through the shrubberies and rose walks. The debate in which he had joined with Sir Robert Peel in speaking and voting against Palmerston's blockade of the Piræus, ostensibly on behalf of the disreputable but mistreated Don Pacifico who claimed British nationality, had lasted through the night. He had slept little, still savouring Palmerston's affirmation of Britain's duty to cast her shield over every British subject, wherever or whoever he might be. *Civis Romanus sum. Civis Britannicus sum.* Disraeli rejected the doctrine, but he liked the theme.

The sun had brought out large numbers of equipages, and Disraeli huddled in the back of his carriage in order not to be distracted by too many salutations. Blagden knew better than to whistle when he drove his master, and the only sound the coachman made was an occasional flick of his beribboned whip.

In the daylight, the night's debate under the sombre gas-lamps seemed like a remembered Grand Opera. For at least four hours, perhaps more, Palmerston had spoken with scarcely an interruption. Peel and Russell had dozed from time to time. But such was the sweep of Palmerston's eloquence that there were always rows of backbenchers to cheer him on, and a relay of those refreshed by a nap to sustain him in the attention of the House.

Disraeli hadn't always admired Palmerston. Long ago in his Runnymede Letters he had written that Palmerston reminded him of 'a favourite footman on easy terms with his mistress'. Then he had spoken of him as the 'Sporus of politics, cajoling France with an airy compliment and menacing Russia with a perfumed cane'. A perfumed cane. Disraeli liked the phrase

269

and savoured it in his mind. But it no longer applied. The courtly Palmerston had exchanged the cane for the gunboat.

All that was far away. Death in Canton. The blazing ware-houses of the Piræus. Here in the Regent's Park the promen-aders had the contented air of citizens of an imperial city, sauntering at their ease within their walls, secure in the insti-tutions that safeguarded them.

Disraeli raised his hat to a lady in a passing carriage and began with some satisfaction to examine himself in a hand looking-glass. At that moment, two well-dressed horsemen trotted alongside his carriage, and one of them said,

'Mr Disraeli, sir – pray forgive the intrusion. I have sad news for you, I fear.'

Disraeli called on Blagden to pull up, and the other rider, more heavily built and straddling a stout cob, said,

'I'm Dr Cullen.'

'Indeed,' said Disraeli. He wasn't sure whether he had heard the word 'sad' or 'bad', but whatever it was it gave him a sudden clutch of terror that the horseman might be referring to Mary Anne.

'I think, sir, you should know – ' he paused, and Disraeli looked at him in fear – 'that Sir Robert Peel has been thrown from his horse and carried home dangerously hurt.'

Disraeli felt himself tremble, half with shock, half with relief. He had seen Peel during the night, cheerful, optimistic, discussing at large in the Smoking Room his plans for his children and his home at Drayton.

'Did you say "dangerously"?'

'I fear so,' said Cullen. 'I was riding near the top of Con-stitution Hill, and saw Sir Robert along with his groom behind him.'

'But Sir Robert is an accomplished rider!'

Dr Cullen reined in his horse. It was restless, and sidling against a privet hedge.

'I'm afraid his animal got out of control when he stopped to greet the ladies. The daughters of Lady Dover, I believe. Their groom's horse was backing, and Sir Robert's began to kick. All of a sudden – hoop la! – he went flying over the horse's head and landed on his face. From where I was, I saw Sir Robert's horse stumble and kneel on his back. It must have crushed his ribs and, I suspect, his chest. He was in great pain.'

'Yes – yes,' said Disraeli. He wiped his forehead.

'We got a surgeon from St George's Hospital, and brought him home in Mrs Lucas's carriage – Mrs Lucas of Bryanston Square – you may know her. Are you all right, sir?'

'Your news has distressed me, gentlemen. I am obliged to you. It's a great tragedy.'

They raised their hats again and trotted on. Disraeli ordered Blagden to return to Grosvenor Gate.

'Yes,' said Mary Anne, laying down her sampler when he arrived and told her of his meeting in the Park. 'I'd already heard the news. You must have some brandy, dearest. You look so pale.'

She poured him a glass of cognac, and added water to it. Disraeli looked at it gloomily.

'I can scarcely believe it. Peel! Such a vital man!'

'They say he's going to die,' said Mary Anne cheerfully.

'That would be a great sorrow for the country.'

He sipped the brandy, and the colour began to return to his face.

'There was no rancour between us, Mary Anne.'

He recalled the Don Pacifico debate, and said, 'He even gave me an occasional "Hear! Hear!" Not a very loud cheer, but all the same, a cheer.'

Mary Anne came over to him and put her hand on his head.

'Darling Ben,' she said, 'you're more forgiving than I am. Peel was harsh and unkind to you. He neglected and spurned you, and he and his friends treated you like a leper.'

'That's true,' said Disraeli judiciously, taking another sip of brandy. 'But it still doesn't merit the death penalty.'

'You brought about his downfall. That was deserved.'

'Nemesis overtaking hubris. But this – '

'Perhaps he'll live,' said Mary Anne.

'I pray so,' said Disraeli.

They were interrupted by a caller.

271

'Lady Jersey,' said the manservant.

They rose as Lady Jersey entered, her handkerchief to her eyes.

'He was to have dined with us last night. Oh, Mrs Disraeli – he's in such agony. That brute of a horse! I'd have it shot. One of my sons tried it out. It seemed such a steady animal. It's unbelievable. Mr Denison – you know, Sir Robert's friend – recommended the beast. He'd ridden it in London traffic. Oh, why are people so officious! If only one could have foreseen!'

She refused Mary Anne's invitation to sit, and said, 'No – I must return to Whitehall Gardens. The doctors are there. Poor Robert! He keeps calling for Harding and Graham. He relied on them so much. Poor Robert!'

At the door where Disraeli escorted her, she turned and said, in a suddenly composed voice, 'I feel as if a mountain of troubles has fallen on me.'

'The unhappy accident – '

'That too,' she said. 'But I want to talk to you before very long about Francis and that woman. It has something to do with the money he's been spending.'

The manservant opened the door and the June sunlight flowed into the hall.

Later that evening, Disraeli entered the Carlton to find Mr Huffam holding court. As always, he was a fountain of news.

'Yes,' he said. 'The situation is dire. Why, the Duke himself has called twice at Whitehall Gardens. Prince Albert came with the Prince of Prussia. Her Majesty – ' he bowed – 'has sent her enquiries.' His voice dropped. 'I have it on certain authority: he's dying.'

There was silence around them. Even Mr Huffam was dignified by the message he brought.

'Who'd have thought it?' said an old clubman. 'To have escaped Macnaghten's bullet – and to have been killed by a horse.'

'In the prime of his life,' said another. 'Alvanley was right after all. He said Peel wouldn't die a natural death.'

'Ah, well, he ain't dead yet. Waiter!'

With that optimistic observation, those present returned to their normal self-absorption, but Huffam wanted to continue.

'The trouble with Sir Robert,' he said, 'was that he had a bad manner. A shy man, I would say. Either too haughty or too exuberant. Nothing half-way.' He lowered his voice again. 'And little capable of enduring pain. Between ourselves, he had a nervous crisis after Drummond's death.'

'I differ from you, sir,' said Disraeli loudly. 'He was a man of great courage.'

'Oh, exactly,' said Huffam, whose audience had grown. 'Great courage! Great courage! Exactly what I meant.'

On an impulse, Disraeli decided to call at Whitehall Gardens and leave his name in the visitors' book before going on to the House of Commons.

Outside Peel's house he saw that a crowd had gathered, and he paid off the cabman. For the most part, the onlookers were working-men and women, staring at the spectacle of the fashionably dressed in their emblazoned carriages calling to pay their respects to a famous statesman on his bed of sickness.

Women in shawls, men in fustian or their labouring clothes, clerks, servants, errand-boys, spoke in whispers as if not to disturb the windows or the shutters or the drawn curtains. When a policeman posted a bulletin at the gates, the spectators surged forward.

> The condition of Sir Robert Peel is unchanged.
> Sir Benjamin Brodie
> Dr Seymour
> Mr Cæsar Hawkins

'Nothing new,' one said, and the words were echoed and repeated, by some with displeasure, as if they wanted something more decisive, like death itself.

Disraeli stood in the evening shadow of a building and recalled the last time he had paused there to watch a crowd waiting to cheer Peel. It was the day of his own triumph, and of Peel's resignation in 1846. A vast concourse had acclaimed

273

Peel all the way from his home to the House of Commons, and Disraeli had followed in its wake.

'It may be,' Peel had said in that debate, 'that I will sometimes be remembered with expressions of goodwill in the abodes of those whose lot it is to labour, and to earn their daily bread by the sweat of their brow, when they shall recruit their exhausted strength with abundant and untaxed food, the sweeter because it is no longer leavened by a sense of injustice.'

They were splendid words, memorable words. Disraeli had read and re-read them in Hansard. It was fitting that the idlers and the curious who attended Peel in these hours should have the appearance of a guard of honour of the people.

He hesitated before entering the house. It looked as if it was dying in the setting sun.

At that moment a carriage arrived, and again the crowd moved forward to see who would alight. A manservant in livery opened the door, and a solemn-faced cleric descended in the silence.

A policeman recognized Disraeli and saluted.

'It's the Bishop, sir. Come to give'm the sacrament. Soon be over, sir. He was a good man, Sir Robert.'

Disraeli turned away and walked slowly down Whitehall.

Chapter Twenty-three

'Sixteen thousand overdrawn at Drummond's, seven thousand three hundred to Messrs Lovell's the contractors – that's for the work on the façade at Hughenden Manor – three thousand and eighteen pounds for sundry *personalia* – and five thousand-odd in bills falling due next month, excluding Mrs Edmonds's bill,' said Mr Rose, adding up the figures.

From the shelves in his library at Hughenden, Disraeli picked a leather-bound copy of the *Aeneid* which had belonged to his father, and without replying examined the tooling on its spine.

'I don't think you're concentrating, Mr Disraeli,' said Rose. 'Does the subject bore you?'

'No – no,' said Disraeli defensively, casting his glance over Rose's shoulder to the Hughenden lawns where Mary Anne in a pelisse-robe of white muslin and a lace-trimmed bonnet was strolling. 'But what are you going to do about it, my dear Rose?'

'Me?'

'Yes, you. You know I rely on you to resolve these bothersome questions.'

'More than bothersome,' said Rose. 'These are critical. You mentioned to me – ' He hesitated.

'Pray continue,' said Disraeli.

'It has been suggested,' said Rose with the small smile he always wore when dealing with matters like defaulting trustees, 'that in the next administration you might be Chancellor of the Exchequer.'

'So they say. *The Times* says so. Stanley says so, although it isn't an office I would have chosen.'

'All the same, your qualifications might be challenged if in your personal affairs you show a lack of prudence.'

'Quite true,' said Disraeli casually. He preferred to dismiss the subject of money from his mind, but Rose persisted.

'You are, sir, on the verge of insolvency. Your paternal inheritance has now been fully absorbed in your disbursements for Hughenden. You have no substantial capital asset which can guarantee further borrowings. And I have to tell you I've just had this letter from Mrs Edmonds. She has returned to London.'

He handed Disraeli a letter that he scanned quickly.

'And on such a beautiful day! What does she want?'

His voice faltered in contradiction of his casual manner. The incubus was back.

'I suppose she wants to bankrupt you. She must like you very much.'

'I wish,' said Disraeli, 'she'd avow her passion more conventionally. Why is it, Rose, that at the very moment when my prospects seem brightest, some postman rushes in like a Greek messenger with a note of doom? What I need is a benefactor to wish away my shackles.'

'I'm afraid,' said Rose, glancing at the accounts laid out on the mahogany table, 'there's a shortage of benefactors. You can't always rely on miracles.'

'What about that madwoman who keeps writing to me from Torquay? Here's another letter. I haven't read it.'

The smile on Rose's face flickered again as he took the envelope from Disraeli.

'If I may say so with respect, Mr Disraeli, statesmen must be careful of casual communications from female strangers. Women are much excited by power – it's a great aphrodisiac.'

'Did you find anything out about her?'

'Only that she was born Miss Sarah Mendez da Costa – a Christian lady descended from the race of Israel, who later married Colonel Brydges Willyams, now deceased, commander of the Royal Cornish Militia.'

Disraeli looked again at the bills on the table, and shook his head.

'Very curious! I have the impression, though, she's a woman of means.'

'Indeed, yes – she is well situated – her letters are graceful

276

and lucid. And unless you think it mad to admire you and share your pride in your Hebraic heritage, quite sane.'

'But the language of her last letter was extravagant,' said Disraeli. He hoped to be contradicted, but Rose tugged at his waistcoat and agreed.

'Extravagant, certainly.'

Disraeli looked downcast.

'Yet sincere,' Rose continued. 'Shall we look at this letter?'

'Yes.'

Rose opened the letter with an oriental dagger that lay on the table, and glanced at the bold handwriting. Then he read aloud:

'Dear Mr Disraeli,   August, 1851

'I have often before addressed you in reference to your political speeches and published work.'

Disraeli sighed at the recollection of her enthusiastic letters.

'But now I will write to you upon a private subject. I am about to make my will.'

Disraeli looked up.

'I have to ask, as a great favour, that you will oblige me by being one of the executors.'

Rose paused for effect, and Disraeli, accustomed to the oratorical device, waited.

'I think it right to add that whoever are my executors will also be my residuary legatees in a sum in excess of £30,000 . . .'

'That's an interesting thought. What age is Mrs Sarah Brydges Willyams?'

'She can no longer be in her first youth,' said Rose.

'In the circumstances, scarcely a disadvantage.'

Rose pondered, a frill of wrinkles in his high forehead.

'Yes, but you realize it's a matter of some delicacy. To be an executor and a beneficiary – that needs a little consideration. And then again, it might seem curious to the world in the fullness of time if you received a legacy from an unknown lady without the foreknowledge of Mrs Disraeli.'

'She already knows of Mrs Willyams's letters.'

Rose thought for a moment or two.

'Then why don't we propose in a week or two to meet Mrs

Willyams? Yes – I think that might be of help . . . The prospect of a legacy is, after all, a security of sorts.' Rose gathered up the papers. 'You'll be glad to know, by the way, that I've obtained Drummond's agreement not to press for a reduction in your overdraft till the end of the year.'

'Rose,' said Disraeli, putting his arm round Rose's shoulders and leading him on to the sun-filled terrace, 'you are my best and dearest friend.'

'But there is another matter, Mr Disraeli. With the prospect of a dissolution – a new government – your own part in it – you are in a constant danger – permit me as your lawyer to say this – from Mrs Edmonds and Tankerton.'

'I realize that. I've always accepted danger as part of my life. It's a challenge to overcome.'

'But there are moments when you're disarmed.'

'It's a risk I must take,' said Disraeli, stopping to look at the statue of a naked Pan set against a privet hedge.

'No,' said Rose, 'you cannot. I've been making some enquiries about Mrs Edmonds and Tankerton from Lawson and his friends. I believe, Mr Disraeli, we must deal with them both.'

'How?'

'We shall see,' said Rose mysteriously.

Disraeli found it easier to talk about politics than about finance, and as they walked he began to expound to his solicitor his ideas for the reconstruction of the Conservative Party. With the enlargement of the franchise, the essential, he believed, was to strengthen the local associations. What, after all, was a Party but organized opinion? He reverted to a long-held view. The present troubles of government lay in the fluctuating alliances inside the House of Commons, which prevented the nation from obtaining definite answers related to general principles. A system of Conservative associations reinforcing clear Conservative policies was, he argued, the only way to obtain a Tory dominance in the country.

'You could well be the man to take charge of the Party in the country,' he concluded.

Rose was flattered.

'Very interesting,' he said. Disraeli mightn't know much about money, he thought, but he certainly knew a lot about people.

On the lawn, Disraeli surveyed the eighteenth-century manor house, the pergola, the classical statues brought from Pæstum, the peacocks stalking one another over a trail of grain cast by Mary Anne, the beechwoods below the eminence of Hughenden, broken only by the folds of the hills and the pasture of the home farm; and beyond them the grazing lands of the estate.

Sometimes on the terrace at Hughenden, Disraeli asked himself by what destiny he had been brought to the leadership of the Party. And he answered, in the privacy of his own mind, with the single word, 'Will!' He had become leader because he had willed it, and married his will to knowledge.

A peacock screamed and the doves fluttered from the dovecote in fright. That too was agreeable, the decoration of the romance he was still composing.

They joined Mary Anne. Rose bade her farewell, and she took Disraeli's arm and together they walked slowly across the lawn down the stone steps, past the grassy slopes leading to the dark colonnade of the walk through the woods to High Wycombe. The fir trees, entangled with larch and beech, left a dusty covering of pine-needles between the trunks, and every now and again Mary Anne paused in delight to look at a vista of the sun-filled valley between the branches.

She clung to Disraeli's arm, and said, 'Darling Diz, you have made me so happy. You could have had all the most beautiful women in London – and you chose me.'

He didn't answer, but kissed her hand, and while she leaned against his chest they stood listening to the stir of the trees.

In his role as a landed proprietor, Disraeli felt sublime. His position in the county, the procession of distinguished and aristocratic visitors to the manor, the letters addressed to the Rt Hon. Gentleman and bearing noble crests that the postmaster reported with deference at the inn, raised him far above the local murmurs about Mary Anne's parsimony.

'When she goes, there won't be a wet eye in the valley,' said the publican. But Disraeli was detached, and she was unmoved.

She carried a black parasol over her right shoulder as they returned to walk uphill through the meadow in the hot July day, and she clutched her husband's arm timorously with her other hand when they were surrounded by a herd of staring, sherry-coloured cows.

'Go away,' said Disraeli, waving his stick, and the cows moved sullenly out of their path. 'And what were you saying, Mary Anne?'

'I was saying you had a mistress.'

'Ah, yes – who is she?'

Mary Anne liked riddles.

'Your work,' she said triumphantly. 'You work all the time. I never see you nowadays. And those elections – those terrible parliamentary papers.'

'You're quite right, Mary Anne,' he said apologetically. 'I've been flirting lately with a few thoughts of a Stanley ministry.'

The rooks were cawing in the elms, and they paused to listen.

'Summertime music,' he said. 'Even the rooks at Hughenden are like nightingales.'

'But you hate rooks,' she said.

'Only in other people's country houses. One nearly gets cawed to death there.'

'How long will this summer last?' she asked.

He looked at her tenderly. In her youthful muslin, she looked fully twelve years older than himself.

'Till the autumn adagio,' he said. 'It's the most beautiful movement of all.'

'You've always protected me, Ben,' said Mary Anne. 'I don't just mean my person. I mean, you have sheltered my feelings.'

Lord Henry Lennox came to greet them across the oval lawn in front of the house.

'Oh, I dislike that young man,' said Mary Anne. 'Why is he always lounging about? Wherever you go, he seems to be.'

'He's very useful – and full of promise. He keeps me very well informed.'

'Is that all?' asked Mary Anne.

Disraeli's manner had stiffened, but then changed as Lord Henry, familiarly addressing him as Diz, greeted them both. Mary Anne felt that when they were together they behaved as if she were no longer present. Walking through an arbour to the terrace on the other side of the manor, they bantered and teased each other, laughing about matters she couldn't understand, and talking of people and places she'd never heard of.

'I think I'll go in,' she said. 'The sun is rather hot.'

Disraeli took Lord Henry's arm and they walked up and down on the lawn as if on the quarter-deck of a ship. He lectured as they walked, and the two peacocks, following their habitual trail of grain across the lawn, strutted behind them.

'The essential, my dear boy,' he said, 'is to remember that we're in a minority, whichever way you look at it. I reckon a General Election would give us three hundred. The Opposition has about two hundred and seventy Liberals – half Whigs, half Radicals – thirty-five Peelite relics, and about thirty of the Irish brigade. And don't forget Palmerston. He's a figure alone.'

Lennox said, 'But really he *is* an old fop. No woman's safe to walk upstairs in front of him.'

'Vigour's a great political asset. We may yet need him. What would you say to a reduction in the malt tax?'

'Very popular.'

'Should we lower the tea duties?'

'Why not?'

'The trouble is we'd have to show a surplus. It's damned difficult unless we borrow.'

'Oh, God,' said Lennox. 'Even I know that if you borrow, you have to add the loan to the debits.'

'What I had in mind,' said Disraeli calmly, 'would be to wind up the Fund of the Public Works Loans Board and put the money in the General Account. You see, the Navy will need another million pounds. Where could we find it, Henry?

The Queen insists she gets her million for the Marines and all
that.'

'What would Stanley say?'

'Oh, he just says "Juggle!" Ever the sportsman!'

They smiled to each other and moved towards the terraces,
where some of the other guests had gathered.

'Oh,' said Mary Anne to Lady Eves as they approached her
in the shadow of the entrance, 'I do wish Dizzy wouldn't waste
time on these young men.'

'But Mr Disraeli looks so happy in their company,' said
Lady Eves.

Lennox joined them, but Disraeli stood apart and took from
his pocket another letter from Mrs Brydges Willyams whose
contents he had concealed both from Mary Anne and his
solicitor.

My dear sir [he read for the third time],

I am obliged to you for sending me an inscribed copy of
your novel *Tancred*, which I have already begun to read with
great pleasure. I am going to London for a fortnight to see
the Great Exhibition with one of my nieces who has seen it
throughout.

If you should happen to be in town whilst I am there,
and could appoint a time and place at the Crystal Palace, I
should be delighted to meet you.

I have taken an apartment at 6 Bryanston Street, Portman
Square.

Yours sincerely,
Sarah Brydges Willyams.

He held the letter in his hand like a talisman.

In London on the morning of his rendezvous with Mrs
Brydges Willyams, Disraeli, lounging at breakfast in his
dressing-gown, gave Baum instructions about his dress. His
coat was to be sober and discreet, yet memorable for those
who could appreciate its cut-away style. Since it was high
summer, he would wear a white waistcoat with only two
chains. Lionel de Rothschild had sent a basket of orchids from

Gunnersbury Park, and although he normally disliked button-hole flowers, he felt that for the occasion a mauve orchid might not be inappropriate.

Baum listened carefully to Disraeli's instructions, and said at the end in a loud voice, 'The Londonderry Suit, sir?'

Disraeli had recently had a specially modish suit made on the occasion of a review to which Lady Londonderry had invited him, and Mary Anne with a touch of jealousy had named it the Londonderry Suit. Disraeli frowned, and Baum backed away.

Mary Anne, entering at that moment and catching his last words, asked lightly, 'Are you going wenching, Diz?'

'Only to the Royal Society of Arts in pursuit of the Muses.'

'See that you don't take one on your knee. Will you be wanting the carriage?'

'No,' said Disraeli. 'I'll be hunting on foot.'

He hurried down the stairs and into Park Lane, where he could see the Crystal Palace of the Great Exhibition, its thousand glass panes coruscating in the sunshine.

He had written to Mrs Willyams asking her to meet him at noon by the fountain, the central and already famous symbol of the Exhibition. All he knew of her was her enthusiasm for his work, and what Rose had told him about her background and means. Though he had received many admiring letters from women, some in society, who had become infatuated with his creations, he had usually ignored them, not wishing to become involved in flattering but embarrassing transactions where the pleasure was fleeting and the disadvantages lasting. But a tryst at the fountain of the Great Exhibition – ! With a woman who wanted to make him her heir! If he had thought of it before, he would have included the situation in one of his novels. Even now, he could still feel something of the same excitement as he had felt long ago on the eve of his first assignation with Henrietta Sykes.

From Apsley House to the end of the Park stretched a long line of cabs, omnibuses, drays, broughams and flies, moving slowly forward while sweating, top-hatted policemen clutched horses by the reins to try and control the traffic, interspersed as it was with farmers on foot, labourers, red-coated Life Guards, streetsellers of gingerbread, hardbake and oranges, women in coloured shawls and beribboned children, 'shilling clubs' of villagers arriving en masse for the cheap entrance day as if in an emigration, barking dogs and hawkers of Exhibition medals, running from carriage to carriage. Disraeli walked fastidiously through the crowd to the main gates, waving his three-guinea season ticket.

He was early, and he strolled to the stained-glass gallery, dawdled in the French gallery in front of the Sèvres porcelain and the Limoges enamel, and paused to admire the iron tubular furniture in the Austrian gallery. He was approaching the Russian salon to examine a huge green malachite vase when he saw Lord Redesdale, a friend of Lord Stanley, staring at it with his hands behind his back. Pretending to raise his hat, but in fact hiding his face, Disraeli turned into the nave of the cathedral-like central hall, and stepped behind the tall elm trees which had been preserved as a decoration, an assurance to those who feared the Exhibition might ruin the Park. From here he could survey the promenaders moving around the fountain directly under the glass roof, where the blue of the sky was framed with an aureole of pink and violet reflections of the scarlet draperies on the wall. The fountain itself, tiered in crystal like a pagoda within a waterfall, rose as high as the lower branches of the elms, and the visitors around it fell quiet to hear its sound.

Until that moment it hadn't occurred to Disraeli that the fountain could be a meeting-place for anyone other than himself and Mrs Willyams; but when he saw a row of well-dressed men and women standing about with no apparent connection with each other, as if waiting for someone who hadn't arrived, he realized that the task of identifying Mrs Willyams would prove difficult. On the other hand, she might recognize him from the print that Colnaghi had recently published in a series about eminent politicians. But his purpose was to see her before she saw him.

He gave a sidelong glance at the fountain as he passed it,

recalling a popular translation of Pushkin's romantic poem, *The Fountain of Bachchisarai*. Did all the maidens standing alone or with their duennas identify themselves with the Khan's daughter, who in the end was to die of love? Not that they looked especially wan. Some indeed wore rouge. Nor did the fountain lend itself to suicide. It was scarcely three feet deep. What a curious gallery for Mrs Willyams to find herself in!

A woman with a rose-coloured parasol in her hand and wearing a heliotrope dress and flowered bonnet slowly took off a glove, and as her naked hand appeared Disraeli saw that she wore a wedding-ring slightly overhung with flesh.

Simultaneously, the clock on the west side of the hall gave a premonitory whirr before striking the hour. Everyone looked towards it. The clock struck twelve, a tinny note in contrast with its imposing size, and Disraeli's glance returned to the fountain. The woman was looking at the ground with a subdued smile, as if ruminating on some private and satisfactory thought. She had a pleasant, intelligent face that fitted well with her fashionable, if slightly ostentatious, clothes.

Disraeli stood observing the fountain, and listened to the restless tapping of the woman's parasol on the floor as she watched each jerk of the clock's minute hand. He approached, hesitated, retreated, consulted his fob watch, circled the fountain again, and at seven minutes past twelve raised his hat and said,

'Mrs Brydges Willyams?'

She looked him straight in the eyes, and replied in a hoarse Cockney voice, 'No, young feller. I'm Miss Ellen Dick. Can I help you?'

Disraeli raised his hat again.

'I fear not, madam.'

'I've been standin' in this bloomin' place for the last hour . . . Five pounds, sir!'

'Five thousand wouldn't be enough. But, alas, I'm already taken.'

She gave a contemptuous flounce, and Disraeli, raising his hat a third time, hurried off to the other side of the fountain.

He felt absurd. It was now nearly a quarter past twelve. Mrs

Brydges Willyams probably wouldn't come. Perhaps it was all a hoax, a crazed woman's jest. It was, after all, ridiculous that an unknown woman should choose him as her heir. How could he find her among all the throng of chattering idlers now surrounding the fountain? Wearing a white waistcoat and carrying a tasselled cane, he felt like some boulevardier eyeing the *lorettes* in Paris. And their London counterparts were now eyeing him in turn. He began to wish he had put on a less identifiable waistcoat.

Then he noticed an elderly lady, dressed in black except for a white lace collar, followed by two pug dogs. She had twice walked round the fountain. He withdrew behind a statue of an Apollo with a shield, called 'Physical Energy', and from behind it he peered at the black bonnet. No, it was impossible. He had visualized a woman of perhaps Mary Anne's age. But suddenly she called to the dogs in a clear and gentle voice.

'Now, Whisky – Chang – come to your auntie at once – come to Aunt Sarah!'

The old lady had again begun her circumnambulation, and Disraeli, submerging himself in the crowd, hurried off to the Carlton. He had always liked women somewhat older than himself. But this wasn't maturity: it was antiquity.

He returned to Grosvenor Gate oppressed by an indefinable malaise, and sat with Mary Anne, listening as she discussed in her customary manner her domestic affairs.

'I saw this chair in the sale-room – the most beautiful petit-point.' Her hands moved more quickly over the tapestry on which she was working.

'Yes,' he said absently.

'So I went in, and when it came up at number fifty-three, I bid ten pounds for it.'

'Yes – I hope you acquired it.'

'I did – for fifty pounds. You see, it was Beauvais.'

'We have eighteen Beauvais chairs for our drawing-room,' he said mildly.

Her hands paused.

'Oh, Ben – are you displeased with me?'

'No – no. Not in the least, my dearest – only displeased that our drawing-rooms have so little space.'

She saw that he was distracted, and rose and stood by his armchair.

'Are you unwell?'

'No, Mary Anne – troubled. I've been thinking very much today of Peel. So many battles – and all that brought to nothing by a frightened horse!'

'Poor Diz!' she said. She put her arms round him.

'What an awesome procession! My mother, my father, Bentinck, and now Peel!'

' "A thousand shall fall beside thee and ten thousand at thy right hand: but it shall not come nigh thee," ' said Mary Anne, holding him closely. 'I learnt that in Wales. Nothing must ever happen to you, Ben. I want you to live for ever and ever.'

He kissed her on the forehead, and she said, 'You must.'

He detached himself.

'Mary Anne – I have something to tell you.'

'Yes, my dearest. What is it?'

He hesitated.

'I visited the Great Exhibition today.'

'Yes – I know.'

'You know?'

'Yes, indeed. Colonel Sibthorp saw you there. And he told Mrs Bulwer and she told me.'

'Ah, I see. Mercury travels fast.'

'By the way, Mrs Bulwer is acquainted with Mrs Willyams.'

'Really?'

'Yes – she told me she's staying in Bryanston Street and that she'll be visiting her.'

'She'll be able to convey our greetings,' said Disraeli impassively.

Mary Anne laid down her needlework.

'I'm going to rest before going to Lady Randall's,' she said.

'I'll follow you soon, my dear one,' said Disraeli. 'But before then, I have to write a letter.'

'Well, write it – but not a sad one.'

After she had gone he sat at his secrétaire and wrote to Mrs Brydges Willyams.

My dear Madam,

By an unhappy fate I was prevented by a sudden influenza from meeting you at the Exhibition. To have met you on this occasion would have been a pleasure which must, alas, be temporarily forfeit. But a forfeit which in the autumn I trust you will permit us to redeem. In the meantime, I am sending you by train from Hughenden to your sunny hill on the western coast some roses which will express my regret, together with the hope that very soon we may follow them.

Ever yours,

B. Disraeli

When he had finished writing, he leaned back in his chair. Whisky and Chang – he saw the two pug dogs trailing behind Mrs Willyams's black skirts as he fled from the fountain. What cowardice! Some foolishness had tempted him to a rendezvous which, even if Mrs Willyams had been Cleopatra, would have been by that degree more reckless. Prudence and chance had enabled him to escape. But all the same – !

He stretched himself, praised the *baraka*, that Divine touch that protected him, and with his conscience half-appeased by his apology, took up a copy of Horace's *Odes* which soothed him on difficult occasions.

Nihil admirari. That was the Stoic motto he had chosen as a pendant to his coat-of-arms. To be surprised at nothing. The phantom inheritance had receded. Instead there was Mrs Edmonds with her accumulating demands, and Tankerton, still waiting for the moment when he could most effectively destroy him.

He shrugged his shoulders and sent for Baum to bring him champagne.

Chapter Twenty-four

'Chancellor of the Exchequer?'

The voices of the Members of Parliament gathered on the Terrace waiting to hear the names of the new administration were incredulous.

'Disraeli Chancellor of the Exchequer? You can't mean it!'

Mr Huffam, wheezing with the effort of being the first with the news, took off his gold spectacles and wiped them. The sun glittering on the Thames in the March morning gave the illusion of an early spring. It shone over the buildings on the other side of the river, brightened the parapet, and touched the neo-Gothic windows of the House of Commons.

'I assure you it's true,' said Huffam. 'I've just been told by a peer very close to Stanley – I mean to Lord Derby – I can never get used to his change of title since his father's death – Diz wanted the Home Office but Spencer Walpole got there first. Walpole's and Perceval's descendant, you know. Prescriptive right!'

'And who's got War and Colonies?' asked a Peelite with some disdain. In constructing the government after the defeat of Lord John Russell, Stanley, now Lord Derby, had declined to negotiate with the Peelites, except for Gladstone.

'Packington – Sir John Packington.'

'Good God,' said George Smythe, 'they've dug up Sir Roger de Coverley. Who thought of him?'

'I hear it's Dizzy's own invention,' said Huffam slyly. 'He always did believe in keeping up appearances. A good old gentleman in riding boots is proof of your attachment to the farming interest.'

'Derby's had to scrape the bottom of the barrel a bit,' said Smythe.

'More than a bit,' said Huffam, who had himself expected at least an Under-Secretaryship but had been disappointed in his hopes. His eyes shone with relish as he prepared his further gossip. He could scarcely wait to butt in.

'I hear,' he said, 'they're calling the new administration the "Who? Who?" government.'

'Who? Who?' said a deaf Member who had just joined them.

'That's it,' said Huffam. 'Who? Who? I was in the Lords yesterday when some luckless peer was on his legs, and Derby was telling Wellington the names of his new men. Each time he spoke a name in his ear, the Duke bellowed "Who? Who?" It resounded through the Chamber.'

The group around him laughed so loudly that the seagulls lining the parapet broke into flight.

'Who? Who?' Some of the Whigs and Peelites took up the cry, and it rippled along the Terrace like musket-fire directed against the new government.

'Diz,' said Smythe, 'will do well as Chancellor. With his experience of creditors, handling the National Debt should be child's play.'

There was a guffaw, but almost simultaneously the half-dozen or so Members raised their hats respectfully. Disraeli had strolled on to the Terrace to take the air after his long discussions with Lord Derby in his room.

He had overcome Derby's doubts and hesitations about forming a government. Secure in his great estates and armoured by his lethargy, Derby, he knew, would have been content to persevere in Opposition. For himself it wasn't a role he relished, nor could he sympathize with the pessimistic and defeated expression that settled over Derby's heavy face whenever politics were discussed. The man who rode fearlessly at every obstacle in the hunting field was, he believed, timorous at heart when power was the goal. As he walked on the Terrace, receiving the deferential and muttered homage of many who till recently had spurned him openly, Disraeli felt the time for greatness had come.

Chancellor of the Exchequer! It was one of the major offices of state. True, he had wanted the Home Office or the Foreign Office. He knew about men and understood the affairs of nations. The management of men, and of women too, depended, he had long decided, on an understanding of their weaknesses; and in that respect there was no difference between cottage and palace. As far as the relations of states were concerned, the only moral course for England was to safeguard her own interests. Let Gladstone dress up his policies with theological sanctions! Let Palmerston interfere in the name of abstractions! The safety of the State was the supreme law. He would have wished as Foreign Secretary to have the opportunity of developing that policy.

But Derby had been cautious. Disraeli would be Leader of the House as well as Chancellor. Tact, diplomacy, fairness – those, he urged on Disraeli, were the essential qualities for the post. Disraeli hadn't demurred, since he could think of no one better qualified than himself in those respects. Finance, on the other hand, was something different. When Derby offered him the Chancellorship of the Exchequer, a huge personal and deficitary balance-sheet presented itself to Disraeli's imagination, the bills dragging on from year to year, the upkeep of Hughenden Manor, the cost of renovation, the expense of political entertainment, all the complicated arithmetic and statistics that Bentinck had revelled in but which were a burden to his spirit.

'I confess,' he said to Lord Derby, 'finance is a branch of government I know little about. Some broad principles – yes. But figures – !'

'Oh, don't worry,' Derby had said in his lordly manner, 'they give you the figures.'

And so Disraeli had accepted office. *They* give you the figures. It was a pleasant assurance. He visualized 'them' as the sum of the solicitors who had always helped him with his intolerable accounts.

But there was far more to it than that. To be Chancellor was ultimately to determine policy, to control every other department of state, to be able to translate into action the programme of Conservative progress. Everyone in the new government would be at his door with partisan cries, the ultras and the bigots, the Protectionists-to-the-death and the No-Popery enthusiasts. His own theme would be to end the rivalry between town and country, to create the one nation that he had often spoken of and written about. The Chancellorship wasn't just a matter of sums; the Chancellor was the nation's adviser.

He saw Herries walking near the Speaker's House, and joined him. Herries, the old man appointed to the Board of Control, answered most questions by calling for more Protection, and Disraeli felt the need to be specially amiable to him as they walked along together, acknowledging the salutes and the murmur of congratulations of passers-by. Disraeli had a great deal to do. The robes of office. The swearing-in at the Privy Council. The kissing of hands at Windsor.

There had been, it was true, a shadow over his appointment. He had been told by Derby that both the Queen and Prince Consort had expressed doubts about his fitness. The Queen had disapproved of the way in which he'd attacked Peel. The name of the late Lady Sykes had been mentioned. In a government in which Disraeli was virtually the only Minister without some formal title of honour, the Palace felt his credentials should be examined very closely. But Lord Derby had gone bail for him to the Queen. Disraeli had no doubt that he could, in his own person and in the course of time, improve on these assurances.

After discussing the weather and the prospects of the new government, Mr Herries left him at the door of the Commons. Disraeli walked on across the tessellated paving in the direction of the House of Lords, where he came face to face with Gladstone, the tall and unsmiling Procrustes of the Peelites.

For most of his rivals and opponents Disraeli felt an indifferent contempt. But Gladstone was something else. He admired Gladstone's mind and disliked his person. Though Disraeli regarded the Anglican Church as a main foundation of the established order, Gladstone's ostentatious churchmanship offended him. He had once said that every time Gladstone was faced with a moral problem he'd have a talk with God and advise Him on how to deal with it. As for himself, he knew that Gladstone neither liked nor trusted him.

Disraeli wondered idly which of the deadly sins Gladstone, the preacher and moralist, attributed to him. Gluttony? No – he wasn't a glutton. Covetousness? But every politician wanted power. Lechery? – that belonged almost entirely to the past. He knew of Gladstone's austere domesticity. He knew that Gladstone, supported by Bishop Wilberforce and Bishop Blomfield, had formed an Association for the Reclamation of Fallen Women. He knew that Gladstone, following this obsessive vocation, could often be seen prowling the streets of Piccadilly, Soho and the Thames Embankment in search of suitable ladies to redeem. But that was Gladstone's affair. Precisely because of his moral and religious fervour, he had great personal authority. In the age of family virtue, exemplified by the Queen and her household, Gladstone's tight-lipped respectability wasn't to be underrated, and Disraeli in his dealings with him tried to adapt himself to his criteria.

'Good morning, Mr Gladstone,' he said.

'Good morning, sir,' said Gladstone sombrely.

Disraeli waited for him to speak, perhaps even to congratulate him. Instead, Gladstone looked morosely at the flagstones. At last he spoke, in a voice that seemed to start in his belly but was controlled and compressed through a number of chambers before it finally emerged in a low, seismic rumble.

'You will understand, Mr Disraeli,' he said, 'that if I do not offer you my congratulations it is because I myself declined to serve under Lord Derby.'

'A regrettable handicap for us,' Disraeli murmured politely.

'But I wouldn't be frank, sir,' Gladstone went on, 'if I didn't tell you that certain other considerations would prevent me from serving in the new administration.'

'Indeed? Doctrinal questions? The question of baptismal regeneration, perhaps? The catholicity of the church?'

Gladstone frowned, and his thick eyebrows twitched. He felt that Disraeli, behind his grave expression, was indulging in irony about a subject that was closest to his feelings.

'Those are matters which governments can only pretend to control. I must tell you, Mr Disraeli, that – ' he paused as if to consider whether the charge was too strong – 'that your own political principles appear to me to be too variable, too uncertain, too unstable for me to associate myself with them.'

'In that case,' said Disraeli with a curt bow, 'I won't trespass further on your time.'

'Besides,' said Gladstone, determined now that he had begun to complete his analysis of Disraeli's character, 'you will recall, sir, that a few years ago Lord George Bentinck accused me of uttering a deliberate lie.' His voice rose at the memory of an old and unresolved grievance. 'He claimed that when I was Colonial Secretary I had lied in saying a certain judge had resigned whereas he had only been "allowed to retire". It was an outrageous, ungentlemanly charge.'

Disraeli, who had half-turned away, shrugged his shoulders impatiently. He had sometimes thought that Gladstone, despite his remarkable intelligence, was mad. Gladstone now seemed to him anxious to establish the fact.

'He was your friend. You supported him.'

Gladstone was trembling with anger.

'He was my friend,' said Disraeli. 'I supported him. He is dead. Good day, sir.'

'One moment, if you please,' said Gladstone, detaining him. 'There's a matter I must refer to, a matter of some personal consequence.'

Disraeli waited.

'It concerns a lady, Mrs Edmonds, with whom I think you're acquainted.'

Disraeli still waited. He observed irrelevantly that Gladstone had hair growing from his cheekbones and nostrils.

'She's a lady who needs help and succour, having been brought into difficulties by the unworthy treatment of her – by certain persons.'

Disraeli looked at him angrily, and said, 'Sir, this is a subject which doesn't concern me. Pray let me pass.'

'It concerns you intimately,' said Gladstone. 'You will see.'

Disraeli thrust his way past him.

At Grosvenor Gate Mary Anne was waiting to greet her

husband when he returned from the Privy Council offices. Before his carriage stopped, she opened the door and, bonnetless, ran down the steps to greet him.

'Dear Mary Anne,' he said, 'you must be more careful. This sunshine is very liberal – more show than warmth.'

She clung to his arm as they entered the house – staidly, because a small group had gathered outside to see the new Chancellor, whose appointment had been announced earlier in the afternoon.

When they were alone, Disraeli said to Mary Anne, 'Shall we dance a jig or a polka?'

'A polka,' said Mary Anne.

They danced through the drawing-room, knocking over a wine-table and an embroidered firescreen, till at last Mary Anne called out breathlessly as she fell on to a sofa, 'That's enough. We have to be at Lady Jersey's tonight. Now tell me everything, Ben!'

Disraeli took her hand, and said, 'You mustn't address me so familiarly. You must call me Mr Secretary of State.'

'All right. Tell me everything, Mr Secretary of State. Did you try on your Chancellor's robes?'

'Indeed I did.'

'All that velvet and gold braid – was it terribly heavy?'

'No,' said Disraeli, standing and admiring himself in an ormolu looking-glass. 'As a matter of fact, I found it remarkably light.'

Mary Anne pointed to a salver piled with unopened letters.

'They've been arriving since midday,' she said. 'You must be the most popular and sought-after man in London. And callers! They've been knocking on the door with all sorts of urgent messages.'

'I shouldn't worry,' said Disraeli in a lazy tone. 'When someone says something is urgent, it means nine times out of ten it's urgent to them.'

He brushed the pile of letters on to the table and noticed Lord Lyndhurst's name. He opened it and read in Lady Lyndhurst's hand:

My dear Ben,

  May I be one of the first to congratulate you on your
appointment as Foreign Secretary. When I recall –

Disraeli stopped reading, and said, 'Lyndhurst has congratulated me on becoming *Foreign Secretary.*'

'Poor Lyndhurst – so old, so blind,' said Mary Anne.

And Disraeli added, 'But he was my first friend in politics,
the first to encourage and guide my ambition.'

'A very dashing old gentleman,' said Mary Anne. 'He used
to be so handsome.'

It was an epitaph.

'Tomorrow, Mary Anne, I go to Windsor, and after that I
am to become the Queen's regular correspondent. As Leader
of the Commons, I must write to her every day.'

'I'll be jealous.'

'You'll become accustomed to it.'

'Will the government last long enough?'

'I've taught you to be ironic,' he said. 'But you're right.
We'll have to have an election before the summer's over. Our
Party is more turbulent than the Israelites in the desert.'

'Who are the Egyptians, Ben?'

'I'll be able to tell you more easily a few days hence. For
the time being, Amalek is Gladstone.'

Mary Anne shrieked at the name.

'Gladstone! But he's always preaching the virtues of brother-
ly love.'

'Oh, in his politics of the Liberal sort that merely means
you must love your country's enemies, not your personal ones.
At any rate, Mr Gladstone let me know today at the House of
Commons that he thought me unfit for office.'

'What a dreadful Pharisee the man is!' said Mary Anne
indignantly. 'Can an Amalek be a Pharisee? When I next see
him I'll give him something to worry about.'

'It isn't worthwhile,' said Disraeli soothingly. 'Gladstone's
very sincere, even if he does give himself the benefit of every
doubt. Like Monsieur Tartuffe.'

'I don't think I know him,' said Mary Anne. 'Still, I'm sorry for Mrs Gladstone. Their daughter Jessy died so recently; meningitis, I believe. They've been distraught this past year.'

Disraeli took her hand and kissed it.

'You have a gentle soul, Mary Anne,' he said.

The new ministry was being welcomed by Lady Jersey with a ball at her house in Berkeley Square, and in the long queue of guests waiting to be presented almost every Tory notable was present, together with ambassadors and their wives, who had come to study the new faces. Unlike Lady Londonderry, a goddess waiting for sacrifice, Lady Jersey after the first hour of reception chose to move from group to group, scattering her attentions like largesse, a stately figure content with her own beauty, requiring nothing but the tribute of admiration.

Most of the new Ministers had arrived early and rapidly established their coteries. An unseen military orchestra, with little brass but many string instruments, since Lady Jersey didn't like loud music, was playing fashionable waltzes, and on all sides there was the mood of optimism that attends a new government. When Disraeli arrived with Mary Anne, every face seemed to turn towards him as he stood at the top of the stairs to be greeted by Lord and Lady Jersey.

'The marriage feast,' said Lady Jersey.

'The honeymoon of hope,' said Disraeli.

'When's the consummation?' asked Mary Anne.

Disraeli hurried her on, and before long she was swept up into an animated circle of politicians' wives, anxious for their husbands' sakes to be of good standing with Disraeli.

Disraeli himself, in a suit of black and a white cravat perfectly knotted by Baum, moved slowly through the ballroom, gravely exchanging greetings with respectful acquaintances, conscious that his distinction had nothing to do with meretricious adornment. Even his gold chains were only filigree strands. He didn't like dancing, since he had never been taught properly, and he intended leaving early in the evening. When the first couples began to dance, he withdrew to the edge of the ballroom floor.

Leaning against a pillar was Lord Henry Lennox, fair-haired, pouchy-eyed, but with a tolerant air that set him apart from the eager dancers and others in search of partners. He was the sort of person who was handsome at second glance.

'You're not dancing, Diz?' asked Lennox, without changing his posture.

'No,' said Disraeli. 'I've always regarded dancing as a form of communion best practised in private. And you?'

'Oh, I've done all that,' said Lennox. 'Danced all the dances. Read all the books. Kissed all the girls. Don't really know why I'm here.'

Disraeli smiled, and Lennox half-smiled, correcting his affectation.

'In that case,' said Disraeli, 'let's sit together in the shadow of this marble pillar and exchange confidences. You know, when I was a youth, Lord Melbourne asked me my purpose in politics. I said rather boldly, "To be Prime Minister." He discouraged me. "That office," he said, "must fall to Stanley." Now tell me your purpose.'

Lennox reflected.

'Have I a purpose? I don't really know. Politics confuses me. It's like chess, that I never could understand. I think I'd have done better in diplomacy. Now there's something for a man. Ambassador in Paris. Of course, it all boils down to the problem of being a younger son. D'you know any heiresses?'

Disraeli looked at him and saw he was in earnest.

'The trouble is,' Lennox went on, 'whenever I find somebody suitable, Father finds her parents are *parvenus*. What about a Rothschild?'

'Generally speaking,' said Disraeli, 'they marry each other.'

Lennox smiled, and as Mr Huffam bore down on them Disraeli said, 'I trust we will meet again before long. Pray call on me at Grosvenor Gate, or Number Eleven, if that's more convenient.'

Lennox stood up and shook Disraeli's hand. His bantering manner had changed into the formal courtesy due to a Secretary of State.

'Now about the Malt Tax, Mr Chancellor of the Exchequer

. . .' Huffam began, his eyes beady behind his gold-rimmed spectacles.

Lennox gave Disraeli a look of sympathy, and withdrew.

'Isn't that Mr Villiers over there?' said Disraeli, anxious to change the subject.

Huffam inclined his head towards him and said in a groan that was intended to be a whisper, 'Lady Jersey ought really to be careful about that son of hers. He's scattering bills all over London like confetti. Acceptances galore. The discount houses – !'

He raised his hands in deprecation.

'And he takes that woman Mrs Edmonds about everywhere. Ever since Mr Hudson got into trouble and she left him . . . Mind you, he told everyone he left *her*!'

Disraeli glanced with a frown across the room at Mrs Edmonds, in a pale mauve dress the laughing centre of a group of men.

'What's she doing here?'

'Mr Villiers insists. His mother will never say "no" to him.'

'Mrs Edmonds isn't without other admirers,' Disraeli said.

'Biggest whore in London,' said Huffam, and before Disraeli could answer he had already moved on to accost the Home Secretary and the Minister for the Colonies, who were walking together in private conversation.

On the day that the ministry was due to be presented by the Prime Minister to Queen Victoria, Disraeli awoke with a migraine, the disease that pursued him like a hobgoblin. Mary Anne brought him a tisane, darkened his room, but an hour before the special train was due to leave Paddington for Maidenhead, the headache lifted like a fog that gives way to bright sunlight.

At the station the Ministers, their secretaries and attendants were already gathered with the station-master, top-hatted and grave, in attendance. The carriages had vases of flowers. A carpet had been unrolled, leading to the Prime Minister's special compartment, and a small crowd was being held at a distance by the police.

The journey itself was short. Soon after they left the station they passed through an opulent countryside, farms, riverside, cuttings and tunnels, till in half an hour they reached Maidenhead, where coaches from the Royal Stables were already waiting to take them to Windsor. The onset of Disraeli's migraines was usually accompanied by a euphoria; after it was over he felt a prolonged apathy. But now it was as if the euphoria had been given a second lease; he was going to Windsor to pay homage to the Queen as one of her Ministers. He was nervous, he had to admit it to himself. But no one else would see it. He would show Derby and the others – the Queen herself – that in receiving him she was giving honour to a statesman who merited it.

Greville, the Clerk of the Privy Council, and one of the court chamberlains had spent a quarter of an hour at No. 10 Downing Street the previous day, explaining the etiquette of presentation. Court dress was naturally essential. Unless directly spoken to, no Minister should speak. On presentation by the Prime Minister, each Minister should take the royal hand briefly, sink on one knee, wait for the space of three seconds with head bowed, rise, take three paces backwards, turn and leave the throne room. No one should cough or sneeze.

Disraeli had carefully rehearsed these procedures at Grosvenor Gate with Mary Anne in the role of the Queen. He was rather dubious about the kneeling part, but at the age of forty-eight he was free from rheumatism and found that he could rise as well as sink without undue difficulty. His only anxiety was the recollection of the Coronation, the moment when old Lord Rolle had sunk to his knee in front of the Queen and was unable to get up. Disraeli, falling on one knee and rising in front of Mary Anne under the critical eye of Baum, was satisfied that it wouldn't happen to him.

There was one other instruction from the courtiers. It was that neither on entering, during the presentation, nor on leaving, were the Ministers to look the Queen directly in the eye.

'What a barbarous idea!' said Mary Anne. 'I want you to look her straight in the face and tell me exactly how she looks.'

In the ante-room the court chamberlains, with a courtesy

that Disraeli both welcomed and resented, were encouraging the Ministers to be at ease. They even raised their voices to a normal speaking level above the ministerial whispers.

The doors into the throne-room where Derby had been invested earlier were closed like the doors of a sarcophagus. Then the tall clock chimed twelve, and immediately the panels were flung open. Disraeli looked myopically into the room as a chamberlain called the names, and Derby, standing close to the seated Queen and the Prince Consort, repeated them to the Queen. They had been told the order of presentation. Was it rank or office that took precedence? Disraeli had forgotten. He waited for his name. Others moved forward, knelt, rose and departed as if they'd done it all their lives.

When he heard his own name, he could scarcely move. He took a deep breath. Nothing happened. Everyone seemed to be staring at him. Then his legs began to move. Ten paces to go. He walked as instructed with his eyes lowered.

He was in front of the throne. He heard his name repeated. Scarcely conscious of it, he took the royal hand and sank on one knee. What was it – three seconds? He would have liked to have rested there. Now came the ordeal of getting up.

One – two – three. He rose slowly as Baum had instructed him. 'From der toe-muscles!' He was up. His eyes were still lowered.

Now three paces back. Steady. He mustn't trip. One. He saw the royal skirt spread in layers of grey silk. Two. He saw the royal lap and the small beringed hands on it. Three. Now it was time to turn.

He looked up and saw that Victoria was scrutinizing him curiously, as if he was an Indian satrap who had just entered her service.

Half an hour later, in the courtyard, Disraeli was stepping into the third carriage when he realized he'd left his papers behind. Until that moment he had shared in the general elation of the Ministers who, having made their formal obeisance, felt that their induction into office was complete. Now he felt clumsy, discouraged.

Ordering the coachman to wait, he rapidly told the chamberlain escorting the Ministers of his difficulty. The chamberlain looked at him as if to say that this was no way to start a new ministry, and then suggested that he should return with him to the royal ante-room.

The ante-room was deserted, but in the corridor they found a household servant who said he couldn't be sure, but he did believe the Queen's secretary had taken some papers to the Private Apartments. Frowning, the chamberlain led the way.

In an outer room, Disraeli saw with relief his red box on a table; and the chamberlain, almost equally pleased to dispose of the matter, handed it to him. At the same instant there was an uproar of voices from within – or, at least, a woman's voice screaming, and answered in a sullen counterpoint by a man's protest.

'Your box, sir,' said the chamberlain as if nothing was happening. Disraeli accepted it, waiting to be led away from the hullabaloo.

A door slammed loudly inside, and the woman's voice became explicit. A voice of complaint.

'You expect me to do everything – everything. No one – no one – gives me any help. He must learn Latin.'

The voice became a shriek and another door banged.

'You've got to listen. Don't run away. Why don't you answer, Albert, when I speak to you?'

The man's voice growled, and a third door closed with a thud.

'Albert! I command you – oh, I'll die of it!'

Victoria's voice trailed away like gurgling tap-water.

The chamberlain, striding past the marble pillars and murals in the corridors, was several steps ahead of Disraeli.

'Ah – my dear,' came the man's voice, appeasingly, from the inner room, 'you excite yourself so quickly!'

The sobbing rose again to a wail, and Disraeli was about to follow the chamberlain when a boy of about twelve with a frightened expression slipped from behind one of the pillars.

'I am Edward, sir,' said the boy, holding out his hand.

'I, sir, am the new Chancellor of the Exchequer – Benjamin Disraeli.'

'There's some difference of opinion in the household,' said the boy, walking alongside Disraeli, 'about the relative merits of Latin and mathematics. My mother prefers Latin, my father mathematics. Which do you prefer?'

'Both, sir,' said Disraeli.

The Prince of Wales's tutor was standing, a hostile expression on his face, at the end of the corridor, and Disraeli bowed and took his leave. It had been an eventful day, and in the carriage and the train that took him back to London he had much to think about.

When he arrived at Grosvenor Gate, a servant was waiting for him with a note. It said:

Dear Mr Disraeli,

A matter of the greatest urgency affecting you personally has arisen. I will call on you at any time of day or night. Pray communicate with me at once.

Yours faithfully,

Philip Rose

Chapter Twenty-five

The House had risen and the clock was striking two as a group of Members of Parliament stood in New Palace Yard discussing the new Tory Government and the latest reports about famine and murder sweeping over Ireland. All around them carriages jostled, coachmen manœuvred for positions at the entrance to Westminster Hall, and other Members were hurrying through the gates while the cry of 'Who goes home?' was still being relayed by the policemen on the door, in a melancholy wail that conjured up thoughts of mortality.

'Diz tells me,' said Lord Henry Lennox, 'the Rothschilds have given a million for the public subscription.'

'Blood money,' said Tankerton. Francis Villiers nodded approvingly.

'Really,' said George Smythe. 'What would you have said if they'd given nothing?'

'I'd have said it was even more typical of their ilk.'

'And if they'd put their cash into Irish railways?'

'I'd have put my own there too.'

Tankerton waved his cane for a cab, and said, 'Anyone for St James's?'

Bulwer said, 'No thanks, I have work to do.'

Tankerton gave a shrug and, followed by Villiers, climbed in.

'Well, what are they doing in Pompeii now, Bulwer?' asked Smythe.

During a dull debate he had been drinking steadily in the Smoking Room and was now looking at Bulwer with a half-hostile, half-patronizing air, unable to understand how this touchy, one-time radical had climbed so steadily in the bosom of the established order, while he himself, more brilliant if more indolent, was beginning to sense that he had failed. Here was Bulwer off to work at midnight while he, Smythe, for whom pleasure was an occupation and journalism a distraction, felt that nothing in the world could persuade him to sit at a desk with a pen in his hand, not even for the *Morning Chronicle*. Besides, he had quarrelled a few days before with his fellow-Member at Canterbury over some trifle, and challenged him to a duel. All he now wanted was to drink himself into forgetting. And he thought, looking at Lord Henry Lennox with his handsome Norman face and his sullen, slightly askew mouth, that he had chosen a proper companion for the rest of the night, except that Lennox wasn't really a friend but merely one of the younger Members, all of a pattern, aristocratic, good-looking and dissolute, that Disraeli seemed drawn to like Narcissus to his own reflection.

'What are they doing in Pompeii, Bulwer?' Smythe repeated provocatively. 'Is your centurion still waiting for his heavenly call? Or is he studying the graffiti?'

Bulwer said, 'I'll bid you good night, sir,' and he too climbed into a carriage.

'Going home to examine his rubbings,' said Lennox morosely.

'Or the pleas in his wife's lawsuit,' said Smythe. 'Poor fellow! The wretched harridan won't leave him alone. She even turned up at the poll to abuse him.'

New Palace Yard had emptied, and they looked up at the spiky mass darkening into a black silhouette as the lights went out.

'Everything's so gloomy. Why don't we visit Mrs Hamilton's?'

'I don't think so,' said Lennox. 'She makes a fellow work too hard. All those damned whores.'

'Come on, Lennox,' said Smythe. 'Let's try Mrs Dill's.'

They took a cab to Duke Street and entered the dark stairway with a single lamp leading down to the night-house. A liveried footman took their cloaks and opened the door to the salon, full of talk and laughter, and heavy with a pleasant smell of cigar smoke and patchouli. At the top table, where the buffet was spread out, Smythe saw above the heads of the guests

Mrs Dill's white aigrette, rising like a bird of prey against the red flock wallpaper, a feathery spread almost as tall again as the distance from her black-dyed hair to her corseted bosom. The two men pressed through the groups of drinkers towards the table, just as Mrs Dill caught sight of them.

She screamed with pleasure and wobbled to her feet, fanning herself as she hurried forward in greeting.

'You naughty boy,' she said to Smythe, 'you've been away too long. Politics – politics! You'll forget how to be a man! Wardle – ' she called to a footman, smacking her fan in her palm – 'champagne for their lordships!'

'You've met?' asked Smythe with his arm around Mrs Dill's fat, moist shoulders, indicating Lennox.

'We heff met,' said Mrs Dill ominously, in the voice that she had learnt some years earlier when she'd worked as a seamstress for Lady Calverly.

'Mrs Dill, I discover,' said Lennox, 'is an old friend. I am much in her debt.'

'What have you got for us tonight?' asked Smythe.

Mrs Dill said quickly, 'No credit, my lord.'

'Cash!' said Smythe good-humouredly. 'But none of your *poussins* that turn out to be boiling chickens.'

'Too tiring,' said Lennox. He looked over his shoulder at a Guards officer who was entertaining a couple of Cyprians at a small table, and the officer gave him a wink. Lennox was pleased, and smiled back.

'What's your pleasure tonight?' said Mrs Dill, pressing a heavy breast into Smythe's elbow.

'Sleep, I would hope. But if that fails, the spectacle.'

Mrs Dill frowned.

'I'm sorry, my lord,' she said. 'The plastic poses are fully booked for the next hour. It's very popular. Ever since I've had the Nubian, the spectacle – '

She spoke with asthmatic interruptions, and the words came out hoarsely. She was apologetic. She didn't want to refuse anything to Mr Smythe. But her reputation rested on her being fair to all. If they could wait till half past three! The ladies would still be enthusiastic, she promised, though perhaps a little tired. Their performance had been especially good lately. But the Nubian – !

She raised her eyes heavenwards and clicked her tongue in rapture.

Two of Mrs Dill's young ladies approached in pink satin dresses with heart-shaped décolletés and crinoline skirts, and she presented them. Lennox took his cigar from his mouth and examined Miss Geraldine and her sister Miss Georgina. Each of them wore her hair parted in the centre, draped around her ears and plaited at the back of her head. In the gaslight neither looked more than seventeen.

Lennox said, 'Do you plan a long stay in London?'

'Oh no, sir,' they said in duet. Then they both giggled.

'We've only today come from the country,' said Miss Geraldine.

'Just a few days – their father – a Northumberland squire – asked me to chaperone 'em while they're in town. So many dangers in London society – eh?'

Miss Georgina, pink-cheeked and bovine, said in a whispery voice, 'I'd like to see the Queen ride past from Buckingham Palace.'

'A very worthy ambition,' said Smythe. Wardle, the squinting footman, brought another tray of champagne, and the sisters lunged to take a glass. Mrs Dill interposed her heavily ringed hand.

'In our – er – residence,' she said, scowling, 'we serves our gentlemen first.'

'Pray continue,' said Lennox, indicating the tray. 'I imagine these bubbles are as good as country air.'

'Oh yes,' said Miss Geraldine, draining her glass. 'Better!'

Her sister sipped her champagne more slowly, turning her beautiful and somnolent eyes to the next room, where a trio of musicians was tuning its instruments for the dancing. The girls both appeared to have added ten years to their age as the champagne flushed their complexions.

'Let us not detain these ladies,' said Smythe. 'Tonight we only wish to contemplate the pleasures of others. We'll drink – we'll observe – we'll vanish.'

Mrs Dill whispered in his ear, and he drank another glass of champagne, his eyes brightening as she pressed her sweating upper lip against his face.

'I don't think there's anything here to distract me tonight,' said Lennox. 'Come on, Smythe. I can't bear to be excluded from your intimacies with Madam.'

Smythe put his hand on Lennox's arm and said, 'Wait.'

'Well?' said Mrs Dill.

'Twenty guineas!' said Smythe.

'Thirty,' said Mrs Dill. 'Champagne – two ladies of your choice – each – and the "special". It's a bargain.'

She leaned forward to put her shoe on more firmly, and her diamond cross on a golden chain dipped into the valley of her breasts where Smythe's gaze followed it.

'All right – thirty – but who is it?'

'You'll see,' she said triumphantly. 'I'll tell you what. If you're not surprised, sir, I'll give you your money back.'

She patted her immaculately piled hair into position.

'Mrs Dill,' said Smythe, lounging in his chair, 'has offered us – in default of the *poses plastiques* – a view through an *oeil-de-boeuf* – a peepshow, you might say –'

'Better,' she said. 'A magic looking-glass –'

' – one of our eminent colleagues in close communion –'

' – secret communion –'

' – with one of her establishment.'

'Who is he?' said Lennox cautiously.

'You'll see,' said Mrs Dill briskly. She didn't want to waste any more time. The orchestra had struck up a polka, and there were shrieks of laughter from the next room mingling with the deeper voices of the men.

'A pig in a poke, so to speak!' said Lennox. 'But we'll take a chance. Thirty guineas!'

'It's only fifteen each.'

'You won't regret it,' said Mrs Dill with a laugh that rippled through her chins and ended in a fit of bronchial coughing. 'Just stay there and I'll send Wardle to fetch you.'

'Tell me, Lennox,' said Smythe, as if the thought had suddenly occurred to him, 'have you ever done anything without reason, without any purpose, and then found you're left with the consequences and that there's nothing to do but go on with it?'

Lennox said,

'Happens to me all the time. What have you done in particular, dear boy?'

Smythe looked gloomily at the champagne glasses.

'I insulted Colonel Frederick Romilly – it was all about nothing. He asked me at the clubhouse if he could pass me when I was standing at the door. I said, "Please do." And then I added, and God knows why, "But pray don't thrust." He said, "That ain't my custom, sir." Well, you know, Lennox, when a fellow calls you "sir" in that situation, there's no alternative but to say, "My impression, sir, is that it is." Romilly then says to me, "My impression, sir, is that you've taken too much refreshment." What would you have done, Lennox?'

'I'd have bowed and walked away. That's what Diz says. "If you meet a ruffian in public, bow and walk away."'

Smythe said in a melancholy voice, 'Trouble is I was the ruffian. At any rate, Romilly and I are going to fight at Epping on Thursday morning. He's got four children, you know.'

Lennox finished his champagne.

'That's a pity, Smythe. You'll either have a bullet through your chest, or a widow and four orphans on your conscience. Call it off, my dear fellow. Apologize! Say you thought he was someone else!'

'Impossible,' said Smythe gloomily. 'He'll think I'm running away.'

'Perhaps you'll both miss,' Lennox said optimistically.

'The Colonel could only miss me,' said Smythe, 'if he faced in the opposite direction.'

He ordered another bottle of champagne. He supposed he should have spent the next forty-eight hours in prayer. But he had to admit that Mrs Dill's night-house was gayer.

While they sat drinking champagne the night-house gradually became more crowded and its visitors more varied. With long experience, the doorkeeper rejected common roisterers and admitted only the 'swells' from Mayfair, the officers from Knightsbridge, the sea-captains from Tilbury and the fancy men with their own women whom Mrs Dill allowed on the premises when business was brisk and she needed reinforcement from outside.

'No, thank you,' said Smythe to Miss Angela, a thin brunette who had invited herself to their table. 'I fear we're suffering from the smallpox and are considering whether to report it to the Central Board of Health.'

Miss Angela gave him an angry look and a swish of her skirts, showing her red petticoat. Smythe took her arm and drew her to a chair.

'We're jesting, dear Miss Angela. Actually, we've come here for a little privacy – my friend and I have a matter – '

Miss Angela drank Smythe's glass of champagne, and said, 'Oo – er! I see!'

She stood up, and neither of the men rose.

'Coming here Monday?' she asked Smythe. She ruffled his hair and said, 'You're a pretty boy!'

'Thank you,' said Smythe, and they both laughed, and Lennox said, 'Let's have some brandy!'

He found the champagne agreeable but he wanted to feel violent. The Guards officer at the next table had risen and was sauntering towards the staircase arm-in-arm with the two girls, his jacket open at the neck.

'Improperly dressed!' he muttered. 'Where the devil's Mrs Dill?'

Smythe ordered brandy, and the two men drank silently.

A young man who looked like a solicitor's clerk tried to pass Smythe's outstretched leg and said, 'Excuse me, sir.'

Behind him, his partner, a blob of rouge on her cheek, waited nonchalantly.

'What can I do for you, sir?' asked Lennox.

'I wish to dance.'

'In that case,' said Smythe, heaving himself to his feet, 'let us dance!' He grasped the young man's hand and began to drag him to the dance floor, crashing against a table and knocking over two glasses.

'Pray, sit!' said Lennox, pulling Smythe down to his chair. The sudden commotion had done no more than make a few heads turn, and the hostess pushed her indignant partner forward, away from Smythe.

'Let us depart,' said Lennox.

'No,' said Smythe. 'Here's Madam herself.'

Mrs Dill advanced, sweeping her skirts like a great merchant ship responding to the winds, a salute here, a flap of sails there. A breeze of laughter followed her, and she seemed carried forward on tides of pleasure.

' 'E's 'ere,' she said in throaty confidence. 'Come in the back way – 'e did!'

As the night advanced, so Mrs Dill's syntax regressed, and she threw away her h's like a craft discharging ballast. Smythe rose to his feet and the room careened, but he quickly resumed his poise. Lennox stood, less comfortably, and rested his hand on the table. But both shared the excitement that Mrs Dill showed, despite her long experience of diversions. Like guests of honour at a banquet, they followed her. All that was lacking was applause as they marched over the thick carpets between the tables to the curving staircase that led to the private rooms, a perpetual thoroughfare of customers and waiters mounting and descending.

On the landing the splendour of the salon, with its gilt chandeliers, divans, marble busts and flower-filled urns, gave way to a series of drab rooms, each numbered as in a hotel. Mrs Dill went ahead, panting a little after her effort in climbing the stairs. She opened the door of number twenty-two with her pass key, lowered the light in the gas-lamp, and when Smythe asked in a loud voice if she had any brandy she put her finger warningly to her lips and then produced a bottle and glasses from a chiffonier.

The only other furniture was a sofa, two armchairs in Louis XV style, a wardrobe, and a tall looking-glass in a gold frame decorated with putti on a see-saw, recessed into the wall opposite the sofa. A red brocade curtain half-covered a small, shuttered window.

Mrs Dill beckoned to Smythe, and he went over to the mirror and looked into its dappled surface. Instead of seeing his reflection, he peered through into a larger, splendidly decorated bedroom with a huge brass bed, sofa-tables, a Savonnerie carpet and two wall mirrors that reflected each other. Smythe drew back, half-embarrassed, but Mrs Dill said,

'It's all right, your lordship – it's one way – see? You can see them – '

She chuckled, and her dewlaps wobbled.

'This is a looking-glass on the other side – but they can't see you. See?'

'Very ingenious,' said Smythe. 'Are you sure?'

'I'm sure,' she answered.

Lennox stared, and said, 'When do they begin?' .

'Any minute now – 'e come in the back way . . .'

She leaned on Lennox's back to point out the special features of the room, the giant bed, the full-length pier-glasses, the gilt lamps.

Lennox disentangled himself from her fat, enveloping arm and said, 'Did you build this – apparatus?'

'My late husband,' she said, 'the late Mr Dill, God rest his soul, was a joiner, and then he became a coachman to the aristocracy. But 'e thought – why drive all the gentry to their pleasures? Why shouldn't they come to me?'

'Exactly – he learned his trade very well.'

'In France – 'e used to drive for the Count D'Orsay, poor gentleman – lost all his money – 'e's in a bad way, they say, in Paris.'

'Your late husband?' said Smythe, who hadn't been listening.

'No, the Count – my husband's in Islington cemetery these last five years, God rest 'is soul. 'E was a good man.'

'And he invented this device?'

'Yes, 'e just cut out the partition and put in the mirror. It's a secret. Even the girls don't know. I keep this room locked.'

'Indeed – but you'll promise never to put me in number twenty-three?'

She gave him a squeeze and said, 'Only if you ask me to. But be quiet now. You can 'ear every word that goes on.'

Her voice dropped to a whisper and she tiptoed away, leaving behind a musky scent that Lennox waved away fastidiously.

'Tell me when something happens,' he said. He lit a candle at one of the gas-jets, and with it a cigar which he puffed, comfortably seated on one of the chairs. At the looking-glass Smythe took up a position like a sentinel. He loosened his white cravat and removed his coat, and for a few minutes he stared into the empty room, while Lennox grumbled, 'Thirty guineas! It's a swindle.'

'Quick!' Smythe said *sotto voce*, and Lennox came lazily to where he was peering. The door had opened in the next room and Miss Georgina came in, humming the tune of a mazurka and drawing off her long gloves. She could never pass a looking-glass without giving herself a careful scrutiny, and she examined herself in a hand-mirror at the dressing-table, poured herself some water at the washstand, where she again studied her face, and then came over to the looking-glass.

Smythe, invisible, looked her full in the face as she opened her mouth to admire her white, perfectly formed teeth, passed the tip of her tongue over them, and then became intrigued by her uvula. She opened her mouth wider and Smythe found himself staring with fascination directly into her gullet. Satisfied with what she saw of herself, Miss Georgina moved over to the bedside table and helped herself to a glass of brandy. Smythe nudged Lennox, who went away to pour a counterpart toast.

Miss Georgina, meanwhile, took a blue peignoir from the wardrobe and spread it out on the bed. Lennox drank hurriedly and they watched her moody expression deepen as she began to unbutton the back of her dress. She couldn't reach the middle button and said in a clear voice, 'Oh, sod it!'

Smythe laughed quietly, and Lennox pushed him a few inches to the left to get a better view.

'Mary!' she called in a harsh, high voice. An elderly maid in a black dress, an irritable expression on her pock-marked face, came in and without speaking undid the remaining buttons and untied the laces of the short, tight corset so that Miss Georgina could step out of her hooped petticoat and the two others beneath it. She stood looking at her firm breasts in the pier-glass, then, with a reflex of modesty in the presence of the maid, held her hands together in front of her.

'Very succulent!' Smythe muttered.

She turned her back, looked over her shoulder into the mirror, picked at a pimple with her nail, and put on the peignoir.

The maid gave her an enquiring look and said, ' 'E's 'ere. Want 'im in?'

'Suppose so,' said Georgina. 'What's he like?'

'One of them devil-dodgers in a high hat . . . From the Rescue Society – I don't think! ' 'Ow's Portsmouth?'

'Still there,' said Miss Georgina, putting cream on her hands at the dressing-table.

'Remember you working at Mrs Rankin's,' said Mary, lingering at the door. 'I 'ated 'er. Only sea-captains good enough for 'er. Ain't seen you, dear, in five years.'

'You wouldn't think it,' said Miss Georgina, 'and me still only fifteen!'

'Each side!' said Mary.

They both laughed heartily, and Georgina fanned her face with the hem of her gown, exposing her long, well-shaped legs.

'Well, you'd better send him in,' she said. She closed her knees and, like an actress arranging herself for the scene, picked up a bible from the bedside table and lowered her eyes.

Mary quickly returned, saying, 'Your gentleman visitor, Miss Georgina.'

'Good God!' said Smythe to Lennox.

'Well, I'm damned!' said Lennox to Smythe.

Behind Mary stood a tall, ruggedly-built man, carefully dressed like a prosperous manufacturer, with a steady expression of stern benevolence. As he entered the room he placed

314

his walking-stick under his arm, doffed his black silk hat to Miss Georgina, and stood waiting.

She looked up timidly and said to her visitor in a childlike voice,

'Be pleased to take a seat, sir.'

The man placed his hat and stick on a table and dismissed Mary with a wave of his hand. They sat without speaking while he studied her head, which she had lowered again.

'My child,' the man said at last, 'you understand the object of my visit.'

Georgina cowered in her chair and didn't reply.

'Do you understand why I have come?' he said more firmly. 'Answer me.'

The girl whimpered.

'I – I have little knowledge, sir, of the world of London. I –'

'How old are you, girl?'

'Fifteen, sir – no, yesterday I became sixteen . . .'

'In that case, I am not too late to offer you my felicitations, though you seem mature for your age. Where d'you come from?'

'From – from Northumberland – my father, sir, is the squire of Ashington.'

'That's what Mrs Dill told me,' Smythe whispered. 'The squire of Ashington is Mr Peters. You are not Miss Peters.'

'No, indeed, sir,' said Georgina. 'It's the other Ashington I was talking about. Would you like some refreshment, sir?'

'No,' he answered gruffly. 'I haven't come for refreshment. Mrs Dill has led me to you. I have come in the hope I can help you to salvation. You read, I see, the Good Book.'

'Daily, sir. It's a habit I sucked in with my mother's milk.'

He frowned.

'Why don't the old hypocrite get on with it?' said Lennox. 'What a story for Diz!'

Miss Georgina stretched out her foot and her slipper fell off.

'Pray forgive me,' she said, and bent forward to put it back. As she did so her corsage yawned a little, and he sat up stiffly in his chair. He reached for his stick and rested his hands on it.

'Now tell me, my child, everything about your past – how you came in your brief life from a home – surrounded, I don't doubt, by a loving family – into the iniquity of Mrs Dill's night-house. How does it happen that one so young – so touchingly fair – has come to this morass?'

Georgina studied him coolly, as if she were a prize-fighter assessing an opponent.

'Very easy, sir – very easy. You see, my father – the squire – he wanted me to marry Sir Henry Bullingdon.'

'Bullindon – Bullingdon? I don't think I know him.'

'He has many disguises, sir . . . I must tell you – he abused me. He left me unmarried with my baby girl.'

She began to cry and he put his hand on her shoulder.

'Continue.'

'Where was I, sir? I'm overwrought.'

'In Ashington, I understand.'

'Yes – I left Ashington with my sister.'

'And your child? Your baby girl?'

'Died – died.'

She began to weep again, and he waited for her to compose herself.

'Too much *récitatif*,' Lennox muttered as he crouched.

'I must leave you briefly,' said Georgina, and hurried out of the door.

'Gone for more brandy,' said Lennox.

As soon as she had gone the man rose and walked around the room, opening the wardrobe, inspecting the cascade of multi-coloured silk that burst out of the cupboards, sniffing their scent like a pointer, and stroking the serpentine brass of the bedheads. His expression had softened to a private content-ment and they craned forward to observe him.

Having ended his exploration, he came to the looking-glass and stared straight into Lennox's invisible face, turned his profile to the glass and looked at himself askew, and brushed his thick eyebrows and side-whiskers with his strong fingers. Then he wrinkled his nose at his reflection, champed his teeth together, smiled to himself and adjusted his cravat. On the other side of the glass Smythe stuck out his tongue.

The door opened for Miss Georgina, followed by Mary with a new bottle of brandy and a carafe of water, and her visitor resumed his censorious expression.

'Let us proceed,' he said when the maid had gone.

'A small cordial?' said Georgina timidly.

He hesitated.

'Christ, too, took refreshment with the Magdalen,' he said, accepting a glass from her hand, appearing white and delicate from the sleeve of her peignoir.

'You were saying, sir – ' said Georgina.

'Yes,' he said, sipping his brandy. 'There is time, my dear child, for repentance. To rescue you from this – this house – would be an act of merciful providence for which tonight my wife and I will earnestly pray.'

'Yes, sir,' Georgina said meekly. 'Sir – '

'Yes?'

'You are so good to me – I am ashamed. I must confess something.'

They were sitting facing each other, Georgina's knees almost touching his.

'Sir,' she continued, 'I – I lied to you before.'

He waited, and she poured them both another glass of brandy.

'You see – the name of the gentleman was Bulstrode, not Bullingdon. And he was older than my father.'

'I see – I see . . .'

'He made me his mistress when I was just turned sixteen. I am eighteen now – not sixteen.'

'Yes, I understand – he ruined you.'

'Yes, sir – but he was very kind to me – he was sixty-one – and he protected me – and I liked it. Never again have I been so happy.'

'Ah!' he said. 'Vice takes many attractive guises.'

'Indeed, sir – he was never the same – him always thinking up something new. Always so kind to me. Called me his Pippin. Then he dropped dead – his exertions, sir.'

'I understand,' he said, and took her hand comfortingly.

'But after that I was all alone – you see – that was how I came to be ruined in the first place. I fled from the manor, sought out my sister – the *cruel* insults! – and I came to London my very first time, and there was this gentleman who took us to Mr Hamilton's – where we were till lately. And Mr Well-beloved – he cared for us at first, him being a Quaker, and then he submitted us to the most harsh abominations!'

The visitor took her other hand sympathetically.

'He beat us – both together. He made us – forgive me – I wouldn't offend your ear – '

'Continue! Continue!' he said urgently.

'He tied us both up, and beat us, and then – like a wild animal – oh, sir! I can't tell you.'

Her visitor's face had flushed brick-red.

'Yes – tell me everything, my dear child.'

'Only yesterday,' said Georgina, 'he bruised my breast.'

She opened her peignoir, and simultaneously the three men on the two sides of the mirror craned forward to see the breast she exposed. It was smooth like an exquisite peeled peach, swelling with a promise of pleasure from the dark cleft to the pert and erect nipple.

'I see nothing.'

'Here,' said Georgina, raising her left breast with her right hand and offering for inspection a tiny bruise below her neck. As he continued to lean forward, she quickly slipped her breast back inside the peignoir, which she drew modestly around her.

'You see,' she said, 'what beasts men can be!'

The man rubbed his hands on his trouser legs. He wanted to address her again, but gulped and sat staring at her. At last he said, 'Have you been subjected to other brutalities?'

'No,' said Georgina. Her invention had begun to fail and she disliked extended conversation. But then she felt that her visitor needed a final encouragement.

'Except,' she said, 'he bit me cruelly.'

'Bit you?'

'In the thigh – I hesitate, sir – '

'Do not shrink from anything.'

318

Georgina looked up, then lowered her eyes quickly. Then she kicked off her shoe and extended her slim foot that contrasted with her heavy shoulders. She raised her peignoir till it nearly reached her calf.

'No, sir – I really can't,' she said, and drew her skirt modestly round her. Smythe whispered an oath and Lennox, leaning over his shoulder, said, 'The bitch!'

'You must tell me all,' the man said in a strangled voice.

He waved his hand. Slowly, centimetre by centimetre, Georgina raised the hem of her gown, and the three men stared, their heartbeats quickening as she stretched out her left leg, half-turning on her side, till it reached the knee. She paused and looked up with submissive eyes. Her visitor didn't speak, but looked fixedly at the skirt now creeping above her knee to her thigh. With a sudden pull, she raised her skirt and exposed her thick, pale thigh, with a red and blue bruise near its inside. Then as quickly as she had drawn it up, she let the dressing-gown tremble down in a ruffled fall.

'She'd wake the Seven Sleepers,' said Smythe.

'Shall I tell you more?' said Georgina.

The man swallowed, and didn't answer.

'Are you struck by my story?' she asked.

He turned the brandy glass in his hand.

'I have so much more to say,' said Georgina. 'I wish I could write books. My friend – he was like you.'

'Indeed – '

'Yes,' she said. 'He was a big – fatherly – man – just like you, Mr – Mr Gladstone.'

The man compressed his lips.

'You are familiar with my name.'

She went on her knees and took his hand, and said, 'It's a by-word among the women you've saved.'

She kissed his hand, and Gladstone said, 'My child, let us pray together for our salvation!'

He sank heavily to his knees opposite Georgina, and they put their hands together in prayer.

Lennox groaned quietly.

'Oh, God,' said Gladstone aloud, 'I pray You that we may

319

be preserved from the lusts of the heart and the flesh, and that we may find recompense – '

Georgina's gown began to slip from her shoulders and her hair, released from its fillets, fell in two swathes around her neck.

' – find recompense – in works that will sustain us – and deliver us from temptation – and the carnal world.'

Gladstone spoke the last words rapidly, and ended, 'Amen.'

'Amen!' whispered Georgina, as he resumed his seat a few inches from where she was kneeling, at his knees. She didn't move, and he put his hand, trembling a little, on her head. Her gown slid to the ground.

At that moment Lennox, pressing with whole weight against Smythe to get a better view, pushed his hand against the looking-glass. With a loud, splitting crack, it shattered into fragments, precipitating Smythe and Lennox into the next room. For a second the four of them stared at each other in shock.

'Run!' said Lennox.

His hand bleeding from the broken pane, he rushed back through the shattered frame into Room 22, closely followed by Smythe.

In Room 23 Georgina was screaming, Gladstone had retreated through the back door, and as Smythe and Lennox, concealing his hand beneath his cloak, though dripping gouts of blood on the carpet, hurried through the corridor, the doors opened one by one as half-dressed men and women peered out to see whether there was a fire or a murder.

Over breakfast at Grosvenor Gate the next day, before Disraeli left for Downing Street, Lennox told him and Mr Rose of the encounter with Gladstone.

'It should be known,' he said, 'how he spends his evenings.'

Disraeli listened solemnly, and said, 'Everyone must find his own way to heaven. Mr Gladstone prefers to save himself through works.'

'That hypocrite! Works?'

'Yes, works. Anyone can bring in a Bill to limit prostitution.

Not everyone would wish to toil, when the House is risen, in the vineyards of Soho and Haymarket. Don't you think?'

Lennox looked up to see if Disraeli was smiling, but he was wearing the graven expression that he had taken to using among the gossips of Westminster and Mayfair.

Chapter Twenty-six

After Lennox had gone, Rose took a second helping of devilled kidneys from the sideboard.

'I think,' he said, 'that small encounter will divert Mr Gladstone for some little time and, I think, keep him silent.'

'It's as well,' said Disraeli glumly. The previous night after he had received Rose's note, he had called at his rooms in Bond Street, and there he had learnt that Mrs Edmonds intended to issue a writ of bankruptcy against him. His parliamentary immunity when the House was in session wouldn't help. It was her purpose, she had informed Rose, to have the writ served after the forthcoming General Election but before the reassembly of Parliament.

Rose wore an unhappy expression that Disraeli was unfamiliar with.

'I've been talking to Drummond's,' he said, 'and I fear they're unwilling to extend your credit – not even the Chancellor of the Exchequer's credit. You see, sir, when one creditor starts foreclosing, it's the beginning of a rush. It gets around. I hear – I have to report this to you – Lord Henry Bentinck and Titchfield may want to call in their loan on Hughenden.'

Disraeli's hand trembled, and the spoon in his coffee-cup rattled.

'Why?'

Rose shrugged his shoulders.

'I don't know – malice, perhaps your success has offended them. But the immediate need is to deal with Mrs Edmonds. We've got to raise ten thousand or so almost at once.'

'Would she surrender the bill? Will she – ' Disraeli had difficulty in bringing out the words – 'will she insist on – '

'The bill is due on the fifteenth. That gives us six days. If she wants to be spiteful, and I expect she does, she can start proceedings the next day. Have you anything to sell, sir?'

'Nothing,' said Disraeli in a melancholy voice.

'Mrs Disraeli's jewels?'

'Never,' said Disraeli firmly. 'I could never agree to that. Besides, they're entailed.'

'Have you anything left to borrow against?' asked Rose.

It was a rumination, not a question. Rose knew the limits of Disraeli's resources.

'How are the devilled kidneys?' Disraeli asked.

'Excellent,' said Rose, speaking through a mush of potatoes. 'But we mustn't lose sight of our purpose.'

'Perhaps,' said Disraeli, 'I could get an advance on a new novel.'

'Too little – too long. What could you get? A thousand, two thousand pounds? You'll need more than that. What you need, sir, is a patron, someone who'll value your genius, your place in public affairs, someone who'll relieve you of the sordid burden of financial anxiety.'

Rose spoke seriously, but his eyes were amused.

'It's exactly what I think,' said Disraeli, maintaining Rose's grave tones. 'The only problem is to find the benefactor.'

'Benefactress?'

'Alas, at forty-eight I've lost the gift of finding benefactresses. You know, Rose, we live in grave days, and grave days require grave statesmen.'

He played with the fob of his single gold watch-chain.

'Twenty years ago I had the art as well as the need of prestidigitation with my finances. With time, it's all become harder.'

Rose took his table napkin from his waistcoat and said, 'I have conceived the glimmer of a hope.'

Disraeli turned to him, and his expression lightened. He knew that Rose wouldn't offer even a glint of optimism if he didn't have some solid reason for revealing it.

'Mrs Brydges Willyams – '

Disraeli's moment of hope was over.

'Oh no. That's out of the question.'

'Not entirely,' said Rose. 'What I propose, Mr Disraeli –

today is Friday – I propose you send Mrs Willyams a telegram, announcing that you'll visit her tomorrow.'

'That would scarcely be courteous.'

'That may be. But vital none the less. You will tell her that as her executor you have an urgent matter to discuss.'

'And what is that?'

'An entitlement, should your situation require it, to use your expectations from her estate as a security against a loan from Drummond's.'

At that moment Mary Anne came into the room and said, 'Heavens, Mr Rose, you look cheerful for so early in the morning. And what a drab morning it is. Why are you looking so out-of-tune with the weather?'

'My dear,' said Disraeli, who had risen to greet her. 'Mr Rose thinks I need a change, and we're going to pay a short visit to Mrs Willyams in Devon. Tomorrow.'

Mary Anne clapped her hands.

'I do so like improvisations,' she said. 'Will we be staying a week or two?'

'No,' said Disraeli. 'A day or two. On Sunday Baum will send us a telegram recalling me to London. Besides, we have to attend Lady Jersey's ball on Wednesday.'

'Ah yes,' said Mary Anne resignedly. 'So much gaiety, and so little time for it all.'

The train rolled southwards towards Taunton, Mr Rose was asleep with his hands over his waistcoat, and gradually Mary Anne teased Disraeli from his gloom.

'Would you like to call on Rosina Bulwer?' she asked in his ear.

Disraeli shuddered.

'The unhappy Bulwer!' he muttered. 'Can you imagine, Mary Anne, anything more odious than a mad wife denouncing her husband?'

'Oh yes,' said Mary Anne. 'Lots of worse happenings.'

'Would you denounce me?'

'Of course I would.'

'What would you say?'

Mary Anne thought for a moment.

'I'd say that whenever we have a party and I'm all ready, you always get into conversation with someone else and I have to wait for you.'

'What else?'

She clung to his arm.

'Too many people want your attention. All those clever young men. Lord Henry Lennox – '

'He's going to stay in Paris.'

'That's the proper place for him. I've always thought him such a *light* person. You always have to be surrounded, Ben, by handsome young people.'

'Mrs Willyams is eighty.'

'I'm so pleased,' said Mary Anne. 'I rarely meet anyone nowadays who's older than myself.'

Disraeli sat back against the buttoned upholstery and thought of the curious history of his connection with Mrs Willyams. After their abortive rendezvous at the Great Exhibition, they had begun to write to each other. He had been moved by the prospect of the legacy. '*Torquay vaut bien une messe,*' he had said to his solicitor. Gradually, though, his correspondence with the old lady had taken on a different significance. As his sister Sarah's letters dwindled, so he found a need to communicate with an admiring audience gratified by his letters.

Well informed, alert and decisive, Mrs Willyams was, as he had soon discovered, not at all so bizarre as he had originally imagined. She was affectionate and outgoing, eager always to learn about his life, a surrogate for his own mother, who had been reserved, undemonstrative and discouraging. Like his father's mother, whom he had always regarded as a demon, she had helped to bring him up with a prejudice against the Jewish faith, and even resented his Semitic features that echoed her own.

By contrast, Mrs Willyams, a respected and secure member of Christian society, revelled in her Jewish ancestry. Drawn to him, as she had first written, by his concern for the race of Israel, she had now decided that both she and Disraeli belonged to the aristocratic Judæo-Spanish family of Lara. The genealogy was as fictitious as their intimacy was artificial. But Disraeli had begun to enjoy it.

Mrs Willyams was waiting to greet them on the steps of her villa, Mount Braddon. She wore a similar black dress to the one she had worn at the Exhibition, with a touch of lace at the neck, her hair drawn back in an elegant bun, and her two dogs – could they be the same ones? – yapping at her skirts. She embraced Mary Anne; gave her hand to Disraeli, who raised it to his lips; bowed to Mr Rose, whom, thereafter, she ignored; and followed by Baum carrying an assortment of gifts, including a trout packed in ice and pressed in fern, cuttings from the gardens of Hughenden, and three pineapples delivered at Grosvenor Gate by an anonymous admirer, they entered the shadowy interior of the large house.

Mrs Willyams was an autocrat. When she appeared, her servants rustled past like ghosts, and even Mary Anne fell silent as Mrs Willyams dispensed tea, mingled with her dicta about the conduct of life. At last Mary Anne congratulated her on her robust air.

'I owe my good health,' Mrs Willyams said, 'entirely to my indifference to doctors. Never consult doctors, my dear Mrs Disraeli. I believe that provided one keeps out of their hands, we can all live to be a hundred.'

Seeing that Mary Anne was about to comment on the disadvantages of longevity, Disraeli offered her a cake, which she took delicately. The vicar, Mr Parks Smith, with the tone of his rubicund face heightened by the sunlight, was announced, and Mrs Willyams presented him. He greeted the Disraelis and Rose cordially. Through Mrs Willyams, he had already formed the view that Disraeli might one day assist in his clerical advancement and help him to overcome the handicap of being suspected of excessively Puseyite leanings.

Disraeli bowed solemnly to him.

'I am already acquainted with the name of Mr Parks Smith. It has become famous in the prints.'

The vicar hurried to explain in a portentous voice.

'Indeed, sir, an unfortunate episode. The Bishop – how can I put it? – is somewhat choleric.'

'Opposed, I understand, to ritual adornment.'

'Indeed, yes – indeed. I think that on that Sunday he was specially impatient – the vase of flowers on the altar – '

'Hardly exceptional!'

'Yes – yes.' The vicar was nervous. 'He was very angry at what he called – mistakenly, I make bold to say – a Popish practice. He shouted, I regret, and tried to sweep the flowers from the altar.'

'How distressing!' said Mary Anne. 'The litter!'

'Well, not exactly,' the vicar explained. 'It was a case of *vox et praeterea nihil*. You see, I'd attached the vase to the marble support with a stout piece of string.'

He looked courteously at Disraeli, and seeing that he and Mary Anne were smiling, smiled himself.

'We are happy to welcome you to the warm clime of Devon,' he said.

There were palm trees growing in the open air outside the window, and Mrs Willyams, following Disraeli's glance, said, 'They were brought here by my late husband many years ago from some campaign or other.'

'Yes,' said Mary Anne. 'My own late husband tried to grow pineapples in Cardiff, but the coal dust, you know – '

She turned to the vicar and said, 'I've been thinking lately about theology, Vicar.'

'Ah, yes, my dear lady,' said the vicar warily, putting down his teacup. Since the episode with the Bishop, he felt somewhat guarded about matters of dogma.

'Well,' said Mary Anne, 'say we all live to be a hundred as Mrs Willyams was suggesting.'

'Yes, of course. Why not?'

The vicar was familiar with Mrs Willyams's theories.

'In that time we could all have a number of husbands and wives.'

'Not simultaneously, of course,' said Disraeli.

'You mustn't make fun of me,' said Mary Anne. 'This is a

very serious matter. Now, Vicar, you believe in immortality – you do, don't you?'

The vicar, accustomed to the question, smiled.

'The Christian doctrine is explicit – together with the doctrine of the Resurrection.'

'Well, this is what I want to ask you. If your first husband predeceases you and you marry again, are you – eventually, of course – united with your first or your second husband – or both – when you go to Heaven?'

The vicar pondered, and Mrs Willyams poured another cup of tea for Disraeli.

'In Heaven,' said the vicar judicially, 'there's neither taking nor giving in marriage.'

'But that's not at all satisfactory,' said Mary Anne. 'I'm not at all sure that I want to go there if I can't be with my Diz.'

'Let us instead,' Disraeli proposed, 'drive through the countryside while the sun is still high.'

Mrs Willyams gave him a benevolent look, pulled at the bell to order the carriage, and the vicar, happy to have been delivered from a metaphysical judgement on a matter about which he had some doubts, excused himself and left, together with Mr Rose who, having met his hostess, felt that Disraeli could deal more effectively with the preamble to their purpose if they were left alone.

Mrs Willyams, Mary Anne and Disraeli drove through country lanes that gave glimpses of the bay, of yachts with white sails moving imperceptibly over a pale blue sea merging at the horizon with a washed sky, and coasters leaving thin drifts of smoke before vanishing beyond the promontory.

Mary Anne was content. Usually the presence of a third person meant that her possession of her husband was diminished. With Mrs Willyams she had no anxieties. She dozed in the afternoon air, listening to the hoof-beats as the other two kept up a lively conversation. Mrs Willyams wanted to know all about the political and social gossip from London and asked Disraeli about Lord Derby.

'I'm afraid,' he said, 'when it comes to power, he's like an eager lover who swoons at the moment before possession. A year ago when he could have been First Minister, he bolted. And now, I fear, in government he's languid.'

Mrs Willyams was flattered by his indiscretions.

'How d'you mean, Mr Disraeli? What sort of languor?'

Disraeli sighed.

'His house always seems closed – he rarely entertains his political friends.'

'And you?'

Disraeli hesitated, unwilling to admit that Derby, while intimate with him politically, only rarely sought to entertain him socially.

'My own connection with him is adequate. But what can one do with a man who's always racing at Newmarket or Doncaster when Europe's in flames?'

Mrs Willyams pointed out a seventeenth-century windmill, and Mary Anne glanced at it and dozed off again.

'Your genius,' Mrs Willyams said, 'is precisely that you confront every obstacle without having to call for help. If Derby were more active, you'd lack the situation for it to thrive in. Don't regret it, dear Mr Disraeli. One man against the world is – divine.'

Disraeli took her gloved hand for a second.

'It's highly flattering for an author,' he said, 'when he hears his written word quoted against what he says.'

'Well, enough of politics!' Mrs Willyams went on peremptorily. 'Tell me about your other friends – Lady Londonderry – Lady Jersey.'

'Ah!' said Disraeli. 'I fear Lady Jersey is unhappy about Mr Villiers and his inamorata.'

'Yes,' said Mary Anne, waking up. 'Our society is very vulnerable to beauty and connections. Yet one wouldn't engage a servant on that basis. Mrs Edmonds appeared from nowhere – her recommendation was that she was married to a Polish count. Diz and I met her in Paris – oh, almost ten years ago. In next to no time she was a reigning beauty, a member of English society, and a friend of the nobility.'

'You knew her personally?' Mrs Willyams asked.

'Oh yes, everyone knew her. She was an intimate of Mr Hudson.'

'That's rather like saying, Mrs Disraeli, she was an intimate of the railway system.'

'Well, in our modern days most liaisons depend on the availability of transport.'

Disraeli intervened. 'And yet, in the case of Mr Francis Villiers and Mrs Edmonds, it seems to be a question of love.'

'What about the time Mrs Edmonds got possession of one of your debts?' said Mary Anne.

Disraeli looked icily at his wife. This wasn't the moment to create doubts in Mrs Willyams's mind about his moral character.

'Bills, my dear, are like currency. They pass from hand to hand.'

They didn't speak until the carriage reached the Royal Hotel, where Disraeli helped Mary Anne down as she wanted to rest before dinner. He then returned to Mount Braddon with Mrs Willyams whose face since Mary Anne's indiscretion had become thoughtful.

'This is Chang and this is Yang,' said Mrs Willyams. 'Chang is two and Yang is three . . . And here,' she said when they reached the bottom of the orchard, 'are the graves of Chang and Yang, their predecessors. I believe in a seemly burial for those I love.'

Disraeli peered at the small headstones, perhaps ten of them, all with appropriate inscriptions. 'Chang – a faithful friend – died aged ten.' 'Yang – always missed – died aged eight.'

After a respectful pause they walked on slowly, with Mrs Willyams holding Disraeli's arm.

'And what about the Jew Bill?' she asked. 'Will Baron de Rothschild ever succeed?'

'Oh, certainly,' said Disraeli. 'Bore people enough, and you can do anything. One of these days the House is going to get tired of saying "No". The opponents will get older. The young men will become indifferent. At that moment, Mr de Rothschild will advance to the Table, take his oath his own way, and nobody will say "No". Boredom, Mrs Willyams, is democracy's version of the *coup d'état*.'

'I pray so – I pray so,' she said. 'It's my great hope before I die to see the rights of Israel's children vindicated. Even here, by the waters of Babylon.'

Disraeli looked at the colonnaded villa with its terraces leading to the cliff, and thought that Babylon took many gracious forms.

'Tell me,' Mrs Willyams asked, 'what recent connection have you with Mrs Edmonds?'

Taken aback, Disraeli said, 'Dear Mrs Willyams – they're the connections of anyone who has shaken her hand – no more than that. The connection of one who has tried to protect an unhappy mother from an unfortunate influence over a favourite son . . . Perhaps you would like to rest?'

'Oh no,' said Mrs Willyams, thinking that she had offended him. 'Pray don't leave. I ask you about Mrs Edmonds only because there's a matter of great importance I want to discuss with you, and I wanted to know exactly your present obligations. Do sit, Mr Disraeli.'

He led her to a wicker chair in the pergola, and she said, 'For some time – ' it was her usual beginning – 'for some time, I've been thinking of my burial place.'

'Oh, come, Mrs Willyams,' said Disraeli, startled. 'You have many years to consider these matters.'

'No – no one can tell. You would, I am sure, like to be buried with your loved ones.'

'It's a subject I don't often consider.'

'But if you did – '

'I imagine – I suppose I'd want to be buried at Hughenden, side by side with Mary Anne.'

'You'll recall what Mrs Disraeli asked the vicar. You said nothing. What is your view?'

Disraeli looked at Mrs Willyams's questioning eyes. They were alert and trusting, as if she were confident he could provide the answer to the mysterious question that troubled her.

'You see,' she went on, as he still didn't answer, 'Colonel Willyams was a very good and kind man – a very brave soldier. But he had very little human understanding. Everything that related to me – to my ancestral past – was closed. He would

331

say, may he rest in peace, "Leave that to the clergy, m'dear," and that would be an end of it.'

'Wasn't that a wise prescription?'

'No – I've always endeavoured to answer these great and universal questions for myself. I would not like to think that if there's an everlasting life, as there must be, I'd have to spend it with the Colonel.'

'Yes – yes,' said Disraeli. 'I do understand all that. Let us hope that in the life to come there's some freedom of choice.'

The two dogs had scampered towards the shrubbery in pursuit of a rabbit. Mrs Willyams, temporarily diverted from eschatological matters, called out, 'Chang – Yang – come here at once!'

'Well, Mr Disraeli,' she went on, 'I've long nourished the belief that our communications haven't been adventitious, but have been prompted by One Above greater than us all.'

'I never doubt that our destiny may be part of a grand design,' said Disraeli noncommittally. He was wondering what new dream had gripped her mind.

'Our kinship – '

She's still involved in her genealogical fantasy, thought Disraeli.

'Your own genius which I detected so personally – '

By no means the first to do so.

'The special affinity which decided me to make you my trustee and heir – '

A moment for watchfulness and prudence. He didn't speak.

'At any rate, all this has emboldened me to ask – '

If she had to be 'emboldened to ask', her request was likely to be bizarre.

'It has emboldened me to ask you that when I die, I may be buried in Hughenden.'

Disraeli was relieved. The request was far-fetched, but not fantastic. But Mrs Willyams hadn't finished.

'I want to be buried in Hughenden in order to be near you, Dizzy.'

It was the first time she'd called him by that familiar name, and it seemed a friendly eccentricity.

'I'll speak to Mr Pigott, the vicar of Hughenden. I'm sure that in the fullness of time – '

'Yes, but there's something further. I want to be buried next to you – by your side.'

Disraeli fumbled with his eyeglass.

'But that, Mrs Willyams, might present difficulties. Mary Anne – '

'She will do what you say,' said Mrs Willyams sternly.

'But the Church authorities – '

'They have no objection to proximity. I would wish to be buried with you and Mary Anne in Hughenden church – that beautiful little Saxon church you've written about so lovingly.'

Disraeli hesitated, and Mrs Willyams smiled to him amiably.

'You see, you're my executor as well as my heir.'

'Indeed.'

'You have agreed to carry out my wishes.'

'Of course.'

'Perhaps you'd like to be relieved of your responsibilities?'

'No, no – to be of service to you, dear lady – but you understand there may be difficulties – the ecclesiastical authorities – perhaps even the Church Commissioners – '

'You'll deal with them, I'm sure. Shall we play *écarté* tonight?'

It was a long time since he had played *écarté*. Crockford's, long liquidated, was a far cry from the elderly lady in front of him. It all belonged to the past, all, that is to say, except for the D'Orsay bill that remained, grumbling, leering and swelling like a jinn escaped from a bottle, a demon to be appeased with occasional tribute which seemed to feed rather than tame it. Now at last, by borrowing against Mrs Willyams's legacy, he had the chance to exorcise it. It would be a pity to forfeit that opportunity over a question of churchyard geography.

Mary Anne came into the sitting-room at the Royal Hotel and saw Disraeli studying a letter with an expression of gloom.

'What is it, Ben?' she asked. 'Do you like my new dress?'

333

It was pale rose, suitable for a young woman, and she had added a special touch of rouge to her cheeks.

'You look radiant, Mary Anne,' said Disraeli. 'The Devon air suits you.'

'But I'll be glad when we get back to our own private air in Hughenden. You look disturbed. Something is worrying you. You can't hide anything from Mary Anne.'

And that was true. In the years of their marriage she had learnt to read the shades of expression in his eyes, and to understand his mood from the space of his silences, the inflection of his voice, even his manner of entering a room.

'What is it, Ben?' she repeated.

'Before I left London, I had this letter from Henry Bentinck.'

'Oh, how is he?'

'Well and friendly. But I'm afraid the letter contains bad news.'

She went over to him and looked up into his face.

'There's no bad news, Ben, so long as you are well and close to me.'

'The bad news,' said Disraeli slowly, 'is that Henry and his brother, Titchfield, want to call in the loan that George gave us for Hughenden.'

Mary Anne sat carefully on a stool, spreading her crinoline skirt.

'But why? They were your friends. Your book on Lord George Bentinck was such a beautiful tribute to their brother. Why should they act so cruelly? What does it mean?'

Disraeli walked to the window and looked out at the declining sun.

'It means, my dearest, that if Titchfield insists – and Henry has shown nothing but goodwill – we may have to leave Hughenden. He wants twenty-five thousand – though he will take an instalment.'

Mary Anne burst into tears.

'But that's impossible. Where can you find twenty-five thousand? Or even part of it? Why should he behave so cruelly?'

'The new Duke,' said Disraeli, 'isn't a generous man.

334

George's tenacity was a noble determination. Titchfield's is a vice. He's a specialist in the vendetta.'

'Why should he have a vendetta against you? You've shown nothing but kindness to the Bentincks.'

'Ah, Mary Anne,' said Disraeli, sitting at her side, 'kindness is often hard to forgive. Dukes in particular don't like to feel obliged. Come now, dry your eyes, Mary Anne. I'm not discouraged. Something always turns up to put matters right.'

He took his cambric handkerchief and dried her eyes.

Then she smiled at him, and he said, 'Titchfield's a very eccentric fellow. Did you know he always travels with the blinds drawn even in daylight?'

'Really?' said Mary Anne. 'I think that's excellent. It's how I'd like to travel with you.'

Disraeli rose again, and she saw that he was agitated.

'Could you,' she asked, 'borrow against your expectations? What about the Rothschilds? One of the banks?'

'I can't ask the Rothschilds for anything. The banks will give me no further credit. And my expectations have been somewhat threatened in the last few hours.'

She looked up quickly.

'But why, Ben?'

'I'm afraid,' he said, 'we are the victims of eccentricity. Our friend Mrs Willyams has put to me a request which I fear you might not favour.'

'And what is that?'

Disraeli went to the looking-glass and adjusted his cravat.

'She has the whimsical idea she wants to be buried with us in a vault in Hughenden church.'

He watched Mary Anne's face in the mirror.

'What a friendly thought!' said Mary Anne. 'So long as I'm on your right, what does it matter?'

That same evening after dinner, when Mary Anne had retired with Disraeli, Mr Rose explained to Mrs Willyams the form in which he proposed, if necessary and with her consent, to draw against the prospects of the legacy. She interrupted him with a hasty 'Yes – yes.' What she was really anxious to discuss were the arrangements for her burial at 'dear Dizzy's side'.

Chapter Twenty-seven

Lady Jersey's summer ball at Berkeley Square was the most important event of the Season before the Budget, and the corridors were a parade-ground of sumptuous display. Not even Mr Huffam's disappointment of office interfered with his pleasure in commanding a respectful audience of Ministers and their wives as he retailed the latest news from the clubs. Mr Gladstone, he was saying, had been involved in a disagreeable scene at White's after making a speech attacking Disraeli.

'Yes,' he said to Lord Naas, the Chief Secretary for Ireland, 'Gladstone has been offering some very *liberal* views – ' there was a snigger – 'when the younger men started hazing him. You know the sort of thing, my lord. He was taking coffee quietly, and one of them said in a loud voice, "Very good coffee at the Reform," and another butted in, "Those Liberals make very good coffee," and someone else proposed in a *very* loud voice that Mr Gladstone should be chaired and carried unanimously to the Reform.'

'Could have been ugly,' said Sir Frederick Thesiger, the sixty-year-old Attorney-General.

'Would have been – would have been if it hadn't been for Mr Disraeli. He invited the young men to take port with him, and – why, here's Mr Chancellor himself.'

Disraeli and Mary Anne paused in their progress.

'Oh, do tell us what happened at White's,' said Lady Olivia Ossulston. 'What happened with Mr Gladstone? Mr Huffam's been telling us all.'

Disraeli dismissed the subject.

'Nothing to speak of. I merely suggested to some of my friends who wanted to try and carry Mr Gladstone that it would be unwise, since I understand his favourite exercise at Hawarden is felling oaks.'

They laughed, and Disraeli moved on with Mary Anne on his arm. She was radiant with the knowledge that her husband's name was on everyone's lips. The words 'reduction of the Malt Tax' accompanied the music of the polka and the quadrille as if they had been composed for each other. Distributed like the masks and bergamasks of a Watteau-like Cytherea, the groups in front of the huge flower-filled vases spoke in statistics. When Disraeli passed the alcoves where the chaperones sat with their charges, there was a movement of naked shoulders and searching eyes, not in pursuit of the poet, or even of the statesman, but of the accountant. The Budget was, after all, something that touched everyone. Next to death, the great leveller. 'Will Mr Disraeli help the farmers?' 'Is it true he was a Radical once upon a time?' 'He voted for the Jew Bill, you know.' As Disraeli and Mary Anne passed on, the whispers stirred like a rustle of leaves behind a curtain of painted fans.

At Lady Jersey's table, Lord Worcester presented himself in front of Mary Anne and invited her to waltz. Disraeli inclined his head and watched with relief as Mary Anne and her partner circled into the dancers. He wanted to feel that she was well bestowed before he gave his attention to more worrying matters.

After supper, he sat in an armchair, the centre of a circle. He raised his eyeglass and watched the dancers for a few moments. At the other side of the ballroom he saw Mr Rose standing by a pillar. Rose gave him a half-smile, and he was glad of the reassurance. They had an uneasy task before them, and Disraeli glanced quickly at Lady Jersey sitting beside him. Her left hand clutched the silk of her dress, and he recognized her anxieties.

'She's here,' said Lady Jersey. Disraeli was about to comment when she leaned towards Lord Naas and said, 'There's nowhere better to make a career than in Ireland. Don't you think?'

'I'd prefer India,' said Naas. 'At least you know there's someone to plunder. Didn't Mr Villiers serve in Madras?'

'Yes,' she said. 'But I don't think he had the wit or the

opportunity to plunder anyone. He was only a military secretary.'

'A very valuable training,' said Disraeli. 'I think Mr Villiers will be of great benefit to our administration in dealing with the Horse Guards.'

Lord Naas was distracted by Lady Georgina Worcester, and Lady Jersey repeated in a tense voice to Disraeli,

'She's here.'

'But that, dear lady, is exactly what we wanted. Don't we agree? It's why you invited her. Is Tankerton with her?'

'I invited him too. Oh, Ben, I hope I acted correctly. My husband dislikes that man so much. So does Derby . . . Look, she's dancing with him.'

Lady Jersey raised her fan to hide the flush of anger that had swept over her neck and her face.

'With Derby? Tankerton?' asked Disraeli, fumbling for his eyeglass.

'No,' said Lady Jersey. 'With Francis – my son.'

Her face was controlled, but Disraeli observed the long sinew of her forearm tighten as she gripped her fan. The music ended, and the couples began to disperse to their tables.

'He's bringing her over,' said Lady Jersey in a smothered voice.

'You must greet her,' said Disraeli.

Mrs Edmonds advanced with her hand on Mr Villiers's, her skirts sweeping with a graceful balancing motion that drew the eyes of everyone sitting in the arc around Lady Jersey. Mrs Edmonds's black hair had been tinted into a russet colour, and she was wearing it set in ringlets that fell on her neck but left her ears with two diamond pendants exposed. Her toilette was a challenge to Lady Jersey's, and outdid it.

At her side, Mr Villiers wore a honeymoon expression. He was both proud and defiant that, having an exceptionally beautiful if notorious woman on his arm, he was presenting her in society in face of the hostility of the wiseacres.

'Mama,' said Mr Villiers as the men rose, 'I think you have seen Mrs Edmonds. Allow me to introduce her.'

Mrs Edmonds gave Lady Jersey her fingers, undaunted by

her cool glance, and then she smiled more boldly to the gentlemen, who despite Lady Jersey's disapproval spontaneously gave her an ingratiating smile.

Disraeli himself greeted her and murmured to Villiers, 'Mrs Edmonds and I are friends of long standing.'

'I think, Francis,' said Lady Jersey in an imperious voice, 'you will stay and talk to me a little. Come – come.' She patted the sofa. 'Mrs Edmonds will release you for a few minutes while Mr Disraeli looks after her. Come, Francis. I know you want to dance with Mrs Disraeli afterwards.'

Villiers brushed his fair hair from his forehead and put his hand on his white cravat as he gave Mary Anne, who had returned, a slight bow.

'That was my purpose,' he said gallantly.

'And do you dance, Mr Disraeli?' Mrs Edmonds asked.

'Only privately,' said Disraeli. 'Perhaps, madam, we can walk and converse.'

She put her hand on his, and they walked together slowly to the conservatory, greeting acquaintances as they went.

Disraeli indicated a place to her in a remote corner beneath the palm trees, almost out of earshot of the music. Mrs Edmonds's expression had become rigid and unsmiling. She waited for Disraeli to speak.

'I am sorry to discuss affairs,' he said, 'on such an agreeable occasion. When I wrote to you – '

'I don't think we need detain each other. You have broken my friendship with Lord Derby – you have tried to destroy my social relations in London.'

Disraeli sighed.

'Ah, Clarissa, you've always misunderstood. I never offered you anything but friendship. Whatever Derby may have thought or done, he has never heard from me anything but good about you.' He took her hand, but she left it inert in his. 'Can't we end this long vendetta? You surely know I never meant you ill.'

She turned her face to his, and the gaslight falling on her hair heightened its unnatural colour. This was the face that had once delighted and troubled and intrigued him, the laughing, adventurous face that had been an interval between Henrietta's and Mary Anne's. 'Greatest whore in London.' Greville's voice overheard. The face was enamelled, the wrinkles around the eyes were masked. It was, he thought, a counting kind of face.

'Oh, Ben, you've done me a great deal of ill,' she said, and the words were a contrast with her disciplined expression. 'I loved you. I'd only just recovered from my husband's death, and you found me grasping the air like someone drowning. You were kind and understanding. You were always like that. And then came the excuses.'

He tried to interrupt, but she went on.

'Those terrible excuses. Why you couldn't come to dinner. You didn't want anyone else to visit me, did you, Ben? You wanted me to sit alone at home, and wait and wait. Just in the hope that at some time you'd come. And then, just as if I wasn't a person – as if I had no feelings – you came and informed me coldly about Mary Anne. You insulted me outside the Abbey on the day of the Coronation. You turned away from me to Lady Jersey as if I was some – some trollop you didn't want to acknowledge. That wasn't very kind, Ben. And you talk about a vendetta!'

Disraeli took his hand from hers as she went on.

'But perhaps it was right for you. You rose and soared and forgot what you didn't want to remember.' Her voice changed. 'Do you think I'm unrelenting?'

He looked at her hesitantly.

'No, I think not. I think, Clarissa, you're a generous and loving person. I injured you. I regret it. In life one has to make decisions. I decided to marry, and that made it impossible for us to continue.'

'I would have cared for you –'

'You had lovers.'

'But never anyone except until afterwards. I wept for you, Ben.'

She raised her fan till only her eyes appeared above it. Tired, he thought.

'Did you ever regret me?'

'I regretted, Clarissa, that I couldn't, alas, have everything.'

There was a silence. Disraeli coughed.

'I wanted to see you about the bill, the D'Orsay bill,' he said. 'I scarcely thought I'd be still further in your debt than when, we parted.'

'Indeed?' She looked up at Colonel Tankerton, still vigorous and aggressive at the age of sixty-four, who as if by a pre-arranged signal had parted the fronds between two palm trees and stood before them.

'You know Mr Tankerton, of course. Pray join us, Colonel. Mr Disraeli wishes to redeem his bill.'

Disraeli stood.

'These aren't matters for general discussion.'

'I think they may be,' said Tankerton. 'If not now, tomorrow. You might care to know I've bought the bill from my friend Mrs Edmonds. It's overdue.' He confronted Disraeli. 'I have to tell you, sir, that I have long regarded you as an unsuitable person in public office. Dammit, a man who can't manage his own financial affairs doesn't deserve to handle the public's.'

Disraeli looked around. Behind him was a wall with a collection of tropical plants. Mrs Edmonds was looking up like a spectator in the stalls at a theatre, and in front of him was Tankerton's drunken face. He recognized that if he tried to move past Tankerton, the outcome might be a squalid brawl. He waited with an impassive expression for the harangue to end. Rose had promised to join him when he spoke to Mrs Edmonds, but his solicitor, last seen in his white gloves standing awkwardly against a pillar, had disappeared. All Disraeli could see were the figures in evening dress moving in the distance between the columns around the ballroom.

'I intend, sir,' said Tankerton savagely, 'to bankrupt you.'

Disraeli was silent.

'And then to expose you as a cheat and a liar. Yes, a cheat and a liar. You lied, sir, in the House of Commons. You denied your application for office. I have it,' he ended triumphantly, patting his breast pocket. 'I have it here.'

'Ah, Colonel,' said Mr Rose in a breezy voice as he joined

341

them. 'I've been looking for Mr Disraeli everywhere. I trust I don't intrude.'

He raised the tails of his evening dress-coat and sat.

'Much too old to dance. May we sit? There's a matter I have to discuss with you.'   ..

'I have nothing to discuss with you,' said Tankerton.

'Oh yes,' said Rose impatiently. 'Sit, pray, sit. It's a matter of some gravity, Tankerton. It affects Mrs Edmonds – yourself. A very grave matter.'

Tankerton sat slowly, and Disraeli said to Mrs Edmonds, 'You will excuse me.'

'No, no. Not yet,' said Rose. 'This affects you too, Mr Disraeli. Ah yes! I understand, Mrs Edmonds, you wish to take preliminary steps in bankruptcy against Mr Disraeli.'

'You can leave Mrs Edmonds out of these matters,' said Tankerton. 'I've bought the bill. I will apply to the Court tomorrow, and I'll publish the proceedings. I don't consider – '

'Never mind,' said Rose calmly. 'I am offering you tonight on Mr Disraeli's behalf to repay the capital and interest of the bill.'

'For God's sake,' said Tankerton. 'You're too late. The bill was due for payment yesterday. I am proceeding in bankruptcy.'

'Why, sir?'

'So that England shall know what manner of a client you have. Besides, I have every intention of handing over his letter to Sir Robert Peel to the *Morning Chronicle.*'

'I see,' said Rose. 'Well, sir, if that is your purpose, there is no more to say.'

Mrs Edmonds looked queryingly at Tankerton, and he bowed to her.

'Madam,' he said, 'let us waltz.'

Disraeli and Rose stood as Mrs Edmonds gathered up her dress. They were both moving towards the ballroom when Rose said, 'But there is one other matter.'

Mrs Edmonds paused, and Tankerton paused with her.

'Mr Francis Villiers's bills!'

Mrs Edmonds turned around with an angry expression.

'Yes,' said Rose sternly. 'Mr Villiers's bills. It would, I think, be in your interest, Colonel Tankerton – and yours, Mrs Edmonds – to return and discuss this matter further.'

Tankerton came back slowly and truculently, and he and Mrs Edmonds resumed their seats.

Rose cleared his throat and spoke again with his customary affected diffidence.

'Er – Mrs Edmonds. You have had a long friendship with Mr Villiers. Is that not so?'

'That is my business.'

'Exactly, madam. Your *business*. That's just the aspect of the matter I want to discuss. Mr Villiers is a young man – under thirty, I believe. Did very well in India. But that's not the point. Not much money in being a Military Secretary. And between ourselves, his father keeps him rather short.'

He wiped his forehead and his neck with his handkerchief.

'I'm afraid I'm unsuitably dressed for a hot-house. If only I had bare shoulders – '

Disraeli frowned. Sometimes, he felt, Rose was lacking in good taste.

'But the point is,' Rose went on, 'Mr Villiers has been spending very great sums of money in the last year or two.'

'Not for me,' said Mrs Edmonds bluntly.

Rose put his fingertips together.

'Yes – for you, madam. Those beautiful diamond pendants in your ears – exquisite – Garrard's – Mr Villiers bought them for you on the basis of a bill, signed by himself and allegedly by some of his friends. There's a lot of this paper about – nearly forty thousand pounds' worth. Did you know, Mrs Edmonds, that Mr Villiers has been issuing a lot of bills?'

'I know nothing – nothing – of his financial affairs,' said Mrs Edmonds stubbornly.

'Alas,' said Rose. 'These things get about.' He turned to Tankerton, who had been silent. 'Tell me, Colonel, have you ever been interested in calligraphy?'

Tankerton compressed his lips.

'You see,' said Rose, 'I've been talking to Mr Lawson – you

know, the banker – or, as you might say, the money-lender. He does a great deal, as you know, of discounting – personal bills and so on. He tells me that some of the Villiers bills have been coming back because his friends' signatures have been – forgive the word – *forged*!'

Mrs Edmonds began to rise.

'This is disgraceful,' she said. 'I'll have no part in it.'

'Disgraceful, yes,' said Rose. 'But you have a part in it. Perhaps, Mr Disraeli, you will inform Mrs Edmonds of your discovery.'

Disraeli thought for a moment.

'The matter is very disagreeable. I must tell you, Tankerton, the Law Officers have established at my request and beyond doubt that forged signatures have been added to Mr Villiers's bills.'

'Oh no,' said Mrs Edmonds quickly. Tankerton's plethoric face had become white, so that the red veins formed a tracery like a river-map.

'They have ascertained with little doubt, from servants apparently – very distasteful – that the signatures were forged by you in the presence of Mrs Edmonds.'

'That's a lie – a damned lie,' said Tankerton, raising his voice.

'No, an ascertainable truth. Great mistake to ignore servants!'

'That is so,' Mr Rose confirmed. 'The only question, sir, is whether to take action against you both.'

'It's a lie and an insult,' said Mrs Edmonds, recovering a little. 'Lady Jersey will have something to say. She'll hardly take kindly to your charging her son with complicity in mis-representation – forgery.'

'Indeed not,' said Mr Rose. 'He thought the bills were being discounted against his own signature. You added the others when the bill left his hand.'

'No,' Mrs Edmonds burst out. 'That's another lie. He was there. It was his idea.'

'You see, Mr Disraeli,' Rose said sadly, 'what happens when accomplices are in dispute.'

Tankerton looked ferociously at Mrs Edmonds.

'There isn't a word of truth in it. Not a word! You're – '

'You, Colonel Tankerton, performed the forgery,' said Rose. 'Mrs Edmonds handled the bills. I think five years in jail will purge your crime.'

'And how many for Mr Villiers?' said Mrs Edmonds coolly. She had put her hand on Tankerton's forearm to restrain him.

'That,' said Mr Rose, 'is a matter for Mr Disraeli's judgment, not mine. But for my own part, I have a suggestion.'

Tankerton had suddenly become sober, and he waited.

'In certain contingencies,' said Rose, 'this troublesome affair can be resolved. You, Tankerton, will accept from Mr Disraeli payment in full for the D'Orsay bill, and you'll deliver it to me tomorrow.'

Tankerton grunted.

'You will then contribute the proceeds to redeeming the fraudulent bills uttered in Mr Villiers's name. That would be fair, would it not?'

Tankerton didn't answer.

'You, Mrs Edmonds, bearing in mind that all worldly possessions are really borrowed and not possessed, will return your pendants to Garrards and make that your contribution to our fund to save Mr Villiers, Colonel Tankerton and yourself.'

She involuntarily felt the ear-rings in her lobes.

'And, as Lord Jersey would be harsher than Lady Jersey in dealing with Mr Villiers, we won't tell him anything about it. Instead, Mr Disraeli, on Lady Jersey's recommendation, will raise from some friendly bankers enough to pay the balance of the bills uttered.'

There was a silence.

'Is that all?' asked Tankerton.

'Not all,' said Rose. 'A condition, sir, of all this is that you return Mr Disraeli's letter to Sir Robert Peel into his own hand. The letter was never yours. It is Mr Disraeli's. You have sought to misapply it. You will bring me all the papers to-morrow.'

He stood, a foot shorter than Tankerton, and eyed him severely.

'I restore Mrs Disraeli to you,' said Mr Villiers, returning with Mary Anne on his arm. 'She dances like thistledown. Mrs Edmonds!'

He bowed to her in invitation. She rose, glanced at Disraeli over her shoulder, and left laughing with Mr Villiers.

'What a lovely couple they make!' said Mary Anne, following them with a sentimental glance.

'Well matched,' said Mr Rose. 'Well matched.'

Tankerton turned his back and left abruptly.

'What a boorish man!' said Mary Anne.

'Yes,' said Disraeli. 'I don't think you'll see him again.'

Rose was looking at him with a contented expression.

'Thank you, my dear Rose,' said Disraeli. 'I repeat, you're a man after my own heart.'

He returned with Mary Anne to the ballroom, where he came face to face with Lady Jersey.

'Well?' she asked anxiously. 'He's dancing with her again.'

'Everything is well,' said Disraeli. 'The matter is disposed of. Pray have no more anxieties. But don't ask me more at the moment. You have my assurances.'

She smiled at him in delight.

'Your husband,' said Lady Jersey to Mary Anne, 'is the kindest of men.'

'And the best,' said Mary Anne proudly.

With Mary Anne's arm in his, Disraeli walked slowly in the interval between the dances towards the ante-rooms. Her card, dangling with a tasselled pencil from her wrist, was almost full, and her face was happy. Lord Derby bowed over Mary Anne's hand, and for a few moments even the most reserved of the aristocratic faces at the tables turned inquisitively towards them. Everyone wondered about the subject of Derby's few words with Disraeli.

Disraeli moved on.

'The malt-tax?' the Attorney-General asked as he accosted them.

'No,' said Disraeli. 'The weather.'

'Here's my cavalier,' said Mary Anne as Lord Naas arrived to claim his dance.

Disraeli was alone, and he withdrew into an open-windowed alcove leading to a balcony with the happiness of one who, diagnosed as suffering from a fatal disease, is informed that the doctor was in error. He, too, was happy and he asked himself: What is happiness? And he gave himself the answer. It was the absence of fear. The incubus had gone. It was true there'd be others to take the place of Mrs Edmonds and Tankerton. That was a law of life. There was no eminence that didn't excite envy and malice. But for this moment there was an interval of peace.

D'Orsay's bill and his own letter to Peel had at last been buried.

He listened to the violins from the ballroom and felt that what the solemnity of this private occasion also needed was muffled drums. For D'Orsay. D'Orsay was dying in Paris. His friend D'Orsay – the Alcibiades of London's drawing-rooms – how many years ago?

And Peel? The passion and the debate was ended. The Corn Laws had disappeared, and would never return. Disraeli contemplated himself in a long looking-glass, lit by candles. He was forty-eight – in the summer of his powers. He had been defeated and harried and blackmailed: and yet he had won. The Right Honourable Benjamin Disraeli, MP, Chancellor of the Exchequer, Leader of the House. Time after time he had endured wounds; and yet he had survived. Life, he believed, was too short for pettiness. Now was the time for greatness. As a youth, he had pledged himself only to serve high purposes. Even while the gross hands of men like Tankerton had tried to sully him and drag him down, he had remembered the advice he had given the workers at the Athenæum Institute.

Aspire!

He had aspired. He had dared to be great. And now, a member of the Cabinet at last, he felt greatness within his grasp. In the morning there'd be a Cabinet. Soon he'd have to present his first Budget. The critic would become a performer.

He peered through his eyeglass at himself in the mirror.

347

And approached closer in order to see better. He adjusted his cravat, visualizing himself at the Despatch Box on Budget Day.

'Mr Speaker, sir . . .' he murmured.

'Not now, Ben,' said Mary Anne, waving her fan. 'I've been looking for you everywhere. Everyone wants to dance with me except you.'

'I will break my rule,' said Disraeli, 'and invite you to dance in public.'

'Oh, Ben,' said Mary Anne delightedly, 'you must follow me – one-two-three-one-two-three – and don't trip.'

The orchestra was playing a waltz, and as the Disraelis entered the ballroom, everyone turned to look.

'Mr Disraeli is dancing.' The words went from mouth to mouth, and the music seemed to quicken. All at once, all the guests were smiling – the women in their turning ball-dresses, the Ambassadors with their sashes and Orders, the officers in red and blue uniforms, and the normally grave politicians in their black tail-coats. The Funds seemed to harden; equities to rise; lovers who had planned to marry in twelve months' time wanted to bring the date forward; Lord Derby forgot to cut Huffam: and Mr Rose took a fifth glass of champagne with Mr Villiers, still enquiring after Mrs Edmonds who had left with Colonel Tankerton.

Mr Disraeli was dancing. From the conservatory and the buffets, Lady Jersey's guests came hurrying to watch. A smile passed over their faces.

Mr Disraeli was dancing.